PRAISE FOR

What Jonah Knew

"A spellbinding literary thriller packed with psychological suspense and profound questions about motherhood, trauma, and how death illuminates life."

—Amy Tan, bestselling author of *The Joy Luck Club* and *Where the Past Begins*

"Barbara Graham is a literary alchemist. *What Jonah Knew* not only grabs you from the first page, it makes the mystical believable and the human predicament shine with wit, wisdom, and love."

—Tara Brach, meditation teacher and author of *Radical Acceptance* and *Radical Compassion*

"Both a riveting mystery and a deep dive into the impact of grief, *What Jonah Knew* offers us not only hope but a fascinating meditation on the nature of love, identity, and reality itself."

—JoAnne Tompkins, author of *What Comes After*

"Barbara Graham's shimmering novel brings new meaning to the concept of inherited family trauma and the very divide between life and death."

—Mark Epstein, MD, author of *The Trauma of Everyday Life* and *The Zen of Therapy*

"Barbara Graham writes with clarity, courage, and heart. *What Jonah Knew* shines light on complicated issues and brings the reader to a new understanding of what it means to be fully human."

—Molly Giles, author of *Wife with Knife* and *Rough Translations*, winner of the Flannery O'Connor Award for Short Fiction

"Barbara Graham is a rare talent who blends comic brilliance with psychological and spiritual insight. *What Jonah Knew* plumbs the depths of the human heart while ingeniously tackling life's hardest questions."

—Mark Matousek, author of *Sex Death Enlightenment*

WHAT
JONAH
KNEW

ALSO BY BARBARA GRAHAM

BOOKS

Eye of My Heart

Camp Paradox

Women Who Run with the Poodles

PLAYS

Jacob's Ladder

Camp Paradox

The Care and Feeding of Poultry

WHAT JONAH KNEW

A Novel

BARBARA GRAHAM

HARPER

NEW YORK • LONDON • TORONTO • SYDNEY

HARPER

WHAT JONAH KNEW. Copyright © 2022 by Barbara Graham. All rights reserved. Printed in the United States of America. No part of this book may be used or reproduced in any manner whatsoever without written permission except in the case of brief quotations embodied in critical articles and reviews. For information, address HarperCollins Publishers, 195 Broadway, New York, NY 10007.

HarperCollins books may be purchased for educational, business, or sales promotional use. For information, please email the Special Markets Department at SPsales@harpercollins.com.

Excerpt from *Jessica* by Kevin Henkes, copyright © 1989 by Kevin Henkes. Used by permission of HarperCollins Publishers.

FIRST EDITION

Designed by Jamie Lynn Kerner
Image on baby announcement page © Lisima / stock.adobe.com

Library of Congress Cataloging-in-Publication Data has been applied for.

ISBN 978-0-06-323018-7

22 23 24 25 26   LSC   10 9 8 7 6 5 4 3 2 1

FOR HUGH AND CLAY,
who teach me more about love every day

Science cannot solve the ultimate mystery of nature. And that is because, in the last analysis, we ourselves are part of the mystery we are trying to solve.

—MAX PLANCK, NOBEL PRIZE–WINNING PHYSICIST,
WHERE IS SCIENCE GOING?

WHAT
JONAH
KNEW

BEFORE

SUMMER 2002

At first it seems like a lucky break, him pulling up in his tricked-out truck with the big-ass tires and honking just as the sky lets loose. It's pitch dark and raining so hard, for a minute I can't tell who it is. "Hey," I say when he rolls down the passenger window. "Were you at the show?" A lot of the time when I'm playing I can't see who's in the house, especially when it's packed.

He shakes his head. "I had some business up here and was heading out when I saw you. You going to stand there all night getting wet or you want a ride?"

If I weren't soaked through to the skin, I might ask him how he could tell it was me walking along this deserted stretch of road, the rain pummeling me like Noah's Ark. "Okay," I say. "If you don't mind dropping me back at the motel, it's only a couple of miles."

"No problem."

Getting into the cab, I wonder what type of business he was doing all the way up here so late at night, but then I see a pile of scorecards from the track. He must be raking it in because he's wearing an expensive-looking leather jacket and he's got this super deluxe ride.

"Sorry to drip all over your seat," I apologize, but there's nothing I can do about it. I was so pissed off by what went down during the second set, I didn't notice the storm about to break when I left the club. I just wanted to get the hell out of there. The one night a producer shows up from the record company we want to sign with, we have our shittiest gig ever.

He reaches behind him, then hands me a towel and says, "I can drive you home, if you want."

"Thanks, but I'm riding back with the band in the morning."

"Up to you."

Just to be polite I pretend to wipe my neck with the towel that reeks of dried puke, then drop it on the floor. I wonder if he's a big drinker as well as a gambler, but I don't smell alcohol on his breath and he looks cleaned up from the last time I ran into him, maybe a year ago. More like a businessman now than some sweaty dude who works odd jobs.

"The motel is up there, on the left," I say. "The Timber Creek, only the K is missing."

As he pulls into the parking lot, I start thinking, maybe it isn't such a terrible idea to get the hell out of Dodge tonight. Blow this rathole. Put the whole fucking catastrophe behind me. "If I went back with you, you'd have to wait while I pack up my stuff. And put on some dry clothes." I can't stop shivering.

"No prob. To tell you the truth, I wouldn't mind the company."

"I just need to text the guys and let them know I'm leaving." But when I take my phone out of my pocket, it's dead. "Shit. No juice."

"Leave it with me, I've got a charger."

"Hey, thanks." I hand him my phone and open the door. "I'll be quick."

"Take your time." Then he turns and grins at me, the blinking lights from the motel making his white teeth sparkle like piano keys. "I've got all night."

Now, I'm a person who usually keeps his guard up, shit detectors on high. I had to be that way when I was a kid and it stuck. But tonight I'm too cold and wet and pissed off about the gig to pick up any weirdness, so by the time I realize that running into him was no random coincidence, it's too late.

PART ONE

2002–2003

ONE

HELEN BIRD WASN'T IN THE HABIT OF BREAKING THE LAW, BUT the heartless creep in the motel office left her no choice. She had to find her son. She had to see for herself if Henry had left something behind, some subtle trace of himself that no one else would notice but would point her maternal compass in the right direction. He'd never been out of touch before, not like this, not when he was expected home two days ago, and especially not now, when his girlfriend, Mira, was due to give birth in a matter of weeks. Luckily, the window in his motel room was open a crack and Helen was able to jimmy it just enough to squeeze through. If the creep who refused to give her the key happened to see her and called the cops, so be it. In a way, she wouldn't mind. Maybe Saratoga Springs' Finest would show more concern than the smug detective in Aurora Falls who tried to convince her that Henry's disappearance was voluntary.

Helen knew better.

Didn't she?

As soon as she was inside, she closed the musty drapes, then turned on the mini flashlight that had been a party favor at her friend Abby's fiftieth and waved it around the room. Nothing jumped out at her, but that wasn't surprising. The woman who'd answered the motel phone earlier in the day told her that Henry had taken all his belongings. She'd also let it slip that number 11 wouldn't be cleaned until tomorrow.

The room was thick with late summer heat, but Helen didn't dare turn on the air conditioner. She undid the buttons on her shirt still dusted with flour, then shined her flashlight in the closet, the nightstand, each of the bureau drawers, and the bathroom, including the shower stall with dark green fur growing around the edges and in the cracks.

Nothing.

She got down on her knees and peered under the desk, then ruffled the covers on the unmade bed. It wasn't until she cast her light on the worn carpet that she noticed a lone gray sock sticking out from the foot of the bed. She picked it up and sniffed. There was no mistaking who the sock belonged to. Her beautiful boy had famously stinky feet.

"Where are you, my love?" Clutching the sock, Helen sat down on the edge of the bed. "Where have you gone?" She tried to feel her way into her son's mind. In the past she'd been able to do that. Together, they'd been through so much—running away when he was five and forging new identities so Kip could never find them—they'd become experts at reading one another's thoughts. "It's like we're in our own witness protection program," Henry once joked. But ever since Stuart Rock, his best friend and Dog Radio's lead guitarist, had phoned this morning looking for Henry, Helen's usually sharp intuition felt jumbled by fear, like a TV signal that turns to snow.

Stuart's explanation simply didn't add up. "We fell apart during the second set on Labor Day. It was a shit show, and Henry was pissed because there was a record guy there, so instead of waiting to ride back to the motel, he decided to walk." Stuart hadn't heard from Henry since and neither had Mira, who'd been visiting her mother at the assisted-living place in Albany. "He probably just hitched or took the bus back and is up at the cabin trying to forget the whole thing," Stuart offered, clearly trying to put a positive spin on Henry's unexplained absence.

Helen did the math. Her son had been out of touch with the people closest to him for thirty-six hours, behavior that was completely out of character for a responsible young man—shit show or no shit show.

"I'm on my way up to the cabin now, and if he's not there, I'm going straight to the police," Helen said, hanging up.

SEEING HOW WORKED up she was, Nico, the duty sergeant, who was a regular at Helen's bakery, the Queen of Hearts, took her in to meet with Will Handler right away. The detective, too, was a fan of the bakery, but Helen didn't really know him except to say hello—and marvel at the quantity of pastries he could consume at one sitting. He reminded her of an out-of-shape boxer—with his big head, a nose with a prominent switchback, and a serious paunch. As a cop, Handler had a reputation for being blunt, but Helen didn't mind blunt. She preferred her truth served neat, not gussied up in ifs and maybes.

When she explained that Henry had been missing since Labor Day, he advised her not to jump to conclusions. "From what his buddy told you, your son was ticked off. Sounds to me like he needed to take a time-out to get his head together." The detective pulled a stick of Nicorette gum from one of the many packs on his desk and popped it in his mouth. "My guess is, he went off by himself. Let's give him a chance to cool off."

"Can't you put out an alert, in case disappearing was not his idea?" Helen asked. "Isn't that standard procedure?"

"Sorry to say, but there's no such thing as an Amber Alert for a missing adult unless they're mentally ill or physically disabled. So, unfortunately, or fortunately, your kid doesn't qualify."

"There must be something you can do. Mira, Henry's girl-friend, is eight months pregnant. He would never be out of touch with her, not even for a couple of days."

"Mm . . ." Detective Handler cocked a bushy brow and nod-ded, as if he'd just been let in on a secret. "You're sure your boy is one hundred percent on board with becoming a dad?"

"Yes. A thousand percent." Maybe what he was insinuating is true for other young men whose girlfriends get knocked up, but not Henry. From the moment Mira announced she was pregnant, he was elated. He even went out the next day and bought pricey cherry to make the baby a cradle, which he'd finished last week. Helen believed Henry saw fatherhood as the chance to repair the painful legacy of his own father.

She glanced at the stack of file folders on the detective's desk and hoped they didn't represent unsolved cases. "You don't know my son," she said, feeling her jaw tighten.

"No, I don't, but my twenty-seven years on the job tells me he knew what he was doing. Most adults who go missing do so voluntarily. I can't tell you how many wander off, then turn up after a few days or weeks." The detective spit his gum into its wrapper, then tossed it in the trash. "You say Henry likes to go hiking up in the Adirondacks, right? Well, if I were a gambling man, I'd bet that's where he is. Had a lousy show and decided to take a little mental R & R. I see it all the time. I'm telling you, ninety-eight percent of missing persons turn up sooner or later. *Ninety-eight* percent."

Helen was too afraid to ask how many of the ninety-eight percenters turned up alive.

SHE PRESSED THE orphaned sock to her chest, recalling the family of sock puppets she'd made for Henry's third birthday, when they were too broke to buy anything more than a few balloons from the five-and-dime. So, just as in the story of Goldilocks and the Three Bears, which Henry loved above all others, Helen created Baby puppet, Mama puppet, and Papa puppet. That was when Henry's real papa was still in the picture. For a long while, the puppet family remained Henry's most cherished treasure, the only playthings Helen had time to grab the night they fled Oregon. Even after he outgrew them, he kept them safely tucked away in his top bureau drawer. His favorite was Chester, the Baby puppet with the big button eyes and red felt grin. "For someday, when I have a kid," he said.

Headlights beamed through the gap in the shabby curtains, jarring Helen out of her reverie. Car doors slamming. Loud voices, male and female, getting closer. Probably the cops coming to arrest me for breaking and entering, she thought, feeling her pulse shoot up. Moments later, though, she felt mildly disappointed when she heard the TV go on in the room next door.

She stretched out on the bed and sniffed the pillow. She could detect Henry there, too. Not smelly like the sock. Sweet, with a hint of his favorite shaving cream. Tea tree and mint. It was the first time since Stuart called that Helen let herself cry.

SHE MUST HAVE drifted off because the rhythmic *thwack thwack thwack* of her neighbors' headboard against the paper-thin wall jerked her awake. And the noise! High-pitched squeals that sounded like randy alley cats going at it. Well, good for them, she thought. *Carpe diem*, because you never know what unwelcome surprises the next *diem* may bring.

She mopped up the sweat pooling between her breasts with the top sheet and tried to figure out what to do next. Obviously, her son had taken his things with him and gone somewhere. But where? Could his mysterious departure really be voluntary? Viewed from a certain angle, Detective Handler's theory made sense. Given Henry's landscaping job, double duty as Dog Radio's fiddler and manager, his relationship with Mira, and a baby coming, he was under massive pressure for anyone, let alone a twenty-two-year-old. Only this was *Henry*, whose maturity and sense of responsibility, even as a young boy, had outpaced his years. Henry was not a person who took time-outs, any more than Helen was a person who lolled around waiting for something to happen. They were scrappers. Survivors. Helen didn't believe her son would abandon her or Mira or the band, or Charlie, the ornery rescue mutt he called his "brother from another mother."

She glanced at the glowing red numbers on the digital clock. Ten fifty! Even if she left this minute, she wouldn't make it home until after midnight, and she had to wake up by four to get the first bake in by four thirty. She forced herself into a sitting position, then liberated the Henry-scented pillowcase from the pillow to take with her and dropped the sock inside.

Deciding she had better pee before taking off, she went into the windowless bathroom, shut the door, and turned on the light. Startled by the sudden brightness, she caught a glimpse of herself in the mirror. Her usually rosy complexion was so pale, the bags under her bloodshot eyes so puffy, and her silver-streaked blonde hair in such a tangle, she looked more like mad Medusa than the woman her lover, Jock, called an earth goddess.

She splashed cold water on her face, then patted it dry with a damp towel. Henry's towel, she imagined, though when she pressed her nose to it and inhaled, she could detect no trace of him and dropped it on the floor. That's when she spotted something in the wastebasket she hadn't noticed before. A crumpled-up piece of paper. Sheet music. She fished it out of the trash. There, on the page, was the start of a letter in Henry's slanted hand.

Dear Kip, the first scratched-out line read.

Then, *Dear Dad,* but that line was scratched out, too.

A blast of adrenaline on top of paralyzing fatigue made the words bleed together. Trembling, Helen sat down on the closed toilet seat. As far as she knew, Henry had never reached out to Kip in the seventeen years since they'd run away from him and Oregon. On the rare occasions when he'd mentioned his father, her response had been firm, unequivocal. *We can never get in touch with him or let him know where we are or our lives could be in danger.* Yet, obviously, her warnings had expired years ago. Henry was a grown man now, free to do as he pleased. Free to get in touch with his father if that's what he needed to do.

Having left her reading glasses in the car, Helen squinted to bring the words into focus.

Dear whoever the hell you are, because honestly I don't know what to call you. Kip feels weird. And though you're my dad by blood, you've never really been a dad to me, so calling you that feels fake. But as long as I'm on the subject, I might as well tell you that your son is about to become a dad himself . . .

Helen pressed the letter to her chest. Why should she be so shocked? It was human nature, wasn't it? The raw animal urgency of bloodlines that must have made her son want to share his big news. But what exactly did he have in mind? Had he written the letter on impulse, then thought better of it and thrown it in the trash? Or was it a draft of a letter he planned to send? Had sent already? A speech he intended to deliver in person?

And where did this ink-splotched sheet of paper leave Helen? Should she share it with Mira? Detective Handler? Book the next flight to Eugene to search for Henry herself?

Questions. But no answers.

Her mind emptied of everything she'd always taken on faith about her son. His loyalty and devotion. His honesty. Their unbreakable bond. She felt like the fool in that old fable, who searches for his keys under a streetlamp, not because he lost them there, but because it was the only place where there was light enough for him to see.

Helen folded the crinkled paper in half and placed it in the pillowcase with the sock. After one last look around the room, she slipped out the door into the still night air.

TWO

The Aurora Falls Gazette
September 6, 2002

Aurora Falls Man Sought After Mysterious Disappearance
BY ALIX BENITEZ

Henry Bird, 22, a musician and manager of the local bluegrass band Dog Radio, has been missing since Labor Day. Bird's absence was discovered when he failed to meet up with his fellow band members on the morning of Tuesday, September 3, to return to Aurora Falls. The group had been performing over the weekend at the Silver Dollar, a club in Saratoga Springs.

According to Stuart Rock, lead guitarist for Dog Radio, Bird told him he "felt like getting some air" after the show on Monday night and decided to walk back to the Timber Creek Motel, where the band was staying. He was last seen leaving the Silver Dollar on foot shortly before midnight, heading in the direction of the motel, a distance of about two miles. The rest of the band—Rock, Damian Barr, Paul Robbins, and equipment manager Luke Attardi—remained at the club until 2 a.m. When they got back to the motel, they assumed Bird was asleep in his room.

"We kept knocking on his door in the morning until finally we got the motel manager to open it just to make sure he was okay, but he was already gone," said Rock, adding that it was unusual for Bird not to phone or text if he had a change of plans.

Henry Bird is the son of Helen Bird, proprietor of the Queen of Hearts Bakery in Aurora Falls. "It's completely out of character for Henry to take off without letting anyone close to him know where he was going," she said. "I'm especially concerned for his safety since learning that two other musicians from New York State have gone missing in recent months."

The musicians Mrs. Bird was referring to are Larry Gustafson, 23, a rapper from Syracuse who goes by 2B.NOT.2B, and whose abandoned car was found near Worcester, Massachusetts, and Aaron Lamb, 29, a guitarist from Ithaca. When questioned, Detective Will Handler of the Aurora Falls Sheriff's Department said there was "no evidence linking Bird to either Lamb or Gustafson." As of press time, the department has declined to launch a formal investigation into Bird's disappearance.

Henry Bird is a 6'1" white male, 170 pounds, with shoulder-length sandy hair, blue eyes, and a small crescent-shaped scar above his right eye. In addition to playing fiddle with Dog Radio, he's employed as a junior landscaper at Perennial Pleasures Nursery and Gardens in Aurora Falls, but did not call in or report for work this week.

Mrs. Bird asks that anyone with information regarding her son's whereabouts contact her immediately at 853-232-6645.

THREE

"OH NO, THIS IS HORRIBLE," LUCIE SAID AFTER READING THE front-page story in the local paper. "He waited on me last summer. There was hardly anyone there, so we got to talking and he told me all about his band. I said we'd try to catch them sometime when we were up here. God, his mother, I can't imagine what she's going through." Huddled in bed naked, Lucie tucked the duvet under her chin. She always forgot how chilly it got in the cottage, even though technically it was still summer.

"He's only been gone a few days, Luce. I wouldn't start worrying yet." Matt dropped his shorts on the floor and took off his T-shirt, still sweat-soaked from his early morning run. "At least now we know why the bakery's closed." Whenever Matt and Lucie came up from the city for the weekend, their first stop was the Queen of Hearts. Though they avoided carb and fat overload at home—especially Matt, who, because of his family history, was fanatical about his LDL/HDL ratio—they refused to pass up the sublime pain au levain, sticky almond croissants, or pillowy brioche turned out by the Queen. But yesterday, the bakery was dark and they had to resort to ShopRite.

"Matt, I'm telling you, I'm good at reading people," Lucie said, chewing on a fingernail. "That day in the bakery he was so friendly, he did not strike me as the type who would just check out without telling anyone."

"Honey, people disappear all the time, for all sorts of reasons, only to show up later. You don't know anything about him, except that his mother owns a bakery and he plays in a band. Anyhow, he looks like someone who can take care of himself. If something suspicious were going on, the cops would be all over it."

"You really think so?" Lucie wanted to believe her husband. She wanted to believe the positive spin he put on just about everything. The guy was born primed for sunshine, while her happiness set point hovered somewhere between partly cloudy and ominous. For Lucie, worry was like a heat-seeking missile: when one target of her anxiety faded, another soon took its place. Usually she and Matt balanced each other out, though at times his glass-half-full attitude seemed like a handy form of denial. Yet, at other times he turned out to be uncannily prescient.

"What about the other two guys who disappeared? Maybe there's some psycho out there targeting musicians," she said.

"Luce, odds are your friend Henry will be back sooner than later, you wait and see." Matt kissed the top of her head. "I'm going to jump in the shower. Don't go anywhere, okay?"

"Okay." She watched the back of his trim runner's body retreat into the bathroom, then turned her attention to the photo beaming at her from the paper. With his blue eyes and winning smile, Henry looked as open and charming as she remembered. Where could he have gone? That day last summer when Matt was off on some mega run, Lucie had gone into the bakery to pick up a loaf of bread but was seduced by the aroma of fresh peach pie. She wound up sitting at one of the little café tables savoring a slice and a cup of tea, chatting with Henry and watching him with his mother, Helen. Lucie remembered being struck by how radiant

Helen looked that day, how content and at home she seemed in her plumpish, apron-clad body. Observing her playfulness with her son, Lucie wondered what it would be like to *be* the Queen of Hearts—having a small bakery in Aurora Falls, free from all the pressures and pretense of New York City.

Like many English majors, Lucie had moved to New York with dreams of working in publishing until she sold her first novel. She'd never planned a career as a magazine editor. Yet, surprisingly, since starting at *Lulu* seven years ago and working her way up from a lowly assistant to senior health editor, she found she liked dealing in actual facts after a childhood brimming with myth and misinformation. But as much as she liked her job, she often wearied of the whole New York gestalt. The ridiculous status thing, based on some mysterious formula involving looks (i.e., being thin!), who you knew and who *they* knew, not to mention the raw ambition to make it, which never seemed to make anyone truly happy when they did. And the noise and suffocating crowds took a serious toll on Lucie's souped-up nervous system.

Aurora Falls was another story. The laid-back vibe took her right back to the funky town in Northern California where she grew up. In fact, Aurora Falls could be the East Coast sister of Point Reyes Station. Even the rolling hills surrounding the town reminded her of Northern California, with the added benefit of staying green all summer, instead of drying out and turning dusty brown. Yet, like Point Reyes, Aurora Falls was originally a farming community that was discovered in the 1970s by hippies and artists and subscribers to *Mother Earth News* and was still a mash-up of the two cultures. An art gallery next to a feed store. An old-fashioned hardware store sandwiched between an independent bookstore and a health food co-op. And Humpty's, a dive saloon kitty-corner from a ritzy wine bar and herbal apothecary.

Most of all, Lucie loved the expansive green in the center of town where kids ran free and adults gathered to play chess and bocce, listen to music, practice tai chi, or just loll around on benches or the grass, reading or doing nothing at all.

Matt didn't share Lucie's infatuation. He was one of those native New Yorkers who thought of Manhattan, especially the Upper West Side, as an enlightened village—sort of like Colonial Williamsburg, only for all the people the nation's forefathers would have run out of Williamsburg. Since 9/11, he'd become even more fiercely New York–centric than before, while Lucie yearned more than ever for a home in Aurora Falls. A place to escape to, if they survived the next terrorist attack.

She'd been on her way to an early morning photo shoot in Tribeca when the first plane roared overhead and she watched as the North Tower was struck—disbelieving, crying, clutching the arms of strangers, until she was swept up in the crush of human flesh swarming north. Borne along by the wave, she couldn't remember if Matt was working at the hospital uptown or downtown and didn't know he was safe until midnight, when he finally showed up at their apartment on West Eighty-Third. Pale as bleached bone, he said that as soon as he'd heard the news, he'd rushed to the ER and waited with the other doctors and nurses to receive the wounded. But the wounded never came.

Even now, a year after the attacks, there were mornings when Lucie woke up gasping, the taste of bitter ash in her mouth.

She returned to the newspaper and tried once more to read Henry Bird's face for clues. Could he really have gone missing on purpose?

"Hey." Matt took the paper from her and crawled into bed. "I'm hungry," he said, kissing her between the collarbones and wrapping one of his slender legs around one of her meatier ones. His longish hair was still damp from the shower and tickled. "But not for one of those shitty ShopRite bagels."

"Mm." Lucie glanced up at the skylight over the bed. Clouds were amassing into a steely fortress. A downpour would soon follow.

"Luce? What's going on? Are you still thinking about that kid?"

"I wish there was something we could do to help find him. Help his mom. They seem like such nice people."

"What do you propose we do?"

"I don't know." Lucie disentangled herself from Matt and propped herself up on one elbow. "Maybe they have posters we could take back with us and put up in the city. Let's check before we leave tomorrow. And . . ." An unreformed nail biter, she dug her teeth into her pinky nail. "When we go into town, I wouldn't mind popping into a few open houses. Just to *look*."

"Again? Didn't we go through this last year?"

"That was before 9/11."

"Luce, I've spent years listening to friends bitch about sitting in miserable traffic for hours every Friday night, only to have to turn around and do it all in reverse on Sunday. I've always sworn I would never be one of those people."

"I just wish we had a place we could go if there's another attack. It wouldn't have to be fancy. It could be a simple cottage, like this." She waved a hand around the tiny refuge they'd discovered during their first weekend in Aurora Falls. With a hot tub and a pond to swim in, it was their favorite getaway. But since being written up in *Lonely Planet*, it was getting harder and harder to book.

"Do you really want to buy a place just in case something bad happens again in New York? Bad things can happen anywhere." Matt eyed the *Gazette*. "Even here."

Lucie tossed back the covers, threw on an old Cal Bears T-shirt, then opened the front door just as the sky let loose with battering rain, bringing with it a shower of golden leaves from the nearby poplars.

"You want half a toasted shitty bagel?" Matt asked after her.

"No."

There was so little they disagreed on, but having a place in the country was high on the list, she thought, noticing how each time a gust of wind rose up, the rain thrashing through the treetops hit the ground at a slightly different angle, in a kind of wild dance. She believed that growing up in the near wild herself had left her with a longing for the natural world, an urgency that was physical, not unlike the craving for sex, but one Matt would never share. She hadn't recognized this yearning in herself until she'd spent a few years walled in by concrete.

"You're getting wet," he said, coming up so close behind her she could smell his bagel breath. Onion.

"I don't care," she said, reaching her arms out in front of her. The rain felt like a thousand tiny needles pricking her skin. "What about our hypothetical child? Don't you think having a place to run around outside would be good for her? Or him?" Ever since his father had had a massive coronary last year, Matt's previously vague desire for a child had turned into a crusade. Lucie had gone off the pill eleven months ago and they'd been tracking her temperature and having sex according to her ovulation cycle ever since, but so far no baby.

"Maybe, if someday we have a child who isn't just hypothetical." Matt shrugged.

"FYI, I made an appointment with that fertility guy Rabia recommended," Lucie said, her back still to him.

"Really, you did? When were you going to tell me?"

"Now. This weekend. I only made it a few days ago. I wanted to surprise you." She reached behind her and patted his chest. "Surprise."

Matt had been after her to make the appointment for months. He came from a family of breeders. Annie and Audrey, his two sisters, had five kids between them. Whenever they got together, Matt spent every minute playing with his nieces and nephews. He was the ideal dad-in-waiting, while Lucie wasn't so sure about her fitness for motherhood. As the only child of a single mom who had gotten knocked up after a Dead concert by some guy called Moondog or Moonbeam—her mother, Phoebe, never could remember which—Lucie hadn't had the world's greatest maternal role model. Besides, compared to her ghostly tribe—in addition to an unknown father, many of her mother's relatives had been killed in Auschwitz—Matt's family tree swelled with leafy branches extending in every direction. Most of the time Lucie felt like a stray twig among the multitude of Pressmans.

"If you really want to, we can go look at a couple of open houses tomorrow," Matt said, shutting the door and leading her back inside. Her jaw was shuddering and she was soaked. He removed her dripping tee, then wrapped her in a towel and hustled her into bed. "There," he said.

"There," she said when he took off his sweatpants and climbed in next to her.

He kissed her wet hair. "You want to know something? You're going to make our actual, non-hypothetical child an amazing mom."

"Oh Matt, how can you possibly say that? How will I even know what to do?"

"Because you will. Animal instinct. Plus, you have the biggest heart of anyone I've ever met. Look how worried you are over the baker's son, who you talked to only once in your life."

"That's because he's somebody else's kid. If something horrible happened to our child, I don't think I could live. You'd have to put me to sleep like an old dog." Lucie removed Matt's tortoiseshell frames and pushed aside the dark brown hair that was constantly falling in his eyes. Then she traced his generous nose and full lips with a fingertip before meeting his warm, dark eyes. It was no wonder his patients adored him. Sometimes, she worried, they adored him a little too much. "You know," she said, "for someone who's such a big-shot eye doctor, I think you see me through rose-colored glasses."

"Did I ever tell you you're beautiful?"

His little schtick. He always told her she was beautiful when he wanted to fuck. Before him other men had told Lucie she was pretty—or cute—but she never quite believed them. She thought she was attractive (ish), but, given her narrow face with the sort of significant nose that drove many women to plastic surgeons, along with a smallish chin and a crown of coarse, frizzy hair, she never felt exactly pretty either—an opinion that had been reinforced by her mother. It was an unspoken agreement in their little family of two that her mother held the pretty card. Not that Lucie could compete with willowy, straight-haired Phoebe, who resembled a Jewish Joni Mitchell. Lucie always assumed her specter of a father must have been short, dark, and hairy like her. No man had ever made Lucie feel beautiful the way Matt did, and after years of him saying so, she'd come to believe she was, at least in his eyes.

"I saw a cute cottage listed in the paper. It's close to town but right on the creek, with a big yard and . . . Not that we're buying right now, but it would be fun to look. Matt?"

But this time he didn't answer. His mouth was slowly working its way along the length of her body and his mind was somewhere else.

FOUR

HELEN AND MIRA WERE PUTTING THE FINISHING TOUCHES ON the "Missing" poster when the doorbell rang.

"Another one," Helen sighed. Ever since the article came out in the *Gazette*, local reporters had been calling and banging on her door, driving her and especially the dog crazy. "I'm glad they're interested, but when there's something to tell, I'll tell them. Jesus. Let me deal with it," she said when Mira started to pull herself up. Helen had insisted that her son's girlfriend stay with her until Henry returned. "Someone eight-plus months pregnant should not be living alone on top of a mountain," she'd offered, and Mira had gladly accepted the invitation.

"Charlie, no! Stay!" Helen tried to mimic Henry's dog-scolding voice, but Charlie wasn't having it. He scrambled down the flight of stairs ahead of her and began snarling at the front door. When Helen peered through the leaded-glass window to see who was ringing the bell this time, she felt like snarling, too. "Just a minute," she yelled, then yanked the dog's collar, dragged him upstairs, and bribed him with "treats" to get him out the back door. Charlie was a large black Labradoodle/German shepherd rescue, with God knows what else in his gene pool. Normally skittish around men who weren't Henry, these days he was even more on edge than usual.

Helen went back downstairs and opened the door partway. Detective Handler was red in the face and waving a copy of the latest *Aurora Falls Gazette* in the air. "What the hell?" he said.

"When you wouldn't do anything, the reporter offered to alert the public in case someone out there has seen my son," Helen said, her jaw rigid. She was convinced that if the detective had done his job, Henry might be home by now. If he hadn't run off to Oregon in search of his father. Which she doubted. In her gut, Helen didn't believe her son would abandon Mira right before the baby was due. Still, she'd booked a flight to Eugene, then canceled it when she realized she couldn't leave Mira alone. The typically spirited young woman was an emotional wreck. Helen also recognized that caring for Mira was helping to keep her own twin demons—grief and terror—at bay.

"You should have come to me before speaking to the press," Handler said.

"I *did*," replied Helen, her eyes boring into his like a hot poker.

The detective sighed. "There are standard procedures for conducting a missing persons investigation, Mrs. Bird, and going straight to the news media isn't one of them." His bulldog demeanor had given way to something akin to resignation. Helen wondered if he felt guilty over dismissing Henry's disappearance as "voluntary," or if he'd been chewed out by the sheriff or some other higher-up when the newspaper article appeared.

"Are you going to let me in or what?" he asked.

MOMENTS LATER, THEY were settled in the living room. The beefy detective on the sofa, Mira in the wooden rocker, Helen on the window seat. The room was bathed in the sweet aroma of cinnamon and cardamon, even though the bakery had been closed for the past few days. Helen was one of the only business owners in town who still lived above her shop.

"So, have you decided to investigate?" she asked, wondering if the detective was serious about looking for Henry or if his visit was a public relations ploy to pacify an angry boss.

"Possibly." Detective Handler cleared his throat. "I need to get some background information first." He pulled a pen and notebook from his jacket pocket and turned to Helen. "You and Henry moved to Aurora Falls when he was in kindergarten, correct?"

"Yes." The man had actually done some research.

"And you came from where?"

"Oregon. I grew up in Ashland and went to college in Eugene," said Helen.

"And Henry's father? Where is he?"

"I don't know. I got pregnant after a one-night stand and I never saw the guy again." Helen's cheeks grew hot and she hoped Handler took the flushing as a sign of shame for a slutty past and not because she was lying. This was the line of questioning she'd dreaded. "I was just out of college and, well, it was back in the day." She glanced at Mira swaying in the rocker and tried to read her face, but her beautiful green eyes were swollen into narrow slits from crying, and Helen couldn't tell if she knew the real story. In Helen's mind, her past—and Henry's—were permanently sealed. Still, she had no way of knowing whether, in a moment of naked bliss, her son had told Mira everything.

"Honestly, our life before Aurora Falls is ancient history and I don't think it has anything to do with where Henry is now." Helen had no intention of showing Handler the letter she'd found in the trash at the motel; it would only raise a million pointless questions and drive the investigation—if there ever were to be one—in the wrong direction. Anyhow, she was on it, just in case. After she'd canceled her flight to Eugene, she'd put in calls to a couple of private detectives in the area and was waiting to hear back. Still, she knew she was playing a dangerous game. If the detective agreed to investigate, then found out about the letter, she could be prosecuted for withholding information from a cop. But it was a risk she was willing to take. Secrets were the currency that had kept her and Henry safe for nearly twenty years. Revealing those secrets now could destroy them both.

"You're going to have to let me be the judge of what's relevant." Handler pressed his meaty thumbs together. "How about your parents? Siblings? Is Henry in touch with them?"

Helen shook her head. "My parents and brother are gone. They died years ago, before Henry was born." This she could prove. She had all three of their death certificates tucked away in the same accordion file folder in the safe-deposit box where she kept Henry's birth certificate and her own—the real ones and the fake ones. Henry was the only other person who had a key.

"Detective, I'm sorry, but I don't see how my dead family is relevant," Helen said, tapping the faded Persian rug with her foot. "Henry walked out of the Silver Dollar five days ago and hasn't been seen or heard from since. He couldn't have just vaporized into thin air. Surely, *someone* knows where he is."

"I'm getting to that," Handler said gruffly.

"Thank you," said Helen. Clearly, the man didn't cotton to having his methods challenged, and she'd better try to win him over. It wasn't his fault that Henry was missing, she just wished he hadn't been so damn cavalier that day in his office. Statistically, with every passing day the odds of finding a missing person drop significantly, and five days is a lifetime in the land of the missing. She glanced at the grinning photo of Henry on the bookcase taken a few months ago, the day his new hand-carved fiddle was delivered. The same shot appeared in the *Gazette* and would be printed on the "Missing" poster.

"What about those two other musicians?" Mira asked. "The ones Alix wrote about in the paper? Do you think there's some kind of weird conspiracy going on?"

"We know the rapper kid, 2B or whatever the hell he calls himself, is heavily into drugs and there's a chance the other one is a druggie, too." Handler narrowed his eyes. "I have to ask and I need you to be straight with me: Is Henry a user?"

"No. I mean, maybe some pot once in a while when he's with the band, but that's it," Mira said, running a hand through her tangle of red hair.

"We'll keep looking into those other two on the off chance there's a connection, but I'm not holding my breath. Meantime, can either of you ladies think of anyone who holds a grudge against Henry? Anyone who might wish to do him harm?"

"No, no way," said Helen. "Henry has always gotten along with everyone. He was never the kind of kid who got into fights at school. If anything, he gives people the benefit of the doubt. And sometimes they take advantage."

The detective fixed his gaze on Mira. "And the band? They all copacetic?"

"Except for Damian. He's the drummer. And a user. He's stoned half the time and Henry's been pushing to get rid of him."

This was news to Helen. She realized that since Henry had moved in with Mira a year ago she was no longer his primary confidante. And probably hadn't been for some time.

"I gotta know," Handler said, his eyes still on Mira, "about the two of you. Any big issues there? It wouldn't surprise me. Henry, out late with the band, drinking, maybe smoking some dope, a bunch of groupies hanging around, flirting. He's a good-looking guy. And there you are, home alone in an isolated cabin, probably waiting up until the wee hours, and with a little one coming. That could put a lot of stress on a young couple . . ."

"We're *good*." Mira's cheeks reddened and she clutched her giant belly, as if at any second the detective might try to snatch the baby from her.

"Okay, happy to hear, but what about old boyfriends? You're a beautiful young woman, Mira. Anyone out there who might still be carrying a torch?"

"Henry and I have been together since our senior year of high school," Mira said, crossing then uncrossing her swollen ankles. "There were a few guys before him. Billy Hallinan, who sort of stalked me after we broke up, but I think he moved away. Jackson Brin, who I've known since we were kids. We broke it off a long time ago and I'm pretty sure he's seeing someone. Oh, and well, Stuart. Rock. From the band. We had a thing, but it was no big deal. Anyhow, Stuart has his pick of adoring fans. He's the one all the groupies go for."

Stuart and Mira? Another breaking news flash for Helen.

"We'll be sure to invite Stuart and Damian and the rest of the band down to the station for a chat."

"Does this mean you're committing to an investigation?" Helen sat up straight.

"Yes, ma'am, that's exactly what it means."

Helen felt her stomach drop and looked away. This was what she wanted, wasn't it? A formal investigation into Henry's disappearance? From now on it wouldn't just be her breaking into motel rooms or calling every hospital in upstate New York. Or Mira getting Stuart to sweet-talk Alix Benitez (one of his groupies) into writing a story for the *Gazette*. So why did Handler's willingness to investigate strike Helen like a body blow?

"Are you saying you no longer think Henry's disappearance is voluntary?" she asked.

"I don't know, but I intend to find out."

Helen knew that as soon as the detective opened a case file, Henry would become a grim statistic, one of 650,000 Americans who go missing every year—a number greater than the population of Seattle or Denver. She had a sudden urge to take the investigation back and continue the search on her own. With Mira's help. And Stuart's. And of course, Charlie's. Find Henry themselves, as if somehow he would be missing *less* if his name wasn't entered into the official rolls of the disappeared. Helen could taste the putrid remains of the hard-boiled egg she'd force-fed herself for breakfast in her throat.

The detective closed his notebook and rose. "Any chance you have a copy of your son's high school yearbook? His college yearbook, too, if he has one."

"They're in his old room. I'll get them," said Helen.

"A couple other things, too. Some of his personal effects—dirty laundry, the dirtier the better. And something of yours, Mrs. Bird, for DNA comparison."

"DNA?" Each request was another gut punch. Helen glanced at Mira. She was folded over her belly, her tumbling chaos of hair masking her face.

"For insurance, just in case we come across an article of clothing or something else that needs to be identified and we bring in a canine unit," Handler said.

"A canine unit?" The only canine units Helen knew of appeared in the British murder mysteries she was addicted to. The dogs endlessly roamed the moors sniffing for corpses—and more often than not, found them.

"All standard procedure. The items will be returned to you, if and when we find him."

"*When*, not if," croaked Mira, wiping her chapped cheeks, then pressing her palms into the seat of the rocker to hoist herself up. "I'll get Henry's dirty clothes. I brought them over to wash so they'll be all clean when he gets back." She returned moments later carrying a wicker basket piled with dirty jeans, T-shirts, boxers, socks, and the filthy denim overalls Henry wore to work at the nursery.

Helen grabbed the basket out of Mira's hands and buried her face in the soiled clothes before the detective gently coaxed it from her.

Then he slipped on a pair of latex gloves, selected several items from the basket, and dropped them one by one into a large plastic evidence bag. Next, he placed Helen's unwashed T-shirt in a separate bag and the two yearbooks in another.

"You will find him, won't you," Helen said. It came out sounding more like an order than a question.

"Soon, *please*," added Mira. "We need him here."

"That's the idea." Detective Handler collected the sealed evidence bags, then handed Helen and Mira each a card with his private pager number and promised to update them as soon as anything turned up.

That was the word he used: anything. Not Henry. *Anything*.

LATER THAT NIGHT, after Mira had fallen asleep in Henry's childhood bed, Helen went outside. She sat down on the back steps and looped herself around Charlie, her arms encircling his large furry frame, her head resting against his. Every nerve running through her felt as if it were on fire, electrified by currents her body could not contain. Even her teeth and eyeballs hurt.

She gazed at the wash of stars lighting up the blue-black night and wondered where in that vast snow globe was her boy. She thought: If only I could get quiet enough, maybe I could sense him, the way I've always been able to sense him, even when we've been apart. Even that summer when he went backpacking north of the Arctic Circle and was out of touch for two weeks. Even then she felt she could detect a cord connecting them, a sort of phantom umbilicus composed of pure energy. But now: nothing. She felt untethered, as if her maternal antennae had been short-circuited by fear.

The fear curdled in her mouth and distorted her vision.

She didn't know how she could go on not knowing whether Henry was alive or dead, because that was the question now. That was always the question when someone disappeared, even if you danced circles around it, even if no one said it out loud. In spite of all she'd been through, Helen's sense of herself as sturdy as an old Western oak with roots deep enough to sustain her through all kinds of trouble felt threatened for the first time.

She wished Jock was there to put his long arms around her, but somehow it didn't feel right to have him sleep over with Mira in the house. Besides, though she longed for Jock's large paunchy body, like a giant, fuzzy teddy bear, she didn't want to have to talk to him. She had no words, and instead of comforting her over the past several days his abundant kindness—part of his job description as a Unitarian minister—had made her feel as though she might break in two.

As if sensing her need for a hairy companion, Charlie nuzzled closer and licked Helen's cheek.

AFTER A SECOND newspaper article appeared, directing inquiries to the Aurora Falls Sheriff's Department, a tidal wave of calls came flooding in from people who claimed to have seen Henry—sneaking across the border on foot into Quebec, boarding a Southwest plane to Cincinnati, buying a pistol in Troy, stealing a six-pack of Bud from a gas station outside Ithaca, climbing into the cab of a semi on a highway somewhere in Michigan—as well as reports of an epidemic of disappeared musicians from Miami to Moscow. There were calls from three or four psychics, too, but none of them could provide any but the vaguest details. After listening to Loretta Sparks, the police department's family liaison officer, recount a call in which a seer "saw" Henry's body buried in the woods near a grove of poplars but couldn't pinpoint where or even in what state, Helen asked Loretta to stop sharing those calls unless the psychics said her son was alive and well or offered specific information as to his whereabouts.

"Henry might still be figuring out his next move," said Will—the detective and Helen were now on a first-name basis—as if that were good news. He and his team had been combing the area surrounding the Silver Dollar and the Timber Creek Motel, going house to house and reviewing the footage from every available security camera, but had failed to turn up any leads.

"Sometimes when people check out for emotional reasons, they feel like they've crossed a line," Will added. "Especially if they get wind that a massive search is on. They feel so guilty about the pain they're causing their loved ones, they're too ashamed to come home."

Fat chance, thought Helen.

———————

SHE GAVE HER employees two weeks' paid leave and shuttered the bakery *until further notice*. Mira, a painter who was getting her degree in studio art at the community college, dropped out of school, and the two women did everything they could to aid in the search. They had thousands more flyers printed and an army of friends and neighbors posted them in nearby towns, while a contingent from Henry's old high school baseball team put them on cars, in bars, restaurants, hotels, motels, and public buildings from Kingston to Albany to Saratoga Springs, and all the way north to the Canadian border. Mira, who was more adept than Helen at using the internet, created FindHenryBird.com. After the first week, Helen stopped monitoring the emails pouring into the website. As with the phone calls being fed to the police, many of the messages seemed to be sent by lunatics and cranks with too much time on their hands. The ones from other parents of missing children and adults were too heartbreaking to read. And Helen preferred not to see the hundreds of condolence notes jamming the site's in-box. Ten days into the search, Mira pitched a segment on Henry to a producer at *America's Most Wanted*, a reality show famous for reuniting family members with missing children.

Mira and Helen both understood that there was only a small window before Henry's disappearance was no longer breaking news. They knew the time would soon come when everyone— including the cops and local reporters—would lose interest and move on to the next case, the next story. The concerned friends and neighbors who dropped off casseroles or helped with the search would congratulate themselves for having done their part and they, too, would move on.

And sooner or later, Helen knew that if Henry didn't turn up, Mira would choose life—as she should, as Helen, under different circumstances, once had—with her child in tow.

Helen, alone, would remain adrift between knowing and not knowing.

Even though she tried not to let her mind wander too far down that path, still it loomed before her, a scary, dark wood.

FIVE

"No way," Lucie said, propping herself up by the elbows, her ankles still tucked in the stirrups.

"Yup, way," said Lucie's gynecologist, Rabia Roubini-Beach, in her silky Jamaican Indian accent that sounded more like music than spoken language.

"But we have an appointment with the fertility guy in a couple of weeks," Lucie said stupidly.

"I suggest you cancel it, sweetness." Rabia rolled the ultrasound machine over to the table and connected it to her computer. "Now lie back down and I'll show you," she said, squeezing icy goop on Lucie's abdomen. "Sorry about that, it'll warm up in a second."

"Are you absolutely sure? I mean, we've been trying, but I didn't think . . ."

"Hear that gorgeous sound?" Rabia said, gently sliding the transducer back and forth across Lucie's womb. "That's your baby's heartbeat. And see that tiny sac right in the middle that looks like a cocoon? That's your baby, baby."

"My *baby*," Lucie repeated. "That's my baby?"

"Looks around seven weeks, give or take. You are pregnant, my friend. Get dressed while I make you a copy of the ultrasound to show your husband."

AS SOON AS she stepped outside Lucie started to punch in Matt's cell but ended the call before the first ring. No way could she tell him over the phone. Plus, she needed time to let the news soak in, to let her mind catch up with her body. She knew how Matt would react, but what about her? Was she thrilled? In shock? Excited? Terrified? All of the above, she decided, feeling her whole body vibrate. She headed for Central Park.

You are seven weeks pregnant.

It wasn't as if she'd had no inkling. Yet she'd been so convinced she couldn't conceive without chemical intervention, she'd been denying the changes in her body like a teenage girl who gets knocked up and is scared to tell her parents. Tender breasts. Nausea. Crushing fatigue. Lately, she'd been falling asleep right after dinner and Matt had been after her to see her doctor and get some blood work done. Lucie laughed out loud at her own thickheadedness. She must have gotten pregnant that weekend in Aurora Falls. They'd never even made it out of bed long enough to look at open houses.

Waiting for the light to change at the corner of Fifth and Ninetieth, Lucie undid the buttons on her jacket and placed her hand over her belly. It felt the same as before. The same and different.

You are seven weeks pregnant.

She called Melina, her assistant, to tell her she wouldn't be in for the rest of the day, then walked south along the path that circled the reservoir. The leaves on the cherry trees were beginning to show their fall pinks and reds. And though it was midafternoon on a weekday, the path was packed with power walkers in business attire and jogging mothers pushing strollers. Soon I'm going to be one of you, she thought, waving at a toddler with corkscrew curls who was babbling nonstop to her mother. Lucie was grateful she no longer had to worry about her fertility or juicing up her hormones, like so many women she knew.

All she had to do was have the baby.

She crossed the footbridge that led south and sat on a bench facing the Great Lawn. Nearby, a father was trying to teach his young son how to throw a football. But the lesson didn't appear to be taking, because the boy preferred to have his father catch him—a scene that ordinarily Lucie would pay little, if any, attention to. But this was no ordinary day, and suddenly, this most ordinary activity struck her as extraordinary: father, son, giggling, falling down, rolling around on the patchy grass in the golden glow of an Indian summer afternoon. She squinted and pretended for a few seconds that Matt was the father playing catch and the kid was theirs. But then she started to panic: What if something went wrong with the pregnancy? So many horrible things could happen, even if she managed to have the baby. Briefly, she flashed on the missing son of the woman who owned the bakery in Aurora Falls and hoped that by now he had returned home safely.

But she would not let herself dwell on it. Lucie vowed that from now on, each time a scary thought arose, she'd banish it from her mind. Last year, after editing a story about the negative effects of excess cortisol and other stress hormones on a developing fetus, she'd promised herself that the anxious wiring she believed she inherited from her nana—which, inexplicably, seemed to have bypassed her mother—would stop with her if someday she had a baby.

Puh puh, she spit over her left shoulder, the way Nana always did to scare away the evil eye whenever she wished for something good to happen.

Lucie wished she could call Nana right this minute and tell

her that soon she would be a great-nana. Even now, ten years after her death, Lucie missed her terribly. She missed her smell, a pungent but soothing potpourri of chicken soup, Chanel No. 5, and mothballs that enveloped her whenever she stayed at Nana's apartment in San Francisco.

Heading for the West Side, Lucie traced the outline of her belly and felt such a rush of love for the tender little fish swimming inside her, she decided that she and the baby could use another shot of good luck for insurance. So she *puh puh*-ed over her shoulder once more and almost got knocked down by a reckless cyclist as she crossed West Drive.

"Asshole," she shouted after him, then clutched her stomach. "Just so you know, baby, your mother is normally not an angry person." This was, she realized, the very first time she'd spoken to her baby.

As she got closer to home, she had to figure out how to break the news to Matt. How to play a scene she'd witnessed only in movies or read about in books? She found her answer in the children's bookstore, then popped into a wine shop and sprung for a crazy expensive bottle of Dom Perignon, even though Matt would be the only one drinking.

THERE HAD TO be champagne. Champagne was the elixir that had brought Matt and Lucie together five years earlier. That night they'd run into each other at the opening of Roots & Shoots, New York's first raw vegan restaurant, where Holly, Lucie's former roommate, was sous chef. Lucie was huddled against the back wall, watching trays of unidentifiable foodstuffs whiz past, when she spotted Matt. He and Holly had had a fling while playing Nick and Honey in a summer stock production of *Who's Afraid of*

Virginia Woolf? The relationship didn't last and neither did Matt's flirtation with acting. According to Holly, after auditioning and waiting tables for a year after graduating college, Matt decided he wanted to do something to benefit humankind, plus he wasn't all that crazy about being broke. So, bowing to family tradition—but not to becoming an anesthesiologist like his father, Gordon, who preferred his patients unconscious—Matt enrolled in medical school. And after completing a fellowship in ophthalmology, he began to satisfy his itch for adventure as well as helping humankind by making twice-yearly trips to Nepal and sometimes Ethiopia to work in rural clinics and see the world, one damaged eyeball at a time.

"I always thought the two of you would be great together and I have it on good authority that he's not seeing anyone at the moment," Holly told Lucie when she called to invite her to the restaurant's opening.

Lucie had met Matt at previous Holly events and had always found him appealing in a nerdy, boyish sort of way, even though he was at least six or seven years older. "He seems like a good guy, but I'm too obsessed with work to get involved right now," she said. Recently promoted from fact-checker to associate health editor at *Lulu*, she was determined not to end up rudderless and broke like her mother, who reinvented herself every couple of years—massage therapist, artist's model, cleaning lady, astrologer, potter, waitress, yoga instructor, etc. Plus, Lucie had just come off a string of miserable fix ups and was taking a break from the whole dating scene. At twenty-seven she had plenty of time to meet someone.

So when Matt asked her to sneak out with him to grab a bite someplace where they served known food groups, she turned him down almost before the words were out of his mouth. "Come on," he prodded, tipping his head in the direction of "pizza" made from ground flax seeds and cashew cheese. "I'm on the verge of passing out. You must be starving, too."

Lucie was feeling a bit wobbly. All she'd eaten since breakfast was a pretzel from a street vendor. "Okay, a quick bite," she agreed.

He took her to a French place on Wooster Street, where she proceeded to wolf down three courses plus dessert, half a bottle of champagne, and a glass of pinot noir—something she never would have done on a real date. On a real date, worried about appearing gluttonous, she would have ordered two appetizers, one glass of white wine, taken two small bites of the guy's dessert—then gone home and polished off last night's leftover sesame noodles. (Though Lucie considered herself a feminist, she was aware that her conditioned female brain sometimes made her act like it was 1952 or even 1752.) But this was Holly's old pal Matt, so she considered it an *un*date and ate with gusto. Drank, too, which probably accounted for why she lunged at him in the cab.

They were married in his parents' backyard in Riverdale a year later.

IN THE TIME she'd known him, Lucie had seen Matt tear up only twice: when he said "I do" at their wedding and a few months later, at his grandfather's funeral. The third time was when he realized she was pregnant. She was stretched out on the sofa when he came in the door, humming as usual. Matt was a major hummer, whose default tune was the theme song from *The Godfather*. Lucie found this habit alternately charming and annoying.

"Hey," she said. "I got you a present."

"Uh-oh, did I forget another big occasion?" he asked, slinging his raincoat over a hook in the entryway. "This isn't the anniversary of the first time we had sex or something, is it?"

"Nope."

"Okay, good, because I'm wiped," he said, kissing her crown of curls, then plunked down next to her. "I was supervising a corneal transplant when my fellow suddenly lost it and I had to take over."

"Maybe this will perk you up." Lucie reached into the bag from the children's bookstore, then pulled out a gift-wrapped parcel and handed it to him.

He tore off the wrapping paper. "Luce, this is so great," he said, holding up a copy of *Where the Wild Things Are*. "You remembered how pissed off I was when my parents got rid of my old one, which I was saving for our hypothetical child, but now we have this. I'll read it to you tonight in bed." He leaned over and kissed her on the mouth.

"Look inside." Lucie's heart was frittering around in her chest. She watched as he opened the book to the page where the copy of the sonogram was hidden.

When he unfolded it, he just stared. Speechless. Finally, he said, "Are you kidding me?"

"Not unless Rabia's kidding me. According to her, I'm seven weeks pregnant. Our hypothetical child is no longer so hypothetical."

Matt looked from the sonogram to Lucie and back to the sonogram. Then he propped his glasses on top of his head and wiped his eyes with his hand so he could see better. "Are you telling me this fuzzy little shadow is our baby?"

"Yessir, that's our baby. I even heard her heartbeat. It was so fast, I think she might be a horse."

"IT'S FREAKING AMAZING," Matt said, trailing Lucie into the bedroom after a dinner of scrambled eggs and toast. "Even though the kid is the size of a blueberry, she already has hands and feet. Which look like little clubs. See." He handed her a printout of a magnified seven-week-old fetus he'd found on the internet.

"Let's not get ahead of ourselves, okay?" Lucie gave him back the printout and started to undress. Now that the initial shock was fading, her mind reeled with ominous facts. "Don't forget, eighty-five percent of all miscarriages happen in the first trimester. You have no idea how many stories I've done on the complications. Gestational diabetes . . ." She was about to rattle off the list of horrors when she stopped herself, remembering the vow she'd made in the park: no negative thinking. "Oh God, Matt, I'm sorry. It's just that I already love the blueberry so much." She began to cry.

"I know you're scared, but honey, I'm telling you, the blueberry is going to be fine and so are you. I promise." He kissed Lucie's wet cheek, then got down on his knees and pressed his mouth to her bare belly. "Hey, kiddo," he said. "This is your dad speaking. You hear me? Your d-a-d."

There it is, Lucie thought, stepping into her pajama bottoms, the main difference between us. Matt's faith in life and my inherent mistrust. Evolutionary biologists call the human brain's tendency to focus on problems our inborn negativity bias. But Matt's brain seemed to run on an alternate program. Lucie knew that tomorrow or the next day he'd start a college fund, then pop into a toy store and buy a teddy bear on his way home from work. She'd always marveled at this capacity in him, his belief that, one way or another, whether by mysterious grace or plain dumb luck, things would turn out fine. Remarkably, most of the time he was right.

Maybe he'd even be right about her being a good mother. After all, without a role model in the conjugal department, Lucie had always believed that marriage was for other people, and she continued to be happily surprised that she'd turned out to be one of those people.

Matt returned to the bedroom carrying two champagne flutes and the bottle of Dom Perignon. He popped the cork, then filled his glass with shimmering golden bubbles and poured Lucie half that amount. "To the blueberry and the blueberry's mama," he said, raising his glass.

"Matt, you know I can't . . ."

"Trust me, you're not going to give the kid fetal alcohol syndrome from a couple of sips. Pretend you're French."

"*Zut alors*," Lucie said, draining her glass in one gulp, then holding it up for him to pour her some more.

SIX

THEY WERE ON THEIR WAY TO THE SILVER DOLLAR. HELEN NEEDED to breathe the air in the place where Henry was last seen, even though it had been three weeks since he'd been there.

She was fed up with sitting around and feeling helpless, frustrated that, so far, Will and his team had yet to turn up a single solid lead, even with the help of the regional FBI office. Nor had anything concrete come from the slew of emails sent to FindHenryBird.com or the thousands of flyers and posters that had been distributed all over the state. Then yesterday *America's Most Wanted* passed. "Not a clear case of foul play. Besides, a twenty-two-year-old man doesn't exactly qualify as a missing child," the producer had said snarkily over the phone. So, after checking with Mira to make sure she felt comfortable staying home alone—the baby could come any day—Helen called Stuart and asked him to go with her to Saratoga Springs. Will had been so insistent on letting law enforcement do its job, Helen had held off on going up there until now. But who knew? Maybe she and Stuart would stumble across some piece of evidence the cops had overlooked.

"I really appreciate this," she said, settling into the passenger seat of the red Corvette convertible that had been a high school graduation gift from Stuart's stockbroker father.

"Hey, it's the least I can do. The po-po are famous for missing critical shit." Stuart put on his mirrored sunglasses and revved the engine.

Stuart wasn't just Dog Radio's lead guitarist and vocalist, he was its leading heartbreaker, too. With his dazzling smile and pitch-dark fluttery eyelids that settled just above half-mast, he appeared to cast a hypnotic spell over the band's small but ardent pack of groupies. He and Henry had been jamming together since middle school but didn't get serious about their music until the summer after college. That's when they put together a foursome with Damian on drums and Paul on bass, and called themselves Dog Radio, inspired by Charlie, who seemed to groove to their bluegrass sound. The band's latest CD had been just starting to attract the attention of a couple of high-profile record producers around the time Henry disappeared.

When Stuart pulled up outside the Silver Dollar, the "Missing" poster with Henry's bright smile greeted them from the club's front window.

"THAT WAS A kickass show, the early set," said the bartender, a stick-thin man named Steve, when Stuart and Helen sat down at the empty bar. "Ginormous crowd. Duke was all set to book you guys for Columbus Day weekend, but . . ." Steve waved his hands in the air.

"Yeah, it was a good night, the first show rocked, but then there was that thing at the beginning of the second set and we sucked after that," said Stuart.

"What thing?" asked Helen.

"Well . . ." Steve looked up from polishing glasses. "The band was in the middle of a tune when this guy came in and started yelling at one of the customers. I think he owed him money."

"It was harsh, but Henry handled it," Stuart said to Helen. "He told the audience we were going to take a short break and we stopped playing until the manager got those two donuts outside. The whole thing couldn't have lasted more than ten minutes."

"I'm no big gambler or nothing, but I've seen that guy who was yelling at the track and I'm pretty sure he's a bookie." Steve held a glass up to the light for inspection. "I told the cops about him, but to be honest they didn't seem all that interested."

"Would you recognize either of the two men if you saw them again?" Helen asked.

"The bookie, yeah, but the other guy, I don't know. I was up to my eyeballs mixing drinks, but maybe Duke could point him out."

Helen was furious that this was the first she'd heard of the incident, especially since Henry was the one who'd taken charge. Maybe the bookie was angry when the band stopped playing and all eyes were on him. Who knew what men like that were capable of? Maybe he'd followed Henry to the motel? "I'm going to bring this up with Detective Handler as soon as we get home," she said when she and Stuart were back out on the street.

FROM THE SILVER Dollar, they walked along the stretch of busy road between the bar and the Timber Creek Motel. The weeds bordering the uneven sidewalk were littered with cigarette butts, liquor bottles, used condoms, and hypodermic needles, and reeked of piss.

"Disgusting," said Helen. "I'm glad Henry never got into drugs, except maybe a little marijuana now and then."

Stuart kicked some pebbles in the dirt.

When he didn't say anything, Helen said, "Right?"

"You know . . ."

"What do I know? Other than the fact that Damian has a drug problem and Henry wants to kick him out of the band? Is there something else I should know?" Helen felt such intense pressure in her head, she might as well be wearing a helmet. "Jesus, Stuart, talk to me."

"We're musicians, you know. We have fans and they bring us treats. Henry is no addict, but Damian isn't the only one who sometimes enjoys a taste." Stuart picked up a spindly branch and started scraping it along the sidewalk.

"A *taste*? Henry likes a taste?"

"Hey, I don't think drugs had anything to do with him going away, but sometimes before shows we smoke some pot, maybe snort a little coke. But not all the time and as far as I know, Henry never shot up. Not like Damian."

"Did you tell this to Detective Handler?"

"Hell, no. I didn't want to get Henry into trouble."

"More like you didn't want to get yourself into trouble."

"Mrs. Bird . . ." It was the first time Stuart hadn't called Helen by her first name since he was twelve.

She started racewalking away from him, questions jamming her brain like an overamped power line. Could drugs be the link to the two other missing musicians? Did Henry have a drug problem and was Stuart protecting him? Or was Stuart the one with the real problem and was he just protecting himself? What, if anything, did Mira know? She'd been Stuart's girlfriend before

Henry. Did Stuart know something about Henry's disappearance, and could Mira be covering for him? Helen knew they'd been talking on the phone almost every day, and Stuart had come by several times to take a walk with Mira and Charlie. Helen was glad Stuart had been so supportive of Mira, who was in a bad way. But now she wondered if Will had gotten the truth out of either of them. If anyone had mastered the art of keeping secrets it was Helen, and now she didn't know who to trust.

Yet deep in her bones she didn't believe her son was a drug addict any more than she believed his absence was his choice. Or that Mira was keeping something from her. At least that's what Helen thought she believed, because in the country of the missing she was finding it hard to be certain of anything.

When she reached the Timber Creek Motel, the *K* still missing, she stood out front glaring at the two-story building in need of a makeover. It looked even more run down in daylight than it had the night she'd broken into Henry's room. Even the name of the place was a scam. There was no creek in sight.

"Want to go in the office and talk to someone?" Stuart asked when he caught up.

"No," said Helen. The last thing she needed was to run into the creep who'd turned her away that night.

"I'm sorry if I upset you. Like I said, except for Damian, the rest of us aren't into drugs in any big way."

Helen turned to face Stuart. The one person she'd always trusted to have her son's back. "When I get home, I'm going to call Detective Handler and tell him what you told me. I expect he'll want to know the names of everyone who ever gave you guys *treats*."

They drove back to Aurora Falls in silence.

A FEW DAYS after the expedition to Saratoga Springs that raised more questions than it answered, Will showed up at Helen's door looking flushed. Even Charlie sensed something different in the detective's demeanor, because instead of barking like his coat was on fire, he jumped on Will and Helen asked Mira to put the dog out back.

"Does this have anything to do with what I told you over the phone?" she asked as soon as Mira was outside.

"I'm having a chat with Stuart tomorrow morning."

Helen tried to gauge Will's expression to see if he was holding anything back, but she still felt so stung by Stuart's revelations, she didn't trust her own sense of things. "But you'll keep looking into it? Drugs could be the key to the whole thing."

"I'm on it," he said.

"What about the bookie?"

"Him, too."

Returning to the living room, Mira sensed something in the air as well. Out of breath, she asked the detective, "What's going on? You found something, didn't you?"

"Well, yes and no, but I don't want either of you getting too excited," Will said in his measured drawl. "I had my deputy run another trace on Henry's cell phone this afternoon, just in case. Turns out that early Tuesday morning, September third, several hours after he left the club, two calls were made from his phone to youth hostels in Canada. One in the far north of Quebec, near Baffin Bay. Inuit country. The other to a hostel near a national park on the northern tip of Cape Breton Island."

"And you're just learning this now?" Helen wanted to scream.

"Why didn't you run a trace before?" The crimson color in Mira's cheeks rose to match her hair.

"We did," Will said, sounding defensive. "But sometimes calls from mobile phones to numbers outside the US don't show up right away. Which is why we run them again. And again. Unfortunately, there weren't any more calls after those two. Radio silence since the morning of the third."

"That doesn't sound like Henry," Helen said, braiding then unbraiding her hair, which she'd vowed not to cut until her son returned home. "He loves the outdoors, sure, and I told you he went hiking up near Baffin Bay a few years ago, but . . ."

She stopped herself midsentence, feeling a buzzing in her chest. Was it possible that Will's original theory was right? That Henry felt so terrified by the prospect of fatherhood that he ran away? And turned to drugs? On some unconscious level, was he repeating the sins of his father, even though he hadn't seen Kip since he was five years old? Helen had always wanted to believe that getting Henry away from Kip's influence would spare him. But maybe that was a fairy tale she'd spun to soothe herself, and it wasn't possible to excise the father from the boy—now the man. Could it be that the sum of her actions—however well meaning—had driven her son away? And made him resort to drugs to blot out the burdens of the past?

"Sometimes we think we know our children better than they know themselves, and then we learn the hard way they're not the people we thought they were," Will said quietly. "Not the people we raised them to be."

Helen knew he was talking about his oldest daughter, Andrea. A few months before Henry went missing, Helen had heard from the town gossipmongers, who chewed over the latest rumors with their morning buns, that Andrea was back in rehab for the third or fourth time. Was Henry a victim of the same epidemic that had claimed Will's daughter?

"So maybe whoever called the police a few weeks ago and said they saw Henry crossing the border into Quebec was telling the truth," said Mira, gripping her belly. "Ow. Sorry. Fake contraction." She took a breath. "At least that gives you something to go on, right?"

"All we know is that Henry—or someone using his phone—called the hostel in Quebec, got voicemail, and didn't leave a message. But the night clerk in Cape Breton remembers a man calling and making a reservation in Henry's name for September ninth, only he never checked in." Will shrugged. "That's all we got."

"Henry's passport is still here, in a file box with mine," Helen said. "Wouldn't he have been stopped trying to cross the border?"

Will snorted. "Security has been tightened since 9/11, but we're talking a border four thousand miles long, with gaps as wide as the Grand Canyon. Anybody wanting to slip through can."

"But even if he didn't make it to the hostels, we finally have a trail, right? He's obviously in Canada." Mira wanted assurance that there was now a clear path forward to finding the father of her baby and bringing him home. A few days before, she'd told Helen she didn't think she could make it through childbirth without him. "So when are you going up there?" she prodded the detective.

"We've alerted law enforcement in Quebec, Nova Scotia, and the rest of the provinces, but until we have something concrete no one's going anywhere," Will said, his jowls sagging. "You're right, Mira, this is something to go on, only we don't know what. Or whether it was Henry who made those calls."

Something to go on, nothing to go on, Helen thought, clasping Mira's hand, which had gone limp. Normally Helen appreciated Will's directness, but she, too, could do with a bit of hope. Especially since learning her son might have a drug problem, might even be part of some drug ring involving other musicians. Something she never would have thought possible.

"I'd like the names of both of those hostels," she said.

"Come on, Helen." Will's granite eyes narrowed and shot her a warning look. "Not a good idea. We're on it, here and up north. As soon as there's a development, if there is a development, you'll be the first to know. Both of you. For now, you need to sit tight, in case Henry turns up."

"What do you think we've been doing for the past three weeks?" Helen did not like being told what to do. When she finally awoke from her trance and marshaled the courage to leave Kip all those years ago, she promised herself she would never let any man boss her around again. Cop or no cop.

As soon as Will was out the door, she logged on to her computer and was hunched over a blown-up map of Baffin Bay when Mira's water broke an hour later.

SEVEN

Rocking in the glider that had been sent over by her in-laws the week the pregnancy became viable, Lucie said, "Let's go to Aurora Falls next weekend, okay?"

"You really want to go away?" Matt looked down from the ladder in the second bedroom, which they'd converted into a nursery, and where, at the moment, he was affixing the Day-Glo solar system to the ceiling.

"Why not? We have four more weeks, plus Rabia says this kid is in no hurry to get out." Which was fine with Lucie. She wasn't in any rush to give birth—the inescapable part of pregnancy that still terrified her. Besides, she didn't mind that her womb had turned into a cramped SRO. She loved the sensation of the baby's fists and elbows, knees and feet, pummeling her from the inside.

"You can't even get a decent night's sleep in our own bed," Matt said, repositioning Pluto.

"So? The great thing about insomnia is that it's very democratic. You can have it anywhere. And Aurora Falls is so beautiful in the spring, everything bursting out of its casing. Like me." Lucie rubbed her mountain of a belly, which Matt had dubbed the Matterhorn because it resembled a horizontal mountain with a very pointy peak.

"Look," she said as the Matterhorn began to jiggle. "The nightly flamenco routine."

Matt climbed down from the ladder and placed his hands on Lucie's gyrating belly, mesmerized. It didn't matter that he was a doctor and had delivered babies; it got to him every time. This was *his* baby. "I'm not sure it's a great idea to stay at a cottage so far out of town," he said when the Matterhorn took a breather. "There's no hospital within at least fifteen miles."

"Okay, so then we'll stay at that cute B and B in town, right across from the green. And if I go into labor early, no problem. You're always telling me how handy you were in the delivery room during your residency."

"If you really want to, but only if Rabia says it's okay."

"I saw her today and she said it was fine."

"All right, I'll see if I can get Mitch to cover for me on Friday so we can leave early."

But on Wednesday evening Mitch sprained his wrist playing pickup basketball, so Matt had to fill in for him and wouldn't be able to leave the city until late afternoon.

Tossing and turning that night, Lucie came up with plan B. She'd take the bus up to Aurora Falls early Friday morning so she could still enjoy the day until Matt got there at dinnertime. In the past, she might have been too nervous to go off by herself in such a vulnerable state, but somehow pregnancy had made her braver. Calmer. After she passed the first trimester mark and got a clean amnio report, she stopped worrying and started knitting, something she hadn't done since Nana taught her how when she was a kid. Booties. Hats. A creamy yellow angora crib blanket. Matt, who'd been prepared to talk her down off the cliff of anxiety and dread, had been amazed. At her urging, in February he'd even made a two-week pilgrimage to an eye clinic in Nepal.

WHEN LUCIE ANNOUNCED her plan to take the bus up Friday morning, he instantly vetoed it. But after going round and round about everything that could go wrong—in a rare reversal of roles, lately Matt was the one whose nerves were ragged—he finally agreed.

TEN MINUTES AFTER the bus pulled out of Port Authority, Lucie was lulled to sleep by its gentle rocking motion as it lumbered north, only to be jerked awake out of a pleasant-dream-turned-nightmare when the driver stopped in New Paltz. Shivering though the bus was overheated, she reached into her bag and rooted around for her dream journal. She'd been faithfully recording her dreams for months, hoping to receive a message from the baby. But so far, nothing. Until now. In the dream, Lucie and Matt were in bed when an adorable little boy with a halo of golden curls burst into the room carrying a small suitcase. He dropped the suitcase on the floor, then hopped into bed between them. Lucie was overcome with joy when she realized this beautiful boy was their son. "Hi, baby," she whispered. "Welcome." He didn't answer because he was just a baby, even though he looked about four or five. He seemed happy and couldn't stop giggling when Lucie kissed his tummy, but when he rolled over on his side and turned his back to her, she saw blood spurting like a geyser from a hole in the back of his skull. In the dream she tried to scream but was unable to make a sound.

Or maybe she did scream, because when she opened her eyes, her seatmate—a pimply young man wearing a neon orange cycling outfit—asked if she was okay. Trembling, she assured him she was fine.

But she wasn't fine. She wanted to call Matt and tell him the dream, but not from a crowded bus. She spent most of the remaining hour to Aurora Falls trying to decipher its meaning. Was it a premonition or a normal expression of the collective fear shared by expectant mothers that something might be wrong with their baby? Or was the dream really about her, in the way that therapists say *all* the characters in a dream are simply aspects of oneself? But what aspect of Lucie did the bleeding boy represent? All she knew was how awful she felt for recoiling when she saw the blood instead of trying to stanch the flow. She promised herself never to recoil from her real baby, not ever, no matter what.

SHE STARTED TO relax as soon as the bus pulled into Aurora Falls, and by the time she was settled in her room at the Inn on the Green, she stopped second-guessing her decision to come up early. The inn's owner, an elderly woman named Vi, could not have made Lucie feel more welcome if she'd been her long-lost niece. And the room was perfect. With its wallpaper dotted with primroses, an old-fashioned washbasin, a green velvet fainting couch, and a four-poster canopied bed, it looked like it belonged in a Victorian dollhouse. Best of all, the room overlooked the village green, which reminded Lucie of the grassy expanse in her hometown, where she'd played while her mother worked at a funky little dress shop nearby. She remembered that year when Phoebe had sworn off men as the happiest of her childhood and decided that later she'd stop by a local real estate office just to see what was on the market. Maybe Matt would humor her and agree to check out a few open houses over the weekend.

She lay down on the dainty sofa, hoping her heft wouldn't reduce it to a pile of pick-up sticks, and gazed out the window. Across the way, gnarled old apple trees, along with dogwoods and cherries, were just starting to show their blossoms, while a few mothers spread out blankets on the grass for a picnic lunch with their kids, only the kids had gone rogue and were running wild in all directions. Watching them, Lucie could not have been more content. This was the first time in forever when there was absolutely nothing she had to do. She opened her old, battered copy of *Middlemarch* and drifted off to sleep before she made it through a single paragraph.

An hour later, she was jolted awake by an intense wave of pressure in her abdomen, which felt hot and hard and rose like a boulder. She wasn't worried, though. It was just one of those annoying Braxton Hicks contractions, which felt like the real deal but weren't—uncomfortable but normal. She'd been having them for weeks. When the contraction subsided, she realized she was starving. She'd had nothing to eat but a toasted bagel on the bus and wondered if the Queen of Hearts had reopened. On her way out she went to ask Vi, but the door to her office was closed and Lucie heard the rumble of snoring on the other side.

THE MOTHERS AND kids had cleared out and the green was nearly empty, save for a man in a suit and tie yelling into a cell phone, a gardener bent over a bed of tulips, and a couple of teenagers with their bodies in a twist. When another Braxton Hicks contraction hit, Lucie found a bench and sat down until it passed. It was unusual to have two false contractions so close together, but she figured it must be on account of nerves left over from her dream. Even though she kept trying to blot it out, the image of the bloody torrent gushing from the baby's skull kept flashing through her mind.

She was also a little nervous about finding out whether the bakery owner's son had returned home safely, as Matt had predicted. Nearing the Queen of Hearts, she had her answer. Taped to the inside front window was a slightly faded "Missing" poster offering a $25,000 reward and the same glowing photograph of Henry Bird that had appeared in the local paper. "Oh no," Lucie sighed, feeling her rib cage sink. But when she peered in the window, she was relieved to see that the lights were on. At least Henry's mother hadn't lost her business.

And when she opened the door, she was transported by the sweet, earthy aroma of cinnamon, the perfume of *home*. Some of Lucie's happiest memories took place in a small bakery in Point Reyes that was owned by a woman named Sierra, the mother of Lucie's childhood best friend, Azalia. The girls spent endless happy hours creating families out of dough, which Sierra baked when the oven was free. The dough families always had a mother and a father, lots of siblings, and a menagerie of pets, and could not have been more different from the girls' own families, each with an only child and a single mother.

Looking around the Queen of Hearts, Lucie saw that just two of the half-dozen tables were occupied, one by a pair of middle-aged women who appeared deep in conversation, the other by a young man tapping away on a laptop. Across the room, a pretty young woman with a tumble of wavy red hair was nursing a baby. Lucie wondered if she was the owner's daughter.

"Be right with you," the woman said in a low voice. "She's just about done. Shh . . ." she cooed, then gently removed the baby from her breast and turned to Lucie, whispering, "Looks like you're about to have one of these yourself."

Lucie patted her belly. "Not quite yet. This kid hasn't even begun to drop."

The young woman settled her sleeping baby into a stroller that flattened into a bed and wheeled it behind the counter, but not before Lucie could take a peek. "So pretty," she said softly. "And with gorgeous red hair like her mom. How old?"

"Seven months." The woman covered the baby with a pink-and-white blanket that looked hand-crocheted, then smiled at Lucie. "So, what can I get you?"

Lucie scanned the menu scrawled on the blackboard behind the counter. "I'll take a bowl of your spring asparagus soup and a plain croissant and . . . Ow, I think I'd better sit down." She grabbed the counter to steady herself. "I keep having these annoying Braxton Hicks things," she said when the wave passed. "This is the third one in the last little while."

"Let me help you. I'm Mira, by the way." She led Lucie to a table by the fireplace. "Are you sure they're just Braxton Hicks?"

"Absolutely. I've been having them for ages. Oops, I better go pee before I sit." Lucie felt her panties and maternity jeans getting soaked. "Oh no." She glanced down at the old-fashioned black-and-white tile floor, where straw-colored liquid was beginning to pool between her feet. "I'm afraid I just peed all over your nice clean floor."

"Don't worry, I'm familiar with the problem," Mira said as an older woman stepped out from the kitchen. Lucie recognized her as Helen, the owner, looking so much paler and thinner than the last time she'd seen her, her hair gone from silverish blonde to pure silver. It was twisted into a long, loose braid, and she was wearing an enormous charcoal gray sweater.

"Oh my," Helen said.

"I think we should call 911," said Mira.

"No, please don't. It's just a little pee." Lucie cupped the Matterhorn from below. "My bladder is completely scrunched. I'll check in with my husband, he's a doctor." She didn't mention that he was an ophthalmologist who had forgotten most of what he'd learned during his OB/GYN rotation.

"You need to be seen." Helen pointed to the growing puddle on the floor that was now tinged pink. "That looks like more than plain old pee."

"Please don't call 911. I know you're just trying to help, but . . . I'm sure this is false labor." Lucie glanced down at the bloody mess that looked like a crime scene and began to cry.

"Just to be safe, I'm taking you to the medical center in Albany to get checked out," said Helen. "It's much better than our local hospital, which is where the paramedics would take you. You can call your husband from the car."

"How about I take her, and you stay with Lola?" Mira sounded concerned. "I just think, you know, you haven't been sleeping all that well and it might be better if I . . ."

"No," Helen insisted. "I'm fine to drive her." Then, lowering her voice, she added, "Please stop worrying about me so much. I'm not an invalid."

Lucie didn't know what to do. Should she let herself be driven to Albany by this ghostly looking woman or let them call 911 and have the paramedics take her to the shitty local hospital? She gripped the back of a chair and moaned as another contraction hit.

After it subsided, with Mira gripping one arm and Helen

propping her up by the other, Lucie found herself being led outside and loaded like a lumpy sack of potatoes into a rusted red
Subaru wagon parked in the alley next to the bakery.

"This old rattletrap may look like she's ready for the junk-
heap, but she's totally reliable," Helen said, securing Lucie's seat
belt. "I'll have you in Albany in twenty-five minutes, half an hour,
max."

EIGHT

HELEN NEVER COULD HAVE IMAGINED THAT THE YEAR HER SON disappeared would be her year for babies. First, the birth of Lola, whose naked fascination with everything from earthworms to her own tiny toes was all that stood between Helen and her shattered heart.

And now here she was, driving a woman she didn't know to the hospital so she could have her baby.

Babies, babies everywhere. Just not mine.

Helen recognized Lucie from the bakery. She and her husband were among the crowd of New Yorkers who flocked to Aurora Falls for a "country getaway." Lucie had always struck Helen as one of the nice ones. Appreciative of what the Queen of Hearts had to offer. Not like the prickly types who managed to slip in a complaint even when they were paying you a compliment.

"Shit," Lucie muttered, dropping her BlackBerry in her lap and cradling her belly. "Matt just got pulled into emergency surgery. Some kid stabbed in the eye with a pencil, which means he won't get up here until late and, oh . . ." She doubled over.

"Squeeze my hand and breathe slowly," said Helen. "In through your nose, out through your mouth, with a big sigh on the exhale." Having recently pinch-hit for Henry as Mira's labor coach, Helen was up on the latest techniques. Which had changed radically since she'd given birth more than two decades before. Back then she'd been instructed to mouth the words to a song during the peak of contractions. She'd picked Linda Ronstadt's "It's So Easy (to Fall in Love)." And it was. Oh, so easy to fall in love with her baby.

"I'm sorry," Lucie said, as the wave passed, and she let go of Helen's hand. "Thank you for taking me. My doctor told me we had weeks, but . . . I'm going to try her, too." She punched in another number on her phone. "Damn. It's ringing through to the answering service."

"Just keep breathing. Nice and slow." Helen was glad to be doing something useful for someone else, even though if she'd acted sensibly, she would have let Mira drive this woman to the hospital while she stayed back with Lola. After dropping twenty-five pounds and barely sleeping for months, she was running on pure adrenaline. Still, it felt good to take control of a situation. It made her feel like a functioning member of society and not some creature trapped between worlds, between knowing and not knowing. Someday she might have to face the fact that she might never again see her son or learn what had happened to him.

But for now she clung to this in-between state like a mountain climber clinging to a fraying rope, even as the various explanations for Henry's disappearance began drying up. The trail in Canada had grown as frozen as the tundra in February, and Stuart's inference that Henry might have gone off in search of drugs turned out to be more about Stuart's habit than Henry's—Stuart was in his second month of rehab. And though the missing-musician conspiracy theory remained an open question, there hadn't been any more cases since Henry vanished. Still, the letter Helen had found in the wastebasket at the motel kept eating away at her. What if Henry really had gone in search of his father?

She'd booked, then canceled, three more flights to Oregon. Each time she imagined facing Kip, she felt her throat constrict and had trouble breathing. Which was why last week she'd hired a second private investigator in Oregon, after the first idiot hadn't been able to turn up anything recent on Kip, let alone Henry. The new guy's name—he swore to her over the phone—was Richard Tracy, "but just call me Dick." Helen was waiting for "just call me Dick" to tell her whether her worst fear had been realized and Henry was holed up drinking and drugging with Kip.

Well, obviously not her worst fear.

"Please tell Rabia it's an emergency. I might be in labor and I'm out of town," Lucie was pleading into the phone. "I'm on my way to the hospital now."

"We'll be there in a flash," Helen said, as they passed a sign for Albany: 18 miles.

"Actually, I think the contractions are slowing down, so maybe this really is false labor," Lucie said, after ending the call. "Maybe they'll just check me out, then I can go back with you and wait for my husband. If you don't mind staying for a little while."

"No problem." The woman was clearly in hard labor, but Helen didn't think it would be helpful to say so.

"Also, I just want you to know, my husband and I, we love your bakery, it's always our first stop, and one time I even had a nice talk with your son . . . And, well, we just happened to be in town right after he, and . . . God, I feel like such a jerk, I'm not sure what to say, except I'm really really sorry," Lucie stammered.

"Thank you, Lucie. And please don't worry, some of my oldest friends don't know what to say to me. I'm a reminder of every parent's worst nightmare. After I reopened a few months ago, a lot of people stayed away. Afraid that having a missing child might be contagious, I guess. Business was terrible until Mira started working the register and I stayed in the kitchen." Helen liked Lucie for mentioning Henry. So many people still tiptoed around her, seemingly afraid that any reference to him might remind her that he was still missing.

"Well, I'm just very sorry, and sorry for putting you out. And with a baby . . ."

"Please. Life goes on, people have babies. Including Mira. Lola's my granddaughter, Henry's daughter. Here, squeeze." She offered Lucie her hand as the next contraction landed. "That's it, deep breath, big sigh on the exhale. Ahhh . . ."

Surprisingly, Helen felt more like her old self the closer they got to Albany. Clearly, she needed to get out more, get out of her own head, do something for other people. Start volunteering again at the soup kitchen. Go back to her book group and the interfaith choir she loved. In the nearly eight months since Henry went missing, aside from searching for him, all she'd done was to get the bakery up and running part time and help Mira with Lola. Too often, the normality of other people's lives struck Helen as garish, unspooling in gaudy technicolor while she slogged along in grainy black and white. She'd tried having dinner with Abby and a few other friends, but found she was incapable of making small talk, and it hurt too much to talk about Henry, so she'd stopped accepting their invitations. And last month she'd gone into the city with Jock to protest the Iraq War. Afterward, he talked her into spending the night at his place, which turned out to be a colossal mistake. Not because it was bad, but because it was so damn good—and she was terrified that if she allowed herself any real happiness, it would mean she'd accepted that Henry was gone. She knew that was deranged; she also knew that sooner or later Jock would tire of waiting for her and move on. Maybe it was time to drag herself to the Parents of Missing Children support group that Will kept hounding her to attend, but which she thought of as the Mothers and Fathers of Perpetual Grief and so far had avoided like a flesh-eating virus.

"You know it's going to hurt, but you never know how much until it's happening," Lucie said hoarsely, when the pain subsided.

"True, but as soon you have the baby, you forget how awful it was. Mother Nature's amnesia." Helen glanced at Lucie. Her cheeks were blooming with bright pink splotches and sweat was raining down from her forehead and temples.

"What scares me is that the baby is barely thirty-five weeks," Lucie said, panting. "Which means her brain could be smaller than normal, other organs, too. I'm just praying it's not a twisted umbilical cord or a problem with the placenta or . . . Sorry, I'm babbling, it's just that I'm in charge of health at a women's magazine and I know way too much about everything that can go wrong."

Helen floored the accelerator. The contractions were coming faster. "Try not to think about any of that right now," she said, trying to sound calm.

"I wish my doctor would call, or my husband," Lucie gulped. "I never thought it would happen like this, without them and . . . Oh God," she howled, gripping Helen's arm. "Big one."

ONE LOOK AT Lucie and the triage nurse grabbed an orderly and together they helped her onto a gurney, then sailed her down a long, brightly lit corridor to the maternity suite and into a room, Helen trotting to keep up. Lucie clutched Helen's arm, then handed her her purse and phone. "Please tell Matt and my doctor what's happening when they call. And please don't go."

Within minutes, the attending OB who examined Lucie was rattling off words like *placental abruption* and *fetal distress*, explaining that he had to perform a C-section stat. "Let's scrub in and get anesthesia down here," the surgeon shouted to the gathering team of medical personnel. A pretty nurse who introduced herself as Amanda had Lucie scribble her signature on a couple of consent forms. Seconds later, as another nurse was inserting an IV line in Lucie's wrist, Matt called.

Helen explained who she was, then gave him a quick update and handed the phone to the doctor. "I'm giving her a general, there's no time for an epidural," he said, then passed the phone to Lucie, who simply sobbed into it until Amanda gently took it from her and gave it back to Helen.

"I'm leaving this minute," Matt told Helen. "Can you please stay with my wife until I get there?"

Helen promised she would, then bent down and kissed Lucie's damp forehead as she was being wheeled out of the labor room toward a pair of massive double doors.

"I don't know how I can thank you," Lucie mumbled, eyes half shut and showing signs of sedation.

"We'll update you as soon as we can," Amanda called out, just as the automatic doors to the OR shut behind her.

STRANGE HOW PEOPLE'S lives crisscross at perilous moments, then disconnect once the peril has passed. Helen sank into a floral-patterned easy chair in the family waiting room, doubtful that she'd cross paths with Lucie after today. Or if they did run into each other at the bakery, they'd exchange warm greetings, but that would be it. The raw intimacy they'd shared was already passing them by, like a tornado after its energy starts to dissipate.

Which was fine with Helen, who wasn't sentimental about such things. She was aware that her relationship with Detective Handler was much the same, an urgent but temporary coupling based on need that would dissolve if Henry returned. Helen caught herself. *When* Henry returned.

Seated across from her on a matching floral sofa, the only other occupants of the room were a man and a woman, both sixtyish. The woman kept tapping her foot and checking her watch, while the man seemed engrossed in a battered copy of *Field & Stream*. Probably awaiting news of a grandchild.

Helen sighed and tried to relax her shoulders now that Lucie was in capable hands. The surgeon had assured her that "the procedure" would take "no time" and soon they would have "their" baby. He probably thought she was Lucie's mother. The Black-Berry vibrated and there was a text from the husband: *just getting on gw brdge*

Minutes later a large woman wearing a turquoise smock festooned with brightly colored butterflies came in and pulled up a chair next to her. The woman's badge read "Paulette Giles, Admissions Administrator."

"I just need you to sign a few forms," she explained, holding out a clipboard. "I assume you're next of kin?"

"Uh, no, I'm just . . ." What was she, anyway? A stranger? A slight acquaintance? She settled on "a friend of the family," adding, "Her husband is on his way up from the city. He can fill out the forms when he gets here."

"Yes, well, I still need to take down some basic information," the admissions lady said with a thin smile. "What's your friend's full name? And any chance that's her purse?" She pointed to the stylish mustard-colored bag in Helen's lap. "If it is, I'd appreciate it if you could check to see if her insurance card is in her wallet."

"Sure." Helen had no idea what Lucie's last name was. She riffled through her bag until she found her wallet with the insurance card inside. "Lucie Pressman," Helen said, as if she'd known her "friend's" name for years. She handed the card to Ms. Giles, who became much nicer as soon as she confirmed that Lucie had health insurance.

"I hope all goes well for your friend and her baby," she said, patting Helen on the knee before scurrying away.

Minutes later a grinning young man in scrubs poked his head in the door and whistled softly. "Who wants to meet their granddaughter? All seven pounds, nine ounces of her?"

"Oh, thank God, I've been worried sick," the woman across from Helen cried, jumping out of her chair and throwing her arms around the young man. "Sweetheart, a baby girl, I'm in love with her already."

"I told your mother, 'Charlotte, honey, don't make yourself nuts, it takes time to have a baby.' But did she listen?" The man winked at Helen as he trailed his wife out of the waiting room.

ALONE NOW, HELEN shuddered, wondering why hospitals always set the temperature to just above freezing. She hugged herself, glad to be wearing Henry's thick Shetland sweater, the one he'd bought on his backpacking trip to Baffin Bay. She closed her eyes and pulled it over her head, then sniffed, yearning for a trace of him. This was the hardest part. Losing his scent. Well, no, not the hardest part, because there were a thousand hardest parts. Losing sight of him. The sound of his voice. His beautiful hands with their long, graceful fingers and thick, calloused pads from years of playing the violin. His slightly off-kilter smile and full-throttled laugh. The light in his brilliant blue eyes that made her feel as if she were gazing at the open sea.

This line of thinking was dangerous, and Helen jerked her head out of the sweater and stared at the Mr. Coffee machine across the room, trying to decide whether caffeine was a good idea or a bad idea. The warmth might feel nice going down, but she was so exhausted in that overtired, jacked-up sort of way, she worried that a shot of caffeine might whack her out even more. She tried to focus on a recent issue of *People* (which, she thought, really should be called *Who the Hell Are These People?*), but her mind wandered to Lucie. How was she doing? Had the baby been born? Was he or she healthy? Yet, as difficult as Lucie's labor had been, at least it was brief. Unlike Helen's, which had been a brutal seventeen-hour assault of such sharp intensity she felt as if she were being ripped in two. She'd tried her best to soldier through, rejecting Demerol (the rural hospital didn't offer epidurals in those days) so she would be fully present when the baby was born, mouthing the words to "It's So Easy" with Kip—sober, on his best behavior—dousing her cracked lips with ice chips when she wasn't screaming. Just before the doctor gave the okay to push, she decided she'd rather die than keep going. But then: there he was. Her perfect baby. Daniel Henry. And suddenly nothing else mattered: not the wrenching pain or the bloody mess or the wicked tear in her perineum. She had him.

And now she didn't.

She'd still been trying to convince herself that he'd soon be back when Lola was born. He'd been missing less than a month then and, as worried as she was, Helen believed that any day he'd come bursting through the door with a good explanation for his absence. He had to come back to meet his glistening pearl of a daughter, born on a full moon. But as the weeks, then months, passed with no sign of him, the darkness that had been dancing around the edges of her mind grew thicker, more urgent, and invaded her body. More and more, watching her granddaughter wake up to the world without her father became unbearable. And so, one day when Lola was thirteen weeks old, Helen simply stayed in bed. She would have stopped eating, too, if Mira hadn't propped her up a few times a day and fed her soup and toast. Helen hated herself for burdening Mira, who had her hands full caring for the baby when she, too, was grieving. Each morning Helen awoke intending to rouse herself and help with Lola but felt pinned to her bed by a force more insistent than gravity. One day her friend Abby, who owned the local bookstore, dropped off a copy of Elisabeth Kübler-Ross's classic *On Death and Dying*, but Helen decided that Kübler-Ross had missed the boat when she left out *not knowing* as the sixth stage of grief, and hurled the book across the room.

Ten days into her bedroom exile, Mira phoned Dr. Sudha Miller, Helen's internist, and the young physician showed up a few hours later with samples of an antidepressant. Though she hated the idea of taking drugs, Helen knew she'd better pull herself together, if only to keep searching for her son, so she gave in and swallowed the damn pills. Five or six days later she began to climb out of the pit. A week after that, at around four o'clock one morning—the hour when she used to turn on the ovens—she wondered how it would feel to bake again. She crept downstairs to the bakery kitchen and set about making the pain au chocolat that Henry loved. She was a little afraid that might send her back to bed permanently, but to her surprise it had the opposite effect. Baking, the thing she loved and did so well, became her therapy. A month after that, with Mira's help, she reopened the business three days a week. But even with the drugs, at times the darkness still beckoned to her, and she had to do everything in her power to resist its siren call.

"Excuse me. Hello?"

Helen must have been dreaming, because at first when she felt tapping on her shoulder, she thought it was Stuart trying to get her attention. "Where's Henry?" he was asking. The band was supposed to be playing a gig but they couldn't find Henry.

"Ma'am, ma'am? Hello?" The voice was growing louder and Helen startled awake.

"Oh my," she said when she opened her eyes and saw Amanda, the nurse she'd met earlier. "Is everything okay?"

"All good," Amanda said, smiling. "Your friend's baby boy is perfect. A little chilly at first, but we warmed him up. He's on the small side, but stellar for thirty-five weeks. His vital signs and color are good and he's breathing on his own. Except for his size you wouldn't know he's preterm. And Mom is doing well, still asleep in recovery. They had to give her a hefty dose of anesthesia, but she'll be able to hold him in an hour or two."

Helen nodded, still dazed from dreaming about Henry.

"Would you like to see him?"

"Who?" Helen asked stupidly. "Oh, the baby. Sure."

"Follow me, he's just down the hall in the NICU. You can hold him, if you want."

"Really, me?"

"It's important for preterm babies to get cuddled when their parents can't hold them right away," Amanda said, leading Helen to a bank of elevators, then up to the second floor. "You don't have a cold, do you?" Helen shook her head. "Then I'll be right back."

There were five babies lined up in a row of incubators in the neonatal intensive care unit. Peering through the window, Helen saw that three of the infants had so many tubes coming out of them you couldn't see their faces. Two others looked normal, just small. A sign at the end of one of the little plexiglass boxes read "Baby Pressman." The newborn inside was swaddled in a blue blanket and appeared to be sleeping peacefully. Helen glimpsed a stooped, disheveled woman staring at her, and it took a moment before she realized she was looking at her own reflection in the glass.

"You'll have to suit up," Amanda said, returning with a green gown, matching mask and booties, a hairnet, and a pair of latex gloves.

The fact that Helen was about to hold this newborn before his mother was making her feel like a burglar. Still, she dutifully suited up and followed Amanda into the NICU.

After settling her into a rocking chair, the nurse gently lifted the swaddled bundle from the incubator and placed him in Helen's arms. "He's a beauty, isn't he?"

"Hello, you," Helen whispered. The baby was so tiny, yet he was all there, so complete and fully human, it knocked her out. Of course, newborn Lola had knocked her out, too. But Helen had been so involved in her birth and then so sad afterward that Henry had missed it, her feelings were all over the place. Holding this little one was uncomplicated in all the ways that holding Lola had been complicated. But when the baby opened his eyes and appeared to gaze into hers, she nearly choked. His eyes were the same striking marine blue as Henry's. Helen knew that most babies' eyes were blue at birth. Still, staring into this little one's eyes was making it hard for her to swallow.

Suddenly, she knew she had to get out of there, even though

she'd promised to stay, even though she'd always prided herself on keeping her word. But this time she couldn't. She wasn't sure why—or maybe it was just so obvious why. What made her think she could hold another woman's newborn baby boy when her own boy was still missing? Who did she think she was, Mary Poppins or some kind of cartoon superhero?

"I have to go," she told Amanda, when the nurse popped back in to check on them.

"Not to worry, newborns make everyone emotional, even when they're not yours." Amanda took the baby from her and returned him to his plastic pen.

Outside the NICU, Helen trashed the scrubs and handed Lucie's bag to Amanda.

"Could you please give this to my friend and tell her I'm sorry, but I had to leave."

Then she turned and hurried down the long hallway toward the exit sign.

INTRODUCING OUR SON

Jonah Daniel

May 1, 2003

5:17 pm

5 pounds 3 ounces

17 inches

WITH LOVE,

LUCIE AND MATTHEW PRESSMAN

NINE

It was true what Helen said about childbirth. How once the baby is born, the agony is forgotten. For Lucie, the memory of the emergency C-section and the terrifying hours that preceded it began to fade the moment she cradled him, his body resting on hers, skin to skin, his spine and ribs as delicate as twigs, his heartbeat as fast and fluttery as a hummingbird's. When she kissed his tender scalp, it tasted like the sun.

"I can't believe he's really *ours* and we get to keep him and take him home," she croaked to Matt, her throat hoarse from being intubated. She had never felt more like an animal. Or more porous, fluids leaking from every part of her body. Sweat. Tears. Milk. Pee. Snot. Unidentifiable substances. On their own and in combination.

Yet there was so much to be thankful for. Unlike many early babies, Jonah started breathing on his own at birth and scored high normal on the Apgar test. The attending pediatrician, a lovely man named Sean Moloney, pronounced Jonah in "remarkable good health for a preterm lad," in a thick Irish brogue.

The day after the baby's birth, Matt and Lucie had two minor wrangles. The first was over his name. Though they agreed on his middle name—Daniel, for Matt's late grandfather—Matt lobbied for Max to be the baby's first name. But Lucie didn't share his attachment to the kid who wore the wolf suit in *Where the Wild Things Are*. She liked Jonah.

"You really want to name him after the guy in the Old Testament who gets eaten by a whale?"

"Yes, because he gets tossed back up on land three days later, unhurt. So actually it's a hero's story." Lucie believed the name would confer extra resilience on their baby, plus the *J* would honor Nana, whose name was Judith. Matt couldn't really argue with that.

The other point of contention had to do with circumcision. Matt, who never set foot in a synagogue unless he was attending a wedding or a funeral, suddenly got religion and wanted to host a proper bris at home and hire a *mohel* to perform the ritual cutting of Jonah's foreskin. But Lucie, so weak she was practically preverbal, wasn't up for any hoopla and wanted to get the procedure over with while she was still in the hospital. And since she was the one who'd suffered through a difficult childbirth, Matt relented and stood by as Dr. Moloney did the deed. Afterward, while the pediatrician applied antibiotic ointment to Jonah's angry red penis, Matt grabbed the little flap of leftover foreskin that looked like the wrinkly tip of a banana, then wrapped it in gauze and stuck it in his pocket. He'd heard from his colleague Ben that some Jewish parents bury their child's circumcised foreskin in their garden for good luck.

WHICH WAS WHY a week after returning from the hospital, they were sprawled out on lounge chairs that barely fit on their cardboard-box-size terrace so they could bury the baby's foreskin in a potted plant. Jonah, having just finished nursing, was sacked out on Lucie's breast, while Matt had the little gauze packet and a trowel in hand. It was one of those perfect spring evenings in New York. Warm but not hot, trails of cirrus clouds streaking across the milky blue sky like hieroglyphics. And the air was refreshingly clean, without a hint of the garbage stink that would soon envelop the city.

"Normal people do this?" Lucie whispered. "Doesn't burying the baby's foreskin seem like the kind of witchy thing my mother would do?" She nuzzled the golden fuzz on Jonah's head, which smelled like ripe apples, then kissed the raised red birthmark at the base of his skull.

"According to Ben, people do it all the time. But it's definitely not something your mother would do, because if you were a boy, your foreskin would still be intact."

"True." When Lucie had spoken to her mother after Jonah was born, Phoebe, a reliable fount of misinformation, immediately launched into a rant about circumcision. "Don't do it, darling, it's barbaric and no one does it anymore." Phoebe bolstered her argument by claiming that the Buddha and his disciples were uncircumcised. Aware that her mother had recently signed on as *secretary* (she assumed lover) to a high-ranking Tibetan Buddhist lama, Lucie refrained from asking how she came by this choice tidbit.

"Maybe we should get on with burying the thing before he wakes up," Matt whispered, holding up the gauze with the little blob of foreskin inside. "We could put it in with the hypericum."

"Good idea." Hypericum, or St. John's-wort, was known to help with anxiety and depression. It was also in the clay pot closest to the wooden statue of Jizo, the Zen Buddhist protector of women and children that Holly had left with the doorman as soon as she'd gotten wind of the emergency C-section.

"I still don't get why you stick it in the dirt," Lucie said.

"I don't know. Something about Abraham and the desert."

"Isn't it always about Abraham and the desert? I thought the whole point was to get out of the desert?"

Matt shrugged, then knelt down and dug a small hole in the pot holding the plant with the tiny yellow flowers. "For Jonah. May he never have to return to the desert." He dropped the packet into the hole and covered it with the loose soil. "Amen."

"That's it? That's your idea of a sacred ritual honoring the birth of our son?"

"All right then, God bless the child and let's eat dinner. I'm starving. And exhausted. Don't forget, I haven't exactly been sleeping either, and tomorrow's my first day back at work."

"Okay, but not so fast. You take him," Lucie whispered, gently passing the sleeping infant to Matt, then grabbing the trowel. From the moment she set eyes on her baby, she understood that there were now so many more ways she could be mortally wounded by love than she'd ever dreamed possible. She wasn't a believer exactly, but having grown up with a mother who spent her life playing spiritual roulette, Lucie was no stranger to rituals—Wiccan, Native American, Hindu, Kabbalist, a virtual delicatessen of prayers and incantations. So, she thought, why not? Maybe motherhood was turning her soft, but as long as they were doing this, she might as well call on all the gods and goddesses, along with Great Spirit and the spirit of Nana to protect their baby. Plus, she remembered her old therapist, Nora, once saying that "courage equals fear plus prayer."

"This might seem weird, but whatever." Lucie closed her eyes and placed a hand over her heart. "I pray to Great Spirit, the spirit of Nana, and all the benevolent forces in the universe that Jonah grows up happy, healthy, and safe, and stays that way until he's a very old man," she intoned in her best witchy voice.

Then, clutching her still raw wound with one hand, she leaned forward and with the other waved the trowel over the hypericum like a magic wand. "I pray that he's free from pain and suffering and never gets a serious illness or is in an accident in the air, on land, or sea." She paused for a moment, then added, "Or in space, on the off chance he decides to become an astronaut. I pray he's never kidnapped or attacked or hurt for any reason, including war, random violence, or being the target of a hate crime, and that he knows love all his life. I pray he's never caught in a fire, a flood, an earthquake, a tornado, a hurricane, a tsunami, a volcanic eruption, a . . . Am I missing anything?"

"I think you nailed it, Luce," Matt said, yawning. "Except maybe being crushed by a falling meteor, but what are the chances of that?"

"Okay, good, no getting crushed by falling meteors either."

Lucie took a few minutes to silently review the catalog of potential catastrophes until she felt certain that all the bases were covered. Then she spit twice over her left shoulder as Jonah began to howl.

On the drive back to town, I try to make conversation. Nothing too personal, no politics, just random blahbeddy-blah to fill the time. The Red Sox, who look like they might actually make the playoffs this year. The new burrito place out on Route 23. Charlie, my crazyass rescue dog. But the dude is none too chatty and I must have fallen asleep, because the next thing I know we're lurching down some bumpy dirt road and he stops the truck and tells me to get out.

"Here? You want me to get out here?" It's pitch dark. I can't see any lights from streetlamps or houses or even other cars. The only light is coming from the sky, big zigzag bolts of it like in a comic strip. The storm is right overhead and I have no idea where the hell we are.

"You're kidding, right? In the middle of this?" I point to the deluge going on outside.

But he just keeps saying "Get out get out get out," like there are no other words in his vocabulary.

"Look man, I really appreciate the ride," I say. "And listen, you don't have to take me all the way home. I can stay at my mom's in town, if that's easier. Or hey, I can just jump out here and hitch the rest of the way." When he doesn't answer, I look around for my phone, and when I don't see it, I start to feel like there's a small rodent clawing the inside of my stomach. I don't know what he's up to, but I'm pretty sure it's not good and I need to get the fuck out of here.

"Hey, thanks for charging my phone," I say, trying to sound casual about the situation. "I'll just take it and grab my stuff and be on my way." I hold out my hand, but he doesn't make a move.

And the next time he tells me to "get out, asswipe," he's pointing a gun at me.

PART TWO

2007–2008

TEN

You SMOOTH THE ICING WITH THE SPATULA, LIKE THIS. THAT'S IT, gently. Like ice-skating, you just glide it across the top." Helen was guiding Lola's hand in the art of icing a wedding cake. And this was not just any wedding cake. This cake was for Lola's mom and Jackson Brin, the man who in a few hours would become Mira's husband and Lola's stepfather.

Kneeling on a stool at the massive marble island in Jackson's—and now Mira's and Lola's—massive marble kitchen, Lola spread the next layer of buttercream as sunlight streamed through the open French doors, sparking off the stainless-steel appliances like shooting stars. When she finished, she grinned at Helen, then brushed the spatula against the cinnamon-colored wave jutting out from her forehead, making it look as if it had just been freshly highlighted.

"Good job, love, you've got the touch. Next layer." Helen gingerly placed tier number three on top of tier number two, then wiped her granddaughter's bangs with a damp dishtowel.

"I want to make the cake perfect for Mommy," Lola said, dipping the spatula into hot water. "But I wish she was marrying Daddy. Why did he have to go away? Before I was even born?"

These are questions Lola has been asking ever since she realized that other kids have daddies as well as mommies, even the ones who don't live with both parents. Lately, as the day of the wedding approached, the questions had been coming more frequently. Helen folded the slender girl into her arms and showered the crown of her head with kisses, inhaling her grapefruit-scented shampoo. She was awestruck that at five, Lola's face was practically a replica of her father's at the same age. Different coloring but nearly identical features and facial expressions. "I wish I had a good answer for you, love," Helen said. "If I knew I would tell you." Five years after Henry vanished, still there were no answers.

"I want to live at your house, Oma. This house is too big. And there's no Charlie."

"This house is new to you, that's all. You'll get used to it, and before you know it, it will feel like your house, too. You have a nice big room and there's a pool," Helen said, feeling like the publicist for a cause she didn't believe in. "And Mommy will be right here with you. Maybe she'll even get you a puppy."

"I don't want a puppy. I want Charlie. Plus, Jackson is allergic to dogs. Their dandruff makes him sick."

"I think you mean dander, sweetie. Anyhow, you can see Charlie and stay with me whenever you want." For years, Helen had known that the day would come when Mira and Lola would move out. Still, she didn't feel any more ready than Lola to break up their little band of three that had been her lifeline.

The girl hopped down from the stool and stared at the floor, her arms crossed, lower lip quivering.

"I'm sorry you're having a hard time, love. Lots of changes, but you're a big, strong girl, and you're going to be happy wherever you are, I promise. Now, let's finish the cake and make it beautiful." Helen held out the spatula to Lola.

"I'm going to find Mommy," she sniffed and ran off.

Helen worried that her granddaughter was picking up some of her own distress over the marriage and knew she'd feel unsettled no matter who the groom was. Jackson and Mira had dated briefly in high school but broke up a year or two before she started seeing Henry. Helen didn't know the details, just that when Jackson started pursuing her two years ago, Mira went on about how much he'd changed, from a teenager who was always getting in trouble to a solid citizen and successful businessman. Not many details then either, but Helen imagined Mira must feel awkward discussing the new man in her life with the mother of the missing man she'd planned to marry.

Even so, Helen couldn't help wondering how much Jackson's money had sweetened the deal. Of course, she understood why Mira wouldn't want to live with her and work at the bakery indefinitely, a life she'd inherited when Henry vanished. And though Helen had done what she could to support her—turning the garage into a painting studio for her, helping her to raise Lola— she was aware that someday lovely Mira would need to break free. Still, Helen worried that by setting aside her art to get her real estate license and join Jackson's company, Mira was sacrificing some essential part of herself in the bargain. Which was exactly what Helen had done when she married Kip. Traded in her dreams for his and lost herself along the way. So, maybe her concerns about Mira were simply projections.

As different as Jackson was from her nature-loving musician son, Helen liked him well enough. He was unfailingly polite to her, though their relationship was mostly limited to hellos and goodbyes when he came to pick up Mira, since his dog allergy kept him from coming inside. Still, Helen would always be grateful to him for stepping up when Henry went missing, driving all over the state, putting up flyers. That was before he became a big deal real estate developer, which was the part she didn't like: the predatory snapping up of old farmland, dividing it into small parcels, then building grandiose McMansions that looked freakish alongside the aging Victorians and modest wood-frame homes that blended seamlessly into the rolling green landscape. Helen would have expected Mira to disapprove as well. Having grown up on a small dairy farm that was an early victim of subdivision fever, Mira used to get so enraged her cheeks would flare as red as her hair whenever they drove past "Strawberry Village." But that was before she took up with Jackson. Helen supposed she would forgive him his greedy capitalist ways as long as he was good to Mira—and, especially, to Lola.

The cake! Helen had been drifting and still had to add the leaves and flowers. She filled a pastry bag with buttercream, then piped fat ruffly leaves around the base of each tier, followed by a sweeping cascade of calla lilies down the sides, Mira's favorite. Helen left it to the caterer, who was frantically stuffing mushrooms and shrieking at her helpers, to affix the plastic bride and groom to the top of the cake, while she rushed off to dress for the ceremony and try to wrangle her runaway hair—uncut since Henry disappeared—into something resembling a do.

HELEN GOT THE idea when Lola swept by in a cotton candy cloud of pink organza, scattering yellow rose petals along the grassy aisle, heralding the entrance of the bride. She knew it was probably insane; still, it stuck in her head like an earworm you can't shake—even though the trip would almost certainly prove fruitless, even though "just call me Dick" Tracy had turned up zip. But that was four years ago, and suddenly it was as if some irresistible force were summoning her back. She supposed it had everything to do with the wedding. Watching Mira float down the aisle looking radiant in layers of pearl-studded white satin was kicking up a dust storm in her mind.

"Do you, Jackson, out of care and respect for your own individual being, acknowledge within yourself that same care and respect for Mira, and pledge to share your deepest truth with her? Will you share with her your hurts, your sorrows, your joys, your happiness? Will you comfort her and be comforted by her, and share with her everything meaningful to you, so long as you both shall live?"

"You bet." Jackson's grin stretched almost to his ears.

Helen couldn't remember ever seeing him look so put together. Instead of his standard uniform—jeans, scuffed-up boots, denim work shirt—he was wearing an expensive-looking French blue suit and his light brown hair was fashionably trimmed on the sides and spiky on top, a style that made her think of porcupines.

Adding to Helen's general state of unease was watching Jock officiate. Her ex-boyfriend minister, aka *The Man Who Got Away*. She wondered what would have happened if she hadn't suddenly pulled back when Henry went missing. By then they were talking about moving in together. Everyone who knew them said they made a great couple. Helen thought they made a great couple, too. As fiercely political as they both were, they managed to be just as silly and sexy when they weren't out protesting wars, endangered civil rights, and all manner of environmental degradation. They'd even gotten themselves arrested a couple of times and thrown in the same jail cell, which they considered a badge of honor and the ultimate symbol of their compatibility. Jock was Helen's first serious relationship since Kip, and Henry had been a huge fan. Things couldn't have been going better. *Before.* After

Henry disappeared, Jock was ready to drop everything to be by her side and aid in the search, but Helen couldn't let him in. It was as if a trapdoor hidden in her heart suddenly slammed shut and she had to go it alone. Which seemed to be her way. And then Mira moved in, and Lola was born, and that was that. But in the back of her mind, Helen kept thinking maybe someday the trapdoor would swing open again. Jock had even waited patiently on the sidelines for the first year or so. But now here he was. Officiating at the wedding of Mira and Jackson, as Sandy, a toothpick of a fourth-grade teacher from Rhinebeck and his wife of three months, looked on from the third row. Helen felt the acid rise in her throat when Jock, his arm around Sandy, had introduced the two women before the start of the ceremony.

"Do you, Mira . . ."

As hard as it was to sit still and watch the bride pledge herself to the groom, Helen had to admit that Mira had never looked more beautiful, her gown radiating wands of light beneath the rose-covered arbor that Jackson had built for the occasion. And though in the logic of Helen's splintered heart, Mira would always be married to the wrong man, she wished the newlyweds well as they set about fulfilling those lofty vows.

But Lola, squeezed up against her mother, was another story. With eyes downcast beneath a knotted brow, she wore the signature frown that usually preceded rivers of tears. It took everything Helen had not to fly out of her seat, scoop Lola up in her arms, and run like hell.

NINE HOURS LATER she collapsed with Charlie on a lumpy mattress at an All-Suites Inn near Lewisburg, Pennsylvania. After the final *I do*s and *I will*s and the extended kiss to seal the deal, Helen knew she wouldn't make it through the reception. Not with Jock and the toothpick joined at the hip or the crowd from town, almost all of them customers or people who knew Henry, including his whole high school baseball team—Henry and Jackson had been teammates—and the members of the band, except for Stuart, who had gotten clean and moved to LA. Even Detective Handler, a classmate of Jackson's late father, was there with his wife, Gail. While the champagne was being poured, he pulled Helen aside. His granite eyes took on a downcast puppyish look when he told her that Aaron Lamb, the guitarist from Ithaca who disappeared a few months before Henry, had turned up in Bangkok living high off the inheritance he'd filched from his siblings. And the rapper, 2B.Not.2B, had reverted to his given name, Larry Gustafson, and would soon graduate from chiropractic school, a tidbit that would have made Helen fall on the ground laughing if Henry hadn't still been missing. She thanked Will for telling her and took the news as her cue. She gave the bride and groom each a quick kiss and blamed her hasty exit on an upset stomach, though it just about killed her to peel off her sobbing granddaughter when she hugged her goodbye.

The rest of the afternoon was a hurricane of activity: begging her assistant, Rachel, to manage the bakery for the next two weeks; stuffing random clothes into the battered suitcase she'd brought with her when she and Henry—then Alice and Danny—had bolted in the middle of the night; gathering enough food for Charlie to last all the way to Oregon; and gassing up the old Subaru, praying it would survive the trip.

Driving through Ohio the next morning, Helen realized that if she'd been in her right mind when she decided to embark on this expedition, she would have bought a plane ticket and rented a car when she landed in Eugene. Made the trip in three or four days, instead of the two weeks it would take her to crisscross the country. But she probably would have rejected the idea, even if she'd thought of it. Though she couldn't say why, there was something as necessary about retracing the miles she and Henry had traveled during their great escape as there was in seeing Rosaleen, Kip's mother. But not Kip. Jesus, she hoped not Kip.

"What do you think, kiddo?" she asked Charlie as they crossed the Indiana state line. "Are we crazy or what?"

ELEVEN

THE FIRST TIME IT HAPPENED, JONAH WAS RUNNING A FEVER. A nasty virus was going around that had decked half the kids in his preschool class.

"Please! Stop! Don't hurt me!" he screamed a few hours after falling asleep, four hours since his last dose of Children's Tylenol. Lucie tried to console him, but he was thrashing so violently she couldn't get close.

"Jonah, wake up, it's Mama. Daddy and I are right here."

But he didn't seem to hear her. Or see her. Lucie and Matt stood by his bed, watching helplessly as his eyes rolled back and he continued to kick and scream.

"I'm calling 911," Lucie cried, panicked. She'd never seen anything like it.

"Hold on, Luce. This looks like night terrors. Sometimes kids get them when they're running a fever."

"He's had bad dreams before, but nothing like this. I'm getting the phone."

"Let's give it a few minutes. I saw this once with a really sick kid during my pediatric rotation. Night terrors aren't the same as nightmares. They're caused by some kind of chemical misfiring in the brain. Scary to watch but not dangerous. He won't even remember it."

"Look at him, it's not slowing down." Lucie appreciated that her husband was a doctor and obviously knew more about medicine than she did. Still, he was an ophthalmologist and she didn't always trust that his knowledge of childhood illness was up to speed. But when she came running back clutching the cordless, Jonah's eyes were closed. He continued to thrash, but less violently, and the screaming had stopped. A few minutes later he rolled onto his side and began softly snoring.

"Poor Bear," Lucie said, kissing the plum-colored birthmark on the back of his neck. "He's drenched."

"Garden variety night terrors." Matt stroked Jonah's forehead and felt his pulse. "It's the virus. Kids' brains do weird shit when they have a fever."

"As weird as screaming, 'Don't hurt me'?"

"Yeah, as weird as that. When the central nervous system goes haywire, it can feel like it's being threatened when there's no real threat."

"One more minute and I would've called 911," Lucie said as they changed Jonah into dry pajamas, then got him to swallow another capful of Tylenol without waking him. "Sometimes I just lose it."

"You're the mom," Matt said, kissing the top of her head. "You get a pass."

Matt always made Lucie feel as if she were perfectly normal, even when she was freaking out. It was one of the ten thousand things she loved about him. Still, maybe any mother would fly into a panic if her kid was in the throes of night terrors. Thankfully, Lucie panicked less often than she used to. She wondered if years of sleeping next to someone as calm as Matt was having a mellowing effect on her amygdala, the brain's panic button, as the latest research suggested.

Yet as amused as she was by the notion of her husband as the human equivalent of Xanax, at the moment she was still in fight-or-flight mode from watching her son throw a fit—garden variety or not. She ran her fingers through his damp curls and decided to spend the rest of the night in his room in case there was another episode. When Matt went back to bed, she curled up in her old glider, then leaned over and kissed Jonah's velvety cheek and breathed in the briny scent of him as if it were the most sublime perfume.

If they were lucky, Matt's mellow brain waves would eventually rub off on Jonah, too. So far, though, his wiring seemed to take more after Lucie's. Even as an infant, he startled easily. Then when he was two and they took him to see the fireworks over the Hudson on the Fourth of July, he started wailing within seconds of hearing the first loud booms. Matt pointed to the colorful display in the sky and tried to assure him there was nothing to be afraid of. But Jonah—face bright red, body trembling—didn't seem to hear him through his screams, and Matt raced home ferrying Jonah in his arms sounding as if he were being tortured. Since that night, they'd done what they could to protect him from loud noises, including having double-glazed windows installed in every room of their apartment. But noise was a challenge in a city plagued by a cacophony of sirens and car alarms, engines backfiring and horns blaring. These sounds, too, could startle Jonah and make him anxious.

If only they could get him out of the city. From time to time, Lucie still checked the real estate listings in Aurora Falls, but Matt continued to resist taking on a second home. And for the most part life was good, there'd been no further terrorist attacks, and she put the idea on hold.

MATT WAS RIGHT about Jonah not remembering anything about the night's high drama. In the morning he was his usual cheerful self, curious and sprite-like—reminding Lucie that most of the time he was not in a state of high anxiety.

"Mama, how come you're sleeping in my room?" Jonah was batting Lucie on the arm with Jolly, his beloved floppy-eared stuffed dog.

"Good morning, Bear," Lucie said, blinking. "You had a bad dream and I came in to make sure you were okay. Do you remember it?"

He shook his head, his long golden curls separated into dried spaghetti strands from sweat, his eyes bright and clear. "I'm hungry, Mama. Can I have breakfast? Am I going to school?"

"Yes on breakfast, no on school," she said, feeling his forehead with hers. "We're staying home, you and me. Come on, hungry boy, I'll make you French toast."

LUCIE WAS GRATEFUL that her job at *Lulu* was flexible, grateful that her boss Diana had rehired her after a four-year hiatus, considering that she'd quit the week before she was due back from maternity leave. At the time, her body, racked by migraines and a testy gut, was screaming *no!* to leaving her six-month-old baby. So were her breasts, brimming with milk. She especially hated the idea of mechanically expressing her bounty like a dairy cow so that some stranger, even a nice stranger, could feed it to her son from a bottle, while she sat at a desk editing copy about breast-feeding and other women's health issues. So she stayed home, aware that her decision ran counter to her plan to always have a job and never be financially dependent on anyone, including her husband.

But that was before Jonah was born.

To Lucie it had always seemed that whatever anxious wiring she'd brought with her into the world had been amplified by her mother's inconstancy, her parade of revolving lovers who sucked up her attention until they spit her out. Phoebe had loved Lucie— she knew that—but as her mother bounced from man to man, job to job, obsession to obsession, she was distracted much of the time. Lucie had done enough stories on attachment theory and the mother-child bond to know that if it hadn't been for Nana's love and devotion filling in the cracks in Phoebe's scattershot parenting, she might be a real disaster.

So until Jonah started preschool, Lucie became the mother she never had, savoring (nearly) every moment of being with him as they set out like explorers discovering a new world. She loved being present the first time he stuck out his tongue and tasted snow or jumped in a pile of fall leaves, squealing with delight at the sound of the crunching. They went to parks, libraries, museums, and zoos, and took boat rides around Manhattan and to every other island in New York Harbor. More than anything, Jonah was spellbound by the Monday morning children's concerts at the New York Philharmonic, and Lucie believed his love of music began in utero, with all the Bach and Brahms she played during her pregnancy.

Shortly before his third birthday, he started begging for violin lessons. Certain he hadn't yet developed the necessary motor skills, Matt told him he would have to wait one more year. But Jonah persisted, Matt eventually caved—and turned out to have been mistaken about his son's motor skills. His first teacher was so impressed by Jonah's natural talent, he referred him to the eminent violin master Elias Fishbein after just a few months.

"I told you I could play," the boy bragged to Matt.

LUCIE WASN'T SURE what to do with herself once Jonah started preschool. All she knew was that she'd never make it as a shopper or a lady who lunches, so she emailed Diana and asked to meet her for a drink. Convinced her former boss was still furious with her for skipping out on her job at the last second, Lucie was prepared to grovel for forgiveness and, fingers crossed, snag a freelance assignment or two. So when Diana threw her impossibly tanned and toned arms around her, then proceeded to offer her a position as editor at large—to be created just for her—Lucie was ecstatic. Though she would make less money and her name would be lower on the masthead than before, the new job was ideal. As long as she met her deadlines and showed up at the office for Monday morning editorial meetings—and occasionally filled in for editors who were sick or on maternity leave—she could work from home editing, as well as writing, the stories that most interested her. "I like the way your mind works," Diana had told her over margaritas, which Lucie interpreted as meaning obsessive bordering on maniacal once she got onto a subject.

So, on the afternoon following the night terrors, after watching several episodes of *Chopped*, Jonah's favorite TV show—the last mystery basket contained pickled pig's lips, grape jelly, lotus root, and reindeer pâté—Lucie scoured the internet for information while he napped. Surprisingly, with all the stories she'd assigned over the years on children's health, the subject of night terrors had escaped her attention. The first thing she learned was that the syndrome went by different names: sleep terrors, sleep terror disorder, night terrors, *pavor nocturnus*. And Matt was right: whatever name it goes by, the problem was caused by sudden increased activity in the brain, usually triggered by illness or stress. Not only that, she learned that night terrors were more common in boys than girls—especially four-year-old boys—and could last anywhere from five to twenty minutes. Typically, kids don't wake up. And though they may appear inconsolable, like Jonah they rarely have any memory of what happened.

By the time he awoke from his nap, Lucie had pitched a feature on night terrors to Diana and volunteered to write it herself.

Diana, who in emails rarely encountered a vowel she didn't love to drop, wrote back three minutes later. "Grt! B sr to inclde yr story, will b mr intrstng 2 rdrs . . . XOD."

"AM I GOING to school tomorrow?"

"Yup," Lucie said, tucking Jonah into bed. "With your cool new look." When he woke up from his nap fever-free, she decided to take him to get a real haircut before the kids at school started to tease him. Her last homegrown attempt had looked like a hit-and-run.

She opened a picture book called *Jessica* that Matt had bought on his way home from work and began to read. "'Ruthie Simms didn't have a dog, she didn't have a cat, or a brother, or a sister . . .'"

"Like me," said Jonah. "I don't have those either."

"That's right, you're an only child, too," Lucie agreed, then continued. "'But Jessica was the next best thing. Jessica went wherever Ruthie went. To the moon, to the playground, to Ruthie's grandma's for the weekend. "There is no Jessica," said Ruthie's parents. But there was.'" Lucie pointed to the illustrations of Ruthie at the playground and at grandma's, but in every picture Jessica was invisible. "It looks like Jessica is Ruthie's imaginary friend. She keeps her company when Ruthie gets lonely, only Ruthie's parents don't believe Jessica exists."

"Did you ever have a friend like Jessica that nobody else could see?" asked Jonah.

"I did. And when I told my mom, she put out a plate with two cookies. One for me and one for my friend." Lucie didn't mention that her invisible friend was the father she never knew.

"If I have one, will you give her a cookie, too?"

"Sure," said Lucie.

"And my dog?"

"And your dog," she said, returning to the book. "'Jessica ate with Ruthie, looked at books with Ruthie, and took turns stacking blocks with Ruthie . . . If Ruthie was mad, so was Jessica . . .'"

"Mama," said Jonah, picking at the elephant decal that was coming loose from the wall next to his bed. "I have one."

"One what, Bear?"

"Somebody like Jessica, only she's not a kid, she's a mama like you."

"Really? Tell me."

"Oops." The elephant decal came off and landed on the bed. "Sorry."

"It's fine. We need to repaint your room anyway. You can peel them all off, if you want."

Jonah went for another one. "I have a dog, too," he said. "Only he and the mama aren't 'maginary, I just can't see them." He turned his head toward Lucie and, with his brow scrunched, said, "Did you know I have another mama?"

"Sweetheart, what makes you think that?"

Jonah shrugged and kept picking at the decals. "I just know. Her hair is yellow like butter and hangs all the way down. It isn't fluffy like yours."

"Hm, do you think maybe this other mom showed up to keep you company while you're at school?"

"And my dog."

"Your dog, too." Lucie's stomach churned the way it did when Jonah clung to her like a barnacle in the mornings when she dropped him off at school. Almost all the other kids had started preschool by the time they were three—the age Matt had pushed to enroll Jonah. But Lucie didn't think he was mature enough and had talked Matt into keeping him at home with her one more year—a decision, in hindsight, she viewed as selfish. "I thought you were really starting to like school," she said, because as clingy as he was in the mornings, he was often reluctant to leave when she picked him up at lunchtime.

"Yeah," Jonah said, ripping off another elephant. "I like it, except for Riley. He spits."

"There's one in every crowd."

"Yeah, but Mama, before when I was big and lived in the yellow house with my other mom and my dog, I didn't have to go to school and my name wasn't Jonah. Don't you remember?"

"No, I don't, Bear, because there was no yellow house or dog or other mom. I'm your only mom and you were a teeny tiny baby when you came out of my tummy and your name has always been Jonah." She stroked his freshly contoured curls. "You know what I think? I think your other mom and dog might be imaginary, like Ruthie's friend Jessica."

"They are *not* 'maginary." Jonah bolted into a sitting position and tugged on his ear until it turned bright red, his go-to gesture when he got angry. "I want to go see them *now*."

He'd been making up stories since he was a toddler. Lucie loved that her son had such a rich imagination but felt she should try to help him distinguish between fantasy and reality, even when it made him mad. "Let's finish the book and find out what happens to Ruthie and Jessica."

"Send Daddy in. I want him to read me the rest," Jonah said, turning to face the wall.

"YOU WERE RIGHT," Lucie said when Matt came back into the living room. She was stretched out on the sofa, staring at the emergency chocolate bar mocking her from the coffee table. Four years on, she had yet to drop her leftover pregnancy pounds.

"Huh?" Matt grabbed the day's sports section from the table, then nudged her in the thigh. She lifted her legs so he could sit. "I can't believe they fucking did it again," he grumbled, waving the paper in the air. "Threw away the whole season in one lousy game." Matt got his heart broken by the Mets every year, but this year had been worse than most. This year, they'd had a real chance to make it to the playoffs but managed to blow it in the last game, which Matt took personally.

"I'm sorry, that's terrible," Lucie said. "But maybe not quite as terrible as our son telling me he has another mother."

"What are you talking about?"

"What I'm saying is you were right. We should have put him in preschool when he was three, like other kids. The separation is harder for him now than it would have been then. He seems to have invented an imaginary mother to be with him when I'm not. And a dog."

"You mean like Ruthie made up Jessica?"

"It's my fault. I've gone so overboard in doing the opposite of everything Phoebe did, I've made him too dependent on me."

"Luce, come on. So he invented an imaginary mom to comfort him when you're not there, what's wrong with that? Pretty clever, if you ask me. I'm sure he would have done the same thing if he'd started school a year ago."

"You really think so?"

"I do. And hey, you didn't get to the end of the book, but Ruthie stops needing Jessica as soon as she makes new friends at school. I bet Jonah's imaginary mom will disappear as soon as he starts spending more time with Jeremy and whoosit, that other kid he keeps talking about."

"Mickey." Lucie leaned over, snatched the chocolate bar from the coffee table, and broke off two squares. "I hope you're right about this being a transitional thing. I just wish I could stop worrying so much."

"I think it's part of the job description and it's called love," Matt said, rubbing her foot and pressing his thumb against the soft spot in the center where she liked it. "Anyhow, you know how Jonah's mind works. Tomorrow, he'll probably bring an imaginary tiger home from school and insist on setting a place for him at dinner." With his free hand, Matt crumpled up the sports section and pitched it across the room.

BUT NO TIGER or other creature came home with Jonah the following day. And when Lucie checked his backpack for loose apple chips left over from his snack, she noticed a balled-up piece of paper and opened it. It appeared to be a picture of his imaginary friends. There was a primitive yellow house with three stick figures inside—a man, a woman, and a black blob with four stumpy legs that looked like it was meant to be a dog. The stick woman was discernible from the stick man by her longer yellow hair, and because the stick man was so tall his head breached the roof and was as big as the canary sun hanging in the turquoise sky.

TWELVE

As LUCK WOULD HAVE IT, THE RADIATOR BLEW JUST AS HELEN HIT Laramie. She and Charlie had to spend an extra two nights at the Mighty Oaks Motel, the same dump where a random flick of her son's finger had decided their fate twenty-two years before.

She tried not to think too much about what coming full circle might signify and tried to focus on the fact that as far as the mechanic could tell, only the radiator had blown, and not a gasket. That would have been the death knell of the Outback, her first-ever new car, which nine-year-old Danny had picked out when the Dodge Dart finally gave up its mojo.

Ever since she crossed the Mississippi, in her mind Henry became Danny again, his real first name and the name she always called him when they were alone. Yet it had been decades since Helen had thought of herself as Alice, her real first name. Way too much baggage.

It WAS AFTER going shoe shopping for Mira's wedding that, on impulse, she'd called Rosaleen. Helen hated shopping and, with her large bunion, buying shoes was torture. As soon as she got home, she lay down on the sofa and promptly fell asleep. An hour later, she awoke from a pleasant dream in which she and Rosaleen had been enjoying afternoon tea at Mad Hatter's near the university in Eugene, just like in the old days. Without thinking, Helen grabbed the phone and dialed the number she remembered, then panicked and hung up as soon as she heard Rosaleen say *Hail-o* in her unmistakable Dust Bowl twang. Considering that she'd run away with Danny twenty-seven years ago, Helen was not expecting a warm reception when she showed up at Rosaleen's front door.

Helen had adored her mother-in-law, loved her quirky, take-no-prisoners style. She was a transplanted Okie, a former Pentecostal turned Zen Buddhist. If it hadn't been for Rosaleen, Helen might not have misread the early signs of paranoia and delusion that should have sent her running from Rosaleen's handsome, seductive son. She might not have swapped her lifelong dream of joining the Peace Corps after college for Kip's impossible dreams. But Rosaleen had been so kind, helping to fill the emotional crater left by the early deaths of Helen's mother, Peggy, from breast cancer, and her superhero big brother, Evan, from a freak skiing accident, that she put blinders on instead.

And kept them on: when Kip, her charismatic twentieth-century literature instructor at the university got fired for insubordination but blamed it on his heroic one-man revolt against the System, personified by the evil department chair; when Kip convinced Helen to drop out of school and become his muse so he could write the *real* Great American Novel on a remote mountaintop where they would live happily ever after in their own private Shangri-La; when Kip insisted on driving Helen the thirteen miles over the mountain to and from her hateful job at the candle factory to make sure she went to work and didn't spend her days screwing her (phantom) lover; when Kip took the call the day Helen's father died and didn't tell her about it until after the funeral. Though not one to give up easily—a trait she now considered seriously overrated—Helen was out the door when she found out she was pregnant. The idea of life in the middle of nowhere with a helpless infant and a raging alcoholic with loose fists terrified her. And so she fled to Rosaleen's, unsure whether to keep the baby or get an abortion and start her own aborted life over. But Kip, one of the world's great undiscovered actors, came crawling down from the mountaintop, weeping, repentant, begging her not to leave him, and Rosaleen brokered the deal: Kip would go to AA meetings seven days a week and treat Helen with the trust and respect she deserved, and Helen would keep the baby and return home with him.

The plan worked so well throughout her pregnancy you would have thought she was the freaking Madonna, the way he waited on her and tried to satisfy her every need. And the longer he stayed true to his word about the drinking and the drugs, as well as controlling his anger and going to meetings, the more she let down her guard. He even got as far as Step Nine, tearfully apologizing for the harm he'd caused her. And for the first time in years, he got a job, working construction in Sisters, the tiny hamlet in the Cascades near their cottage. Both Rosaleen and Helen were optimistic that, at last, Kip had mended his ways.

It wasn't until a few months after Danny was born that things started to go bad again. That's when Kip realized he had a permanent competitor for Helen's love and attention, a rival he had no chance of beating. He started drinking, on the sly at first—Helen discovered empty bottles of vodka and rum rattling around in the spare-tire compartment of his pickup—and then openly, in a fuck-you, you-can't-control-me-bitch sort of way. He quit his job and his temper blazed, worse than before. When Danny was eleven months old, Helen was forced to return to her old minimum-wage job at the candle factory and put the baby in day care.

Still, for a time she tried to convince herself that if only she could help Kip finish his great bildungsroman, things would improve. He would go back to AA and the witty, brilliant man she'd fallen in love with would suddenly step out from the shadows and banish his evil twin. That fantasy ended when Kip's fists found Danny, the night of his fifth birthday. Helen hated herself for sticking around long enough to let it happen, but in another way was grateful. That was the night she finally awoke from her seven-year trance and plotted their escape.

Her friends, who had plenty of money troubles of their own, managed to scrape together nearly two thousand dollars in a couple of days. Mac found her a beat-up but solid Dodge Dart in Bend for twelve hundred and Julie stuck a map of the United States in the glove box. Which was a good thing, because Helen had no idea where she was headed. All she knew was that it had to be someplace way off Kip's radar. She drove for fifteen hours straight before she felt safe enough to stop for the night at a cheap motel, the Mighty Oaks, in Laramie, Wyoming. The next morning, she got the map out of the car and folded it so that only the part of the country east of the Mississippi was visible—she wasn't taking any chances on returning to the West—then laid it on the bed and told Danny to close his eyes, say *hocus pocus abracadabra* three times, then let his finger drop. A random gesture seemed as good a way as any to find their new home. Helen closed her eyes, too, and when she opened them, Danny's little finger had landed on a small town in upstate New York called Aurora Falls. They picked out new names, too. By switching their middle names with their first names and adopting a new last name, they went from being Alice and Daniel Rogers to Helen and Henry Bird.

Alice let Danny, who loved birds and believed that someday he would grow wings and fly, choose their surname. All the way across the country, they laughed and sang and felt as free as a couple of jailbirds on the loose.

HELEN WAS GOING stir crazy. There had been one thunderstorm after another since she and Charlie got stuck in Laramie and except for brief walks between downpours, she'd been cooped up in the motel room watching shit TV with the dog, who desperately needed a bath. She decided rain or no rain, she needed to be around humans. So, on their last night, she threw the celadon silk tunic she'd worn to the wedding on over a pair of jeans and twisted her long silver braid around her head. Studying her face in the mirror as she applied lipstick and a touch of eyeliner, she decided she looked more alive than she had in some time. The color had returned to her full cheeks and the heavy bags under her eyes had retreated into normal-looking circles. Even her deep-set hazel eyes seemed to have lost some of the opaque glaze that made her look so sad.

"You know what, Charlie?" she said. "I'm starting to think that getting out of Aurora Falls for a while was the right idea. What do you think?" The smelly dog was splayed out on one of the two double beds looking mopey. She scratched under his chin and kissed his head. "Sorry, boy, but this time I can't take you with me." She slipped her brown leather bomber jacket over the tunic and left the Weather Channel on for the dog, who, like some old coot, seemed to be soothed by it. Then she borrowed an umbrella from the manager of the Mighty Oaks and hoofed it the half mile to the Lazy Stirrup for a much-needed glass of wine.

The second Helen was inside, she started scanning faces.

Looking for her son was a reflex now, as automatic as blinking. Sometimes she thought she caught a glimpse of him. The shape of his head from behind, the swipe of a grin out of the corner of her eye, the way he often stood on one foot and drifted to the right. The whole way across the country, she was on the lookout. She could tell Charlie was, too, the way his ears pricked up and he wagged his tail excitedly before leaping out of the car at every rest stop and gas station, sniffing, expectant, as if *this* time Henry would be there: pumping gas in Toledo, working the take-out window at McDonald's in South Bend, handing over room keys at the Days Inn near Des Moines, or hiding in the bushes at a truck stop outside Omaha. Each time Danny wasn't there, the dog's ears would droop, and with his tail tucked between his legs, he'd drag himself back to the car as if he'd just aged a decade in dog years. He and Helen were a real pair. And now here she was, checking out the customers and the guy mixing drinks behind the bar. Helen hadn't really expected to find her son in any of those other places. But Laramie was where the compass of Danny's five-year-old finger had set their course for Aurora Falls. Helen believed that if his finger had landed anyplace else—Maine, New Jersey, Pittsburgh—he wouldn't be missing now.

She sat down at the bar and ordered a glass of the house red.

As soon as she did, a rangy-looking cowboy type took the stool next to her and offered to pay for her drink.

"No thanks, I'm good," she said, avoiding his eyes. She needed to be around other humans, not relate to them, especially not some country redneck. This guy looked like an extra left over from *Gunsmoke*, her father's favorite TV show. She took a gulp of the rotgut the bartender had just set down on a napkin.

"You're not from around here, are you?" the man persisted.

"Just trying to have a quiet drink," Helen muttered. "What

are you, some dime-store cowboy who preys on lone women passing through?"

"Nope, not a cowboy, though I do have a bunch of horses. My name is Randy, and believe it or not, I'm actually a nice person. The answer to your question is no, I'm not in the habit of preying on lone women. Or anyone, for that matter. But if you don't want company, I get that." He tipped his head in her direction.

Helen turned slightly and looked at the man's face. It was a kind face. Sixtyish, tanned, with a full head of silver hair and green eyes surrounded by laugh lines so deep they looked like tattoos. Helen estimated he was sporting about two days' worth of stubble.

"Well," she said, thinking that, after all, it might not be so bad to talk to another human. "Before you go in search of your next victim, maybe you can clear something up for me. I've always wondered why people who raise horses are called cowboys and not horseboys?"

The man laughed, a low, unrestrained belly laugh. "Good question. I'll bring it up with the Fraternal Order of Cowpokes next time we gather round the ole' campfire and sing 'Home on the Range.'"

Helen flashed him a smile. "Guess I had that coming."

"You said it, not me."

"Do you really raise horses?"

"I do, but that's not my day job."

"Oh." Helen pictured him selling RVs or tractors, or maybe something more outdoorsy, like working at a feedlot. "So what is your day job?" she asked.

"I own a software company."

"Really?" She couldn't tell if he was putting her on and swiveled her stool around to face him.

"I don't lie any more than I prey on pretty women passing through." He pressed his tongue against the inside of his cheek so that it stuck out, and stared at Helen, as if trying to decide how much to tell her. "I moved here about a year ago from Silicon Valley," he said, less jokey than before. "Got tired of all the traffic and the noise and especially the smug twenty-year-old geniuses who made me feel like Methuselah's older brother. I just woke up one day about a year after Candace, she was my wife, died, and realized there was nothing holding me to that life. My daughters were grown, one living in Brooklyn, the other in Denver. And I could run my business from anywhere on the planet. So, why not Wyoming? I've always been a sucker for horses and mountains, and you might have noticed we got ourselves one hell of a sky out here." Randy shrugged his shoulders and smiled, a winning, faintly asymmetrical smile. "That's it. So now that you know my whole life story, which, believe it or not, I don't usually tell strangers in a bar, who may I ask are you?"

"Well . . ." Helen hated to lie to such an obviously nice man, but she could hardly tell the truth: *I'm an accidental baker living under an alias whose adult son went missing five years ago and, really, I'm so far beyond brokenhearted, there isn't a word for what I am. And I don't know what to call myself. Helen? Alice? No, not Alice.* Helen polished off the rest of her wine and out it tumbled: "Colette. My name is Colette."

"Colette," Randy said, elongating the *ette*, the way the French do. "After the writer?"

"Uh-huh, yup, *c'est moi*. My mom was a big fan. And she was French, on her father's side." (True!) She waved at the bartender, fluttering her crimson fingernails in the air to get his attention. "Could I have another glass of the house red, please?" She'd had her nails painted for the wedding, an out-of-character move for a woman whose hands were usually buried in dough, but definitely in character for Colette. She tapped the fingernails of one hand along the bar as if she were practicing scales on a piano.

"So, Colette, what brings you up to the High Plains?"

"Well . . ." *Jesus*, Helen thought, someday she really would love to unburden herself and tell someone the whole truth and nothing but, only her truth was too complicated, too sad. "I work in the um . . . movie business. I'm a location scout." (She knew about scouts from the Queen of Hearts; she'd rented the bakery out twice, once for a local commercial and another time for a movie that went straight to video.) "I'm checking out locations for an upcoming TV series."

She was amazed at how easily the lies came spilling out of her mouth. But really, she shouldn't have been so surprised. Her life in Aurora Falls for the past twenty-seven years had rested on a foundation of lies. Thank God for Nessa Stokes, the original Queen of Hearts. Nessa had had her own share of violent, angry man trouble, so when she took one look at a washed-out Helen and her sketchy application to work the counter at the bakery, Nessa got the picture. She offered her a job on the spot, as well as a room for herself and Danny in her house above the shop. (A good thing, since they were down to their last eighty-seven dollars and were sleeping in the car.) Then, with the aid of a guy who knew a guy who knew a guy over in Kingston, Nessa helped Alice and Danny Rogers become Helen and Henry Bird, papers and all. And when Nessa died of cancer three years later—after sharing her carefully guarded secrets concerning the mysteries of dough—she left Helen the Queen of Hearts.

Helen took a generous slosh of wine and realized that she felt freer than she'd felt in years. For a little while at least, she could be someone else. Someone not plagued by constant sorrow. Colette.

A freewheeling location scout from LA who was enjoying her wine and the attentions of—she had to admit—a seriously appealing man. She'd never see him again, so what real harm could her spontaneous little improv do?

"Actually, I'm up here scouting ranches. Maybe I should take a look-see at yours." The wine was definitely loosening her up. Maybe she'd take up smoking again, along with other fun, nasty habits.

"You're welcome to, but I have to warn you it's not a typical working ranch. I adopt wild horses from the Bureau of Land Management and then let them run free, except for the few we break and train. They make the best riders. You like to ride?"

A horse rescuer? Who the hell was this guy, was he running for saint? Could any man really be this perfect? "I love to ride," said Helen. Which was the only true thing that had come out of her mouth all night, aside from her maternal grandfather being French. "Can you take me to see the horses? Right now?" She was as surprised as he was by her request.

"I guess. But you won't be able to see the wild ones at night."

"At least I'll get some idea, because I'm leaving first thing in the morning. I just have to stop at the motel on the way and pick up Charlie, my dog, if that's okay. Only I have to warn you, he doesn't much care for men."

HELEN HADN'T MEANT to sleep with him. She told herself she was just curious about the ranch. And the horses. She'd never met anyone who saved wild horses before. Or lived on a giant spread bordering the Middle Fork of the Laramie River. Not that either attribute was on her checklist for the ideal man, because she had no such checklist. Nor had she felt a ripple of desire since pushing

Jock away. But somehow stepping out of her identity as a grief-stricken mother liberated her. She felt bold, unafraid. As a burst of sexual energy like a wayward storm overtook her during the half-hour drive to the ranch, waking every cell from her fingertips to her toes, she realized that the physical pain of loss had been so acute, she'd clamped down against the flow of sensation itself. Only now she was remembering what it was like to be a living being with a body. She imagined that if people who'd opted to be cryogenically frozen just before death were ever revived, this would be how they'd feel when they woke up.

"I see what you mean about the sky," she said, climbing out of Randy's Jeep and looking up. The thunderclouds had given way to a knockout explosion of stars and a crescent moon so luminous it appeared to be vibrating.

"Told you. But be careful, Colette, so you don't sink into the mud." Randy offered her his hand. "We can start in the barn with the trained horses. The wild ones are way out there, hunkered down for the night." He motioned to the vast darkness beyond the corral. "I doubt if we'll see any. C'mon, Charlie, c'mon, boy. This way." After greeting him with the usual warning growls, Charlie was treating Randy like an old friend. Helen supposed that the dog, still grieving the loss of his master, craved male company as much as she did, and his superior shit detectors had given Randy a pass.

"Please, can I see your house first?" Helen said. "I'd love to use the bathroom. And I wouldn't mind another glass of wine." It was all she could do to keep from wrestling the man down in the mud.

"YOU ARE ONE conundrum of a woman, you know that, Colette?" Randy said when they were settled on a worn leather sofa in the high-ceilinged great room, with Charlie contentedly curled up at their feet like a throw rug and a fire blazing in the massive stone fireplace. "First, you bite my head off and accuse me of being a dime-store predator. Next thing I know, you're dying to come with me to my ranch late at night. And you've yet to tell me anything about yourself, other than you're a location scout. Are you married? Divorced? Have kids? On the lam? A terrorist, or maybe the leader of an international spy ring?"

Helen gazed at the fire. She couldn't bring herself to tell any more lies. But she couldn't tell him the truth either.

"Hey, I like you anyway, whoever the hell you are." Randy shrugged. "I can tell, you're good people. I've been around enough bad ones to suss out the difference."

"I promise I'm not a terrorist or on the lam. I'm not an alcoholic either, this is the most I've had to drink in . . . well, a very long time. Let's just say I've had a pretty rough few years." Helen set her wineglass down on the wooden trunk that doubled as a coffee table and inched closer to Randy. "When I was a kid, I did dream of joining a spy ring. But that was mostly because of the trench coat and sunglasses," she said, barely able to breathe, every nerve in her body on fire.

She was the first to make a move, and then they were all over each other, a tangle of limbs and mouths, eyes gazing and hands exploring, juices flowing, tender and awkward, hungry and laughing as they slid off the slippery leather sofa and crashed onto the floor, sending Charlie whimpering across the room. Randy let out a holler when he landed on his bad knee and Helen pulled a muscle in her torso trying to get the tunic over her head, but none of it mattered. What mattered, Helen thought when they were done—the first time, after which, mercifully, they relocated to Randy's enormous bed—was that even though each of them had been broken by private sorrows, they were able to see one another apart from their stories, naked and whole.

And for a little while Helen was able to see herself that way, too, even if it was only for one night.

"You don't have to go," Randy said, helping her down off Frankie, a chestnut mare so agreeable, it was hard to imagine her ever roaming the plains untamed.

"Oh, but I do," said Helen. "If I don't leave now, I'm afraid I'll never go."

"Works for me."

She rose on tiptoes as he brushed the curtain of loose hair away from her face and bent down to kiss her. It hadn't been until that morning when he got out of bed to open the shades that she realized how tall he was.

"I'll call you," she said, an hour later when he dropped her and Charlie at the garage so she could pick up her car. "I promise. I just have to take care of a few things first."

"Could you at least give me your phone number or email?" he said, handing her his card. "How am I supposed to find you? Stand under the Hollywood sign and holler Colette?"

"I'll text you my number," Helen said, staring at her feet. She was still wearing the silver sandals she'd worn to the wedding. "I am so grateful to you, you have no idea."

She buried her head in his neck, breathing in the sharp leathery scent of him, then walked away as fast as she could, relieved that he drove off before he saw her and Charlie climb into the dinged-up Outback with the New York plates.

THIRTEEN

JONAH WAS FULL OF QUESTIONS ON THE FLIGHT TO KEY WEST. "If I run really fast and flap my arms, why can't I fly?" he asked, shortly after takeoff. And when the plane was buffeted by thick clouds as it climbed, he wanted to know if he "could walk on them since they are fat and fluffy and you always tell me I'm light as a feather," he giggled. "How much does a feather weigh? I weigh thirty-seven pounds."

Lucie had stayed up late finishing the night terrors story and had to drag herself out of bed for the predawn taxi ride to LaGuardia. As soon as they were on the plane, she closed her eyes and let Matt, who was used to keeping surgeon's hours, take over. Had it been up to her, they would have rented a house in Aurora Falls and gone snowshoeing and played board games by a roaring fire. But it wasn't up to her. Every winter between Christmas and New Year's, Matt's parents rented a big house near Key West for the whole family, and attendance was mandatory. As she drifted off, Lucie heard Matt explain where the sun went at night and why the plane would not be flying through outer space on the way to Florida, and that Jesus H. Christ was the same guy as Jesus Christ but some people liked to say the H, especially when they were really mad. The last thing she heard before being awakened by the flight attendant announcing their descent into Key West

International was Jonah asking, "Will my other mom and dog be in Florida, too?"

FOR DINNER ON New Year's Eve, Nan, Matt's mother, made bouillabaisse, and Jonah worried it might contain dolphins. There had been a lot of discussion earlier in the day about the fact that dolphins are whales, but that not all whales are as nice as dolphins.

"Come on, Jonah, I promise, no dolphins," Matt said. But Jonah wasn't having it. He sat cross-legged on his chair, scowling. "Nana slaved away all day in the kitchen, so how about just one little bite?" Matt took a spoonful from his bowl and held it up to Jonah's sealed lips.

"Enough." Lucie kicked him under the table. Though Matt was generally laid back about food and claimed that kids are biologically programmed to get the nutrients they need, he had regressed—as he usually did—when he spent more than fifteen minutes with his parents.

"Dolphins live in pods and they're really sweet to each other," said Isabelle, Audrey's nine-year-old daughter, in an obvious attempt to deflect attention from Jonah. Audrey was Matt's younger sister.

"We had a marine mammal unit, too," said Kira, Matt's older sister, Annie's, ten-year-old. "Dolphins are really smart and even though they don't have ears, they communicate like this." She clicked her tongue to demonstrate.

Lucie shot her nieces a thumbs-up for trying to rescue Jonah.

"Enough yammering," said Matt's father, Gordon, who got antsy when he wasn't in motion. He tossed his napkin on the table and rose. "Come on, kids, last one down to the beach gets only one scoop of ice cream."

Matt and Gordon immediately took off for a jog, while Rufus, Annie's husband and an astronomy buff, tried to teach the kids about the constellations, with little apparent success, because they were too busy collecting seashells. "A starfish, I found a starfish!" Lucie heard Jonah cry, as thrilled as if he'd just struck gold.

"Thankfully, it only happened the one time, so I guess Matt was right that it was because of the fever," Lucie said, describing Jonah's night terrors to Audrey, as the two women stood at the edge of the shore, bathing their feet in the warm waves. Without Audrey, Lucie didn't think she could make it through these Pressman extravaganzas. Audrey was the designated black sheep—a trauma therapist in a family that didn't believe in therapy, the daughter who'd left her dolt of a husband for the brilliant Nina, a disability rights lawyer. "A handful," according to the senior Pressmans. Lucie was certain that behind her back she was considered "a handful," too.

"I can see how that would be really upsetting," said Audrey. "I'm glad it was just the once."

"Me too," said Lucie, about to ask her sister-in-law her thoughts on Jonah's imaginary mom and dog, when a series of deafening bangs, crackles, and pops punctured the rhythm of the breaking waves. Lucie turned and saw fireworks being launched from the beach in front of the house next door. "Shit, Jonah's going to freak. Aren't fireworks illegal here?"

"Probably, but that doesn't keep the assholes from setting them off," said Audrey.

"Mama, mama!" Jonah dropped his starfish and came running. "Mama, I'm scared!" he shrieked. "Make them stop." Ever since he'd had a meltdown on the Fourth of July when he was two, Matt and Lucie had been vigilant about keeping him away from fireworks.

He'd become almost too heavy for Lucie to lift, but somehow she managed to pick him up and carry him inside kicking and screaming, as Matt raced down the beach toward the neighbors' house, shouting and threatening to call the cops if they didn't "stop the goddamn fucking fireworks *right now!*"

IT TOOK THEM half an hour to calm Jonah down and another half hour for him to fall asleep, curled up between them.

"I hope the cops arrest those fuckers," Lucie whispered. "Jonah hasn't gotten that spooked in so long, I was hoping loud noises wouldn't bother him anymore."

"It was probably just a fluke because of the fireworks. Happy New Year, Luce, it must be 2008 by now," Matt said, yawning, then falling asleep so fast it was as if he had an on-off switch.

An hour later, Jonah began shaking and screaming, "Stop! Don't hurt me!" just like the first time he had night terrors. Only this time he added, "Don't kill me!"

And just like the first time, Lucie panicked, Matt talked her down, the whole episode was over in twenty minutes, and Jonah had no memory of it the next morning.

You really couldn't make this shit up, Lucie mused a few hours later when she read Diana's email in response to her article on night terrors.

"Grt wrk!!! Smrt, hrtflt, infrmatve! U naild it. So gld ths only hppnd 2 Jnh 1 tme! XOD"

THE NIGHT TERRORS happened twice during their first week back from Key West, and this time there were no simple explanations, no fevers or fireworks to pin them on.

Matt had two theories. One: They were caused by residual trauma left over from the fireworks on New Year's Eve and would soon stop. Two: Jonah's brain and nervous system were still slightly immature from him being preterm, and he was working out some kinks while he slept.

"You might be right about the fireworks," said Lucie, "but in all my research, not one expert said anything about immature nervous systems causing night terrors. I think it's something else."

Lucie's theory was based on the epigenetics story she'd just started researching. Reading up on it, she realized why, in spite of having done everything she could to avoid passing her anxious wiring on to Jonah, she'd failed miserably, in an uncontrollable, epigenetic sort of way. Her baseline nervous system, like her nana's and now Jonah's, seemed programmed to react as if a band of Nazis was about to come storming through the front door and send them to their deaths. Lucie wondered if Jonah screaming *Don't kill me* during the last couple of episodes of night terrors had been triggered by unconscious ancestral memory.

"Luce, come on, you can't blame yourself for what's going on with Jonah," Matt said after she told him her theory.

"I'm not blaming myself. I know I'm not responsible for my genes, but let's face it. A lot of bad shit happened to my family."

"Bad shit happens in a lot of families, but not every kid has night terrors. It's a neurochemical thing." They were sprawled on the sofa after putting Jonah to bed, worn out. The latest episode had kept them up the night before.

"Maybe, but did you know that everyone has a genetic blueprint that doesn't just affect height or eye color or whether you get cancer, but emotions, too? There's a lot of new research that shows how traumatic events in someone's life can change the way their DNA is expressed and then gets passed down to future generations. In some studies, mice whose grandparents experienced trauma were born more anxious than mice whose grandparents were happy. Well, as happy as mice can be, which might mean a nice chunk of cheddar and no cats." Lucie stopped and strained to hear if any sounds were coming from Jonah's room. It was at about this time—ninety minutes after he fell asleep—that the night terrors started. "The point is, even though the studies on humans aren't conclusive *yet*, some researchers think the same is true for us. Our ancestors' genes could be altered by trauma and passed down at least three generations. So maybe Jonah and I have messed-up genes inherited from Nana."

"Even if what you're saying turns out to be as true for people as it is for mice, and I'm not saying it will be, what can you do about it?"

"I don't know, maybe some kind of PTSD therapy? For me it's just helpful to have science confirm what, on some level, I've always sensed."

"Don't forget, Jonah has my genetic blueprint, too," Matt said, sweeping Lucie's curls aside and massaging her neck. "Most of the time he's just a regular kid. A little sensitive, but he's not you or your Nana. And what about your father? For all we know, he was some happy-go-lucky guy. So try not to project your emotions onto Jonah. Not good for either of you."

Lucie jerked away and slid to the far end of the sofa. Sometimes her brilliant doctor husband acted like a thick-skulled dimwit. Or, giving him the benefit of the doubt, maybe he just seemed that way to her because they were so different. She was focused on making sense of her life, as if it were some elaborate jigsaw puzzle—a futile pursuit, since so many pieces were missing—while the pieces in Matt's life were all out on the table.

"This stuff is important, and not just for me. Inherited family trauma could explain so much about the human psyche. You really don't get it, do you?"

Matt took off his glasses and rubbed his eyes. "I'm trying, but, Luce, as interesting as this is, until there are credible studies with humans it's just another theory."

Studying her ragged fingernails, Lucie was trying to decide whether to go on. "Okay," she said after a few minutes, "when I think about this terrifying nightmare I had as a kid, starting when I was two or three, about dying in some giant, pitch-dark bathroom-like place that made me wake up screaming and gasping for air, where did that come from? I had no idea Nana's parents and brother had died at Auschwitz. I'd never heard of it, but I must have somehow metabolized her trauma—and maybe Jonah has, too. The difference is, I remembered my nightmares. Only my mother, who never acknowledged what happened to her family, ignored what I told her and decided the gasping meant I was allergic to dairy. Which she cut out of my diet, but it didn't help, since the only time I had trouble breathing was during the nightmares.

"And then I became completely obsessed with the Nazis when I was a teenager and read every book I could get my hands on. *The Last of the Just. Treblinka.* Primo Levi. But it wasn't until I was getting ready to go to college that I learned what happened. I was fishing around for something in Nana's sewing drawer when I found an old photo of an adorable little girl in a white organza pinafore standing next to a taller, very serious-looking boy of about eight, who was wearing knickers. I asked her about it, and that's when she broke down and told me that was her and her older brother, Isaac. She told me about the Kindertransport, how her parents managed to get her on a train in Vienna, but Isaac stayed behind with them. They were all supposed to meet up in England a few months later."

She took a breath and met Matt's eyes. "In the past, when I talked about this I always felt like I was describing something that happened to someone else's family, like characters in a play. I didn't want to go near it. But knowing there's a real explanation for how scared I sometimes get for no reason makes me feel less afraid."

"Lucie, one of the things I love most about you is how sensitive you are. You pick up on things outside the margins I'd never even notice if it weren't for you."

"I know, but it's never been you, Matt. It's always been me who believed something inside me was broken." She leaned over and laid her head on his shoulder, feeling calmer, lighter, scrubbed clean, the way you do when suddenly you realize some basic truth about yourself, some essential piece of the puzzle that's been eluding you, and you tell someone you love.

"Did I ever tell you you're beautiful?" And this time when Matt reached for her she didn't resist.

A FEW HOURS later, unable to sleep, Lucie stood on their terrace in her bathrobe, the frigid air licking her bare legs. On that narrow slice of bluestone floating twelve stories above the earth, it was so quiet the city could have been swaddled in flannel. She opened her mouth to let the fat snowflakes that appeared to be falling upward melt on her tongue. And though she knew it would pass, she longed to hold on to that moment, or at least remember it, because at that moment she felt fearless. Unbroken.

If only she could give Jonah a transfusion of the fearlessness she felt standing there, trembling in the freezing cold, the thickening snowfall turning her dark hair white.

FOURTEEN

HELEN WAS STARTLED AWAKE WHEN THE OLD MAN RAPPED ON her car window with his cane. Bleary-eyed from driving straight through to Eugene from Laramie, she rolled down the window. "Can I help you?" she shouted over Charlie's barking.

"I think the question, miss, is, can I help you? You've been sitting outside my house for two-plus hours and I'd like to know why. See that sign over there? The one with the big black eyeball?" The man waved his cane at the Neighborhood Watch sign that was nailed to a tall cedar across the street. "I'm the block captain and I'm watching you." With his forefinger and middle finger in the shape of a V, he motioned to his cloudy eyes, then pointed them at Helen.

"So sorry to bother you. I'm just waiting for one of your neighbors to come home. An old friend. Rosaleen Rogers."

"Her car's in the driveway. The blue Toyota. Have you tried ringing the bell?"

"Yes, well, no, I mean, I wasn't sure that was her car. I haven't seen her in a while and well . . . I thought I'd just wait for her to get home from work and surprise her."

"She retired years ago. I'll walk you over."

"Oh. Right. Thanks. My mistake." Helen left the window rolled part way down for Charlie, then, feeling like a criminal,

trailed the man across the street and down the block to the familiar yellow Craftsman bungalow with the jumble of rosebushes
and hydrangeas out front. Apart from the trees and bushes being
much taller and denser than before, the house looked the same.
Helen just wished she'd driven away when Mr. Nosy Block Captain started interrogating her. How stupid to tell him the truth.
She wasn't ready. She'd hoped to catch a glimpse of Rosaleen
before meeting her face-to-face; it had been more than twenty
years since she'd last seen her mother-in-law. Who, for all Helen
knew, was her ex-mother-in-law, if Kip had ever gotten sober
enough to file for divorce. This was not how Helen had pictured
their reunion. She'd planned to observe the comings and goings
at the house long enough to make sure she wouldn't run into
him. Shivering, her arms gooseflesh despite the warmth of the
late morning sun, she asked the man if, by chance, he'd seen Rosaleen's son recently.

"Not my beeswax," he snapped, groping the railing as he
climbed the few steps to the front porch, then rang the bell several times.

"She must be out," Helen said after about a minute. "I'll come
back later." She started to retreat just as the door opened.

"Sorry it took me so long, Joe. I was out back turning the
soil for bulbs. The weather people are predicting an early frost."
Helen was stunned by Rosaleen's appearance. The woman may
have turned eighty-one last year, but apart from being an inch
or two shorter and wider than the last time Helen had seen her,
she looked remarkably robust. Her tanned face was practically
unlined and even her wiry gray curls were streaked with black.
By contrast, having not slept the night before, and with her long
hair half pinned up, the other half hanging past her waist, Helen
looked like an aging waif.

"This young lady claims she knows you. She's been sitting in her car watching your house since early this morning. I was about to call the cops, but thought I'd better check with you first. You know her?"

Rosaleen wiped her hands on her green plastic gardener's apron, then glanced suspiciously at Helen. "Nope, I don't think so, I . . ." She stopped in midsentence, took a step closer, and squinted. Then it was as if a shadow swept across her face, eclipsing the sun. "Alice?"

Helen nodded. She'd imagined this scene so often, she couldn't believe it was actually happening. In the years following her flight from Kip, she'd wanted to believe that Rosaleen would understand why she and Danny had to run and would welcome her back, if Helen ever felt safe enough to return. Losing Rosaleen felt like losing her own mother all over again, and she'd imagined that Rosaleen must miss her, too—even though she'd deserted her son and fled with her grandson. But later, as Alice settled into her new identity as Helen the artisanal baker and single mother of Henry, she more or less stopped thinking about ever seeing Rosaleen again.

That changed when Danny disappeared. Besides Mira, Rosaleen was the one person in the world Helen most longed to talk to, to cry with. Danny's only living grandparent. But she'd been too frightened to reach out, too scared that Rosaleen would tell Kip, and he'd come after her. Until now.

Once Rosaleen got over the shock of seeing her, her face lit up. "Is Danny with you?"

"THEN HE WAS just gone," Helen said. After liberating Charlie from the car, she sat facing Rosaleen across the red Formica kitchen table where she'd sat a thousand times before, the dog asleep at her feet. "He wasn't Danny anymore. When we left Oregon, I changed our names. You have no idea how much I wanted to let you know we were safe, but I was terrified that Kip would find out where we were and kidnap Danny to get back at me." She tapped her fingernails on the table. The polish was now so chipped, her nails looked as if a mouse had clawed at them.

"After about a year the detective told me they were putting the investigation on the back burner. I begged him not to. He said he was on my side, but the sheriff wouldn't let him keep devoting so many hours to a 'cold case.' He still keeps an eye out, but . . ."

Helen was having trouble reading Rosaleen's face. It was a broad, inscrutable tabula rasa; her expression gave nothing away. Which shouldn't have surprised Helen. Rosaleen was famous for projecting steely neutrality, even in the midst of hearing bad news. Because of her seeming indifference, she scared a lot of people, including Helen when they'd first met. Back then she'd assumed that Rosaleen's disregard had to do with the fact that she was just one of a pack of young women who'd fallen for her charismatic son, so why should she bother showing any particular interest in her? But later, when Helen got to know her better, she came to view Rosaleen's demeanor as more of a Zen thing. The woman seemed to listen to what people had to say without passing judgment. Or offering phony encouragement. Eventually Helen realized that as the daughter of fundamentalist preachers who roamed Oklahoma from town to town, Rosaleen's only chance of psychological survival had been to grow a thick outer shell. But now, Helen was desperate for a sign.

"After the cops threw up their hands, I hired a private detective," she went on. "Two, actually, when the first one turned out to be an idiot. The second guy combed the Cascades near Sisters and couldn't find Kip or Danny, then he staked out your house, too. I guess he was better at stakeouts than I am, because as far as I know your neighbor never busted him." Helen smiled at Rosaleen, hoping for a smile or even a friendly nod in return, but got nothing. Clearly, Rosaleen hated her and she'd have to leave soon, so she had better ask the question she'd come all this way to ask.

"Even after the detective turned in his report, I still wondered, did Danny ever get in touch with you or show up here? Was he so furious at me for taking him away from Kip, he made you promise not to tell?" Helen's mouth felt parched, her tongue thick with fur. She reached inside her purse and fished out the letter Danny had started to his father and handed it to Rosaleen. "I found this in the trash at the motel where he stayed right before he went missing."

Rosaleen scanned the letter, then gave it back to Helen. "I haven't heard from Danny since you ran away with him. And neither has Kip. Don't you think if he'd found his way here, I'd have made sure to let you know?" Her eyes narrowed and the skin around her taut lips went white. "A separation I could have understood. Kip was drinking again. But taking off like that, in the middle of the night? You were my *daughter*."

Of course Rosaleen could never forgive her, and Helen didn't blame her. Why had she even come? Did she really think the mother-in-law she'd deserted would welcome her back after decades of silence? Or that her fantasy of finding Danny would have more substance than smoke? She'd better pull herself together and get out of there before she caused Rosaleen any more pain, but she could barely hold her head up. She didn't think she'd ever felt this weary, this hollowed out.

"I am so sorry," Helen said, her voice sounding coated with rust.

HOURS LATER WHEN she opened her eyes, it was dark. At first, she didn't know where she was. Then she remembered: Eugene. Rosaleen's house. In Kip's old room. She looked around in the dim light cast by a lamppost out front, then ran a hand over her body. She was still wearing the jeans and tunic she'd had on since Laramie. Lying on top of Kip's childhood bed, an old Hudson's Bay blanket covering her, she recalled the two weeks she'd spent in this room the first time she left Kip, after learning she was pregnant. It was here that she'd made up her mind not to go through with the abortion. She rolled onto her side and dragged herself out from under the blanket and opened the blinds. The sky was streaming with ribbons of burnt orange and gold.

"I'M SORRY, I must have passed out on you. I should just go." Helen stood in the doorway to the kitchen.

Rosaleen, always an early riser, was already dressed and seated at the table drinking coffee. Charlie, curled up on the floor beside her, was lazily licking his paw.

"Sit," she ordered. "You're not going anywhere."

Helen did as she was told, taking the same worn vinyl seat as the day before.

Pointing to Charlie, Rosaleen said, "I made an appointment to take this stinkbomb to my old dog groomer's later this morning. I told her it was an emergency."

"Oh. Thank you." Even if she hated her, Rosaleen had always

been a dog person and would never take her feelings out on Charlie. "He's Danny's dog," Helen said.

"I got that. Coffee?"

"Yes, please."

Rosaleen rose shakily, leaning on the table to steady herself, and then hobbled over to the stove. "It's worse in the morning. The arthritis. It eases up during the day."

"Rosaleen, you're the last person in the world I ever meant to hurt. You have no idea how many times I picked up the phone and . . ."

Rosaleen set a cup of coffee in front of Helen, clearly doing her best not to spill it. "Still take it black?"

"I do. Yes." The ticking of the old grandfather clock, inherited from Rosaleen's prairie preacher grandfather, made the silence thicker.

"I can't tell you how enraged I was at you," Rosaleen said finally. "Every cell in my body, screaming. After you left, Kip started using meth and God knows what else on top of the drinking, and I blamed it all on you. If only you'd stayed, we might have been able to rescue him from himself. That was my story and I was sticking to it." She bent down and stroked Charlie's head. "Until one day I found him in my bedroom packing up what little jewelry I had to take to the pawnshop. I threw him out and told him not to come back unless he got sober, then had the locks changed within the hour. That night I went to the Zendo to meet with my teacher and told her the whole sorry saga. When I finished, she said she understood why I was so hurt by Kip and furious at him, but she wondered why I was still so angry with you. Did I have all the information? Was there more to the story than I was telling myself? Could something have happened that I knew nothing about? How could I continue to judge you so harshly when I didn't know what drove you away? And I had to ask myself: Had I turned a blind eye to you and Danny in order to protect my son?"

"No, you never . . ."

"Let me finish." The expression on Rosaleen's face softened. "It was so much easier to hate you. But talking to my teacher that day, I realized I couldn't be faithful to the truth and keep pretending to know what I had no way of knowing. Admitting that just about killed me. Because underneath the rage was grief. I'd never felt so weighted down by grief, not even after Kip's dad hung himself. You and Danny were gone. Kip was killing himself one way or another. And there was nothing to do but accept things as they were, as awful as they were. There's a saying in Zen, *Welcome the unwelcome.* It sounds like a silly platitude, but you don't get how radical it is, or how hard, until you're faced with unimaginable loss."

Rosaleen rubbed her knobby hands, then said, "But that's what saved me. It sounds simplistic, but realizing there was nothing I could do except what I could do kept me from going crazy. I could plant my garden, go to work, take poor old Bo out for walks, and help Kip as best I could, without expecting any miracles. And I had to stop hoping that one day you and Danny would come home. I had to let go of pretty much everything except what was right in front of me." Rosaleen smiled at Helen for the first time since she'd arrived, then stood with less obvious discomfort than before and watered the row of potted herbs lined up on the windowsill above the sink. The sun dusted the tender leaves, making them appear incandescent.

"What about Kip?" asked Helen. "I hope by now he's gotten himself cleaned up."

"I doubt it." Rosaleen shrugged. "Last I heard, he was living on the street in Portland. That was ten months ago."

"Oh God," said Helen.

"It's not your fault, Alice. Or mine." Rosaleen sat back down. "Nothing either of us could have done to stop him from destroying himself. Only he could do that. I tried, of course. I'm a social worker, right? A professional. If I couldn't help my own son, what good was I? But he didn't want my help."

"Maybe he would have been okay if I'd stayed. I would have divorced him, but if he'd gotten sober he could have seen Danny."

Rosaleen shook her head. "You realize that line of thinking will get you nowhere?"

"I can't help it. Ever since Danny disappeared, I've agonized over what would have happened if I'd made a life for us here instead of running away. Kip would have had his son, you would have had your grandson, you and I would have had each other. And Danny would still be here. And I have to live with that." As she said it, Helen realized this was the first time in decades that she hadn't been hiding her real identity or her past. She wept with relief, but also for the toll that years of living a lie had taken, as well as all that had been lost. Was still lost.

Rosaleen waited for the tears to subside, then said in her no-nonsense Rosaleen way, "Alice, it's time you quit your agonizing. There's so much we all have to live with. Who knows what would have happened to Danny if you'd stayed? He could have skied off a cliff and broken his neck like your brother. You know as well as I do that loss is the price we pay for love." Rosaleen took Helen's hand in hers. "Something I've learned is that if you let the grief be, if you don't try to make it go away, even though it's unbearable, worse than death, especially when it's your kid, at some point the loss stops defining who you are. Because I'm telling you, Alice, who you are is bigger than losing Danny and there's life beyond your suffering. Maybe it's nothing like the life you planned for yourself, but it's the only one you have."

Stuffing her bag into the overhead compartment for the flight to Albany, with Charlie smelling like wintergreen and sedated in his new crate in the belly of the plane, Helen felt that something in her had shifted on that trip, but she couldn't say exactly what, because so much had happened: the frantic drive west in the failing (now officially dead and junked) Subaru, the wild night of lovemaking with Randy that seemed like a madcap sex comedy starring a stranger called Colette, or the precious few days she'd spent with Rosaleen.

But as she thought about it, the shift, if there really was one, had to do with what Rosaleen had said about grief. How we're bigger than our grief, but only if we stop trying to make it go away. Maybe that's it, maybe I'm starting to let it be, Helen thought, as the plane rose and banked east over the Cascades and the tiny town of Sisters far below.

Dying feels like being on an airplane that's out of control and then the pilot comes on and says, "Sorry folks, I hate to break it to you but we're going down." Because once the dying starts there's no stopping it. You want to, for a while you even think you can. You think, this can't be happening. Not to me. I'm too young. So you try as hard as you can to stop it, but you can't.

Your body starts feeling heavy, heavier even than gravity, so heavy it seems as if the earth's surface is too flimsy to hold you. Like you weigh a gazillion pounds. And you feel yourself sinking, sucked down to God knows where, you haven't a clue because you can't see the bottom. Actually, you can't see at all because your eyesight is shot.

Still for a minute you think, okay, I can handle this. Being blind isn't the worst thing that can happen to a person. Plus, you realize, it doesn't matter if the world has gone all blurry, since in your mind's eye your vision is still twenty-twenty. You see everything and everybody whirling past and you try as hard as you can to grab on to the people you love and tell them you love them, you don't want to leave them, but they just keep flying by like planets orbiting farther and farther away from you, so you shout as loud as you can, only they can't hear you, and now you can't hear you either because your hearing is gone along with your voice, and you're melting into night with no stars to guide you.

And you're thirsty, so thirsty, and cold, so cold, you've never been this thirsty or cold before. You can't feel your hands or your feet or your legs or your arms, nothing that just minutes ago was <u>you</u>. And that's when you know you're fucking toast.

No body.

PART THREE

SPRING 2010

FIFTEEN

For his seventh birthday, Matt and Lucie decided to let Jonah plan the day from start to finish. Instead of having a party, he wanted to take his best friend, Jeremy, to *The Lion King*. Lucie had tried to talk him into skipping his Saturday violin lesson so they could attend the matinee, but he refused.

"Matinees are for babies," he scoffed.

When Lucie bought tickets for the evening performance, Jonah was so excited he promised to take a nap in the afternoon.

He wrote down the day's schedule with a Sharpie on two sheets of lined notebook paper and proudly handed a copy each to Matt and Lucie.

SATERDAY MAY 1 JONAH IS 7!!!!!

930–GO TO SARA BETH FOR FRENCHE TOST AND HOT CHOCLATE

11–VIOLIN

1230–EAT LUNCH GIRLLED CHEES PLEESE

2–TAKE NAP I WILLL!!!!!!!!!!

430–PICK UP JEREMY AND GO TO TOYS ARE US

630–DINNER CARMINE SPAGETTI MEETBALLS

8–LION KING!!!!!

It was a perfect spring day, warm without being sticky. Petals drifted down from the branches of the cherry trees like pink snow as Matt, Lucie, and Jonah circled the Central Park reservoir between brunch at Sarabeth's and Jonah's violin lesson. Matt and Lucie went for a second, speedier lap while waiting for the lesson to be over. When they picked him up, Jonah was beaming. Elias Fishbein had presented him with a hand-carved bow for his birthday.

The afternoon went off without a hitch, too. Even though he was excited about the evening, Jonah went down for a nap without protest. In fact, he fell into such a deep sleep that Lucie had to wake him when it was time to pick up Jeremy. They found him waiting in front of his building with his dad, looking more wide-eyed and Harry Potterish than usual. A small boy—smaller even than Jonah—Jeremy had thick black hair that his mother cut short to keep it from falling in his eyes, and he wore round tortoiseshell glasses. As soon as he caught sight of Jonah, Jeremy dropped his father's hand and raced to catch up with his friend. The boys skipped all the way to the subway at Eighty-Sixth Street.

They took the train to Times Square and headed to the Toys "R" Us flagship store, with its giant Lego replica of the Empire State Building. Both boys were in awe of the towering model, as well as the amusement park–size Ferris wheel. And though Jonah had asked for only the Empire State Lego kit for his birthday, Matt, ever the proud New Yorker, bought him the complete architectural set, which also included the Chrysler Building, the Flatiron Building, and One World Trade Center. And Jeremy, who was not expecting a gift at all, was thrilled when Matt presented him with the Empire State kit. Lucie and Matt practically had to drag the two boys out of the store to make their six thirty dinner reservation at Carmine's.

While they waited at the light to cross Seventh Avenue, Lucie noticed a crowd of people congregating near *The Lion King* marquee.

"Look at all those people, they must be trying to get tickets to the show," she said to Matt. "Good thing we got ours months ago." She squeezed Jonah's hand.

"Ooh," squealed Jeremy. "Look, a policeman on a horse. Maybe there's a parade."

But the grim expression on the mounted policeman's face did not suggest he was part of a celebration. It wasn't until Lucie, Matt, and the boys made it across Broadway that Matt noticed a smoking car parked at an odd angle in front of the entrance to the Minskoff Theatre, where *The Lion King* was playing. "Luce, look, I think that car is on fire. That must be what all the commotion is about."

"Probably an accident," she said. "I hope no one's hurt."

But seconds later, the smoking car burst into flames, accompanied by a battery of deafening popping noises that sounded like cannon fire.

"Daddy, Mama, what's wrong? I'm scared," Jonah cried.

God, please, don't let it be a bomb, thought Lucie. *Please, not a terrorist attack.* But what she said to Jonah, talking fast to cover her own fear, was, "I think it's just a little car accident, Bear, nothing to worry about, right, Matt?"

"Right, but just to be safe, I think we should move." The look on Matt's face belied the calm in his voice and didn't fool Jonah, who was starting to hyperventilate. Matt picked him up and

Lucie pulled Jeremy close as a line of cops sprang out of nowhere and began pushing people away. Many of the officers were wielding guns.

The scene turned to chaos: people close to the burning car screaming, shoving, running; sirens blaring from all directions; the arrival of more cops in full riot gear and carrying shields. No one seemed to know what was happening, only that it was bad, and the frightened crowd was scrambling in all directions, making it difficult to move.

"Take your kids and get the hell out of here," an officer shouted at Matt.

Lucie watched terrified as Jonah's eyes rolled back in his head, the way they did when he had night terrors. He began shrieking, ear-piercing shrieks. Clutching him, along with the giant shopping bag of Legos, Matt started running south, pushing his way down Broadway through the mob of gawkers, away from the rising pandemonium. Lucie, holding tight to Jeremy, followed Matt, hobbling in uncomfortable heels until she kicked them off, then picked Jeremy up and sprinted in her tights, sticking as close to Matt and Jonah as she could, eyes fixed on the ground to dodge broken glass. She watched them round the corner at Forty-Seventh Street and head west toward Eighth Avenue. By the time she and Jeremy caught up, Matt was standing in the street frantically waving his free arm until, at last, he flagged an unoccupied cab.

Wrapped tightly in his father's arms, Jonah trembled and cried and punched the air all the way home.

It was a car bomb. Crudely assembled from gasoline, propane, and fireworks, it smoked and started to detonate but failed to explode. The cacophony of loud popping sounds were hundreds of firecrackers going off inside. Apparently, a T-shirt vendor had noticed smoke coming out of an SUV parked near the entrance to the theater and alerted a cop. When he investigated, he smelled gunpowder and immediately called for backup, including a bomb squad.

"We are very lucky," Mayor Bloomberg said in a televised news conference at two a.m. "We avoided what could have been a very deadly event." Lucie, still shaken and unable to sleep, was in the living room watching TV and reapplying alcohol and Neosporin to the gash on her heel she got from running through the streets without shoes.

The Lion King and other Broadway shows were canceled that night.

On Sunday Jonah refused to leave the house.

Nothing Lucie or Matt said could convince him he was safe. That no one was hurt. That what happened was a one-time thing and that, in fact, the rapid response of the police had kept everyone safe.

"It's over, honey," Matt told him before he would consider getting out of bed. "There's nothing to worry about."

"What about the bad men with the guns?"

"They were policemen. They're good guys. They carry guns to protect *us* in case something bad happens. And that's just what they did. They did their job and kept us safe." Matt didn't mention that the bad men who had tried to blow up Times Square were still on the loose.

"I hate guns and I'm never going outside again. What if they try to shoot me?"

Matt scooped Jonah in his arms. "No one's going to shoot you, Bear, no one. Mama and I will make sure of that. We've got you."

"No, you don't. The bad men pointed their guns at me. I heard them go off. They were going to kill me."

Of course the guns were never pointed at Jonah. The sounds he heard were the firecrackers exploding inside the SUV, sounds that in his mind seem to have been conflated with the weapons carried by the police.

"Daddy's right, no one tried to hurt you, Bear," echoed Lucie. "But you're right, too, guns used improperly can be scary."

Jonah had seen guns before, on television and tucked into police holsters on the street, and even then, he averted his eyes. Lucie and Matt had been proud of his natural inclination toward nonviolence. But the Times Square incident was different. Jonah had never seen huge semiautomatic rifles before. And though his reaction had mimicked his behavior during night terrors, unlike the night terrors, which he never remembered and hadn't experienced for more than a year, images from the previous night's near catastrophe seemed burned into his psyche.

From stories she'd worked on, as well as her own interest in the subject, Lucie knew something about trauma. She knew it was important to get the traumatized person—whether a child or an adult—to talk about the experience as a step toward healing. But other than being fixated on the noise and the guns, Jonah refused to talk about it.

"It's too soon, you can't push him," Matt said. "The memory is still too raw. He needs time to integrate it. He'll talk when he's ready."

Jonah spent most of Sunday curled up on the living-room sofa clutching Jolly and watching old episodes of *Chopped*. Before dinner, when Matt asked him how he was feeling, he said, "Those stupid chefs are trying to bake Alaska."

ON MONDAY HE claimed his head hurt too much to go to school, and Lucie convinced Matt to let him stay home. She argued that he needed some sense of mastery over his life, regardless of whether the headache was real, and arranged to skip her Monday morning meeting.

Before lunch, she set out several large sheets of paper and Magic Markers on the dining-room table, then sketched her version of the scene in Times Square. Her crude rendering included *The Lion King* marquee, a car filled with firecrackers parked in front of the theater, and a few policemen aiming their guns at the car. Figures of Lucie, Matt, Jonah, and Jeremy stood nearby, watching. No guns were pointed in their direction.

Lucie used her picture to talk about what she'd seen. Jonah listened, but when she encouraged him to draw his own version, he tugged on his ear and stamped his foot. "Okay," she said, lightly running a hand along his spine. "You don't have to, but can you look at my picture and tell me how it's the same or different from what you remember?"

But all he said was "Can I go back now and watch?" Ordinarily, Lucie and Matt were strict about screen time, but cooking shows seemed to be able to soothe him in ways they couldn't, so she said yes.

Jonah obviously still felt threatened. And Lucie felt in over her head.

After lunch she got to work finding him a therapist. She put in calls to Audrey, Matt's trauma therapist sister; her former therapist, Nora; and her friend Ellie, whose daughter suffered from panic attacks—and got everyone's voicemail. Luckily, Lucie remembered Dr. Miriam Zager. She'd interviewed the psychologist after 9/11 for a story about helping children cope with the attack and had been impressed both by Dr. Zager's insightful observations and her practical suggestions. Miraculously, Dr. Zager was able to squeeze Jonah in late Thursday afternoon. Lucie just hoped Matt would go along. Like many adults who had reasonably happy childhoods, he was less drawn to therapy than Lucie.

That night when he got home, he went directly into Jonah's room and explained that the bad man who put the firecrackers (he avoided the word *bomb*) in the car had been caught and would never cause trouble again.

He hoped this information would allay Jonah's fears, but it did not.

ON TUESDAY JONAH woke up complaining of a headache, refused to get dressed for school, and for the first time ever begged Lucie to cancel his violin lesson.

"I'm not playing anymore," he announced, handing Lucie his violin case and the new bow he hadn't yet tried. She couldn't imagine how the instrument he loved had anything to do with what happened on his birthday, but knew enough not to question him about it.

"I'll keep it safe for you," she said.

He wouldn't go near his Lego kits either.

"Maybe in his seven-year-old mind not doing what he loves will protect him from further danger," Matt said, when Jonah went back to his room. "Because on Saturday the danger happened when he was doing something he loved, which he'd planned all by himself."

"Yeah, maybe. Or maybe Nana's brother or parents got shot by the Nazis and it's their trauma that got triggered on Saturday. I was afraid of guns when I was a kid, too."

"Luce, that was a pretty scary scene. I don't think you can pin Jonah's reaction on your family history. Jeremy was terrified, too."

"But not like Jonah. I haven't seen him like that since the last time he had night terrors, and he's obviously still freaked out."

"True, but we don't know why he got so upset, the same way we never knew exactly what caused the night terrors and probably never will. So why don't we figure out how to help him get past this, instead of focusing on some untested theory about ancestral trauma?"

Lucie couldn't believe Matt was still so dismissive, when more and more good research was coming out all the time. In one mind-blowing study, pregnant women who were near the World Trade Center on 9/11 had children who showed heightened distress when faced with new stimuli. Of course, until the studies were double blind and could be replicated in multiple labs, Matt would remain irritatingly skeptical. "I wasn't suggesting we don't do everything practical we can to help Jonah," Lucie said, her throat tight. "But as usual I'm more interested than you in getting to the root of a problem. Which is how real healing happens. Jesus."

"Thanks a lot. You treat me like I'm some slug who just crawled out of a cave and never heard of psychology," Matt said, his olive skin turning an unusual shade of pink. "Maybe inherited trauma is a factor, I don't know. But what can we do about it? Go in there and tell Jonah he's upset because your great-grandparents were murdered by the Nazis?"

Lucie threw her half-eaten bagel in the trash, then retreated to her study and started playing online sudoku.

A short time later, Matt stood in the doorway dressed for work and said, "Luce, let's stop this. I hate fighting with you."

"I hate fighting with you more," she muttered, crossing her arms and sticking out her tongue.

"Right now you look about five years old." He leaned down and kissed her on the temple. "We'll figure this out together, okay?"

She nodded, thankful that when she told him about the appointment with Dr. Zager, he agreed that taking Jonah to a trauma therapist was a good idea.

SIXTEEN

It was in early May, mud season, when Helen got the call. The gruff voice on the other end of the line belonged to Detective Will Handler. Though officially Will hadn't been working the case for years, he continued to keep his eyes and ears open.

"During the snowmelt a couple of teenagers stumbled across some human remains near a creek in Saratoga Springs, close to where Henry was last seen," he said in typical Will fashion, no *hi-how-are-you?* warm-up. "The remains appear to be male, and the timing could be right. I'm going to take Henry's dental records up there when the M.E. does the autopsy, probably early next week. I thought you'd want to know."

It was a Tuesday, a day the bakery was closed. Helen was stretched out on the window seat in her front room, rereading *Mrs. Dalloway* for her book club and thinking about how unlike Clarissa Dalloway she was. As she prepares for her party, Clarissa puts on a cheery face as if she were applying makeup, in spite of her grieving heart. Helen dropped the book on the floor and looked out over the green. The dogwoods and tulips were in bloom, and the cherries were starting to bud. "Oh," was all she managed to say.

"Hey, I know we've been down this road before and each time we turned up zilch. But because of the location and the condition of the remains I think this one is worth taking seriously." When Helen didn't respond, Will said, "Hello? Petunia?"

As their early mistrust of one another had morphed into something akin to friendship, Will had taken to calling Helen Petunia whenever he was worried about her. She assumed it was because of the window boxes jammed with cascading petunias outside the bakery in summer.

"I'm coming with you," Helen said, surprising herself. Since returning from Oregon nearly three years ago, she'd done everything possible to reboot her life. Book club. Choir. Trips to the fall antiques fair in Vermont with Abby. The usual letter-writing campaigns and protest marches, plus three days of sit-ins across from the New York Stock Exchange during Occupy Wall Street. On one of those days she'd even ridden into the city with Jock and the toothpick, whom she'd stopped hating after her one-night stand with Randy. In fact, Helen believed her life was now on a slow crawl toward some form of normalcy, and she avoided any activity that would set her back. Which was why she'd stopped tagging along with Will whenever he went to check out some newly excavated pile of bones, because whatever the results of the inquiry, she wouldn't be getting her son back alive.

Why it seemed urgent for her to go with him now, she couldn't say. Just something in her body was telling her *go*.

"I think that's one bullcrap idea," Will huffed into the phone. "I wouldn't have told you if I thought you'd want to come. Stay home and let me do my damn job."

"This stopped being your job years ago."

"Okay then, my hobby."

"Let me know what day you're going, so I can make sure I'm covered at the bakery," said Helen.

"Oh, good Lord," said Will.

ONE OF THE nice things about being with Will was never having to make small talk, because at the moment Helen was too frazzled to make any sort of talk at all. They were clipping along on the Thruway in his standard-issue copmobile, an old black Ford Crown Victoria. It didn't matter how many of these missions she'd been on, each one reduced her to emotional rubble, and she still couldn't explain what made her want to come this time. She loosened her hair from its mooring on top of her head and repinned it for the third time since Will had picked her up. Would she feel even a shard of relief if today's corpse turned out to be Henry?

The few times she'd dragged herself to the Parents of Missing Children support group in Albany, she'd felt out of step with the other parents. They all craved an ending to the nightmare, even if it meant identifying the body of their missing son or daughter. They prayed for a funeral. A burial. A circumscribed period of mourning to mark the end of not knowing.

Helen longed for an ending, too, just not that one.

SHE POSITIONED HERSELF on a bench between bird droppings in a sketchy little park across from the police station, trying to remember to breathe while waiting for Will to return. She couldn't understand what was taking so long. Unless . . . When at last she saw him emerge from the station, she couldn't tell if his gloomy expression meant something or if it was just his usual poker face.

When he sat down on the bench, he didn't say anything, just shook his head. Which in their silent lexicon meant: *not Henry*. While he waited for Helen to absorb the news, he popped a stick of Nicorette in his mouth. Then he said, "You ain't gonna believe this."

"Is it about Henry?" Helen could feel the skin on her arms grow cold and start to prickle.

"Not exactly, but it's not exactly *not* about Henry either. When I walked by the holding cell on my way to the morgue, there was Damian Barr, looking thin and scraggly, glaring at me, all bug-eyed. Turns out he was collared in a raid last night and is being held for trafficking in opioids and possession of illegal firearms. Felonies, both."

"Damian, Jesus." Helen couldn't believe the drummer from Henry's band, a kid he'd met in elementary school, had committed such serious crimes. True, he'd always been something of a fuckup. And a druggie. Which was why Henry had wanted to kick him out of the band. "But what does Damian dealing drugs have to do with Henry?" she asked.

"I'm getting to that," Will said, scratching his cap of brownish-gray hair. "The FBI agents who searched the shithole where Damian lives found something in his underwear drawer. They knew of his connection to Henry, so they showed it to me and I had to wait for them to copy it." He reached into his briefcase and pulled out several sheets of paper that had been stapled together. "You recognize these?"

Tears clouded Helen's vision, but she didn't need to be able to read to know what she was looking at. It was a photocopy of Henry's address book. In his unmistakable scrawl. She clutched the sheaf of papers to her chest. "So, is Damian a suspect again? This is evidence, right?"

"We don't know yet. The guy is such a loser. Turns out he's part of a ring of losers, and now he's looking at eating slop for the next ten to twenty. As soon as the Feds are done processing him, I'll get to question him, find out if there's any connection between the address book and Henry's disappearance. But we needed you to ID it first."

Helen nodded.

"I'd like you to look through it, see if anything pops out. Just try not to jump to any big conclusions. We know what it is, but we don't know what it means."

WHEN THEY WERE back in the car, Will said, "You okay, Petunia?"

Helen sighed and shrugged and picked at the stray smidges of flour stuck to her cuticles. It seemed that every time she let go a little bit more, some new piece of information came to light. Another body in the woods. Another heart-stopping search to identify the remains. And with each new discovery, the pattern was always the same. Her emotions spiked, then fell like a fever. And now this.

But this was different. Henry's address book. The first real sign of *him*.

A FEW DAYS after the trip to Saratoga Springs, Helen was seated in a booth at Village Sake, the good Japanese place, waiting for Mira. She'd been looking forward to their dinner for weeks. She couldn't remember the last time they'd spent more than a few fleeting minutes together or had a chance to really talk. Though they saw each other often, for the most part their contact was transactional, limited to Lola pickups and drop-offs. At those times Mira dashed in and out, usually rushing off to show a property.

It was a cold night and Helen had ordered half a carafe of hot sake. She'd just started on her second tiny cup when she saw Mira walk in. From a distance she looked lovely as always, draped in a cream-colored cashmere poncho over skinny black leather pants and high-heeled black leather boots. But when she sat down, Helen noticed dark shadows under her eyes. When she asked if everything was okay, Mira's response—"Fine"—betrayed the pinched expression on her face and the catch in her voice. "Sorry I'm late," she apologized. "Traffic."

Helen wanted to probe—something that in the past she would have done without thinking. Until she married Jackson, Helen had been Mira's closest confidante, especially as Lois, her widowed mother, retreated deeper into early dementia and Mira had to move her from assisted living to memory care. In those days Helen had offered Mira the same kind of unconditional loving support Rosaleen had given her. But since the marriage, Mira had pulled back and Helen hit a wall whenever she started asking questions.

She missed the old Mira. The wry, bighearted girl who didn't worry over a few extra pounds and dreamed of a career as a painter. The rescuer of wounded animals, including Charlie, whom she'd found cowering in a corner at the shelter where she volunteered. When she first knew Mira, Helen would have laughed if anyone had predicted that this spirited, creative girl would end up marrying a developer and selling real estate. Nor would she have believed that Mira would make frequent trips into Manhattan to buy designer clothes and get her magnificent red hair disciplined at Bergdorf's. Helen wondered whose idea that was—Mira's or Jackson's?—but didn't dare ask. Most of all, she would have flat out rejected the notion that one day Mira would seem more like an acquaintance than the surrogate daughter she adored.

Before Mira's marriage to Jackson, Helen would have told her about the trip to the morgue, Damian's arrest, and the discovery of Henry's address book. And if she'd wept in the telling, Mira would have held her hand and wept along with her. Together, they would have chewed over the latest trail of bread crumbs and tried to figure out what it meant. But tonight Mira appeared so drawn and, Helen was convinced, clinically depressed, she didn't bring it up. Nor did she mention that Lola had let it drop recently that her mom and Jackson had been "fighting like screechy cats."

Still, Helen couldn't stop herself from probing a little. "So, how are things at home?"

Mira shrugged, scanning the menu.

"Whatever happened to that studio Jackson was going to build you? Wouldn't it be wonderful if you could get back to painting, even as a hobby?" Helen asked.

"Back burner. Let's order," Mira said, signaling the waiter and the end of the discussion.

Helen poured herself another cup of sake. She hated feeling like a pest and decided to forgo asking any more questions. But seconds later when she looked up, tears were streaming down Mira's cheeks and the dark pockets under her eyes were stained black with mascara.

"Oh, sweetheart," Helen said.

Mira fished around in her oversized suede bag until she pulled out a fistful of tissues to swab the tears.

Helen hated to see Mira suffer; at the same time, she was relieved to see a fissure in her perfectly turned-out armor. In fact, she thought Mira's red puffy eyes and splotchy cheeks, with all the makeup washed away, left her looking more beautiful, more like herself, than she'd seen her in some time.

At last, thought Helen, we can talk. "Things not so good on the home front?" she asked, when Mira's weeping turned to intermittent choking sobs.

The question brought on another cataract of tears, just as the server arrived with their plates: an assortment of nigiri rolls for Helen; plain sashimi, no rice, for Mira, who always seemed to be starving herself.

"I'm sorry," Mira mumbled.

"Sweetheart, there's no need to apologize. Please just tell me what's going on, no judgments, I promise."

"I mean I'm sorry I *can't*, not now." Mira shook her head, a pleading look in her eyes.

Helen recognized the look. She realized that Mira wasn't apologizing for crying, but for not being able to talk about whatever prompted the flow of tears. Helen recalled a similar scene at a café in Sisters with her friend Julie, not long before she left Kip. It took place one rainy day when Helen was still making excuses and, on some primal level that preceded language, believed she'd disintegrate if she dared to admit the truth, as much to herself as to Julie.

Helen wanted to say something about the terrible bargains women sometimes make, and especially about how those bargains don't have to turn into life sentences. There was so much more she wanted to say than: "You know I'm here, Mira. Always." But that was all she said.

Mira tipped her head to one side and pushed her plate away. "I just have to figure some things out." She threw on her poncho, then reached into her bag and pulled out a hundred-dollar bill and left it on the table. "I really am sorry," she said, before bolting out of the restaurant.

HELEN WASN'T MUCH of a drinker, but on the rare occasions that she allowed herself more than one glass of wine, her heart would pound wildly, then skip beats and seem to sprint all over her chest. She lost her appetite when Mira ran out of the restaurant and didn't take more than a few bites of her own dinner. But she did manage to polish off the sake, forgetting that rice wine has a much higher alcohol content than wine made from grapes. She was lucky to make it safely home.

And now lying on top of her bed, trying to ignore her skittering heart, she realized she was lonely. This came as something of a revelation. In the eight years since her son went missing, she'd been so fixated on finding him, so swamped by grief and then, later, devoting herself to Lola and trying to forge some semblance of a life, that she'd never allowed herself to feel the hollow pangs of loneliness.

Until now.

Which was why, reeling from too much sake, she decided to call Randy.

EVEN THOUGH SHE'D forgotten to take his card out of the glove box when she junked the Outback, it was a snap to find him. All she had to do was google his name. His phone number and a link to his company email popped right up.

He would have every right to hang up on her. She was pretty sure that by now he must have found someone, maybe even remarried. A guy like him on the loose—a rich, good-looking widower who saves wild horses, for Christ's sake—would be catnip to the unattached. Nearly three years had passed since Helen had blown through Laramie on a gust of lies and disinformation, and she could hardly expect him to still be carrying a torch for her.

But lately he'd been showing up in her dreams. And she really needed someone to talk to. She glanced at her bedside clock as she punched in his number. It was midnight in the East, which meant ten Mountain Time. Mercifully, the call went straight to voicemail. Listening to his warm greeting gave her chills, even though the night she'd spent with him now seemed more like a hallucination than something that had actually happened. But hearing his voice, her body remembered. Oh, did her body remember. She took a breath, aware that if she didn't start talking, she'd never work up the courage to call him again.

"Hi, Randy," she blurted between hiccups. "It's me, Colette. Only my name isn't really Colette. It's Helen. Well, there's a story there, too . . . Anyway, I'm calling to tell you I'm not really a Hollywood location scout. And I'm sorry I didn't tell you my real name. Or what I do. Or where I live. I'm sorry I lied to you about, well, everything. And that I left in such a hurry. I was afraid if I didn't go then, I'd never go, only I couldn't stay. Not that you really *asked* me to stay or anything," she sputtered, hiccuping a few more times. "Sorry about that. Have you ever drunk sake and forgotten how much alcohol is in it? I think it's a lot. Anyhow, to be honest, the only thing I'm not sorry about, Randy, is spending that night with you. I realize it's taken me a little while to get in touch, well, more than a little while, and I'm sorry about that, too. But if you ever feel like talking. I mean, if you don't one hundred percent hate my guts, if you think you could give me a chance to explain a few things, well, here I am. In upstate New York. I remember you saying you have a daughter who lives in Brooklyn, so if you're ever, you know, and you're not, um, married or *with* someone, maybe we could . . . I don't know, talk? Anyhow, I'm sorry for calling so late and leaving such a long message. I just wanted you to know that, well, I think about you, Randy, I do, and I'm sorry, and, well, that's really all I called to say."

Jesus, she thought, hanging up. That was pitiful. If he didn't hate me before, he hates me now. Then she realized she'd forgotten to leave her number. Or tell him her last name. Or even the name of the town where she lived. She thought about calling back to tell him those things, but she couldn't. At the moment she couldn't do anything except shut her eyes and lie as still as possible, hoping the room would stop spinning, too wasted to remember that these days everyone had caller ID.

SEVENTEEN

JONAH SAT SCOWLING BETWEEN MATT AND LUCIE IN DR. MIR-
iam Zager's office. He was tugging his ear and refusing to say a
word, not even hello. He'd started clamming up in the cab on the
way across town after Lucie explained that they'd be visiting a
nice lady who plays with kids who sometimes get scared. She'd
been careful to avoid the bad word: *doctor*—but he was onto her.
It was his first time out of the apartment since Times Square.

"Well, I'm very happy to meet you, Jonah," said the tiny
woman with the big reputation. She sat in a low chair opposite
Jonah, close but not too close. "We don't know each other yet,
but I look forward to spending time with you." With her short
blonde hair, warm green eyes, broad toothy smile, and a manner
that was high energy without being pushy, Dr. Zager appeared
much younger than her seventy-four (according to a *Psychology
Today* profile) years.

"You want to know something?" she said. "Lots of kids feel
shy when they first come here, but I'll let you in on a little secret.
Pretty soon they can't wait to come back because we have so
much fun together. We play with puppets. We draw and paint.
And sometimes we make up stories and act them out. See that
big box over there filled with sand? The one with the little peo-

ple and animals and cars and all sorts of cool things, just waiting for you to play with them?"

Jonah snuck a quick peek at the sand tray, then went back to staring at his feet.

"Well, I have a feeling they'd like to play with *you*. And someday," Dr. Zager added in her Long Island lilt, "when we know each other a little better, we can even talk about what happened the other night when you were on your way to *The Lion King*. Because I promise you, you don't have to feel that scared ever again."

Lucie had to muzzle her excitement when a few minutes later Jonah cautiously approached the sand tray, then knelt on a red cushion and began moving some pieces around. Dr. Zager held back for several minutes before taking a seat on a low navy ottoman next to him.

"Wow, that's quite an interesting story you've got going," she said. "I see a big blue monster with a gun on one side and some little people on the other side, and one of those little people is lying down on the ground. It looks to me like the monster might have hurt that person, is that what happened?"

Without looking up, Jonah gave a slight nod of his head.

"We have to stop now, but I'm so glad you like my sand tray, Jonah. It will be waiting for you next time you come, maybe even tomorrow, would you like that? Because I would."

Again, an almost imperceptible nod of the head.

THE NEXT DAY Jonah headed straight for the sand tray and re-created the same scene, only this time there was a dog next to the person who lay on the ground.

"I really like your sand tray," said Dr. Zager. "But I wonder what would happen if the people who are standing got together with the person who's down on the ground and held a meeting. Maybe they could come up with a plan to get rid of that monster so he can't hurt anyone ever again. Just something for you to think about."

The psychologist winked at Lucie as she and Jonah headed out the door after scheduling three more appointments.

WHEN LUCIE REPORTED Jonah's progress during Friday's session to Matt, he was pleased. He was also pleased that Jonah had buckled down and caught up with his homework in preparation for returning to school on Monday, even though he still refused to touch his violin or the new Legos.

"I think we can start to relax," Matt said. They were sacked out in bed earlier than usual, both exhausted. "This has been a bad week, but the signs are all good. And," he said, scooting closer, "I know how much you'd like to take a place in Aurora Falls and skip Maine this summer, but Jonah is expecting to be with his cousins, and honestly, I don't think the situation warrants changing our plans. In fact, I think it would give him the wrong message. Look at what he's accomplished in just two sessions with Dr. Z."

That was Friday night.

SATURDAY SEEMED LIKE old times. It didn't take too much convincing to get Jonah to go with Matt to pick up bagels at H&H. On their way home they stopped at Pet Patrol to look at puppies. There were a couple of goldendoodles, a litter of Jack Russell terriers busily nursing, and three sad-looking cockapoos. Since his latest sand tray had included a dog, Dr. Zager suggested feeling him out to see if he might like to have a dog of his own.

Jonah observed the animals with interest, but when Matt asked him if he wanted to get a puppy, he shook his head and said, "I just like Jolly."

WHEN LUCIE GLANCED at the clock Sunday morning, it was nine thirty—an unusually late hour for her to be getting up. Still, it was the first decent night's sleep she'd had all week. She listened for Matt and Jonah, but the apartment was quiet. When she finally threw on her robe and went into the kitchen, she found a note in Jonah's boxy, all-cap letters on the counter.

MOM WE ARE GOING TO SEE BOTS FROM JONAH

It was the normalcy of the note that got her. On any other Sunday she would have been grateful that her son and husband had gone down to the Seventy-Ninth Street Boat Basin and let her sleep in, but it wouldn't have been such a big deal. This morning, though, Jonah's words spread through her body like warm honey.

She took her coffee into the living room and threw open the doors to their terrace. The birds of spring were back. The usual robins and sparrows were helping themselves to brunch at the feeders suspended from the overhang, and she spotted a small bird with a red triangle on its white breast poised on the railing, waiting its turn to eat. She looked it up in *Birds of the Northeast* and thought it might be a rose-breasted grosbeak, a member of the finch family that, according to the book, sounds like a robin who took opera lessons. Listening for its song, Lucie thought there is beauty even in the midst of crisis. Better yet, maybe the crisis had passed.

The good feeling carried her through the day. It stayed with her when she went down to the boat basin with Jonah so he could show her the tall sailing ship that had docked that morning, and afterward, when they visited the lush community garden at Ninety-First Street to see how many flowers they could name. Later, the three of them went to dinner at the original Carmine's on Broadway to make up for the doomed meal at the Times Square branch. When they got home, Jonah went right to sleep, his clothes neatly laid out for school the next day, his books and homework tucked in his backpack, ready to go.

The screaming started just before midnight. At first Lucie's reaction was one of sleepy disbelief. How could Jonah be having night terrors after such a perfect, stress-free day? But disbelief was soon followed by anguish.

This time the words he cried out shredded her heart.

I want my mom. I want my mom. I want my real mom.

"LUCE, COME ON, he didn't mean anything by it," Matt said, climbing into bed after sitting up with Jonah until the episode had run its course. "It was just his reptile brain firing off random neurons left over from Times Square. But it's good you got him in to see Zager." He rested a hand on Lucie's heaving back. "And if you really think getting him out of the city for the whole summer will help him settle down, then okay, let's do it. Why don't you see what you can find in Aurora Falls? We can make a cameo in Maine when I get back from Nepal."

LUCKILY, MATT DIDN'T start until nine on Monday, so he got Jonah up and off to school while Lucie, who had lain awake until five, slept through the alarm.

j fine, just a little tired, no memory of last night, Matt texted after dropping him off. *don't worry, just take care of you xxx*

The first thing Lucie did when she woke up was to put in a call to Miriam Zager. She knew she shouldn't take Jonah's words shouted at the peak of insensible panic personally. Still. *I want my real mom* was hard to take any other way.

After leaving a voicemail for Dr. Zager, she called Mira Brin, whose name and number she got from someone named Katy at the Queen of Hearts when she phoned to ask for a referral to a local realtor. Mira called back ten minutes later.

"I'm so sorry, I don't know what's going on this year, but the rental market has gone bonkers. Basically, anything with four walls and indoor plumbing has been booked for months."

"Could you please put me on your cancellation list?" asked Lucie. "I'll take anything, sight unseen, though plumbing would be nice." Mira promised to give her a call on the "needle-in-a-haystack chance" that something opened up.

LUCIE WAS NAPPING when Dr. Zager rang back just before noon. As soon as she heard the psychologist's warm, soothing voice, she began to sob. After a minute or so she pulled herself together enough to fill her in on Jonah's latest episode of night terrors.

Dr. Zager immediately tried to assure her that Jonah's cry for his real mom was symbolic. "It's not about you. In the arche-typal world of dreams, the word *mom* is associated with a sense of safety. And Jonah is telling us loud and clear he feels unsafe. But we know that, don't we?"

"I guess," said Lucie.

"I actually think your son's cry for his 'real mom' was a good sign. As painful as it was for you to hear, it strikes me as a clear signal that he's trying to restore a basic sense of safety that got disrupted at Times Square. He's going through what we call a healing crisis. I'm sure you're aware that often in therapy when we get close to the source of a problem, symptoms heat up before they diminish. Now that Jonah's seeing me and acting out his fears, I'm not surprised that the night terrors are back or that he's making statements he hasn't made before. From my perspective it's all good, because similar images are likely to show up in his sand trays, and together we can work through them. Over time his autonomic nervous system will get the message that he's no longer in danger and retune itself. Maybe knowing that can help you hang on to the big picture, give you a bit of faith."

"I'm trying," Lucie said. "But I still don't get where this is coming from. The situation at Times Square was scary, but the night terrors started when he was four, around the same time he started making up stories about having an imaginary mom. But he never cried out for her before. And he's always been terrified of loud noises. Could his reaction on his birthday go back to the fireworks that freaked him out when he was two? Or even further?" Lucie took a breath. "Sometimes I wonder if inherited family trauma is to blame. Several of my family members died in the Holocaust and my grandmother got separated from her family, though some people, including my husband, think it's a pretty far-fetched idea that Jonah . . ."

"Well, not to worry, because I'm not one of those people," said Dr. Zager. "And who knows, ancestral trauma may turn out to be one source of Jonah's distress. But it doesn't really matter, because our work together would be the same. Right now I'm trying to guide him through the strong emotions and bodily sensations he experienced on his birthday since they're still fresh. When he's ready, I'll help him recast the story of that night from a more empowered place. And if there are other sources of trauma, including those that might be inherited, what we do now will have retroactive benefits. That's one of the most rewarding aspects of this kind of therapy."

"Wherever it came from, I just hope he doesn't have to keep reliving the trauma over and over."

"Of course, and trust me, he won't. But I do know how helpless it can make you feel to have a child who's hurting." Lucie could hear Dr. Zager inhale, followed by a long outbreath. She knew from a mutual acquaintance that the psychologist had two grown sons. "And, Lucie, just in case you're tempted to blame yourself for what's going on with Jonah, as we mothers tend to do, I want to be very clear and make sure you hear me. *It's not your fault.*"

Lucie felt the Gordian knot in her chest start to unwind, reminding her how the best therapists also seem to be mind readers.

EIGHTEEN

Randy showed up at the Queen of Hearts late one Sunday afternoon in May clutching a brown paper bag stuffed with bagels.

"I'm afraid this is like bringing coals to Newcastle," he said, taking in the artfully arranged pastries in the case and the cornucopia of breads on wire racks behind the counter. "They're from the Bagel Hole, which my daughter Georgia swears is the best in the five boroughs."

The moment she saw him, Helen felt her face flush. "I love a good bagel, and I promise you there are none to be found within a hundred miles of the city." Out of the corner of her eye, she saw Katy, her manager, pucker her lips and wink as Helen led Randy through the kitchen and up the inside stairs to her flat.

"Beware of dog," she warned, opening the door and fully expecting Charlie to perform his usual bark-and-growl routine. "I doubt if he'll remember you." But remarkably, he did seem to remember Randy, because he went right up to him and slobbered all over his hands and face.

After the royal canine welcome, Randy stood in the center of the living room holding the bag of bagels, and Helen wondered if he was having second thoughts about the visit. Was she? Now that he was more than a phantom, how long would it take for him to disappoint her? Or, more likely, her him? She was older, flabbier, and not nearly as witty and carefree as Colette. Colette had sparkled, while Helen was a lonely fifty-two-year-old woman with grief etched into her face. The night she'd spent with him in Laramie seemed like time out of time, a drug trip minus the drugs. They might have been better off preserving the memory of that one perfect night without subjecting themselves to the awkward test of real life. The missing son. The beloved late wife. Two thousand miles separating his home from hers. What did they even have in common? Other than a brief hug when he came into the bakery, they hadn't so much as shaken hands.

"Please, make yourself at home," Helen said, taking the bagels from him and trying to sound relaxed. "I'll just heat up some soup."

While she puttered in the kitchen, she could see him studying the photographs on the mantel. Henry as a baby in Helen's arms. Henry at three back in Oregon, dressed up as a pumpkin for Halloween. Henry with his kindergarten class soon after they'd arrived in Aurora Falls. Henry grinning, with Mira turned sideways to show off her pregnant belly. And so many more, crammed together. Was it sick, this massive display of photos of her lost boy?

Helen wasn't sure why she felt so gloomy after the rush of joy she'd felt when she first saw Randy. She was pretty sure it had nothing to do with him. He seemed as genuine and kind as she remembered. Handsome, too—even more so than she remembered—but just as tall, with soulful green eyes and an unapologetic smile that said, *What you see is what you get*. What she could probably get, if she wanted it. If she let herself.

THEY HAD SPOKEN a few days after she'd left her drunken rant on his voicemail. She was in bed reading when he called. She apologized again, then told him the story. Not the whole story, just the unadorned facts about her missing son.

After that, she didn't expect to hear from him again. In her experience, most men weren't interested in a grieving mother. But Randy wasn't like other men. No stranger to grief himself, he seemed refreshingly unafraid of it. Still, Helen was surprised when he called a week later to say that his Brooklyn daughter had just been invited to show two of her sculptures at a pop-up gallery in Greenpoint in mid-May. He was planning to fly East for the opening and wondered if Helen would be up for a visit later that weekend.

"I'd like to find out what this is," he said. "If it's anything. I've dated a lot of women since that night. And though I'm pretty sure none of them misrepresented themselves, at least not on any grand scale like you, no one got to me like you. *Colette*, my ass," he laughed. "I'd like to find out if you're just some crazy fantasy I've been harboring or if you're for real."

THEY SAT EATING their carrot-ginger soup and toasted bagels, making small talk. Helen was surprised to learn that this part-time cowboy was a vegetarian.

"If you saw what I saw out on the range, you'd stick to plants, too," said Randy.

They quickly blew through the easy subjects—the latest dictates from the Bureau of Land Management on caring for wild horses, Georgia's art show, the challenge of finding steady help for the Queen of Hearts, the devastating food and water shortages in Haiti since the January earthquake. When the topics started to thin out and the pauses grew longer, Randy said, "Kinda strange seeing each other after all this time, isn't it?" He set his soup spoon down and leaned in closer. "So, Helen, tell me, who are you really?"

She swirled her soup around with her spoon. Aside from Rosaleen, there was no one on this earth who knew the whole story. But if there was to be anything between her and this man, anything at all, he needed to know the truth. And more urgently, she needed to tell him, even if it sent him running. One by one, she pulled the irritating pins out of her hair and let it drape across her back like a heavy cloak. She still hadn't cut it since the day her son disappeared.

"Okay," Helen said, looking into Randy's eyes and noticing for the first time a golden halo like a ring around his pupils, making them glow.

She took a breath and felt a sharp sensation in her chest as she began by telling him about Alice and Danny. She told him about Kip and Rosaleen. She told him about how she, lost, motherless, and brotherless at a tender age, had given herself over to seductive, charismatic Kip, cashing in her dream of joining the Peace Corps and traveling the world for the dream of rescue. At first, Kip had reminded her of her brother. The way he made her laugh, his irreverence, his habit of turning the most ordinary experience into a party. Soon after they got together, Kip even took her rafting on the Rogue River, which Evan used to do every summer until he died. It wasn't until later, after she'd succumbed to his spell, that Helen realized Kip was nothing at all like her big-hearted big brother. She told Randy she'd been so out of her own mind and body then, she let herself become his punching bag.

She told him how, mercifully, the moment his fists found Danny, she woke up out of her trance and fled, changing their identities so Kip could never find them. And then, her voice breaking, in choppy sentences she told him about Danny aka Henry, about his musical gifts, his love of nature, his quirky sense of humor, his tender heart. How much he was like her big brother, for real, always trying to take care of her, even as a little boy. She described the search for him, how sooner or later every lead turned to dust. Her life, she said, had been like some kind of dizzying high-wire act, teetering between trying to find out what happened to him and letting him go.

And then she took a breath and told Randy how terrified she was to let her frozen heart thaw, how the very idea of it felt like an abandonment, a betrayal, a breach that would cut her off from her son forever.

Helen told Randy everything. She wept and laughed and wept some more until there was nothing left.

And when he was sure she was finished, he pulled her to him and she felt her body dissolve into his.

NINETEEN

Y**OU'RE NOT GOING TO BELIEVE THIS."** M**IRA** B**RIN WAS CALLING** a few days after telling Lucie there was zero chance of finding her family a summer rental in Aurora Falls.

"Really?" Lucie's heart rate shot up.

"Well," Mira said, "it's kind of a sad story, but good for you." She explained that one of the old-timers in the village had recently fallen and broken her hip. Her two children, both of whom lived in Boston, had decided to move mom to an assisted-living place near them. "The son just called and asked if I could rent the house for the summer. And between us, he also said they'd probably put it on the market come fall, so if you love it, you could consider making a preemptive bid. To be honest, I have other people ahead of you on the waiting list. But after our conversation the other day, it just seemed meant to be. If you still want it. No pressure."

"Want it? God, yes."

"I don't think you'll be disappointed. It's an adorable cottage. Three smallish bedrooms and one bath. Not updated, but charming, with lots of light and a nice big yard right on the creek. We'll do a major cleanup and you should be able to move in by the third week of June. Feel free to drive up and take a look."

———

LUCIE PRACTICALLY BURST into song when she saw the post-and-beam cottage at the end of the long gravel driveway. With its broad lawn out front framed by leafy sycamores, it looked perfect. They wouldn't be moving in until later in the month, but she'd brought Jonah along to give him a preview of where he'd be spending what, she hoped, would be one of the most memorable summers of his childhood.

"Wake up, sleepyhead," she sang. He'd fallen asleep on the drive up and his head was drooping to one side.

"Where are we?" he asked, eyes half-open slits, Jolly in his lap, along with a tattered copy of *The Adventures of Captain Underpants*.

"We're home. Well, our home for the summer. Let's go check it out." Parked next to her Volvo wagon in the driveway was a silver Mercedes SUV that she assumed belonged to the realtor.

She was unbuckling Jonah's seat belt when the front door opened and a striking young woman came striding toward them, followed by a pretty little girl with a turquoise feather boa wrapped around her shoulders, who started doing cartwheels across the lawn.

"It's great to see you again, Lucie."

Lucie stared at the woman. Was she supposed to know her?

"You probably don't remember me, but I was with Helen at the Queen of Hearts the day you went into labor. I thought I recognized your name when you called, but I wasn't sure until I saw you."

"Oh my God, you're *that* Mira," Lucie said. "And this must be the baby you were nursing that day." The girl was now doing double backflips.

"Yep, Lola. Eight going on eighteen."

If Mira hadn't told her who she was, Lucie would not have recognized her. Seven years ago, with her waterfall of red hair and dressed in overalls, she looked gorgeous in a laid-back country sort of way. Now she was much thinner and, with her sleek bob and olive wrap dress, she looked like she'd had a makeover by the editors of *Vogue*. Yet despite her glamour, she seemed wearier now than she had as a new mom whose fiancé was missing.

"And this must be the boy who was born that very same day." Mira peeked around Lucie's shoulder to where Jonah was hiding. "Hi there. I'm Mira. Who are you?"

"Jonah," Jonah said in a small voice. He snuck a quick glance at Mira, then returned to his lookout behind his mother.

"Well, it's very nice to meet you, Jonah. And that girl running around on the grass is my daughter, Lola. Why don't we all go inside and I'll give you the grand tour?"

Lucie waved at Lola, who came bounding toward her.

"Is that your kid?" she asked, pointing a finger at Jonah.

"It is." The pretty baby Lucie saw that day was now a pretty girl with reddish braids, a spray of freckles, a heart-shaped mouth, and an expression that said, *I don't take no for an answer.*

"I'm not human, I'm a mermaid, but my mom says I have to wait until I'm sixteen to meet my pod," Lola volunteered, kicking the gravel. "Except I might get my powers sooner, if my papa comes home first. This is his." She pointed to a large watch wrapped around her wrist. "My Oma got me a new band to make it fit, but I have to give it back to him when he gets here."

"Oh, sweetie," said Mira.

A HAND-CARVED SIGN by the front door of the cottage said *Brookhaven*. Inside, the furnishings were worn and the kitchen and bathroom hopelessly out of date. But the place was spotless, and in spite of its shabbiness, it felt to Lucie like a home that had been well loved. Her friend Holly would say it had *good energy*.

"We brought in new mattresses, a couple of lamps, and some dishes, and got rid of a truckload of junk. But otherwise what you see is pretty much what was here," Mira explained after showing Lucie and Jonah around. "The place is kind of funky. I hope it's okay."

"More than okay." Lucie opened the French doors that led off the kitchen to a stone patio and gazed at the creek that ran behind the cottage. The setting reminded her of one of the houses she'd lived in as a kid. The topography was different, but that house had overlooked a narrow slice of Tomales Bay. Lucie had spent countless hours down by the water with her friend Azalia, taking turns being Cinderella and Prince Charming. Lucie also spent countless hours alone by the water, imagining that at any moment a tall ship would sail up with a handsome prince on board, who would rush down the gangplank and sweep her up in his arms. Of course, that prince would be none other than her lost father, who'd been sailing the seven seas searching for her. Never mind that nothing wider than a kayak could make its way up the spindly tributary or that her father didn't know she existed. When her mother asked Lucie why she spent so many hours by the water, she told her she liked to watch the pelicans dive for fish.

"You could blow out the side, add another bedroom and master bath, along with a couple of skylights and a family room, and the house would be awesome," Mira was saying. "We'll know in a month or two if the owner is going to sell."

"Actually, I love it the way it is," Lucie said, stepping back inside and looking around for Jonah. She'd been so transported by the view of the creek that she'd forgotten about him. "Have you seen Jonah?" It wasn't like him to leave her side in an unfamiliar place.

"He's with Lola. In the bedroom with the ancient bunk beds. Bought many years ago for the owners' grandkids."

The door to the bedroom was closed. Lucie opened it and saw Jonah crouched by the window, the feather boa slung over his shoulder. First Lola rushed past Lucie and out the French doors, followed by Jonah, boa flying.

"We're going to play pirates. I'm Captain Hook. Yo ho ho and a bottle of rum," Lola shouted, in her deepest, most piratey voice.

"Ho ho ho and a bottle of . . . something," Jonah shrieked, tailing her down the hill to the edge of the creek.

Lucie was thrilled. She'd never known her son to run wild with someone he'd just met. Or, for that matter, with the boy cousins he'd known his whole life who were always trying to get him to join in their raucous games. Worried about injuring his hands, Jonah had never been much for running wild, period. Maybe his taking a break from the violin would turn out to be a good thing. This was exactly the way childhood should be, she thought. Free range.

While the kids were playing pirates, Lucie was tempted to ask Mira if there had been any news about Helen's son. She'd wondered about him from time to time, though she supposed that Lola's comment about gaining her mermaid powers "when my papa comes home" answered the question. Regardless, she looked forward to introducing Jonah to Helen, who no doubt had saved his life by insisting on driving Lucie to Albany the day he was born, though she would spare him the details.

Yet as much as she looked forward to reconnecting with Helen, she was wary about meeting up with another local—her mother. Phoebe and her Tibetan lama had recently taken up residence at a monastery near Aurora Falls.

It had been three years since Lucie and Phoebe were in the same room, and their visits were always fraught: Lucie, painfully reminded of her mother's careless neglect during her childhood, and Phoebe, yearning to connect while more or less rewriting the past and clearly hurt by Lucie's lack of responsiveness. And now they were going to be neighbors. Sort of, though Lucie had yet to return Phoebe's phone call announcing her move to the monastery, along with a plea to get together *soonest*.

Oh well, thought Lucie, just because her mother would be living nearby didn't mean she suddenly had to reinvent herself as a devoted daughter. She could see Phoebe once or twice and that would be that. It might even be nice for Jonah to get to know his maternal grandmother, whom he'd met only once. In any case, Lucie would deal with her mother later. For now, she couldn't be happier. The house was perfect. Jonah had found a friend. And she felt confident that, along with seeing Dr. Zager, a summer in the country was just the medicine he needed to soothe his tender nervous system and heal the trauma that got unleashed on his birthday.

"I see playdates in our future," Mira said, pointing to Lola and Jonah, who were now taking turns making each other walk the "plank"—a fallen log by the stream.

Lucie smiled. She couldn't believe her luck in landing this funky slice of heaven.

It was going to be a good summer.

TWENTY

HELEN AWOKE ON A BLINDINGLY BRIGHT MORNING IN JUNE knowing it was time.

Time to pick up—not where she'd left off eight years before, that was impossible—but where she was now. Time to get the cracked ceiling repaired, she thought, surveying the elaborate network of lines over her bed that resembled the road map of a small country. Time to knock the damn cobwebs out of the corners, get the whole house repainted, replace the leaky refrigerator, regrout the kitchen counters, reupholster the saggy sofa—or, better, buy a new one—and refinish the scratched and pitted wood floors.

Time to chop off the weighty mass of hair that was deforming the vertebrae in her neck and spine.

Time to let go of the last filament of hope that kept her cracked heart loosely knit together—even if that meant allowing the fissure in her heart simply to be.

Which was what Rosaleen had said that day in Eugene. How loss is the price we pay for love, and if we just let it be, we realize we're bigger than our losses. But except in fleeting moments, loss had not made Helen feel bigger. If anything, being stuck inside a husk of unrelenting grief had made her feel smaller. And she didn't want to live there anymore. Randy was part of the reason, but not the whole story. If she was ever going to have a life that included grief but wasn't defined by it, she needed a new story.

Henry's thirtieth birthday was a month away. Every year since he went missing, Helen had marked the day by baking his favorite dessert, an ambrosia layer cake made with oranges and coconut, topped with homemade marshmallows and fresh strawberries. She'd adapted the recipe from Nessa, her mentor, and had been making it since Henry turned seven.

This year she would not bake the cake.

In the first few years after he vanished, Mira and Lola had joined in the annual ritual. For Lola's benefit, Helen and Mira had tried to lend notes of gaiety in the form of silly hats and balloons to the otherwise heart-shattering occasion. Understandably, Mira had declined to participate after marrying Jackson. Then starting last year she kept Lola away, too, claiming that the *"uncelebrations"* were too distressing for the girl. Yet that wasn't the only reason. Helen knew from Lola that Jackson had been campaigning to get her to call him Daddy. But Lola refused. "My papa is my papa," she insisted. "And he's coming back for me."

Helen knew she was largely responsible for Lola believing that someday her father would return. But she could no longer bewitch her mind—or her granddaughter's—into denying what she knew in her bones.

It was time.

As IF TO underscore the point, later that morning Will showed up at the bakery clutching a manila envelope.

"We need to talk, Petunia," he said.

They went outside and sat on a bench in front of the window boxes where Helen had recently planted actual petunias. "What's up?" she asked, her stomach rising to meet her throat. She knew Will wouldn't interrupt her during the morning rush with his bushy brows in a twist if there wasn't something he needed to tell her.

Without meeting her eyes, he said, "Nothing. Nothing's up. That's the problem. We've cleared Damian of any wrongdoing in connection with Henry's disappearance. Oh, he stole his address book all right, snatched it out of his backpack before the last show in Saratoga. 'My insurance policy,' he told me. Apparently, his big plan was to blackmail Henry with all the clubs and promoters when he got kicked out of the band, which he knew was coming. But then Henry was gone, the band fell apart, and the loser decided to embark on a more promising career as a drug dealer. To tell you the truth, the guy is in shit shape and didn't make a whole lot of sense. Looks like he's headed for an all-expenses-paid trip to Dannemora," Will said, offering Helen the manila envelope. "After all this time, I wish I had something more to give you than this."

She knew without opening it that tucked inside was her son's address book. "I know," she said, pressing the envelope to her chest. And then she lay a hand on top of Will's, which though large with knuckles the size of cherry tomatoes, was surprisingly soft to the touch. "Honestly, I never expected much to come from this Damian business. You've done everything you could, Will, everything, and for that I'll love you forever." Then, still resting her hand on his, she leaned close to his ear and whispered the words she couldn't have imagined saying even a month ago, the day they'd gone to the morgue in Saratoga Springs. "It's time, Will. To stop. Henry is just . . . *gone*."

Later that morning, she made an appointment to get her hair lopped off the day after his thirtieth birthday.

———————

HELEN SPENT THE evening stewing over how to pay tribute to him while also honoring her decision to . . . what? *Move on* wasn't right. Moving on wasn't possible, because as long as she was alive, he was alive inside her. *Closure* was as despicable a word as it was dishonest, and *letting go* wasn't right either. But maybe that was it—*not* letting go of Henry or her love for him but letting go of her urgent need to learn what had happened to him.

When she awoke the next morning, she knew what she had to do.

IT WAS A little risky, ascending the steep falls alone. Well, not exactly alone; she had Charlie with her, though she wasn't sure if he would be an asset or a liability along the narrow trail, especially if they ran into any men. Even worse, she was woefully out of shape, in spite of keeping off the weight she'd lost after Henry disappeared. She couldn't remember the last time she'd gone for a serious hike. And the climb up to the falls that gave the town its name was notorious for the number of reckless day-trippers who, determined to reach the top of the thunderous waters with an elevation higher than Niagara, had ignored the big yellow warning signs and plunged to their deaths. Henry was one of the lucky ones who had reached the highest point and lived to tell the story. Helen was thankful he never told her about his perilous expeditions until after the fact.

"It's amazing, the water is so loud the mind goes blank and you're just there, part of it, which must be what heaven is like," he told Helen and Mira with a look of rapture on his face after his last ascent. At which point Mira made him promise not to hike to the top of the falls ever again, at least not until the baby she was carrying graduated from college.

As if that would keep him safe.

And now, just after sunrise, Helen parked in the small lot at the foot of the trail. Hers was the only car there. Feeling slightly panicky, she opened the door for Charlie. "Oh well," she said to the dog, as she adjusted the straps on Henry's backpack over his old jeans jacket, then put on her wide-brimmed straw hat. "What's the worst that can happen? We could die, so what? We've already been through worse, right, boy?" Charlie hung back, looking at her quizzically, then began trotting alongside her.

The first part of the trail, though steep with switchbacks, was fairly wide and hiker friendly. Helen admired the watery gorge flanked by sandstone cliffs dyed a rainbow of oranges and pinks by the rising sun. This isn't so bad, she thought, until the path narrowed. Now, instead of enjoying the view of the cliffs from a safe distance, they were skirting the edge of a precipice, with only a rickety wooden railing between them and the crater below.

Was she a fool for attempting this climb by herself? Suicidal? Randy had wanted to fly in and go with her, especially after reading online about all the people who had lost their footing and died along the way. Helen was grateful for the offer but declined. Same with Abby, who had volunteered to be her guide. Abby was a seasoned hiker familiar with the trail. She was also a big talker, and Helen needed to go it alone. In silence, with only Charlie and the crashing din of the falls for company.

It took them forty-five minutes to get to the pool at the base of the first drop. Out of breath, Helen looked up at the even snakier trail that led to the upper falls. She smiled as she imagined her sure-footed son, with his long legs and nimble gait, dancing up the treacherous footpath like a billy goat.

"We're no billy goats, are we, Charlie?" Cowering at her feet with his ears pressed to his head, it was pretty clear that the dog agreed. Henry had never taken him on this trail, and now Helen understood why. And though it may have been rash for her to set out on this mission alone, she wasn't a complete idiot. Nor, in spite of everything, did she harbor a death wish. "I think this is the end of the line for us, kiddo," she said, patting Charlie's head.

The sun was up but it wasn't yet hot when she began searching for a spot to bury the map. Other people honored their loved ones by burying their bodies or spreading their ashes under a favorite tree or tossing them into the sea. But Helen had no body. No ashes. No remains. Just love that pulsed with every heartbeat, along with the gap in her heart that had become as much a part of her as the organ itself. Still, she needed something to bury and had spent half the night trying to come up with a worthy object. She considered his first violin and his baseball mitt—but those things would be too cumbersome to stick in the ground. Nothing seemed quite right, until she hit upon the old map. The map they'd brought with them from Oregon that had decided their fate.

After giving Charlie some water in a paper cup and taking a swig from Henry's Boy Scout canteen, Helen found a semi-level patch of dirt between the hemlock and spruce trees that bordered the path. She pulled a trowel from her backpack and set about digging a shallow hole. Then she opened the map and, with her finger, traced the route they'd taken from Sisters in Oregon through Laramie and on to Aurora Falls. She was probably off by a state or two because she couldn't see very well through her tears, though when she got to the Mississippi she stopped and wondered what would have happened if instead of folding the map so that only the states east of the great river were visible, she'd folded it along the Mason-Dixon Line. Would they be living in Louisville now? North Carolina? Richmond, Virginia? Would her son be playing fiddle with a bluegrass band someplace down south and coming over to Helen's with his wife and kids every Sunday for roast chicken and dumplings? The thought brought on another rush of tears and Charlie, whose head was burrowed in her lap, let out a few mournful yips of his own.

Hocus pocus abracadabra. Like an incantation, Helen said the words Danny had chanted as he'd waved his little finger around in circles before setting it down on Aurora Falls. She repeated the chant three times, then refolded the map and kissed it before placing it in the ground. A few shovelfuls of dirt later, the burial plot disappeared.

She gathered some stones and erected a cairn to mark the spot, then after one last *hocus pocus abracadabra*, started down the mountain with Charlie at her heels.

At first I thought it was just me. Stuck in this nowhere place. Like a waiting room, only it's not a room. There are no walls or floors or ceiling. And I'm not alone, there are a whole lot of us here. Babies, old people, teenagers, just hanging around.

To tell you the truth, I'm getting pretty restless. Like, is this really it? Do I have to stay here forever? And I'm not the only one who feels this way. There are all kinds of opinions about why we can't leave.

Some kid from Bolivia says he's stuck here until his parents wash his clothes in the river, then burn them. Only every night his mother sleeps with the clothes he was wearing when he got stabbed and she refuses to wash them or set them on fire the way she's supposed to.

And some wiseass from California just keeps saying over and over like a broken record, "It's the bardo, stupid, get used to it."

Well, what the hell is that supposed to mean?

It isn't until this sweet old Japanese lady says what she thinks is going on that I start to get why I'm still here. In Japan, she says, people believe that the souls of children who die before their parents can't cross the river to the afterlife as long as their parents are suffering.

Oh.

Now, I don't know if this place is the bardo or if I have a soul or what river the Japanese lady is talking about, but this is the first thing I've heard since I got here that makes any sense.

PART FOUR

SUMMER 2010

TWENTY-ONE

THE SUMMER WAS TURNING OUT TO BE EVEN BETTER THAN LUCIE had imagined—and they'd been in Aurora Falls only a few days. Though she was embarrassed by her extreme reaction to Jonah's cries for his "real mom," without her *agita* Matt might not have agreed to take a house up here. So maybe just this once her souped-up wiring was good for something, because she'd never seen Jonah happier, thanks in large part to Lola the Brave.

Looking out the window of the tiny alcove off the kitchen that she was using as a study, Lucie marveled as she watched Jonah and Lola playing down by the creek and wondered: Why do some people have instant chemistry, while others grate on each other's nerves from the minute they meet? Pheromones? Some other mysterious mash-up of chemistry and attraction?

Maybe this was a story for the magazine, she thought, as outside Lola flapped her mermaid tail on the grass while Jonah awkwardly tried to follow suit with his merman fin—ordered online the day he met Lola. But what's the angle? The science of friendship? Lucie would poke around to see if there were any interesting new studies. God forbid you should pitch an article to a women's magazine that didn't offer some sexy new scientific tidbit to transform the lucky reader's life forever after.

"Now take off your flipper and be a pirate," Lola ordered. "Pirates are scared of mermaids."

"Why do I have to be the pirate?" complained Jonah. "You be the pirate."

"I'm a mermaid in real life, so I can't be the pirate!" Lola countered, hips jutting forward.

"Well, I'm a merman and neither can I!" Jonah flapped his fin extra hard.

"You're a pirate just pretending to be a merman so I won't steal your booty."

"What's booty?"

"You know, like gold and jewelry and stuff."

"No way am I giving you my booty!" Jonah grabbed a few twigs and stones and clutched them to his chest.

"OMG, okay," Lola muttered. "You can stay a merman and we'll both steal the booty."

Good for you, Jonah, standing up to that bossy girl, Lucie silently cheered. She could get used to this. Living in the country. Working from here. All this running around and fresh air were exactly what Jonah needed. What she needed, too. Being in Aurora Falls was taking Lucie right back to her childhood, the good parts. And though she knew it was a losing proposition, she wished Matt could see himself as a country doctor, because with each passing hour she felt the rocks in her neck and shoulders melt a little more.

The percussive sound of kitchen cabinets flying open, then being slammed shut, interrupted her bucolic fantasy. When she glanced over from her makeshift desk, Jonah was standing on the counter peering into one of the cabinets, and Lola had her head in the refrigerator.

"Careful, Jonah. *Basta!* Get down from there this minute," Lucie called.

"I'm hungry," whined Jonah, even though he and Lola had polished off cream-cheese-and-jelly sandwiches and half a watermelon a short time ago.

"I'm hungry and bored," Lola said, slamming the refrigerator door. "And hot."

"Yeah, I'm bored and hungry and hot," echoed Jonah. He was crouched on the counter, glaring defiantly at Lucie.

She tried to hide her amusement. Seeing him with Lola was like watching a tadpole turn into a bullfrog: behavior that was so different from the quiet intensity with which he played Legos with Jeremy or video games with Mickey. Or practiced his violin. Well, past tense on that, since he kept insisting he'd never play again. Matt and Lucie didn't believe him but were careful not to make a big deal out of it, as Dr. Zager had suggested.

"I want to see Oma. We can walk from here. I know the way. C'mon," Lola said, tugging on Jonah's shirt. "She'll give us good stuff. You know, cupcakes and cookies and *whatev.*"

Jonah hopped down from the counter and was trailing Lola to the front door when Lucie stopped them.

"Hold on, you two, you can go to the bakery, but I'm coming with you."

"You don't have to. I know the way." Lola flashed Lucie a big fake smile, a look of cunning in her eyes.

"I'm sure you do, but as long as you're our guest, I'm in charge. Anyhow, I'd like to see your grandma, too." Lucie wasn't used to having her authority challenged and supposed it had to do with the difference between boys and girls—at least her usually sweet, agreeable boy and this headstrong girl. She was also aware that the headstrong girl had her reasons for trying to exert control, including having a father she pined for vanish right before she was born. Lucie could identify.

"Sunscreen, people," she said. Jonah was used to being slathered and submitted without a fight. At first Lola pouted when Lucie turned to her with the tube of creamy white goop, but seconds later she held out her arms and legs. Then Lucie handed each child a hat: Mets for Jonah, her old Cal Bears cap for Lola. Putting on her own big straw hat, she said, "Hats, check. Sunscreen, check." She opened the front door and was slammed by a wall of scorched air.

It was only a ten-minute walk from the cottage to the Queen of Hearts, but by the time they made it to the village green, they were drenched in sweat. Waves of heat rippled up from the sidewalk and the sky had turned a blistering, cloudless white. Lucie's feet were so damp, her leather sandals had turned into slip 'n slides and she nearly tripped. She couldn't wait to be inside the air-conditioned bakery, but Jonah stood stiffly on the sidewalk staring at the building and refused to budge, even after Lola went racing right in.

"Come on, Bear, let's go inside and get some nice cold lemonade," Lucie said, her hand gently prodding the back of his sticky *I went to spring training!* blue tee with the orange Mets logo. "It's too hot to stay out here."

Jonah gave a little shrug.

"Well, I'm going in, are you coming or not?" She held the door open for him. "One, two . . ." On three he reluctantly shuffled inside, but stuck close to the back windows.

"What's up, Jonah?" Lucie couldn't imagine what was causing her son, who minutes ago had been a pushy merman, to grow suddenly quiet and withdrawn.

Again he didn't answer, but after looking around the bakery, he seemed to be watching Lola, who was parked behind the glassed-in pastry counter as if she owned the place. Lucie wondered if Jonah felt more comfortable having her in his space than being with her at the Queen of Hearts, where clearly she was the reigning princess.

"Where's Oma?" Lola asked the Goth-looking teenager behind the counter. The girl was ringing up a loaf of bread for an elderly woman who was painstakingly counting out pennies.

"Why isn't Oma here?" Lola whined.

"She had an appointment, honey. She'll be back soon. What can I get you and your friends in the meantime?"

"We'll take three lemonades and three of your fabulous chocolate chip cookies," Lucie told the Goth girl when it was her turn at the counter. But when she took out her wallet, the young woman, who introduced herself as Izzy, refused to let her pay. "Helen would chop my head off," she said, gagging, then pretending to slit her throat. Her tongue had a silver stud punched through its moist, pink center.

Lucie dropped her hat and backpack on one of the empty tables, then collected the cookies and drinks. Jonah shambled over a few minutes later, while Lola hung back behind the counter, frowning.

"Mama, when was I here?" Jonah asked.

"You were never here, Bear, this is your first time. Well, technically you were here, the day you were born. But you were still in my tummy then, so you couldn't see anything."

"I was so here. I can tell by the smell. Don't you remember?"

"Maybe we went to a different bakery that smelled like this one, and that's what you remember. Sometimes our memories play tricks on us and we get places mixed up." Lucie knew of many excellent studies proving that fetuses form memories in utero, but she'd never seen any research that showed them having visual or olfactory memories of the world outside the womb before birth. That would be physically impossible.

Jonah yanked his ear until it turned bright red, then said, "Where's the dog? I need to see the dog."

"Dog? There's no dog here, sweetie. Dogs aren't allowed in places where they serve food. It's against the law, unless it's a guide dog for a blind person."

"It's not that kind of dog." He shoved his untouched cookie across the table.

Just then an attractive fiftyish woman sporting a spiky silver pixie cut came into the bakery. It was midafternoon and only a few tables were occupied, but the conversation in the room stopped and all heads turned toward the newcomer. It took Lucie several seconds before she recognized her. Jonah just stared.

"Oma!" Lola shrieked, breaking the silence and running out from behind the counter into her grandmother's arms. "Where is he? Where's Papa? I knew he would come for me. Oma, I knew it!"

TWENTY-TWO

ONE OF LIFE'S GREAT IRONIES IS THAT THE THINGS YOU DO TO save yourself almost always hurt someone else. And when that someone is your grandchild, the person you love most in the world, how can you ever forgive yourself? If only Helen had told Lola about her haircut ahead of time. If only she hadn't been so caught up in what she needed to do for herself.

If only . . .

Still in bed at the scandalously late hour of seven a.m. the day after the haircut, she didn't think she'd slept all night. Thank God she'd trained Katy and Geo to manage the four thirty bake without her, though the point had been to lighten her load, not make it possible to lounge around in bed tormenting herself.

"Oh, Charlie," Helen mumbled to her bedfellow, who glanced at her sideways with his sleepy brown eyes. "Whatever was I thinking?"

She hadn't been thinking, that was the problem. All these years she'd made such a big deal about not cutting her hair until Henry came home. How did she expect Lola to react? Helen was glad the dog couldn't talk.

She'd been in a daze when she left the salon, her head feeling as weightless as air. Stopping to study her reflection in the window of the variety store, she wouldn't have recognized herself if she hadn't known who it was staring back. For a second, she panicked and thought: *What have I done? What if my son doesn't recognize me?*

As soon as she walked into the bakery and saw Lola, she realized exactly what she'd done. Helen scooped her granddaughter into her arms and somehow managed to cart her up the stairs to the house without falling and breaking either of their necks. She apologized over and over, then had to explain that the haircut didn't mean her papa was coming back.

"But you said, Oma, you promised. No haircut until Papa comes home. You promised," Lola choked between sobs. "You lied to me. I hate you!" She ran into her old room and slammed the door so hard a tremor like an earthquake rattled the house.

Helen's worst crime, worse than lying to herself all these years that her son might yet return, was letting her granddaughter believe it, too. She stood in the hallway outside the closed door, tallying up all the half-truths and outright lies she'd told Lola about her father. It didn't matter that they were spun from love. Or rather, equal parts love and delusion—a deadly combination. Mira had understood years ago what until very recently Helen couldn't acknowledge. Henry was never coming back. But because of her willful blindness, grandmother and granddaughter had been stranded in the unmarked territory between hope and grief. So much better for the child simply to have been allowed to grieve.

Helen opened the door a crack. Lola was curled up in the beanbag chair in the far corner of the room, a shuddering pretzel, her skinny arms and legs twisted around herself. Helen dropped to the floor and sat silently beside her until, with her hair masking her face, Lola inched closer, then crawled into her grandmother's lap. Helen rocked her and sang "All the Pretty Little Horses," as she'd done when Lola was a baby. They stayed that way until Mira came to pick her daughter up and take her home.

THE NEXT MORNING Helen was brewing her first cup of coffee when Mira called to ask if Lola could come over and spend the day with her. "She's supposed to have a playdate with that little boy, Jonah, but she insists on being with you. That okay? Are you in the shop all day or do you have time?"

In the background Helen could hear: "What did she say? What did she say? Can I, Mommy, can I?"

Helen had hoped to have more time to think about what to tell Lola next, but the words "absolutely" and "of course" came tumbling out.

"OMA, DO YOU think it's okay if I don't cut *my* hair?"

"Of course, love. You can keep your hair as long or as short as you like."

"But I was letting mine grow, too. Until Papa comes home. If I don't cut it, maybe he'll still come. Mommy says no, but I think she's lying."

They were seated at the dining table with an assortment of croissants and morning buns from downstairs. Helen was nursing her second cup of coffee, while Charlie, strategically positioned under the table, vacuumed up the flaky crumbs.

Still fuzzy from lack of sleep, Helen took her time answering. She knew that what she said next would have serious consequences, and she'd already caused enough harm. But how to poke a hole in Lola's magical thinking without breaking her spirit?

She took another sip of coffee and said, "Sweetheart, you can love your papa forever, as I will, because he'll be your papa forever. You can look at his picture and tell him what you're up to and how much you love him. You can even write him letters. But cutting your hair or not cutting your hair won't bring him back. He's not coming back. Not because he doesn't love you, but because he can't. If he could, he would."

"Now you sound like my mom. I don't believe you either. You always said he *might*. My whole entire life."

"I know, love. That's what I hoped for, too. But now I know that's not going to happen."

"How do you know?"

"I just do. If Papa was able to come back, he would have by now."

"So then why should I talk to him or write him a letter if he's not going to answer? OMG, that's just stupid, like writing Santa Claus." Lola took a bite of a cinnamon twist, then threw the rest on the floor for Charlie, a move that under normal circumstances would not be tolerated.

"You don't have to write him or talk to him. You don't have to do anything unless you want to."

"Do you think he didn't come back because we stopped making him birthday cakes? Maybe if we bake him a cake . . ."

"No, love. Nothing we do can make him come back. I wish we could, but we can't." Helen took a breath, trying to think of something more upbeat to say. "In a funny way, Papa is always with us, because he left me you. He'll be part of you—and me— forever." Helen leaned over to stroke Lola's cheek, but the girl jerked her head away.

"So why don't you just say it then. Why don't you just tell me he's dead?"

Lola was right. The time had come to say the D-words. *Died.*

Dead. Death. Deceased. Departed. Done. The words she'd been so careful to avoid while saying that other D-word: *disappeared,* along with *missing, vanished, cold case*—words that had left her son's fate uncertain and therefore open to speculation and its stepchild, hope. It was time to say the D-word out loud, for the child's sake as well as her own.

"Yes, darling." Helen felt her body go cold, as if plunged into icy waters. "You're right, Papa is dead. He probably died a long time ago. We just don't know how or where and we won't ever know. I'm so sorry, baby."

Helen stayed seated as Lola crawled under the table and curled up with Charlie, who put his front paw over her, an unofficial therapy dog.

When she poked her head out some minutes later, the half-moon-shaped crescents beneath her eyes were puffed out like little pillows and her eyelashes were dewy with tears.

Helen reached for her, but Lola pulled away. "Can I go downstairs and get a cupcake?"

"Sure." Helen watched Lola scamper down the inside stairs to the bakery kitchen, as if she couldn't get away fast enough. Was she desperate to hang on to some remnant of magical thinking or simply digesting the new reality? Out of habit Helen went to grab a thicket of hair to twist around her finger, but that too was gone.

She glanced down at the old cherry table and skimmed her fingertips over the surface, feeling the hieroglyphics carved by her son's hand as he pressed down with his Number Two pencils while doing his homework. Helen used to get on his case, scolding him for ruining the soft wood. But now she was glad he had. The table had become a treasure, more wondrous to her than the prehistoric drawings on the cave walls at Lascaux. She'd been awed by their magnificence during a trip to France the summer after graduating high school, a gift from her father a year after her mother died. Helen had fallen hard for France and imagined herself someday living there between Peace Corps stints in Africa or Asia. But then she met Kip and fell even harder for him.

She shut her eyes and pressed her cheek to Henry's scratchings. She was at a loss. What else could she say or do to help Lola, now that the golden carrot of hope had been snatched from her?

The sound of Charlie gagging, then puking up the remains of the cinnamon twist, brought her right back. "Oh, Charlie, you're like someone's demented old uncle," she said, her hand cupping the panting dog's head. "How many pastries must you eat before you remember they make you sick every time?"

She was on her knees cleaning up the puddle of canine vomit when Lola came running up the stairs. "Oma," she yelled. "I'm bored! Can Jonah come over?"

"If you want," said Helen. "I'll call his mom and see if he's free. And please put Charlie outside. The last thing we need is for him to try to bite that little boy's head off."

TWENTY-THREE

PLEASE, CAN I GO SEE THE DOG?" ASKED JONAH.

The boy was staring at Helen. Surprisingly, his eyes hadn't changed color the way most babies' do over time. His were the same startling marine blue as the day he was born. The day she had held him, rocked him, then handed him back to the nurse and ran out of that hospital like her hair was on fire. She'd forgotten how spooked she'd been by his eyes.

And now those eyes were staring at her. "Pretty please, can I go see him?" he asked again, looking out the window.

"Unfortunately, that mutt isn't very friendly," said Helen. Charlie was going nuts outside, barking like crazy.

"He hates boys. He'll bite your head off and eat you up," said Lola.

"Lola, you may not be rude to your guest or you'll need a time-out," Helen warned. Then she turned to Jonah and smiled. "I'm sorry, but your friend is right. I wouldn't want that silly dog to hurt you."

"He won't hurt me, pinky promise," said Jonah.

"Enough, Bear. Didn't you hear what Helen said? Anyhow, you're not all that crazy about dogs, so what's the big deal?" Lucie shot Helen one of those children-are-mystifying looks.

"I like Charlie," Jonah said, his pleading eyes still fixed on Helen.

"How do you know his name?" Lucie wondered, but Jonah didn't answer.

"We're pretty sure Charlie was abused by his male owner when he was a puppy," Helen explained. "He bonded with my son after he got him as a rescue, but he's never stopped being scared of most men and, unfortunately, boys."

"Please please please," Jonah begged. "He's not scared of me, I promise."

"Jonah, stop. *Now.*" Lucie turned to Helen and shrugged. "He went on about the dog yesterday, too. I've never seen him so worked up about an animal."

Helen looked from Lucie to the boy to the dog leaping around the yard. "Okay, here's what we'll do," she told Jonah. "I'll go outside with you, and you stay behind me on the porch. And if Charlie so much as growls once, even a tiny growl, you go right back inside, okay?"

"Double pinky promise," Jonah said, locking both pinkies with Helen's.

Lucie looked worried, so Helen said, "I won't let Charlie near him if I sense trouble. C'mon, Jonah. Follow me. Lola, you stay inside until we see how this goes."

Fists jammed against hips, Lola snorted but did as she was told.

It was a good thing the dog didn't attack the boy, because as soon as they were outside Jonah did not keep his promise. He sprinted right past Helen, down the stairs into the yard, and she couldn't say who pounced first, the slight boy or the fifty-seven-pound dog. All she knew was that within seconds they were all over each other, rolling around on the grass, Charlie licking Jonah's face and wagging his tail so hard it looked as if it might break off. Charlie hadn't been this excited since Henry disappeared. *Who is this kid?* Helen wondered.

"Hi boy, hi Charlie," Jonah said, scratching under the dog's chin in the sweet spot where Henry used to scratch—the spot that made Charlie go limp.

A moment later Lucie was out on the porch, shouting. "Jonah, be careful! That dog looks out of control!"

Clearly this woman knows nothing about dogs, thought Helen. She couldn't recall ever having witnessed such a love-fest between human and beast, certainly not since Mira brought Charlie home from the animal shelter as a birthday present for Henry. The man-hating mutt with the sorrowful eyes had been found tied to a tree a few weeks earlier and was slated for doggie death row if no one adopted him within the month. Thankfully, the dog's aversion to men had skipped Henry. Then Randy. And now, this boy.

"You have nothing to fear," Helen called to Lucie. "Charlie will never hurt your son."

Lola ran down into the yard and watched from the sidelines, frowning. "I bet Charlie thinks Jonah is a girl," she said, tossing her braids dismissively.

Jonah is definitely not a girl, thought Helen, feeling the skin on her arms tingle and wondering once more: *Who is this kid?*

TEN MINUTES LATER they were wilting in the midday sun—good for her dahlias and Russian sage, but hard on humans—and Helen ushered everyone inside. They were seated around the table drinking lemonade and eating lunch: Lucie and Helen, gazpacho and a still-warm baguette from downstairs; Lola and Jonah, hot dogs and cherries. Charlie was resting his head on Jonah's thigh, and out of the corner of her eye, Helen could see the boy sneaking him bits of hot dog, but for the second time that day decided to keep her mouth shut about feeding Charlie from the table.

"It's funny," Lucie said. "For years my husband has offered to get Jonah a puppy, but he never seemed all that interested. Honestly, I didn't think he even liked dogs, except for Jolly, his stuffie. Guess I had that wrong. Goes to show, right, Bear?"

But Jonah didn't answer. He was standing in front of the fireplace on tiptoes, and with Charlie stuck to his leg like Velcro, studying the photographs lined up across the mantel. The same photos, except for one or two, that Helen was planning to take down and store—another heartrending but necessary decision, like burying the map, chopping off her hair, or adding the D-word to her vocabulary.

"I really like this one," Jonah said, pointing to a shot of Henry giving Charlie a bath in the backyard. It was one of Helen's favorites, taken in the late afternoon a few weeks before he vanished. She'd captured the pair from the back steps midbath. The dog had his front paws perched on Henry's shoulders, both of them drenched and dripping with suds, Henry laughing.

"That was a fun time, wasn't it, Charlie?" Jonah stroked behind the dog's left ear and scratched under his chin, then turned to Helen. "It was before I got killed in the head and had to go up in the sky," he said quietly.

"Jonah," snapped Lucie. "Don't make up stories."

"Excuse me?" said Helen, finding it hard to swallow her soup.

"That was the day I got all wet and you had to bring me a towel before you let me back in the house. You said me and Charlie were so soapy we looked like snowmen."

"No, no, that's not possible," said Helen. "That's a picture of my son, Henry, with Charlie, taken before you were even born."

"And *my* daddy," Lola added, jumping up and trying to snatch the photo from Jonah.

"I'll take that," Helen said, retrieving the embattled picture.

"And that's my daddy *and* my mommy. And me, in my mom's ginormous tummy, see?" Lola tapped the photo next to the one Helen had just returned to the mantel.

"Right." Helen would never forget the evening she took that picture, though there were moments when she envied people with dementia, like Mira's mother, and wondered if losing your mind might actually be an adaptive strategy for blotting out unendurable loss. That night, just a week before Henry vanished, Helen had gone over to the green with him and Mira to listen to a baroque chamber group. The late summer concert was packed with families, but the crowd parted like the Red Sea for Mira and her massive belly. In the photo, she's sprawled out on the grassy carpet, and Henry is glowing, his head on her shoulder, his hand cupping her belly.

And now, still trusting in the generally accepted order of the universe, Helen said to Jonah, "That's Mira, Lola's mom. The picture was taken when she was pregnant with Lola, and she's there with my son, Henry, Lola's dad."

"Why do you keep saying Henry?" Jonah asked. "You always called me Danny."

HELEN MUST HAVE blacked out, because some time later—seconds? minutes?—when she opened her eyes she was slumped on the floor next to the fireplace and Lola was crying, "Oma, Oma, wake up, Oma, I'm scared!" while Jonah and Charlie hovered to one side of her and Lucie, crouched on the other side, looked as if she'd eaten a bad shrimp.

TWENTY-FOUR

ARE YOU, MAMA?"

"Am I what?" Lucie's head was spinning. On the walk back from Helen's she was clutching Jonah's hand, sufficiently aware of their surroundings to keep them from getting mangled by oncoming traffic, but that was all.

What the hell?

They'd stayed at Helen's long enough to make sure she wasn't about to faint again. Lucie had offered to take Lola home with them, but the girl understandably insisted on staying with her Oma. Lucie was relieved. She needed to get a handle on what was happening.

"Mama, are you?"

"Am I what, Bear?" Lucie asked, as they turned toward their house. The air was so steamy and still, even the leaves on the sycamores appeared to be napping.

"Mad at me?"

"No, I'm not mad. Of course I'm not mad at you, Jonah. But I am trying to understand what you said. About how that was you in that picture. And how Charlie used to be your dog and your name was Danny and Helen was your mom. Do I have that right?"

Jonah was zigzagging back and forth across the driveway, kicking up little tornadoes of gravel along the way.

"Is that right?" Lucie unlocked the front door, relieved to have made it home after the bizarre scene at Helen's, even though without air-conditioning, their rental house turned into a steambath in the heat.

"Yeah, I guess," Jonah mumbled.

"Honestly, sweetheart, I don't see how that's even possible." Lucie had heard of spiritual leaders like the Dalai Lama who were supposed to be reincarnations of holy men. There had also been a lot of silly stories in the media about regular people who went through past-life regression therapy in order to get in touch with their former selves. Who almost always turned out to be famous historical figures such as Nefertiti or Napoleon, never your average peasant or working stiff. She'd once gotten a query at the magazine from a woman who had just discovered her past life as Lucrezia Borgia and wanted to make amends to her deceased victims in print. Lucie was certain that the Dalai Lama and other saintly types who reincarnated were exceedingly rare, while the gullible bunch who claimed past-life flashbacks were probably seeking otherworldly explanations for their present-day misery. But Jonah didn't fit either category.

"I could see that you and Charlie really liked each other," Lucie said. "Which is lovely. But that doesn't mean he used to be your dog or that Helen was your mom or that it was you in those photographs."

"Can I have some ice cream, Mama? Please? I'm too hot."

"Okay." Lucie dug the Rocky Road out of the freezer and piled two generous scoops on a sugar cone, then sat down with Jonah at the kitchen table and watched him lick methodically from bottom to top to minimize drips. She wondered how it was possible to love someone as fiercely as she loved this boy, a boy who had grown from a speck to personhood inside her body, yet still be so mystified by him. She supposed that's what love is: the kind of surrender that surpasses all understanding. Because this time she couldn't explain away his behavior with her echoes-of-relatives-killed-at-Auschwitz theory. And she wondered: Could traces of memory be passed between people who weren't related, like Jonah and Helen's son? Could Jonah be having one of those collective unconscious experiences Jung talked about, a concept for which he was ridiculed during his lifetime but now seemed to be supported by quantum theory?

When Jonah finished his cone, Lucie gently wiped the goatee blooming on his chin with a paper napkin, then said, "So, can you tell me why you think Charlie used to be your dog and Helen your mom?"

"I tried to tell you, Mama, but you and Daddy always said I was making it up. Like Jeremy who pretends he's from Mars to get out of broccoli because they don't have vegetables on Mars. But I was not making it up."

"I'm sorry I didn't believe you, Bear."

Jonah reached for Mancala, one of his favorite games, then took the blue and green glass beads from their nests in the board and began lining them up on the kitchen table. "I told you there was a dog when we were at the bakery."

"You did." Lucie took a breath, then said, "So, do you think Helen was the mom you talked about when you were little, and Charlie was your dog and you lived with them in the house above the bakery?"

"Yeah, only the house was yellow, not blue like now." Jonah snuck a glance at Lucie but didn't meet her gaze.

"Can you tell me anything more about that time?"

Jonah shrugged, then started rearranging the beads into a

snake. "It was before I was me. Jonah. I got killed in the head and when I was up in the sky I picked you to be my mama and Daddy to be my daddy. You looked so nice and I could tell you really really wanted me."

"You're right, we wanted you more than anything." Lucie paused. "But I'm a little confused. Helen's son was Henry, so why did you say his name was Danny?"

"I don't know. Do we have to keep talking about this?" Jonah whined.

"No, we don't. But I'd like to hear more when you're ready to tell me."

"Can we go get Charlie and bring him here? Please? He wants to come."

"Not today, Bear, maybe another day. If it's okay with Helen." She stopped herself from adding, *It's her dog.*

"I can get him myself, I know the way."

"I said, not today," Lucie said, sounding harsher than she intended. Of all the things she'd worried about since becoming a mother, hearing her son talk about his previous life and getting killed in the head were not among them. She needed to talk to someone. Now. Someone who could help her sort out what was going on. Miriam Zager, if she could get through. "How about I set you up with some drawing stuff, then later we can go splash in the creek?"

Jonah stuck out his lower lip and blew a loud raspberry, a recently acquired skill of which he was terribly proud. "Okay," he said.

Lucie kissed his shaggy curls that stank of dog, then set about collecting all the art supplies she could find—enough to buy her some phone time.

THINGS LIKE THIS aren't supposed to happen to people like us, she thought, scrolling through her contacts for Dr. Zager's number. By *us* she meant highly educated professionals who live on the Upper West Side and have memberships at all the museums. Which was disgustingly elitist, she knew; still, it had always struck her that weird, unexplained phenomena, like ghosts and UFOs and people with "memories" of past lives, happened to people who lived in Nevada or New Mexico, the wide-open N-states out west. Or maybe some of the stoners she grew up around in West Marin.

Lucie expected Miriam Zager's phone to go straight to voicemail, so she was surprised when the psychologist picked up. Luckily, her next patient was running late and she listened as Lucie unloaded the story in one long run-on sentence.

"So, crazy, right?" Lucie was crouched under the eaves on the back patio to avoid being in the direct line of the sun; still, rivulets of sweat dripped from her brow, stinging her eyes and blurring her vision. "Have you ever heard of anything like this? Do you think maybe Jonah, who we know is highly sensitive to the feelings of others, could be picking something up from the collective unconscious about Helen's missing son? Who he says was killed?"

"An interesting theory," Dr. Zager offered in her reassuring lilt. "Possibly, maybe. But," she added, "Jonah's account of being killed fits with his last sand tray, where his miniature stand-in got shot in the back of the head and died."

"Like when he had night terrors and woke up screaming, 'Don't kill me'?"

"Exactly. Which until now I've understood as a symbolic expression of his anxiety, source unknown. I'm planning to have him recast the ending of that story so he can turn it around. But his distress may be less symbolic than I thought."

"You don't think he's delusional or hallucinating or, I don't know, psychotic?" Lucie felt as if the air had been let out of her just saying those words.

"Not at all. You have no worries on that score, but he does present like someone with PTSD. And after what you just described . . ." Dr. Zager paused. "I have to tell you, Lucie, I've never seen it in my own practice, but I have heard of cases of children who recall the lives of people who've passed away. These kids seem to know all sorts of detailed information about the deceased that they couldn't have learned in any of the usual ways."

"And you really think that might be what's going on?"

"I don't know," Dr. Zager said. "Ten years ago, even five, I would have dismissed it as a creative way of managing his distress. But after some of the cases I've read about, I'm not so sure. It could be that the source of Jonah's PTSD symptoms took place in a previous lifetime."

"Wow," said Lucie.

"Very wow, indeed."

"And Helen? You think she could have been the other mom he started talking about when he was four? The *real mom* he cried out for that night?"

"Again, I don't know, but it's possible. It's also possible that the blasts he heard in Times Square triggered some unresolved trauma he picked up from her son and made him cry out for her."

"So much for my inherited family trauma theory."

"Hard to say. It may turn out that the altered genes passed down by your grandmother have affected you more than Jonah."

"So when he starts talking about this other life, how should I respond? Hearing him say that Helen was his mother and he got killed in the head is kind of freaking me out."

"I understand, but I suggest you just listen. If you probe too much, he might shut down. And try not to take his comments personally," Dr. Zager said. "Because whatever is going on is not about you or your husband. I wish I were more of an expert on this sort of thing, but there is someone, a psychiatrist at the University of Virginia medical school, who studies kids who claim to remember a previous life. I believe he's written some books. Tell you what, I'll try to find his name and email it to you. You might want to reach out to him. Sorry, there's the buzzer, my patient is here. Please keep me in the loop. If nothing else, I can help Jonah integrate whatever new material comes to light."

Lucie hung up and stared at the sluggish creek, stymied by the heat. But what she felt was the force of an incoming wave, a thunderous tsunami headed straight for her and Matt and Jonah.

"MAMA? DO YOU want to see my pictures?" Jonah stood by the French doors, waving a sheet of construction paper.

"Course I do." Lucie stumbled as she rose. The leg that had been curled up beneath her was asleep. "I always want to see your pictures," she said, following Jonah into the kitchen.

"Here." He handed her his drawing, then started worrying a scar between his knuckles that he'd sliced on a broken glass when he was five.

She could feel him watching her as she studied his picture. "What a lovely drawing, Bear," she said in as neutral a tone as possible. "Thank you for showing it to me."

And there it was. A crude but colorful replica of the photo that had captured his attention at Helen's house. Both the man, who had yellow shoulder-length hair, and the black dog were grinning through oversized teeth and their bodies were dotted with round turquoise circles meant, Lucie imagined, to be drops of water. The man held a long snaky-looking thing that looked like a hose. A turquoise waterfall gushed from a hole at one end of it, and a wide yellow-orange sun with squiggly rays was smeared across the top of the page.

"You really like it?"

"I do. It reminds me of the photograph you were looking at when we were at Helen's."

"Mama, I tried to name my stuffie *Charlie*, but I was so little when I got him, it came out Jolly."

"And all this time Daddy and I thought you named him for your cousins' collie." Lucie hesitated, then asked in her best Chipper Mom voice, "Is there anything you can tell me about that day in the picture?"

Jonah went back to rubbing his scar, then said softly, "Me and Charlie were just having fun. He made me all wet. Do you want to see my other picture?"

"Sure."

He ran into his bedroom and returned with another sheet of paper. This picture featured the same stick man from the first drawing, only now he was holding a brown oval object with a long handle that resembled a big spoon. In his other hand, which looked like a claw, he seemed to be grasping a stick. He was surrounded by curvy black lines that rose to the top of the page. The scene appeared to take place at night, because overhead six-pointed Jewish stars were scattered across the sky. The mood was in stark contrast to the first picture and struck Lucie as something the young Edgar Allan Poe might have drawn on an especially bleak day.

"Do you mind telling me what the man is holding?" Lucie asked, thinking it might be a gun.

"It's a violin, can't you tell? And that's my bow," he said, pointing to the stick.

My bow . . .

"Come here," Lucie said, setting the drawing on the kitchen table.

Jonah hopped onto her lap and buried his doggy-smelling head in her neck. "You're my mama, Mama," he said in a tiny voice just below her ear.

"Yes I am, Bear. Of course I am."

She wasn't sure if he was trying to reassure himself or her. Probably both, she decided. Until a few hours ago she believed she was his one and only mama, forever and ever, case closed. But now? There were so many questions she wanted to ask him, but she was afraid she might say or do something to make him clam up again.

"Now can we go get Charlie?" Jonah pulled back and flashed her his goofy grin that was as manipulative as it was endearing.

"Like I said before, maybe another day. If it's okay with Helen."

Lucie studied her son's face, his blue eyes so bright, so earnest. Whatever he believed to be true, he believed with his whole heart.

Now she just had to figure out the truth for herself.

TWENTY-FIVE

AFTER MAKING IT THROUGH THE MORNING RUSH AND A WALK with Charlie up in the hills, it was still only eleven o'clock. Which meant eight o'clock on the West Coast. Rosaleen used to stir at dawn, but at eighty-four she was three years older than when Helen last saw her, and she didn't want to risk waking her. She needed Rosaleen's help. Her Zen wisdom. Her unsparing clarity of mind.

Helen had had another sleepless night; it was as if her mind and body had been hot-wired and couldn't shut down.

And *Danny*, Jonah saying she called her son Danny? That blew her mind most of all. Because there was no way the boy could know Danny was Danny before he was Henry.

Ten thousand questions, all pointing to one: If Jonah "remembered" the day in the picture when Danny gave Charlie a bath (and Charlie seemed to "remember" Jonah), did the boy also remember what happened to Danny the night he walked out of the Silver Dollar?

Yet how ironic that this little boy showed up after her big ritual on the mountain when she'd buried the map, then admitted to Lola that her father was dead; when she was ready, finally, to find out what sort of life was possible if her identity was no longer based on motherhood. Or its absence. When she stopped being a walking synonym for loss.

Before calling Rosaleen, Helen wondered briefly if she should run over to the police station to tell Will about possible new information. But, really, what new information? What was he supposed to do with it? Question a seven-year-old kid based on a few bizarre comments?

Helen was on her third cup of coffee when she punched in Rosaleen's number. The last time they'd spoken, a few months before, Kip was still missing and Rosaleen said she'd abandoned all hope of him ever returning.

"Hail-o."

Just hearing Rosaleen's Okie twang shook loose the river of tears that had been dammed up since the day before. When she was able to get the words out, Helen filled her in. Boy. Dog. Photos. *Danny.* The way the child looked at her, the color of his eyes, his uncanny statements about things he couldn't possibly know. "What *is* this?" Helen pleaded. "Please. Tell me."

Rosaleen didn't answer right away. When she did, her response was not what Helen was expecting.

"It doesn't matter," Rosaleen said. "Not a hair on a skinny rat's ass."

"What do you mean? Why doesn't it matter? How can this kid know things only Danny knew? Don't you Buddhists believe in reincarnation?" Helen let herself say that word for the first time. One of the psychics she'd heard from years ago had predicted that someday her son would return, but in an altered form. At the time Helen had dismissed the idea as a load of airy-fairy crap.

"Oh, you're thinking about the Tibetan Buddhists. They make a whole production about reincarnation and rebirth. In Zen we don't mess with it," Rosaleen said. "There's no point, because by definition reincarnation means that there's been a past and there will be a future. But there is no past and no future, only the present moment. Each moment arises, then it's gone, and we're on to the next moment. Then the one after that. That reincarnation business was inherited from Hinduism. Dogen, the founder of the Zen tradition I practice, called reincarnation a non-Buddhist idea that got spliced onto Buddhism. Hang on a sec. I'm going to read you something Dogen wrote."

Rosaleen set the phone down and Helen heard shuffling in the background. Suddenly she felt overcome by exhaustion. As if the electrical current jolting her system since yesterday had just short-circuited.

"Here it is. 'Firewood, after becoming ash, does not again become firewood. Similarly, human beings, after death, do not live again.' That's the nub of it, toots. In other words, focus on the present moment. Live your life right now. Be thankful for it and don't waste your time indulging in a wishful fantasy that this little boy might be Danny come back to you."

"Then how could he say those things? As if he were really remembering them?"

"Who knows? On some level, we're all connected. Atoms, like Einstein said, are neither created nor destroyed. So on that level Shakespeare is part of us, so are all the stars in the galaxy and the chair my saggy butt is sitting on. And the same may be true of consciousness, but so what? It's when we start believing that our so-called souls travel from one lifetime to the next that we get into trouble. Heaven, hell, what good does it do anyone? When we focus on the past or the future, we lose the life we have. Maybe the kid is picking up some spillover consciousness from Danny, but he's not your son, is he?"

"No. He's not Danny."

"In Zen it gets drilled into us that sooner or later we humans can't escape being separated from everything we hold dear. Including the people we love." Rosaleen cleared her throat. "It hurts, sweetheart, but that's just how it goes. For everyone."

Listening to her, Helen was reminded of how at times, now as in the past, she wished Rosaleen would gild the truth. Even a little. "But what if Jonah knows what happened to Danny?"

"Come on, Alice, what if he does? Do you think that'll bring Danny back?"

"No."

"Well, then. Does this little boy have his own mother?"

"Yes."

"Does she love him?"

"Yes."

"So there you have it. He's someone else's beloved child, not yours. That's all you need to know."

But was it really?

Yes, Jonah had his own mother, but that didn't explain what he'd said. Or the instant love affair between the boy and the dog. Didn't that take place in a (recent) present moment? Besides, Helen didn't see how embracing the present moment—which, frankly, she didn't care for all that much—would help her make sense of any of it. Her mind felt like a chopped salad with too many ingredients.

"I'm so tired," she said.

"Then pay attention to what your body is telling you. All that other crap is just a bunch of thoughts messing with your mind. No wonder you're exhausted. Have mercy on yourself, dear Alice. Rest. This child is not Danny."

After they hung up, Helen lay down on the sofa. She had no clearer idea of what was happening than she'd had before speaking to Rosaleen. Yet maybe that was the point. No way the boy's comments, memories, whatever the hell they were, would bring Danny back.

What got her the most before drifting off to sleep was that even after doing everything she could to banish hope, there was a chamber deep in her heart still longing for magic.

TWENTY-SIX

"WHY DIDN'T YOU TELL ME WE WERE GOING TO VISIT GRANDMA Phoebe?"

"I didn't tell you because I didn't decide until late last night, after you were asleep," Lucie said, trying to sound enthusiastic.

"Don't you want to see your mom?"

"Of course." As usual, Jonah was onto her. Just the thought of seeing her mother was making the muscles in her neck spasm. It had been three years. Lucie couldn't imagine three months without seeing her child—or, someday, her grandchild.

"How come you hardly ever see your mom? Don't you love her?"

"What are you, a spy for the FBI, asking me so many questions? We didn't see her for a long time because she lived far away. But now she lives closer."

"I always want to see you. Every day, my whole life. I'm going to marry you, Mama."

"Oh, Bear." Lucie glanced in the rearview mirror. Jonah was arranging his Lego firefighters in his Lego fireboat that patrols the harbor and keeps the citizens safe. "Ahoy, mateys," he growled in his boat-captain voice.

She may have felt undone by the scene that took place at Helen's the day before, but Jonah didn't appear all that fazed by it. And when she finally got Matt on the phone and related the day's events, he was watching a Mets game that had just gone into the bottom of the thirteenth inning with runners in scoring position and was so obviously distracted, she might as well have been giving him the weather report. All he said was that he'd "get to the bottom of the situation" over the weekend, as if by applying his brilliant scientific mind he'd solve the riddle of Jonah's uncanny behavior the way he diagnosed rare ophthalmic conditions or cracked arcane crossword puzzle clues. Frustrated after hanging up, Lucie had just started googling to see if she could dig up anything on the doctor Miriam Zager had mentioned, when she remembered that there was someone nearby who might be able to help.

Now that she was living at a Buddhist monastery, her mother was the only person Lucie could think of who might know something about reincarnation. And if not Phoebe, then maybe her guru. But so much had been going on, Lucie had yet to respond to her mother's phone message left weeks ago and was worried about how her call would be received.

But Phoebe answered on the first ring and sounded thrilled to hear that Lucie, Matt, and Jonah would be spending the summer nearby. When Lucie explained her reason for calling, Phoebe offered to arrange a meeting with Rinpoche "soonest," perhaps as early as the next day. "If anyone can shed light on what's going on with Jonah, he can," she said, adding, "Thank you for calling, darling, thank you. To be honest, I wasn't sure you would."

Turning onto the mountain road, Lucie said, "Grandma is really excited to see you, and I thought you'd like to see her, too. Plus, she has a special friend who's sort of like a rabbi, only instead of being Jewish he's from a place called Tibet, which is near

China, and he teaches people about his religion, which is called Buddhism."

"Isn't Grandma Phoebe Jewish like us?"

"Yes. Well, she was born Jewish, but now she likes this other religion, Buddhism, too. But that doesn't mean she still isn't Jewish."

"Is her rabbi Buddim and Jewish, too?"

"No, sweetie, he's just Buddhist. That's the religion he was born into. He believes in Buddhism, and he isn't called a rabbi, he's called a lama."

"Llama?" Jonah giggled. "Big and hairy like in the zoo?"

AN IMPOSING TWO-STORY white building with maroon and gold columns, the monastery was set on the highest point of a mountain, with orange geraniums tumbling out of baskets lining the wide front steps.

"Wow, look at all those," Jonah said, climbing out of the car and gazing at the rows and rows of colorful banners fluttering between the trees.

"They're called prayer flags. I think they're supposed to bring good luck. Maybe we should have Daddy bring some back for us next time he goes to Nepal."

Suddenly, a woman came rushing down the steps to greet them. She looked practically angelic, the way she seemed to float through space, dressed in white from neck to toe like a modest bride. Her hair was long and white too, and she radiated calm. Lucie felt herself tense.

"Hello, my darlings, hello, hello, *tashi delek*," Phoebe said, crouching down and pulling Jonah close. "Oh my, what a handsome young man you are, so big and grown up. And you know what else? You look so much like your mother when she was your age, you could pass for twins. Except her eyes—like mine—are brown and yours are a beautiful deep blue, like the ocean."

Interesting, Lucie thought, watching the woman who had never been on easy terms with motherhood turn into an adoring granny. Jonah was eating it up.

"I can't tell you how excited I am you're here, darling," Phoebe fussed, pressing a palm over her heart. "It's been such a long time, you probably don't even remember your *Momo*—that's Tibetan for grandma. But I remember you. And the wonderful day we spent at the Cloisters. You drank two big hot chocolates with marshmallows and whipped cream, and then we spent hours walking and watching the boats go up and down the river. The great thing is, now that we live so close, we can spend many more wonderful days together. If you'd like that. I know I would. If it's okay with your mom, of course," she added, rising.

"It's good to see you, darling." She gestured to Lucie with open arms but flinched slightly, as if worried that Lucie might as soon strike as hug her.

"Hi Mom," Lucie murmured, surprised by how glad she was to see her mother. She was even more surprised when her body went slack and swelled with tears when she let her mother embrace her.

"Oh darling," Phoebe whispered into Lucie's hair. "My darling girl."

"FOLLOW ME," PHOEBE said once they were inside the building. She removed her shoes and motioned to Lucie and Jonah to do the same. "We need to be quiet," she whispered, and then opened one of two massive wooden doors that led to an enormous temple. The hall was thick with the pungent scent of incense and bursting with color—walls lined with vibrant hanging tapestries in reds, purples, oranges, and gold, bright fabric-swaddled pillars, chairs and maroon meditation cushions dotting the floor (occupied by a smattering of people, a few in maroon and yellow robes, most in street clothes), tall multicolored objects that looked like kites suspended from the ceiling, and at the far end of the room, a huge luminous golden Buddha seated atop an altar. It was almost too much to take in, and the effect was both stunning and gaudy. Lucie had never been to a Tibetan temple before. Her only experience with Buddhism was at a stark Zen center in the West Village where she'd gone a few times with Holly. The two places were like the difference between a black-and-white documentary and a Bollywood extravaganza, and Lucie couldn't imagine how they served as sanctuaries for the same religion.

"Whoa," Jonah said, eyes open wide.

"Come with me," Phoebe whispered, taking his hand. She led them to a narrow platform next to the altar, where rows of golden, oil-filled lamps flickered. She put a match to three of the unlit wicks, then uttered some phrases in an unfamiliar language that Lucie took to be Tibetan. When they left the shrine room, Phoebe explained that she lit three lamps every week to ensure the safety, good health, and happiness of Lucie, Matt, and Jonah, in this lifetime and the next.

Lucie was having a hard time reconciling this loving vision in white with the flaky mother of her childhood, when an elfin-looking creature with a shaved head and wearing robes came scurrying toward them.

"This must be Lucie and Jonah," exclaimed the person in a thick Brooklyn accent that was decidedly female. "You have no idea how happy I am to meet you. Welcome, welcome. *Tashi delek*. Sonam has told me so much about you both."

"Really?" Lucie said, turning to her mother. "Sonam? It wasn't enough to change your name from Phyllis to Phoebe?"

"Sonam Dawa is my refuge name, given to me by Rinpoche," Phoebe said shyly. "In Tibetan, 'Sonam' means merit and 'Dawa' means moon. There was a full moon the first night I heard him speak. I was pretty lost at the time, and it was as if I were suddenly moonstruck. Not in a romantic way," she added, obviously aware of what Lucie must be thinking. "But it was true love. Love of the dharma, the thing I'd been searching for my entire life, only I didn't know it until that night. And this," she said, putting an arm around the tiny woman, "this is my dear friend Sangye Wangmo, who noticed me huddled in a corner the first evening of my first retreat. Sangye marched right over and introduced herself, then led me into the dining hall and ate dinner with me. She made me feel so welcome. That's when I knew this community was where I belonged."

"I can't tell you how thrilled we are that your mom and Rinpoche are going to make this their permanent home. It was either here or England, and we nabbed them," Sangye said, sounding giddy. "And did you know that the main reason Sonam pushed so hard for here was so she could be near you?"

Lucie stared at her mother. In what universe was it a priority for Phoebe—Sonam—to be near her?

"Rinpoche is ready for you," Sangye said to Lucie.

"Go, darling, go," her mother trilled, with an ecstatic look on her face that suggested Lucie was in for the treat of her life.

As she followed Sangye down a long corridor, feeling as if she were off to meet the Wizard, Lucie turned and watched her mother and son walk off in the opposite direction, hand in hand.

Do most adults continue to see their mothers the same way they did when they were five? she wondered. Who was the real mother? Phoebe then or Sonam now?

IF IT WEREN'T for the tapestry of the fire-breathing deity with multiple arms or the shelves lined with books in unrecognizable characters, Jampa Rinpoche's small, simply appointed study looked as if it might belong to an overworked, underpaid community college instructor. Lucie had imagined something grander, more in keeping with the flashy meditation hall. Plus, she'd been half expecting to see the guru equivalent of the Hollywood casting couch. After all, she'd heard the stories: vulnerable young women plucked then later discarded by predatory "spiritual" teachers who behaved as if enlightenment had granted them immunity when it came to sex. But there was no couch, just a weathered oak desk and matching chair, a large wooden bookcase, a green upholstered armchair, and a rust and celadon tribal area rug. The single window looked out on a community garden with a knot of people bent over, weeding or harvesting. She quickly scoured the field to see if her mother and son were there but didn't see them.

Jampa Rinpoche took her hand and greeted her warmly. Instead of wearing robes like the Dalai Lama, he was dressed in black trousers and a blue short-sleeved shirt with an ink stain on the pocket that resembled a mouse. To Lucie's eye, he looked more like someone's pudgy old uncle from the old country than a revered sage with devotees all over the world—and hardly, as she'd been imagining, her mother's latest boytoy. With his broad unlined face, it was impossible to tell his age; he could have been fifty or seventy. He graciously offered Lucie the easy chair, then took the desk chair himself and nodded for her to begin her story.

Until yesterday, she explained, she believed Jonah's night terrors and phobias of guns and loud noises were caused by trauma inherited from her murdered relatives. But now, after everything he'd told her and the way he reacted to Charlie and Helen, as well as to the photo of her son and the dog taken before *I got killed in the head and had to go up in the sky*, she didn't know what to think.

"That was the first thing that really threw me, because he talked like that was him in the picture. Him, giving the dog a bath, a dog he says is *his* dog. And then the part about getting killed and going up in the sky? As if he were describing his own death." Lucie shuddered. "To be honest, it's pretty upsetting. And confusing."

Several moments of silence followed, punctuated by deep-throated *mms*. When Jampa Rinpoche finally spoke, his voice was gentle and a little scratchy. "You see, when the physical body dies, our mind, that is to say, our consciousness, separates from our body. That can happen fast or slow, the time varies for each person. But consciousness, awareness itself, is never lost. At the time of our physical death, the awareness we had while our body was alive keeps going, sort of like a film loop without a beginning or an end, and it passes through several stages that we Tibetan Buddhists call bardos. Except for a very few enlightened people, sooner or later our consciousness enters what we call the bardo of becoming, a disembodied in-between state, and it stays there until the conditions are right for that consciousness to be reborn in a new body. You see?"

"Not really. I'm sorry, but I don't see at all," Lucie said. "I mean, of course I've heard of reincarnation, but it always seemed like some vague concept to help people feel less scared of dying. Except, of course, for holy people like the Dalai Lama," she added, not wanting to insult him. "Whatever is going on with Jonah seems very different."

"My bad. I'll try to explain better," Jampa said, smiling.

Surprised by the use of the idiom delivered in his hard-to-pin-down accent, with traces of Oxbridge as well as Tibet, Lucie smiled back.

"Most people are confused. Even if they believe in reincarnation or any afterlife at all, they usually imagine we each have an individual soul that we cart around with us from one lifetime to the next like an old steamer trunk." The image obviously tickled him, because the spiderweb of lines around his dark eyes crinkled and he laughed before adding, "But what actually happens after we die is that our consciousness searches for a new body that will help it achieve what we call karmic continuity. So even though we don't continue on as individual souls, we do carry traces of our karma, our prior life experience, into our next rebirth. Which explains why highly evolved lamas and tulkus, such as the Dalai Lama, have memories of previous incarnations, but most people don't. Like me," Jampa chuckled. "I'm just a lowly lama who doesn't remember too much about my last life, even though growing up I was assured by the higher-ups that I was the reincarnation of the Jampa before me. It took awhile and a bit of teenage rebellion before I believed them," he said with a wink.

"But," he added, drawing his thin eyebrows into a long dash, "occasionally an ordinary person's experience leaves such a strong impression that memories and images from a former lifetime cross the stages of the bardo between death and rebirth and pass into the present-day consciousness of a new being. That seems to happen most often when there's been some form of shock in the previous life. So, you see, your notion of inherited trauma isn't wrong, though its source in this case may be different from what you imagined."

"You think Jonah might really be the reincarnation of Helen's son? She doesn't even know if he's alive or dead, just that he disappeared."

"I'm saying that, yes, if he has passed away, it's possible your son carries memory traces that arose from his consciousness. But to be clear, your son is not Helen's son reborn. There's a world of difference. Jonah is his own person with his own individual karma."

"I get that your religion teaches about karma and reincarnation, but in my religion, Judaism, the emphasis is on leading an ethical life, doing good here and now, and not worrying about what happens later."

"That's excellent advice. Ethical behavior in the present lifetime leads to a favorable rebirth, so you see we're all on the same page."

"Yes, but . . . I'm used to putting my faith in science," Lucie said. "So is Jonah's father, who's a doctor. Controlled studies and all that. There's no way to prove that when the body dies anything is left over. Inherited trauma makes sense, because it's based in biology, genes that get passed down. But rebirth? How can you even prove it exists?"

"You're one hundred percent correct. Rebirth has yet to be established in scientific trials. But perhaps that's only because science has yet to catch up with what the Buddha realized over twenty-five hundred years ago, and that is that *everyone* has had countless rebirths. Because of this, sages advise treating every human being with the same loving kindness you would show your own mother. Some even say that every person you meet might have been your mother during a previous incarnation, so you'd better be nice," he chuckled. Then, his expression becoming more solemn, he added, "Western psychology is quite good at identifying many causes and conditions of suffering, but it fails to look beyond the circumstances of the present lifetime. However, there are occasions when a bigger perspective could help get at the root of a problem. Do you understand?"

If she were being perfectly honest, Lucie would have to admit she didn't really want to understand. She liked it better before, when she didn't have to think about any of this. When Jonah was just *her* son, hers and Matt's, not some floating cloud of fairy dust that settled into body after body, lifetime after lifetime.

As if he were scanning her mind, Jampa said, "Please don't misunderstand me, my dear. Your son is your son. He came to life inside your body. He carries your DNA and your husband's. He's your child and will be until the day he dies. But like everyone else, there is also the consciousness he brought with him into the present lifetime, consciousness that did not originate in your womb. What matters is that he was drawn to you and your husband like a magnet because you offered the best possible conditions for his growth." He smiled. "That is very good news, because it works both ways. Your son came into your life to offer you a precious opportunity for your own growth, too. And that is a great blessing."

At the moment it didn't feel like a blessing. Lucie's vision was slightly blurred and she hoped it didn't signal the onset of a migraine. She closed her eyes, took a couple of breaths, then said, "So you really think that when Jonah says Charlie is his dog or Helen used to be his mom or he was killed in the head, I should stop looking for symbolic meanings or a deeper psychological explanation? I should just believe what he's telling me are actual memories?"

"That would be most wise. Children have fantastical imagi-
nations, but they rarely make up stories about things that really
matter. The fact that your son is having these memories doesn't
mean he loves you any less." Jampa was regarding her with such
kindness, Lucie felt as if she might dissolve in tears for the second
time that day. "All you and your husband need to do is listen to
him. Just listen and believe him when he tells you he remembers
something. That's it, no big deal, and before long he won't bother
so much about the past."

Listening to him, Lucie realized that Jonah had been telling
the truth all along, at least what he believed to be the truth. But
by refusing to believe him, she and Matt had shamed him into
not talking about it, while concocting all sorts of elaborate psychological and neurological theories to explain away what they'd
seen and heard. Would Jonah have suffered less if they'd believed
him? Did his memories manifest as night terrors because they
didn't accept what he'd told them? "Oh God," she said.

As if once more seeing into her mind, Jampa said, "You are a
loving mother, that's clear. You'll only create unnecessary karma
if you waste energy blaming yourself or your husband for past
actions. What's done is done. It's not too late to believe your son.

"And by the way," he added, rising, "some of your Western scientists have been researching reincarnation for decades.
You're not the first mother who's come to see me when her child
started talking about a past life. It happens." He shrugged, then
searched the bookcase until he found what he was looking for
and handed Lucie a worn paperback.

"You may find this helpful. And now I would very much like
to speak to your boy," he said with a little bow.

Lucie bowed in return.

TWENTY-SEVEN

Momo's rabbi Jampa is really nice. He laughs a lot for a grown-up and he's not too good at checkers. I beat him two times and I do NOT think he's letting me win just because I'm a kid.

"Do you know how to play chess?" I ask him. Not that I'm good at chess, I'm terrible. My dad is trying to teach me, but I lose to him every time. He doesn't EVER let me win games if I don't win "fair and square." But maybe if this rabbi guy is so bad at checkers, he's also bad at chess, and I could beat the pants off him. Which is what my dad says about tennis. He's always getting the pants beat off him by his friend Lou. When I was little, I used to worry that if I played a game and lost, I would have to go around all day without any pants.

"I know how to play chess," Jampa says. "I learned when I was a boy in the monastery in Tibet, but I'm better at checkers." Then he cracks up with one of his big *hahaha*s and his giant belly rolls up and down.

"Where's Tibet?" I ask him, and he shows me on his globe. He looks sad when he tells me his monastery isn't there anymore because of China and he had to run away in the middle of the night when he was just "a wee monk," and how he can never go back to see his family.

That is so terrible, I think, the WORST. I want to cheer him up, so I say, "But now you have this place and that's good, right?"

"It is good," he says, but he still looks sad.

Right away I think, maybe I could bring Charlie over to cheer him up. Jampa is so nice and even though he's a man I think Charlie would like him. "Do you like dogs?" I ask.

"Sure," he says. "Dogs are the best. They have a lot to teach us. Your mom told me there's a dog you really like who you used to know before you were Jonah."

"Yeah. Charlie. I got him when I was Danny."

Yesterday when I said that, my mom and my old mom got funny looks on their faces and then my old mom fell on the floor. But this Jampa rabbi acts like it's okay if you talk about your old life.

"You know," he says, looking right at me with such a big smile I can see a bunch of gold choppers in his mouth, "I remember a time before, too, when I was a very old lama. When I got reborn and was a little kid again, I had to prove to some big-deal monks that I remembered things about the life of that other guy, even though I was now somebody else."

"REALLY?" Like me! Except I'm just a kid, not a lama like him or the kind in the zoo. "How did you prove it?"

"A search committee came to my parents' house and showed me some bells and prayer beads and books, and I had to pick out which ones belonged to the old teacher who died."

"And did you? Pick the right ones?"

"I did," says Jampa, patting his belly that's so big it looks like there's a giant balloon in there. "As soon as I took one look, I recognized which things were that old teacher's, the same way you recognized Charlie."

"And Charlie recognized me. Even though now I'm Jonah."

"Yes, you are. You are not that other boy."

"So why do I know all this stuff about him that makes my stomach feel funny?"

"Sometimes people like you and me remember things that another person once knew. It can be a little scary, can't it?"

"Yeah," I tell him, but I look at my new sneakers because if I look in his face I might cry.

"I'm going to let you in on a little secret. You're not alone, Jonah. Everybody has had many lives, only most people don't remember them."

I can't believe it. "EVERYBODY? Even my mom and my dad? They do NOT act like it."

"It's a funny thing," Jampa says. "Often the people who don't remember have a hard time believing the people who do. It's not their fault. There's just nothing that sticks in their mind from their life before this one. But that doesn't matter, because even if they don't remember it, some teeny-tiny part of their awareness from that time stays with them, even though they have different parents and they're a different person in a brand-new body. Just like you and me. Do you think knowing that might help you feel better?"

"Sort of," I say. But I still can't believe it. "My mom and my dad?"

"Yup," he says, then his head goes up and down like a bobblehead. "But sometimes parents who don't remember anything from a previous life worry that if their child does, that child might think he is that other person, not *their* child, and they feel a little sad or jealous."

"But I know I'm Jonah, not Danny, and I don't want to be him."

"And I promise you, you're not. You know what else? I bet someday soon, you'll be so busy being Jonah, you'll forget all about Danny."

"That's okay," I tell him. "I already forgot about him, but then I came here and started to remember again." And then I have to know, "Did somebody kill you too? When you were the other guy?"

"No. I was lucky. I grew old and died in my sleep."

"Do you remember it?"

"Yes. I do. But that death wasn't as scary as getting killed."

"I hate that part. I want it to go away." All the sudden, I feel tears drizzling down my face.

"I'm going to let you in on another secret. It's good that you remember being Danny. Good you know there's something inside you that never dies. Lots of people spend their whole life searching for what you already know, so you're way ahead of the game."

He hands me a tissue and I wipe my snotface. I don't know what game he's talking about.

"I'll tell you something else," he says. "I had a good talk with your mom and now you can tell her what you remember without worrying about upsetting her. It helps to talk about it. Makes it less scary. And pretty soon Danny will seem like someone you knew a very long time ago, if you remember him at all."

"Good," I say. "I just want to be me, not Danny, but me WITH Charlie. Did you have a dog when you were that old teacher?"

He goes *hahaha* again, one of those big bellyrolls. "Not that I remember. But I bet you can visit Charlie, even if you can't have him all the time."

"But I want him all the time," I say.

"I know." Then he pats me on the knee and looks all serious.

"But Charlie was Danny's dog, and if you can't have him all the time, then maybe your mom and dad will get you your own dog. Because remember, part of the secret is that it's only the smallest part of us that goes from one life to the next. Sort of like a river that starts out as a tiny stream, then gets bigger and bigger as it flows from the mountains through the forests and canyons until by the time it reaches the ocean it's so big it hardly remembers that once it was a tiny stream or even a river."

"I'm like a river? I'm going to tell my mom." I blow my nose and wipe my eyes, and then I ask him, "Now can we play chess?"

TWENTY-EIGHT

By THE TIME LUCIE FELL ASLEEP, SHE WAS IMMERSED IN THE WORK of Ian Stevenson, MD. A psychiatry professor at the University of Virginia medical school who died in 2007, Stevenson wrote the book that Rinpoche had loaned her—*Children Who Remember Previous Lives*—and was the same doctor Miriam Zager had emailed her about earlier in the day. Lucie skimmed the book, then checked him out online. Among the entries, she found several critiques of Stevenson's four decades of research.

There was simply no way to prove his theory that reincarnation was the most feasible explanation for the "memories" expressed by the twenty-five-hundred children he'd studied, who, like Jonah, seemed to recall detailed information about a deceased person's life that they had no way of knowing. As astonishing as the accounts were, before yesterday Lucie would have scoffed along with the skeptics and dismissed Stevenson's conclusions as well-meaning but wishful quackery. Without the usual scientific guideposts to light the way through the tangle of the unknown, how could she—or anyone—separate the truth from a con?

As if addressing her doubts, she came across an interview with Stevenson that had appeared in the *New York Times* in 1999.

"Science develops ideas of what is so," he said, "and it becomes very difficult to force scientists to take a look at new data that may challenge existing concepts. I'm not trying in any way to replace what we know about genetics or environmental influences. All I'm offering is that past lives may contribute a third factor that may fill in some of the gaps in our knowledge."

Stevenson's point was similar to Jampa's when he suggested that science hadn't yet caught up with the Buddha's understanding of how consciousness gets transmitted from one person to the next. And Lucie had to admit that with every significant scientific discovery there was always a period of time—often centuries—between the emergence of an idea and its acceptance. (See: Leonardo da Vinci's sketches of flying machines from 1485.)

What if Stevenson and Rinpoche were right?

Would acknowledging Jonah's past life help heal his PTSD?

Did other parents feel as flipped out as Lucie when their kids started talking about living before? Having another mother? Getting *murdered*?

Obviously, some did, because in the *Times* interview Stevenson told the reporter that even in India, where just about everyone believes in reincarnation, 40 percent of parents actively repress their child's past-life memories. Not only that, he added, some of those children "are tormented, struggling with torn loyalties between two families. They often want to go back to the other family and reject their parents. Very often the child is placated by meeting the previous personality's family."

Had Jonah been *tormented* all these years? Did he feel *placated* now that he'd met Helen and Charlie?

Lucie felt somewhat better—though not exactly placated—

when she read what Stevenson had said about how acceptance of reincarnation might change the world: "It would lessen guilt on the part of parents. They wouldn't have as much of a burden that whatever goes wrong with a child is all their fault, either through genes or mishandling during the child's infancy."

Maybe so, but that didn't mean she and Matt were off the hook. Because even if they weren't to blame for the terrifying images and memories that had been flooding Jonah's mind since he was a baby, he'd suffered. And more than anything, Lucie wanted that to stop. Whatever it took—even if it meant over-riding her knee-jerk skepticism, her confusion, her feelings of jealousy toward Jonah's *real mom*, and accepting as true, or at least as possible, something that a week ago she would have dismissed as a paranormal fairy tale. She was scared for Jonah and, at this point, open to any explanation that could help him, even if it lay beyond the reach of science. Even if it ran counter to the currently accepted understanding of the human psyche. Even if Matt refused to go along. Even, hardest of all, if it upended Lucie's beliefs about motherhood—one mother, one kid, a singular, sacred bond—as well as her beliefs about who we are to each other. Every belief she held dear.

To her great surprise, she felt waves of relief when she realized she didn't need to know—and couldn't possibly know—the absolute truth about any of it. Because if she didn't need to know, she no longer had to tie herself in knots defending against the immensity of everything that was unknowable, as if her life depended on it. She wondered what was left after that. Perhaps only love? Or God? The thought made her think she might be having a mystical experience and that made her laugh out loud.

Still, there were things that could be inferred, even if they could never be proved in a lab. She turned back to the book and zeroed in on the chapter where Stevenson outlined the qualities common in children who remember a previous life.

He could have been talking about Jonah when he described how these kids spontaneously start speaking about their former life at a very young age in a matter-of-fact tone of voice, unlike the playful tone they use when engaging in make-believe. They often exhibit exceptional talent, such as playing a musical instrument, that fits with the person whose life they remember. (Check.) When she read the next few traits, Lucie felt as if a swarm of bees were colonizing inside her head. According to Stevenson, the kids frequently give detailed descriptions of how the previous person died and suffer phobias related to their death. Not only that, in three-quarters of the cases death was often sudden and violent, and some of the children seemed to relive the person's passing in nightmares or night terrors. (Double check.) And birthmarks: Stevenson claimed that among the most convincing signs that a child remembers the life of someone who died are birthmarks that correspond to wounds sustained during that person's death. Some of these matches have later been confirmed by autopsy reports or medical records.

Lucie got out of bed and shut the window. The lightning and dull claps of thunder that had been puncturing the night sky from a distance were growing louder.

Obviously, there was no autopsy report for Henry, because Henry's body had never been found. But Jonah had been born with that rounded, red, slightly raised birthmark at the base of his skull. Sometimes at night when Lucie gave him a back rub to help him fall asleep, he whimpered when her hand brushed the tender spot. Did that mean he was assaulted by images of being shot in the back of the head when she touched it or he heard loud noises or during the episodes of night terrors? And what about the nightmare she'd had on the bus to Aurora Falls the day Jonah was born? The one where blood came gushing out of the baby's head? Where did that come from?

"Poor Bear," she said aloud, as a deafening drumroll of thunder pierced the air and lightning seemed to split the sky in two. Expecting Jonah to wake up and start howling, Lucie ran to his room and crawled into the narrow, saggy lower bunk beside him and held him close.

Which is how Matt found them when he showed up early the next morning.

"We need to talk," Lucie mumbled, then promptly fell back to sleep.

MATT FOUND HER still sacked out when he and Jonah returned home hours later.

"Luce?" He shook her gently. "You okay?"

"Mm. Is Jonah up yet?"

"He's been awake since I got here. At eight o'clock this morning." Matt crouched on the edge of the narrow bed in order to avoid hitting his head on the top bunk.

"Oh. What time is it now?"

"Three. *P.M.*" He gave up on the bed and slid to the rag rug on the floor.

"Seriously?" Lucie propped herself up on one elbow. "Jesus, I haven't slept this late since I had mono in tenth grade." She licked her lips. Her mouth tasted like sand.

"Well, Jonah and I have had quite the day, too. After breakfast, we went to see about joining the community pool where, he casually mentioned, his swim team used to practice when he was *big*. I tried to get him to say more, but he just shrugged and told me he didn't really remember anything else about it."

"I hope you didn't try to talk him out of it," Lucie said, bumping her head against the top bunk as she tried to sit up, then, like Matt, gave up and joined him on the floor.

"No. But Lucie, what the fuck?"

"I told you we needed to talk," she said. "Where's Jonah now? I don't want him to hear."

"Outside. Playing fetch with Charlie."

"What?"

"Okay, so after our trip to the pool, we actually had a few normal hours. I took him to Theo's for pepperoni pizza, then we played a round of mini golf, which he won. Fairly. But then things started getting weird again. We were on our way home when he begged me to stop by the bakery, where, he informed me, he used to live with his *old mom*. He wanted to see if her dog, which he seems to think is *his* dog, could come over to our house. At first, I nixed it, but he kept pleading and said he *really* needed to see that dog, so finally I gave in. Helen was behind the counter, not looking all that happy to see us. And what the hell happened to her hair? She looks like she got scalped since I was in there last week."

"Long story."

"Anyhow, she said yes and took Jonah outside to get Charlie. I don't think I've ever seen any human and dog so excited to see each other. Only I could tell by the dog's snarls that he wasn't all that excited to see me. But then I think he got that Jonah and I are a package deal, so he decided to let me live. I tried to talk to Helen about what's going on, but she wasn't too chatty. She just went inside to collect the dog's leash and some food and one of those plastic ball-tossing things. As we were leaving, I asked her again if she was sure she was okay letting her dog come home with us. And you know what she said? 'Charlie was never really my dog.'"

Matt waved his hands in the air like a conductor. "Do you think we have a dog now?"

IT WASN'T UNTIL later, after Jonah and Charlie were asleep, snuggled like a couple of honeymooners, that Lucie was able to fill Matt in on the events of the past two days. They were out on the front porch, rocking on the creaky glider. The air that had been rinsed clean by last night's thunderstorm was still fresh, while overhead stars were popping up like sparklers. In every way but one, the scene matched Lucie's fantasy of summer nights in Aurora Falls.

She lit a citronella candle, then told Matt about her conversation with Jampa Rinpoche and Stevenson's research. She tried to describe her mystical flash of insight (awkwardly, because how can you describe such a thing?) that little in this world is truly knowable, including who we believe ourselves to be.

When she finished, Matt took off his glasses, blew on the lenses, and wiped them on his T-shirt, then put them back on. "I'm sorry, Luce, but this sounds more like science fiction than science. I can't believe you're buying that Jonah is the reincarnation of Helen's son."

"If it helps Jonah, then yes, I think I am. As impossible as it sounds." She massaged the back of her neck. "Quantum physicists now say that past, present, and future are nothing more than mental constructs, a handy way of organizing time in our minds, but in reality, all three happen simultaneously."

"Yeah, well, we happen to live on planet Earth, where life is divided into yesterday, today, and tomorrow, so their theory isn't all that helpful. Plus, if there really is something to what these so-called experts say, why hasn't Jonah been talking about his quote 'memories' before now?"

Lucie stared at Matt. The silver strands in his dark hair appeared iridescent in the moonlight. "He *has* been talking about them. All that stuff he said about his other mom, his dog, the yellow house, we heard in a way that made sense to us. Imaginary friends. An amazing fantasy life. But both Stevenson and Rinpoche . . ."

"Your insane mother's guru? You really trust this guy?"

"Yes. I liked him. So did Jonah. He seemed very rational and reasonable, well educated, too. He says the best way to help Jonah is just to listen. So he'll feel safe talking about what he remembers, even if we can't prove any of it. Even Dr. Zager thinks it's possible the source of his anxiety comes from a previous life. And before he died, Stevenson gave an interview to the *Times* where he said that kids whose parents are accepting have a much easier time letting go of their memories. Usually they forget them and move on. Which is what we want, right?"

"So what are we supposed to do now?"

Lucie was relieved that Matt seemed to be going along, even if he still believed it was all a crock of voodoo. "Dr. Stevenson has a successor at the University of Virginia medical school, a psychiatrist named Jim Tucker. I think we should try to meet with him or someone on his team." When Matt didn't respond, she said, "So? Okay?"

He slapped at a mosquito that had just landed on his wrist, then said, "I guess. Or maybe there's some toddler running around who is Stevenson reborn and can give us some tips."

Lucie poked his thigh with her bare foot.

"Seriously, what about Helen? Have you spoken to her about this?"

"No."

"Well, don't you think you should? It's her son Jonah says he remembers. If we end up talking to this Tucker guy, don't you think she needs to be involved, too? If his so-called research is at all credible, wouldn't he want to confirm Jonah's statements with her?"

"You're right." Ever since their fateful lunch at Helen's, Lucie had been so fixated on trying to make sense of Jonah's revelations and figuring out how to respond that she hadn't given much thought to what Helen must be going through. First, to lose a child, then to have some strange little boy show up and claim he was her son *before he got killed in the head and had to go up in the sky*? It scrambled Lucie's mind just thinking about it. She wondered: Was it simply an accident of timing and geography that Helen had been the one to take her to the hospital when she was in labor? The first one besides the surgeon and the nurses to hold Jonah after he was born? Had something else been going on all this time that was bigger than any of them? Impossible to know. And even though she wasn't crazy about the idea, if Jonah had to remember having another mom, Lucie was glad it was Helen; she felt certain that Helen had been a wise and loving mother.

"I'll talk to her first thing tomorrow," she said, then leaned over and brushed the hair from her husband's eyes and kissed him on the temple.

LATER THAT NIGHT when Matt went to make sure the big hairy dog wasn't smothering Jonah, he noticed a sheet of paper poking out from under the mattress on the top bunk. He pulled it out and saw that it had been crumpled up, then took it into the bathroom and turned on the light. What he saw when he opened it made his usually slow runner's pulse rev up like a jackhammer.

The picture was drawn in Jonah's unmistakable hand. Filling most of the page was a large dark rectangle. A man crudely drawn in yellow crayon was splayed out on top of the rectangle. He had yellow hair but no features, which made it appear as if he were lying facedown, and squiggles of red crayon radiated from the back of his head. There were a few objects off to the side that Matt had trouble identifying because of the dark blue background, though he could make out a couple of sticklike trees. The scene obviously took place at night, because the sky was dotted with Jewish stars.

Lucie had shown Matt a couple of pictures that Jonah had drawn the day they had lunch at Helen's, but not this one, which he'd obviously hidden.

Matt didn't know what the picture meant, but there was no mistaking its subject.

TWENTY-NINE

SUMMER PEOPLE," HELEN BITCHED TO KATY AND GEO WHEN THE knocking started. "Honestly, with all their fancy degrees, you'd think they'd know how to read." The hours posted on the front door of the Queen of Hearts couldn't be clearer: Open 7 a.m.–3 p.m., and it was six thirty Sunday morning. The first batch of croissants, morning buns, and pain au jambon wouldn't be out of the oven for another fifteen minutes, and Izzy, who worked the counter, wasn't in yet.

"I'll go and tell them to come back later," said Katy.

"No, you and Geo finish getting the next bake ready, I'll go." Helen was in a state, had been since Jonah's declarations on Thursday, followed by her conversation with Rosaleen on Friday. Of course Rosaleen was right, because in spite of everything this little boy seemed to know, however he came to know it, he was not Danny, never would be, could not fill the gap in Helen's heart.

Wiping her hands on her flour-caked apron, she was more than happy to give the latest entitled customer a piece of her mind. She switched on the lights in the front of the shop and pointing to the sign was about to yell, "Can't you read," when she saw who it was.

Lucie. Clutching a book to her chest.

Shit, thought Helen, unlocking the door.

"I'm sorry it's so early," Lucie stammered, "but I was hoping to catch you before you got busy. I can come back later, if . . ."

"It's fine." Helen studied Lucie's face. She could see Jonah in it. Its long, narrow shape, the full lips, the slight curve of the nose, even her toothy smile. But not Jonah's big blue eyes. They were nothing like his mother's. "Did you want to pick something up for breakfast?" she asked, certain that wasn't the real reason why Lucie had shown up at this hour looking nervous.

"Do you think we could talk? There's something I'd like to ask you. It won't take long."

Did she want to hash out what was going on with Jonah? What would be the point? If anything, Helen needed to snuff out whatever faint hope got fired up by Jonah's comments. She'd been silently repeating *he's not my son, he's not my son,* as if it were a mantra. And it wasn't as if she and Lucie were friends. They'd spent one intense half hour together on the way to the hospital in Albany. That was it. So who were they to each other? Helen didn't think there was a word for it.

"We can talk, but let's go over to the green. I'd like to keep this between us," Helen said, tilting her head toward the kitchen. She'd been unusually testy with her staff for the past few days, and she knew they sensed something was up, but she hadn't told them anything about Jonah and didn't plan to. What would she even say?

SHE LED LUCIE across the street to the gazebo near the bandshell, so that not even a lone jogger running by would overhear their conversation. The last thing she needed was for the town's gossip mill to get revved up over this.

"This must be as weird for you as it is for me," Lucie started, when they sat down.

"I have no idea how your son seems to know what he knows about my son. Or about me. And the dog. The *dog*." Helen shook her head.

"The whole thing is mind boggling. On top of you saving Jonah's life. And mine." Lucie picked at a hangnail. "And now this."

"Yes. Now this." Helen gazed through an opening in the wooden gazebo. Though the sun had risen over an hour ago, beads of dew still sparkled on the grass like tiny diamonds.

"It seems like more than just coincidence," said Lucie.

"Maybe, but to be honest I'm not sure where we go from here. If there's anywhere to go."

"That's what I wanted to talk to you about." And then it all came out: Lucie's conversation with the Tibetan lama, Dr. Stevenson's research, the possibility of meeting with his successor, a Dr. Tucker. "My guess is that if we end up seeing him, he'll want to talk to you, too. So you can confirm—or deny—what Jonah says he remembers."

"Oh," said Helen, feeling her body heat up, as if struck by sudden fever. "When?"

"I don't know. I haven't reached out to him yet. I wanted to talk to you first. Maybe you could take a look at this?" Lucie handed her Stevenson's book.

Children Who Remember Previous Lives: A Question of Reincarnation. Helen stared at the cover photo, which showed two children accompanied by three women in long dresses with full skirts, everyone wearing Victorian-style hats.

"The stories are amazing," Lucie said. "All these little kids talking about a person they say they used to be, much of the information verified. It made me understand so much about Jonah. Like many of the children in the book, he's always been anxious, like someone with PTSD. And though we've spent years trying to figure out why, we never dreamed he might have picked up residual trauma from another person." Lucie stopped fidgeting and looked directly at Helen. "Your son. Jonah's been talking about his other mom and his dog since he was a little kid. We just never took it seriously. It sounds unbelievable, I know . . ."

"Unbelievable is right. And, frankly, pretty unsettling. But how can you prove there's any truth to the idea that Jonah picked up, what did you call it, residual trauma, from my son?"

"Dr. Stevenson and his team have spent decades correlating the children's claims with facts. Names, dates, that sort of thing. All over the world. Many of the kids were obsessed with meeting their previous family, and usually when they did, they felt happier and became better adjusted to their present life."

"And what about the family from the previous life? Were they happier, too?" Helen's tone was sharp. She felt like she was being set up.

"I don't know the answer to that, but I'm sure Dr. Tucker could tell you. Also . . ." Her voice faltering, Lucie said, "Just in case you think I'm some woo-woo nut, until three days ago I'd have thought this reincarnation stuff was a crock. My husband still does."

Helen studied her calloused hands, trying to formulate what she had to say. "I appreciate your reasons for wanting to let Jonah explore his memories with this doctor, Lucie. I'd probably do the same if I were you, but I'm not sure I can be involved. Because regardless of whatever stray bits of information Jonah is pulling up out of the ether about my son, he's your child, not mine. I don't know what happened to mine, just that he's never coming back." She glanced across the street. A line was forming outside the bakery.

"Please understand. I've been grieving for eight years, and it's only very recently that I've begun to make peace with the fact that I'm never going to see my boy again. That he's dead." Just saying the word made Helen's whole rib cage ache.

"And I am so sorry. The last thing I want is to cause you more pain. I just thought that maybe talking to this doctor could help you, too."

"I'll take a look at the book," Helen said, rising. "But in the meantime, why don't you see if you can meet with him without me?"

"Sure. Of course."

Lucie was regarding Helen with such a plaintive expression on her face, it made Helen wonder how she would have reacted if one day her son had suddenly announced that he had another mom. Not all that well, she imagined.

"No matter what you decide, I hope we can be friends," Lucie said. "Ever since Jonah was born, the way it happened, I'm just so grateful to you . . ."

In that moment Lucie looked as lost and undone as Helen felt, so Helen wrapped her arms around the younger woman and held her close before turning to go.

THIRTY

To someone who didn't know the backstory, it would have looked like a classic Sunday in summer: Matt and Jonah playing wiffle ball while Charlie raced back and forth between them, barking and trying to eat the ball; a family lunch of grilled cheese sandwiches and lemonade out on the patio, followed by a dip in the creek; and after that, an animated game of Clue, which Lucie won. Miss Scarlet in the Billiard Room with the Dagger.

By five o'clock, Matt's legs were twitching and he was desperate for a run. He promised Lucie he'd be home in time for dinner, but he wasn't wearing his watch and nearing Humpty's on his way back through town, he decided what the hell, what's the harm in one lousy beer? He deserved it. Because as devoted as he was to his wife and son—and he would step in front of a firing squad to protect them—he was at a total loss. Nothing in his training as a physician had prepared him for this. In medicine it's understood that when the body dies, the mind goes with it. Snuffed out, end of story. But more than anything that Lucie had told him or Jonah volunteered, he was spooked by his son's drawing of what was unmistakably a grave.

Lucie was probably right. They should talk to this doctor who studies kids like Jonah and find out what they could. But then what? What were they supposed to do with the information? How could they help their son let go of his "quote" memories and return to *this* life? These were the thoughts jamming Matt's brain that the endorphins released during his run had failed to obliterate. Panting, doused with sweat, he opened the door to Humpty's. A beer would help.

All the stools facing the bar were occupied by a bunch of men and two women pounding their fists and yelling at the TV. Matt took off his shades and squinted at the Yankees game on the screen. "Come on, Derek, baby, we need a friggin' base hit!" shrieked a woman with blue hair. Matt hated the Bronx Bombers. As a teenager, rooting for the Mets was his big act of rebellion, since his father had season seats at Yankee Stadium, right behind home plate. Matt's devotion to the Mets had started out as a joke to needle Gordon, but the more his father tried to convert him into a Yankees fan, the more rabid Matt became about the Mets. They could laugh about it now—yet the laughter still had an edge. Which is why Matt tried to show some restraint in his efforts to turn Jonah into a fan of the "Lovable Losers."

He noticed a vacant seat at the far end of the bar, where he'd be spared a full-on view of the game, and asked the guy on the stool next to it if it was taken.

"Nope," the guy said, his nose in his drink.

Matt ordered a Corona. Humpty's was your basic throwback saloon. Filthy linoleum floor, ancient pockmarked wooden bar, so dimly lit that when you entered during daylight hours you saw mostly shadows. Matt spent enough of his life in rarified settings; when he had the chance, he preferred to enjoy the odd brew in seedy watering holes—yet another way he set himself apart from his father, whose favorite drinking establishment was Bemelmans Bar at the Carlyle Hotel.

"You're not a Yankees fan either?" Matt asked his neighbor, who looked like he was in his early thirties.

"Hell, no. I was on the baseball team in high school, but it's a fucking snooze to watch. Give me football any day."

"Fair enough," Matt said, guzzling his beer. "You live around here?"

"Just my whole life. Born and bred. You?" The man half turned toward Matt but didn't make eye contact. He had a neatly trimmed beard and what little light there was in the bar made his white teeth shine. To Matt he seemed like one of those muscular types who never set foot in a gym. The kind of guy who could fix anything. Matt sometimes operated on men like that who'd injured their eyes doing construction. Their strength, even when they were down, fascinated him. Matt was fit, a runner since cross-country in middle school, but these guys struck him as a different breed. They seemed to be able to smoke and drink and raise hell—until their bodies broke down prematurely, usually by the time they turned fifty.

"I live in the city. Manhattan," Matt said. "Up here for the summer."

"Yeah?" the guy said, turning to face him. "You looking to buy?"

Matt ran his finger along the sweaty rim of his beer glass. "Nah, I don't think so."

"Well, if you change your mind, there are some pretty sweet properties for sale. Brand new, hardly any upkeep, enough land for a nice garden or infinity pool. You gotta get out of the city sometimes, right?" He called to the bartender. "Hey Mick, another round for my friend here. And a double and a Sam for me." The guy opened his wallet and pulled out a business card. "Full disclosure," he volunteered. "I happen to know these properties are top of the line because I built 'em. Well, my guys did, and they're the best in the tristate area. Ultrasolid construction, roof to foundation. Jackson Brin." He handed Matt his card.

"I'm sure they're great," Matt said, glancing at the logo, a drawing of a McMansion-type place in a development called Bella Vista Estates. That's just what they needed right now, to buy a house in this haunted burg.

"Hey, no pressure. Just thought I'd let you know in case you're in the market. These babies are going fast. And because there's no middleman, I can cut you a hell of a deal."

All of a sudden the crew watching the game let out a collective groan. The Yankees failed to pull it out in the ninth and lost to the Twins, 4–3. Matt silently cheered.

"So, what are you anyway?" the real estate guy wanted to know. "Lawyer? Stockbroker? CEO?"

Matt laughed. "I'm a doctor. An ophthalmologist. Matt." He extended his hand.

"Pleased to meet you, Matt. So how do you like our little corner of the world?"

"I like this joint," Matt said.

"Well then, you got good taste. Humpty's is the hometown fave. I've been coming here since I was a teenager. Don't usually see too many of your city compadres, though. They go to 212North. But Mick ain't no pussy mixologist, are you, Mick?"

"Hell, no," Mick replied, with a facial expression that might be a grimace or the lopsided grin of a stroke victim, hard to tell.

Matt hated being lumped in with other well-to-do New Yorkers, even if he was one. Still, in all honesty, as soon as he sat down, he pegged this Jackson guy as a construction worker or a member of the trades—and he wasn't that far off. We're all just a bunch of walking stereotypes, he thought ruefully, which was why the world was in such a fucking mess. He didn't usually socialize with guys like Jackson and was finding it refreshing. The beer was relaxing him and he motioned to Mick for another round, even though he'd just started on Corona number two.

"You got any kids?" he asked Jackson.

"One, a daughter. You?"

"A son."

"I bet he likes it up here. Gives him a chance to run around and breathe some fresh air, am I right?"

"I guess," said Matt. "It's been a little weird, though."

"Yeah? Weird, how?"

Matt took a long swill of beer. He wasn't in the habit of confessing his business to strangers in bars. If anything, he was a stickler for privacy. On the other hand, he needed to talk to someone and his family was out. He could just imagine Gordon's reaction to the news that his grandson was being stalked by a ghost. And if he said anything to his doctor buddies, they'd think he'd gone off the deep end. Maybe a stranger was the right idea, a half-drunk guy in a bar who'd forget what he heard by the time he made it home.

"The whole thing sounds nuts, but the Cliff Notes version is that my seven-year-old son believes he lived in this town in a previous life. At least he seems to think he has memories of some guy who used to live here."

"No shit? Man, that does sound nuts."

"Yeah, well, my wife has done some research and thinks he might be onto something."

"Still, sounds like bullshit to me. No way would I let my wife indulge my kid in that kind of crazy."

"As weird as it sounds, there might be something to it. Who

knows?" Matt had to admit there were enough bizarre coincidences that made it hard to say what was true and what was bullshit. And that drawing, Jesus. He just wanted his son back. And his wife. He downed the rest of his beer.

"Your kid say anything else?"

Matt shrugged and popped a couple of mini pretzels in his mouth. He was starting to feel a little woozy. "There's this dog that supposedly was his dog in his past life and the woman who owns the bakery was his mother and . . . The whole thing sounds like science fiction, right?"

"Which bakery?" Jackson asked, running his finger over deep grooves in the bar where people had carved their names. "There are a couple."

"The good one, across from the green. The Queen of Hearts."

Jackson let out a long, low whistle, then polished off his shot. "Man, if I were you, I'd give the kid a good talking-to about the difference between make-believe and real life and shut the whole thing down. And if that doesn't work, maybe get him to a shrink and check out what's up with the hallucinations." He slid off his stool, pulled a wad of bills out of his pocket, and dropped a fifty on the bar. "Hey, great to meet you, Doc. And don't forget, if you decide to buy, I'm your man."

Matt watched as Jackson flashed Mick a military salute on his way out the door.

Fuck, he thought, pushing his third, untouched beer aside. What the fuck was wrong with him? He'd never done anything like this before in his life. He was always getting on Lucie's case for "oversharing" with Holly. *Jesus.* Where did he get the idea that telling some guy in a bar about Jonah would make him feel better? Aurora Falls was a small town. Why would he confide in a local who probably knew the story of Helen's missing son, chapter and verse?

He was pissed at himself, but what's done is done, he thought, stumbling his way along the length of the bar and out into the blazing sunlight. At least he hadn't given the guy his card or told him their last name.

THIRTY-ONE

THESE ARE FOR LOLA," HELEN SAID WHEN MIRA OPENED THE front door. "A peace offering." She held up a box filled with a mixed dozen of snickerdoodle cookies and red velvet cupcakes, Lola's favorites.

"Come on in, I'll make us some coffee. Jackson's out," Mira said. "I'll tell Lola you're here, though I can't guarantee she'll come down. She's pretty upset about Charlie."

"Well, she has every right." Helen stood in the entryway and watched Mira sprint up the broad curved staircase to the second floor and knock on Lola's bedroom door. Instead of her usual designer getup, she was barefoot, wearing jeans and a frayed blue-and-white-striped man's shirt that looked so much like one of Henry's Helen felt her stomach heave. *Stop it*, she warned herself, the shirt obviously belongs to Jackson. Still, with her long red hair loose and unencumbered by gunk or flattened by one of those hot irons, Mira looked like a paler, skinnier version of her old self. Which cheered Helen, in spite of the troubling scene with Lucie earlier, not to mention her guilt for letting Jonah take Charlie home without first telling Lola.

Most Sundays, she got up for the first few bakes but arranged staffing so she and Lola could spend the afternoon together. While Mira and Jackson ran around to open houses, Helen and

Lola took Charlie on walks up in the hills or along the river, and sometimes they went to a movie or a museum. But when Helen spoke to Lola over the phone Saturday night and carelessly mentioned that Charlie was sleeping over at Jonah's and would be spending Sunday with him, Lola grew hysterical and hung up on her. Mira had called early this morning to say that Lola was refusing to leave the house.

"The market's dried up, so regardless of what Jackson says, it doesn't matter if I stand around all day pouring prosecco and looking like Barbie. No one's buying and I'm staying home with her," Mira added.

Helen had been struck by her candor. She couldn't tell if it was because of the talks they'd had recently about why Helen had cut her hair, or her admission to Lola that her papa was dead. And that was before Jonah showed up and bloody hell broke loose. Still, remembering how miserable Mira had been at their dinner a few months back, Helen wondered if something else was going on with her. Some internal shift making her more open than she'd been in a long time? Whatever the reason, Helen was thankful. She needed someone else in her life right now who had known and loved her son.

"LOLA SAID TO give you, and I'm quoting here, *the 411* that she *hates snickerdoodles and red velvet cupcakes,* and she's *never eating them again* in her *whole entire life,* even when she's *one hundred years old,*" Mira reported when she came downstairs.

They were in the kitchen, Helen seated on a stool at the long marble counter, shivering. She always forgot that Jackson insisted on keeping the AC set to freezing.

"She's upstairs playing with her American Girl dolls, something she hasn't done in a while. It's been a rough week, and I think she's just trying to absorb the news about her dad, plus what happened the other day with Jonah," Mira said, frothing milk for cappuccinos. "Anyway, my guess is that her *whole entire life* will last around ten more minutes. I've never known her to resist red velvet cupcakes."

"Letting Jonah take Charlie without telling her was a mistake," Helen said. "I haven't been thinking very clearly the past few days."

Mira set the cappuccinos on the counter. "Lola is just hurting and confused. I'm kind of confused myself. So what do you think?"

"About Jonah?" Helen shrugged.

"I saw a TV show a few months ago about this little boy who insisted he was a fighter pilot in World War Two," Mira said, resting her elbows on the counter opposite Helen. "He said he was killed when his plane was shot down by the Japanese. I don't remember much else about it, except this doctor who studies kids with memories like his checked out his story. Supposedly, the boy had all the details right, down to the guy's name and where he was from. Jackson thought it was a bunch of hooey, but watching it gave me chills. So maybe what Jonah says is true."

"Interesting." Helen wiped the froth from the corners of her mouth, then fished a book out of her bag. "Lucie stopped by this morning and gave me this." She handed Mira the copy of *Children Who Remember Previous Lives*. "She wants to know if I'd be willing to meet with some psychiatrist who works with these kids. Maybe it's the same guy you saw on TV. She thinks he might be able to help them sort out what's going on with Jonah. And if he meets with them, she thinks he'll want to talk to me, too."

"What did you tell her?"

"Nothing definite yet, but I'm leaning toward saying no. Maybe that's selfish, but I'm just starting to grow back a thin layer of skin and I'm afraid if I say yes I'll be ripped open again."

"Are you sure? Because what if talking to this doctor and hearing what else Jonah has to say helps you get some clarity? What if he knows what happened to Henry?"

"Oh, sweetheart, if he does, maybe, but what are the chances of that? I don't think we'll ever know. Anyway, I think the time has come for me to stop putting what's left of my life on hold trying to find out." Helen stirred the dregs of her cappuccino with a finger. "Also," she added, "I've met someone. A man. It's still early days, but . . ."

"Helen, really? That's wonderful, I'm so . . . oh." Mira stood up straight and cleared her throat. When Helen turned around, she saw Lola in full mermaid regalia wobbling toward them, her tail dragging behind her.

"Mommy, can I have my cupcake now?"

Mira and Helen watched as Lola demolished one cupcake, then another, her face turning into an abstract painting, cream cheese frosting spread across her nose, mouth, and cheeks. When she reached for a snickerdoodle, Mira stopped her and wiped her down with a damp napkin.

Then Lola, who had pointedly been ignoring Helen, shot up into her lap, winding her arms around Helen's neck and burying her face against her shoulder.

"I am so sorry, love," Helen whispered. "I should have told you I let Jonah borrow Charlie for the weekend."

"Uh," Lola grunted, slapping the stool with her tail.

"How about next Sunday we take him to that park you love with all the sculptures, then go to Holy Cow for mint chip?"

"Next Sunday is the Fourth," said Mira. "I promised Jackson we'd ride in the parade."

"Well okay, then Monday the fifth." Helen kissed Lola's hair, which smelled of chlorine laced with sweat.

"Charlie is *my* dog. Mine and Papa's. He's not Jonah's, right?"

"Yes, he was yours long before he met Jonah," Helen said, trying to be diplomatic without lying. Even if Jonah's "memories" turned out to be false, she didn't question the bond between the boy and the dog. As for Lola, Charlie was more of a symbol to her than a beloved companion. Most of the time when she was at Helen's, she ignored him.

She gave Lola a squeeze as the girl wriggled out of her grasp and hopped off the stool. Watching her readjust her mermaid tail, Helen was glad that after venting their anger, children were naturally so forgiving, so naked in their need to make sure they were still loved.

They were naked in their honesty, too. Lola looked up at Helen and made a face. "You should wear lipstick, Oma, otherwise your bald hair makes you look like a boy."

"Lola!" Mira snapped.

Helen laughed. "Like a pretty old boy, huh?"

"We're going for a swim. Why don't you join us? I can loan you a suit," Mira said, then turned to her daughter. "Ready to jump in the pool, Miss Mouthy?"

"Duh." Lola waddled off to collect the plastic fin that fit inside her tail.

"You enjoy the time with Lola," Helen said, picking up the reincarnation book. "But thank you for listening, you're the only one I can talk to about this." *Something that might not have been possible even a month ago,* she thought, recalling again how tense and weepy Mira had been at the Japanese restaurant. Helen was tempted to ask what was going on, why the sudden openness, but knew from past experience it might only make her shut down again. Still, halfway out the front door, there was one question she had to ask. "That shirt you're wearing, is it . . . ?"

"It is," said Mira, stroking a length of the faded blue-and-white-striped cotton. "I grabbed it the day we moved out of your house, but I never wore it until today. I hope it's not upsetting you to see me in it."

"Oh no," said Helen, smiling. "Not a bit."

WHEN JACKSON ROLLED in around nine thirty, Mira had just tucked Lola into bed and was seated at the kitchen counter enjoying a red velvet cupcake.

He hung over her, huffing and snorting before he said, "I thought you swore off carbs."

"Yeah, well, I'm revisiting that decision," she said, holding up the box of cookies and cupcakes without looking at him. "Want one?"

"You know I don't eat that shit. And I don't want you eating it either. Sugar causes cancer. Boom, and you're dead." He punched his fist into his palm to drive the point home. "I don't want you getting sick, babe. I couldn't deal if something bad happened to you."

Mira turned her head to the side so the hot, drunken kiss aimed at her mouth landed just below her ear. She was about to say something about the sugar content in alcohol but decided not to go there. He was already annoyed at her for bailing on today's open house. "There's leftover pizza in the fridge, in case you're hungry."

"Pizza? You ordered pizza, too?" Jackson opened the refrigerator and pulled out a Sam Adams, then sat down on the stool next to her. "I'm glad you and Lola got to spend a nice day together carbo-loading, but I really could have used you at Bella Vista. Without you, baby, nada." He took a long swig of beer.

"No bites, huh?" Mira carried the plate with the empty cupcake wrapper over to the sink and started loading the dishwasher.

"As a matter of fact, I did get one. Some optometrist from New York I met at Humpty's. He seemed pretty jacked up about buying a house, so I gave him my card. We'll probably hear from him, maybe even tomorrow. Didn't you rent Irene's old dump to some New York doctor? I think this might be the same guy."

"What's his name?"

"I don't know. Matt something. I didn't catch his last name. But baby, you want to hear something really weird? He told me his kid thinks he used to live around here in a past life. Reminded me of that hoax TV show we saw. You know anything about this?"

Mira shrugged. Her back was to him and she was glad he couldn't see her face. She was shocked that Lucie's husband mentioned Jonah to a stranger in a bar. Especially this stranger, and in a dive like Humpty's.

"Because the funny part is, the kid seems to think his mother from his previous life owns a bakery in town. And you'll never guess which one. The Queen of Fucking Hearts. Did Helen say anything about that when she delivered the truckload of shit?"

"Hmm, that does sound like it might be the people renting Irene's house. They're a nice family. Lola's had a few playdates with the boy. She likes him. He's a little younger and lets her boss him around, her favorite kind of playmate," Mira said, sponging off the counter. "Did the dad say any more?"

"Nah, just the thing about the bakery. Does Helen know about this?"

"I don't think so. She didn't mention it." Mira was aware of how easily the lies flew out of her mouth. She'd once tried tracing time in reverse to figure out when lying had become her default survival strategy. Maybe around the same time she started hiding her birth control pills, after promising him she'd stopped taking them? Which was around the same time he started drinking heavily. She couldn't remember the exact timeline, because for the first two years of the marriage, she'd been like a lump of wet clay, letting him remake her into an image that sprang from his fucked-up mind but had less and less to do with her. Until she all but vanished. Like Henry.

"Yeah, well, I forbid Lola to play with that kid ever again," Jackson was saying. "He sounds mental and I don't want our precious pumpkin exposed. Grab me another beer, will you, baby?" he said, his words turning to slush.

Mira didn't move. She waited a minute, then said, "Jackson, number one, Jonah is not mentally ill. Number two, even if he were, mental illness is not contagious. And number three, don't you think you've had enough to drink for one night?"

His head was drooping and would soon make a crash landing on the counter. He was one of those drunks who never seem tipsy until they collapse.

It was getting worse. His drunkenness. The threat of violence. At first, she'd tried to rationalize it: the downturn in the real estate market, the fact that the business was on life support. If he hadn't turned into such a controlling asshole, she might feel sorry for him. She might even try to help him come up with a plan to turn things around. Sell the house, whatever. But now she needed to come up with a plan B for herself and Lola. Just thinking about leaving him lifted her spirits. Clearly that, not drugs, was the cure for her depression. With him passed out on the counter, she fished the unopened bottle of Wellbutrin from her purse that her internist had just prescribed and washed the little orange tablets down the garbage disposal. Then she went outside.

The sensation of heat on her skin, the warmth of the stone underfoot, was such a relief from the icy tundra indoors that it felt like a homecoming to her own body. She stretched out on a wicker chaise facing the firepit and the arbor beyond, where she and Jackson had stood nearly three years before, vowing to share their deepest truth with one another.

Not.

Over the last few months, as she sank deeper into a depression that made her body feel as if it were coming apart bone by bone, Mira sometimes wondered if her psychological withdrawal was a sign of true clinical depression or just another survival strategy, like the way snapping turtles retreat into their shells and pretend to be rocks when under attack by predators.

She gazed up at the night sky. Vega had just made its showy appearance, followed by Deneb and Altair—the "summer triangle." Henry had been a devoted stargazer and spent hours teaching her the constellations during their last summer together, when she was near to bursting with Lola. Mira had forgotten most of what he'd taught her, but those three had stuck. Vega. Deneb. Altair. Still up there, burning bright, but no Henry by her side to marvel at them with her.

Most of the time she didn't let herself imagine what life with Henry—with Henry and Lola—would have been like. It made her too sad. She might not have stopped painting, and who knows, maybe if she'd kept at it, a decent gallery would have taken her on. Henry would have had his music, and even if the band never scored a big record deal, he would have been happy. He was like that. His childhood had been harsh. "After that," he told her, "everything else is Christmas morning."

Was. Was Christmas morning. For her, too. With him.

"Where oh where are you, Henry?" Mira directed the question to the stars.

Though Helen questioned the whole concept of reincarnation, Mira was a believer. There was something in Jonah's manner, the wide-open look in his blue eyes, the sweet air about him that conjured Henry, even if he hadn't seemed to recognize her. *Yet.* Mira had a soft spot for discarnate beings. She often sensed her dead father nearby, trying to protect her. Maybe this thing with Jonah was a sign that Henry was there too, looking out for them all. Bring it on, she thought, because something in her was waking up that had long been dead. Just putting on Henry's old shirt today had made her feel more alive. So did defying Jackson by staying home, not to mention eating that red velvet cupcake and a couple slices of pizza, then washing the antidepressants down the drain.

She never should have married him. Her body had tried to warn her. But instead of listening to the spasms in her gut, she went on a bland diet and ignored the fact that, sooner or later, Jackson was likely to behave as her husband the same way he'd behaved as her boyfriend in high school. He wanted her too much. Worshipped her too much. Tried every which way to control her. Even though he'd managed to keep his possessiveness in check until after the wedding, she should have known better.

The corner of her mouth felt raw. She could feel the cold sore coming. She may have married the guy for all the wrong reasons, but back then she wasn't sure what else to do. How long could she and Lola keep living above the bakery with her not-quite-mother-in-law? Mira loved Helen, but she was afraid to turn into her: a single mom waking up at four every morning to turn on the ovens, then spending the day wrestling mounds of dough into submission. At the time, Mira was considering a move to New York or Boston, then going back to school and getting a degree in studio art, but how could she do that and support Lola? Besides, how could she take Lola away from her Oma? She didn't think Helen could withstand another devastating loss. And if Mira were being completely honest, she would have had to admit that Helen was more of a co-parent than the average nana who babysits once in a while.

Mira's future had been a great big question mark the day Jackson came strutting back into her life. Of course she'd seen him over the years, in the bakery or driving his shiny Range Rover around town. He'd even been on the front lines in the search for Henry. From a distance, Mira had watched as he transformed himself from a cocky teenager into a construction jock and, later, a player in the local real estate market.

The day he dropped by the bakery toting an armload of yellow tulips and asked her to join him for a glass of wine at 212North, she figured, what the hell. Maybe he really had grown up. He certainly looked grown up. Taking in his neatly cropped hair and beard and a look that was still more cowboy than businessman but appealing in its cleaned-up way, she said yes to the drink. A week later, she said yes to dinner. She was skittish about getting involved with him, but he continued to remain on his best behavior. Solicitous without being pushy, sweet to Lola, more relaxed and self-confident than she'd ever seen him, staying off the heavy sauce. A couple of months in, he offered to help her get her real estate license—a career move that would free her from the bakery until she could get back to painting. She wasn't wildly in love with the guy, but she liked him okay, especially since he'd upgraded his skills as a lover since they fumbled around as teenagers. Besides, Mira was certain she'd never feel the same uncontrolled heat for any man that she'd felt for Henry, so why not? She convinced herself that her feelings for Jackson fell into the category of adult romance, the sort of relationship that involved compromise and acceptance of one another's imperfections. Finally, after a year of being seduced with Michelin-star dinners, horseback-riding lessons for Lola, and trips to exotic islands, as well as a five-thousand-square-foot "dream house" built especially for her—with a separate painting studio to come—she said yes to marrying him.

Shivering though it was balmy out, she remembered Helen once telling her that she felt as though she'd been in so much denial when she was with Henry's father, she might as well have had a lobotomy. Lucky for her, the lobotomy turned out be reversible and she'd escaped with Henry.

Now Mira just had to figure out how to escape with Lola without getting maimed in the process. It was hard to know the lengths to which Jackson's obsession with her might take him.

First, she just had to get through the Fourth of July. Ride in the damn parade.

She gazed skyward. The early-to-rise summer triangle was smothered amid a web of brother and sister constellations, but in spite of Henry's patient tutorials, apart from the Big and Little Dippers, she could not name a single one.

I was starting to get really pissed. It seemed like everybody and their grandmother, including a boatload of grandmothers, was allowed to get out of this place.

Everybody except me.

That sweet old Japanese lady hoping to make it across some river? Gone. And the kid from Bolivia's mother must have finally washed and burned his clothes, because he's history, too. Ditto, that annoying dude from California who kept saying, "It's the bardo, stupid!" Well, he took off, along with that cute Indian girl with the ponytail and so many others, coming and going all the time.

But I'm still stuck here, even though I now have a pretty good idea why. So I should be able to make a break for it too, right?

Wrong. Not happening.

Then I thought, okay, if I just can find the entity or spirit-in-chief or whoever the hell is in charge and explain my situation, they'll let me go. So I kept asking everyone, even the new arrivals, who's the head honcho? What do I have to do, who do I have to sleep with (haha) to be able to move on? I asked and asked, but nobody could tell me.

That's when I started to get it. No one is in charge. There's no big cheese, no CEO, no sheriff, not even a rookie traffic cop to show me the way out.

My only hope is that when the time is right, the exit will appear.

PART FIVE

SUMMER 2010

THIRTY-TWO

"WHEN WAS THE FIRST TIME JONAH SAID ANYTHING THAT STRUCK you as unusual?" asked Ben Skinner, the tall, gawky, past-life expert from Minneapolis. Wearing a blue work shirt and wrinkled khakis, topped by salt-and-pepper hair and a beard—both of which could use a trim—he could easily be mistaken for a middle-age graduate student or bookstore clerk instead of a renowned child psychiatrist with a formidable pedigree.

"And Jonah, please, jump in any time." The man who had studied under the late Dr. Stevenson smiled through large wire-rimmed glasses. "I really want to hear what you have to say. And just so you know, I've talked to lots of kids who remember being someone else before they were born."

Jonah, apparently transfixed by the twirling blades on his Lego helicopter, didn't look up. He sat scrunched between Lucie and Matt on the worn denim sofa in their rented living room. Across from them, Dr. Skinner was seated in a matching club chair. His two tape recorders—"Just in case," he'd explained—lay on the coffee table next to a platter of breakfast pastries from the Queen of Hearts.

"Well, there were quite a few things, but Daddy and I thought you were making them up, didn't we, Bear?" Lucie said, trying to involve Jonah in a conversation that until a few days ago would have seemed unimaginable. "You talked about your mom and a dog, which we thought you invented. But we were wrong about that, weren't we?" Lucie paused, giving Jonah a chance to chime in. When he didn't, she said to Skinner, "Also, when Jonah was a toddler, he had strong reactions to loud noises, and the night terrors started when he was four, but we didn't connect any of that to"—she waved her hands in the air—"well, *this*."

"Whatever *this* is," added Matt.

"If it's any consolation," said Skinner, "the last thing most parents consider is that their child's behavior might be influenced by memories from a previous lifetime. That concept doesn't exist in the West, and goodness knows, you won't find any mention of it in the DSM."

"Yeah, they skipped that part in *What to Expect When You're Expecting*, too," Lucie said, trying to keep the mood light. "And well, looking back, there were lots of other things. Like the summer when Jonah was two. We were in Maine with Matt's family and Jonah's Aunt Audrey gave him a stuffed dog he named Jolly. We thought he picked the name because he loved his cousins' collie. Collie, Jolly, it sounded the same to us in toddlerspeak." She turned to Jonah. "We didn't get that you were trying to name your stuffie *Charlie*, did we?"

"That's because I couldn't say my *r*'s. I was just a baby," Jonah said, looking up, then returning to his helicopter.

"I bet you were surprised this summer when you met up with the real Charlie?" Dr. Skinner asked.

"Yeah, but only a little because I know him from before," said Jonah.

"What about the dog thing?" Matt, master of the single arched eyebrow, asked the psychiatrist. "It's nice that Jonah and

Charlie have bonded, but the first time he saw that dog was just a week ago."

"I have to admit the dog is a fascinating new piece for me. But maybe it's not so far out of the box as it seems. Animals, as we know, have sensory capabilities that far exceed those of humans."

"Hmm," Matt murmured.

Jonah grabbed a chocolate croissant from the platter. "This is my second," he told the psychiatrist, popping the crusty end in his mouth, crumbs raining down on his faded T. rex tee. "The lady who used to be my mom makes them, but I don't help her because she's not my mom anymore. *She* is." He poked Lucie's arm.

Though typically shy around strangers, Jonah seemed to be warming to Dr. Skinner. His manner was so mild, his voice so soothing, he reminded Lucie of a gangly Mister Rogers, minus the cardigan—a refreshing contrast to most of the nerdy researchers she'd interviewed over the years, who seemed to care only about their data. And maybe Jonah was finally starting to feel safe enough to talk about what he remembered—and no doubt would have done so long ago had she and Matt not stifled him.

Matt was even more surprised than Lucie by Jonah's openness. As a man of science, he accepted that all matter in the universe was recycled and that human bodies were part stardust and all that. But he remained skeptical about the credibility of past lives, even if Skinner's research was funded by a major university.

LUCIE HAD EMAILED Ian Stevenson's successor, Dr. Jim Tucker, right after Matt showed her Jonah's drawing of the stick man in what was obviously an open grave. Dr. Tucker was out of the country, but his assistant sent her a few names, including that of Dr. Skinner. Lucie reached out to him, and after hearing her account of recent events, he suggested that in order to help clarify what was going on, he'd need to interview Jonah, as well as Lucie, Matt, and hopefully Helen—in situ, the sooner the better, since Jonah's memories had been flooding back since coming to Aurora Falls. Matt had rescheduled a whole roster of patients so he could be in situ for the interview.

OVER THE PHONE the night before their meeting, Matt questioned the wisdom of having Jonah present. Dr. Skinner explained that secrecy was unnecessary, since Jonah was the one with the memories. "He already knows more about the previous personality than anyone. And if you can listen without judgment to what he remembers, the better for him. As with any trauma, the key to healing is being heard and believed. A girl I worked with who recalled drowning in a previous life is no longer afraid of taking a bath or going for a swim. I encourage you to trust the process."

"As a physician, I rely on treatments whose efficacy has been established in randomized controlled trials. How can we be sure that the source of Jonah's"—Matt cleared his throat—"*difficulties* came from a previous life?"

"Point taken," Dr. Skinner replied. "It's also true that many protocols in medicine are effective, but *how* they work is often a mystery. In our area as in yours, the accumulation of evidence is key. We conduct controlled tests in which the children being studied are shown a variety of objects—some belonging to the previous personality, others not—and the kids are asked to choose the right ones. That's one way we gather evidence."

"That may be, but since Jonah has already been to—what did you call him?—the *previous personality*'s home and identified his dog and a number of other objects, how can your sample be clean?" Matt pressed.

The point was to help Jonah, not engage in a pissing contest over scientific protocols, and Lucie had had it with her husband's pigheadedness. Dr. Skinner was more generous. "Because every situation is different, depending on the child's exposure to the previous environment, we take pains to collect as much information as possible from multiple sources," he explained. "With some children the evidence is so strong that the most plausible explanation is that the memories have somehow—and we don't claim to know how—been transferred from the consciousness of a deceased person to the consciousness of a child. But unlike ordinary memories, which get revised over time, these memories generally remain stable in the child's mind until sooner or later they fade away."

"That fits. Jonah's description of the yellow house, his mom, and the dog have been consistent ever since he started talking about them years ago, and we look forward to seeing you tomorrow," Lucie said, ending the discussion before Matt could voice any further objections.

MATT KNEW HE'D been testy with the guy over the phone and had promised Lucie to be more agreeable in person. "And when Jonah was three, there was the thing with the violin," he said.

"Daddy, I told you I could play. Maybe not perfect but *good*." Jonah turned to Skinner and added, "I already knew how when I lived here. Not *here* here"—he motioned to the cottage—"but with my old mom. At the bakery. Not *in* the bakery, but over it. Only it was yellow then, not blue. And I was Danny and Charlie was Charlie and my old mom was my mom, but now she says her son was Henry. I don't know why, do you?"

"No, I don't, Jonah. But there must be a good reason. We'll ask her about that." Skinner scribbled something in his notebook.

This wasn't the first time Matt had heard Jonah mention the discrepancy in the names, and he had his own theory. "Jonah's middle name is Daniel, after my grandfather, so that must be why he's confused."

"I am not confused. Not *this* Daniel," Jonah said, rapping his fingers against his chest like a bongo drum. "The *other* one. From before."

"As you said on the phone, memory is nothing if not capricious," Matt suggested.

"True, but memory is also highly selective, as I'm sure you know. The amygdala tends to lay down memories that have a strong emotional association, such as fear. In most cases, we find there's a reason why kids get the names of people and places mixed up."

Skinner turned to Jonah and smiled.

Looking directly at him, Jonah said in a voice that was just above a whisper, "I remember how I died. When I was big and the wolf killed me."

Lucie and Matt locked eyes. The wolf? What wolf? This was the first they'd heard of any wolf.

But Dr. Skinner didn't miss a beat. In his smooth Mister Rogers voice, he said, "That's wonderful that you remember that, Jonah. Just wonderful. Can you tell me more?"

Jonah looked from Lucie to Matt, as if seeking their permission to go on, then settled his gaze on Skinner. "He took me in his truck because it was raining and dark out and then we drove and drove. It was raining hard with a big thunder and lightning." His words started coming faster. "And then all the sudden I was in the woods, like a big forest. And I had to walk, and the thunder got bigger and the lightning and I was all wet. There was nobody there except me and the wolf and he was pushing me with his gun."

"That must have been so scary," Skinner said. "And you had no way to escape, did you? It wasn't your fault that you couldn't get away."

Jonah was digging the plastic blades of his helicopter into his palm. "It was really *really* scary. I just wanted to go home, but I couldn't. The wolf wouldn't let me."

Lucie longed to fold Jonah in her arms but held back. If the key to healing trauma was reliving the shock and terror in a safe space, she'd do her best to stay out of his way. But not Matt. He couldn't keep his mouth shut.

"Jonah," Matt said, "do you want to keep talking about this? You can stop any time."

"I am not finished," Jonah said, his gaze still directed at Skinner. The next part tumbled out almost in a single breath. "I wanted to run away so bad because I could tell the wolf was going to shoot me, but I couldn't. And I felt really sad, 'cause I didn't want to go. But then he pushed me in the hole with my face in the dirt and I heard this big POW POW so loud, and then something hit me . . ." Tears raining down his cheeks, Jonah fingered the birthmark at the base of his skull. "Here. And then all the sudden I was flying up in the wavy trees and I wasn't scared anymore but I was really sad. And mad. I didn't want to go."

Lucie let out a little whimper, then covered her mouth. How could a mother comfort a child who had experienced trauma in a previous lifetime? A boy who remembered being marched to his death and murdered? Yet as chilling as it was to hear Jonah's description of being killed, Lucie's thoughts flew to Helen, who still didn't know what had happened to her son. Helen, who would never again see, touch, kiss, smell, breathe in the molecules that were Henry—or Danny—while Lucie and Matt had Jonah, the miraculous fact and flesh of him.

"After I died, I picked you to be my mom and my dad. From the sky," Jonah said, curling himself into a ball in Lucie's lap. She blotted his wet cheeks with a tissue, then kissed his golden curls.

"And you were just the boy we were waiting for," Matt said. His voice sounded as if he'd swallowed broken glass.

After a few minutes, Dr. Skinner said softly, "Just so you know, Jonah, lots of kids who remember another life talk about being up in the sky and finding their parents that way. But not every mom and dad are lucky enough to learn that their child chose them. That's pretty special."

Hearing that seemed to help Jonah relax.

"I'd like to ask you a couple of questions. Is that okay with you?"

Still curled in Lucie's arms, Jonah nodded.

"When you say the wolf killed you, you seem to be talking about a man. I'm wondering why you call him the wolf."

"I don't know," Jonah said. "It just came out. But it was a man."

"Do you think this man was someone you knew?"

Jonah wrinkled his brow. "I think maybe, but I don't really remember. I'm sorry."

"No need to apologize. Very often, these old pictures we carry around in our mind are fuzzy and we can't remember all the details. Especially when what happened was so scary." Skinner leaned closer to Jonah. "Do you know if the place where you were killed when you were Danny was familiar to you, somewhere you'd been before?"

"No, it was just some forest place and I couldn't really see because it was so dark out."

"Last one," Skinner said, asking the question that had been haunting Lucie since that day at Helen's, making her heart rate quicken and her muscles cramp, but that was so terrifying she hadn't let herself dwell on it. "Have you seen this wolf man since you've been in Aurora Falls?"

"Nope." With that, Jonah shot out of Lucie's lap like a missile, nearly knocking the plate of pastries to the floor. "Now can we go get Charlie, Daddy? Please!"

As PROMISED, THE minute Jonah said he'd had enough, Matt—who was more than ready to blow this surreal tribunal—took him to fetch Charlie from Helen.

Dr. Skinner stayed behind to pack up his gear. "You okay?" he asked Lucie.

She clasped her hands. They felt like ice packs. "I'm not sure *okay* is the right word for how I feel. I keep thinking, if only we hadn't rented a house up here, Jonah wouldn't be going through this." Lucie wished she could undo that decision. If they hadn't taken this place, they'd soon be off to Maine with Matt's family and she'd be miserable, but it would be ordinary misery. Eventually Jonah would forget that he ever had another mother. Another life. Suffered a gruesome death. And, Lucie thought selfishly, she wouldn't have to deal with it either.

"From my perspective, you and your husband did a good thing by bringing Jonah here, even though you had no idea what you were getting yourselves into. Because it's clear he has unfinished business. Recalling the painful memories near where they took place should help him work through them."

"God, I hope so."

"We may never solve the mystery of how one person's memories show up in the mind of another, but we do know that it happens most often when the previous person died violently. Like

Jonah, some of the kids I've worked with had an urgent need to complete the earlier life cycle before they could let it go. But as soon as they had permission to express what they remembered, the memories began to lose their power, their actual stickiness in the brain, until eventually they seemed as ordinary and forgettable as last Thanksgiving dinner at Grandma's."

"To quote my nana, from your lips to God's ears," said Lucie. "I just hope that tomorrow at Helen's, Jonah won't have to describe getting killed again. For her sake, as well as his. To be honest, I'm surprised she agreed to be part of this."

"At first she hesitated, but then she decided she might learn something about what happened to her son. She also told me she hopes to be able to help Jonah. And you, Mrs. Pressman." Dr. Skinner slid his recorders and notebook into his rolling briefcase, then zipped it shut. "When I meet with her this afternoon, I'll play her the tape of today's session. I expect she'll need time to digest it."

"Thank you," said Lucie. "And I need to ask. Have you ever had a case where the killer was still around? Where a child was threatened because of his memories?" She made no effort to keep the panic out of her voice.

Dr. Skinner took off his glasses and wiped the steamy lenses with a paper napkin. "I know of no child who's ever been threatened or harmed because of his memories. And since Jonah's recall of the young man's murder is so fragmented, the way it often is with trauma, it would be virtually impossible for him to identify the killer, especially since he refers to him in classic archetypal terms: *the wolf.*" He rolled his briefcase to the front door, then turned and said, "Mrs. Pressman, in my opinion you have absolutely nothing to worry about."

As soon he was out the door, Lucie spit over her left shoulder. Twice.

THIRTY-THREE

"WOLF, TRUCK, RAINY NIGHT? GETTING SHOT IN A FOREST?"
Will shook his head when the tape was finished. "Petunia, even
if we give the kid the benefit of the doubt and believe what he's
saying, what do we got?"

"I know it sounds vague, but it's something, Will, *something*,"
said Helen. "More than we had before."

The detective sighed. "It ain't much more. We knew eight
years ago it was a rainy night when Henry disappeared. So the
only new information, if it isn't all made up, is that the guy
he hitched a ride with drove a truck. Which, for all we know,
he drove straight to Montana or Canada, someplace where there
are a lot of forests with wolves running around. Or maybe the
guy had a wolf tattoo. Who the hell knows? But Danny? Why
does the kid keep calling him Danny? How do we even know he's
talking about Henry?"

Helen felt her heart pinballing around in her chest. She'd
been so stunned by hearing the boy's account of being murdered,
she borrowed the tape from Dr. Skinner and rushed right over
to the station, thinking: Will needs to hear this, too. Without
considering the fallout.

"I'm just trying to get my bearings after listening to the tape,"
she mumbled.

"I can see that. What happened to the mop?" Will motioned to her shorn head.

"I had it chopped off," Helen said, relieved to delay the inevitable grilling over the names. "Right before Henry's thirtieth birthday. Well, what would have been. You look different, too."

Will patted his chest. "Got the old ticker upgraded. They put in a pacemaker and a couple of stents, so now I have to eat bird food."

Helen realized she hadn't seen him at the bakery since he returned the address book more than a month ago. He must have dropped at least fifteen pounds, his droopy jowls a testament to the fact that the fruit cobblers he used to devour whole were no longer part of his "health" regimen.

"Well, I'm glad you're okay," she said.

"And hey, I like the new look. But come on, kid. Henry. Danny. What's with the names?"

Secrets were toxic, Helen understood that now. But a quarter of a century ago, when Kip threatened to kill her if she ever tried to leave him, secrecy was her protection—hers and Danny's—and she'd clung to it for so long she'd almost come to accept it as the truth. But now she felt her face grow hot, flushed with shame as she backtracked through history and explained how Danny came to be Henry.

"Jesus mother, Helen. Or whoever the hell you are." Will practically spit out the words.

"Alice. I used to be Alice," she said, looking at her flour-stained palms. "It became automatic for me to call him Henry around other people and Danny at home. I thought it was important for us to remember our real names. And who we were and where we came from and why we had to leave."

"But you didn't think it was important to tell the detective investigating Henry's—pardon me, Danny's—disappearance the truth? What if your psycho husband had kidnapped him? What then?" Will was looking at her with such undisguised fury, Helen wouldn't have been surprised if he locked her up for obstruction of justice.

"It wasn't a total lie. Henry and Helen were our middle names. We just switched them around and picked a new last name. Well, Danny did. From the time he was little, he always loved birds." Helen had seen the blustery detective lash out plenty of times, but never at her. "I shouldn't have lied to you, Will, but I was scared that if I told the truth, somehow word would get out and Kip would find me. Or if you knew about our past, it would muck up the investigation. It wasn't rational, but I wasn't thinking very clearly when Danny disappeared. But just so you don't think I'm totally irresponsible, I hired a couple of private investigators in Oregon to make sure he wasn't with Kip. And then I went out there myself a few years back to make double sure."

"I *trusted* you," Will said.

Helen forced herself to meet Will's gaze. "Everything else I told you was true. And everything that little boy said on the tape is true. Not about being killed, I don't know about that, but the rest. When he came over the other day, he knew it was him, Danny—Henry—in the photographs. Plus, the whole business with the dog. What if he knows something about what happened to my son? Shouldn't we try to find out?"

Making her case to Will now, Helen felt the same hollow sensation in her chest that she'd felt at her wedding when her father, in her eyes as principled a lawyer as Atticus Finch, told her how disappointed he was in her for marrying that "no-good, bloodsucking worm." She had hotly protested and didn't speak to him for a year, but of course he was right. As Will was now. Did she really think he could solve the riddle of her son's disappearance based on Jonah's vague comments about how he'd died? The man was a detective, not a wizard.

"Jesus H. Goddamn Christ, Petunia," Will said, just when she thought he might never speak to her again. "You're lucky I almost croaked. Because, without going into the gory details, if I hadn't had a little near-death experience of my own, I don't think I could ever forgive you. But I got lucky and so did you, because I'm not going to prosecute. Or kick you out of here on your sorry ass and scare you into never coming back. But since I now know what a genius you are at keeping secrets, I'd appreciate it if you kept your trap shut about what I just told you. I don't want any of our local citizens getting the idea that I've gone soft."

"I'm so sorry, Will. I never should have lied to you."

"Stop. Enough with the mea culpas, you obviously did what you thought was right, as dumbass as it was. And what the hell, if the kid comes up with anything real, any names or places, you let me know."

It wasn't until Will stood that Helen saw his shrunken frame. He looked like a clothes tree with a pot belly.

"Thank you, my friend," she said softly.

She could feel his eyes on her back as she let herself out.

THIRTY-FOUR

So, AS I EXPLAINED YESTERDAY, WE'RE GOING TO KEEP TODAY'S session easy peasy," Dr. Skinner said, taking in the alarmed expressions on the faces greeting him in Helen's living room: The grieving mother, who had only just learned the details of her missing son's fate. The boy's mother, who seemed to believe her son but appeared both worried and threatened by his revelations. The doctor/dad who distrusted the whole idea of past-life memories because they can't be confirmed in controlled trials. (Skinner was sympathetic. He used to be in denial, too, before his daughter Jenny's memories turned his own mind inside out.) Then there was Jonah, the central character in the unfolding drama, clearly concerned about upsetting his parents and no doubt his "old mom," too.

"Jonah, you may recognize some objects but not others," said Dr. Skinner, bending his frame into a shape that resembled a shepherd's crook to get closer to the boy's level. "Or you might not recognize anything. And that's fine, too. There's no right or wrong, no way you can make a mistake. On the other hand," he added, straightening up and addressing the adults, "we're going to keep things as easy on Jonah as possible. So, please, no suggestions, comments, or questions until after he's had a chance to explore and see what, if anything, he remembers."

"Don't forget, you can stop any time," Matt said, tousling Jonah's hair. "No pressure."

Jonah nodded, staring down at the zigzags on his sneakers. He could feel the grown-ups' eyes stuck on him like superglue, not a feeling he enjoyed. He couldn't wait to get back to Charlie, who was still over at their house, because Dr. Skinny said he couldn't come to the meeting. Like the dog might give him some big hint or something. Anyhow, if there really was *no pressure*, why did he have that awful tickle in his stomach?

Across the room Helen leaned against the back of the sofa, feeling as if she might tip over. She'd gotten three, maybe four hours of sleep, and had been startled awake by a terrifying dream. But she couldn't let herself think about that right now, because the scene taking place in her living room was stranger than any of the scenarios she'd conjured in her head to explain her son's disappearance. She thought it might be good if she did topple over and blanked the whole thing out.

"So," Dr. Skinner asked Jonah in his Mister Rogers voice, "anything in particular you'd like to see?"

"My room," Jonah said, his gaze still directed at his sneakers.

Lucie hoped he hadn't noticed her flinch.

"I mean, my *old* room," he corrected himself.

"Can you show me where it is?" the psychiatrist said.

Jonah led the way out of the living room, past the kitchen and bathroom, and down the hall to the first bedroom on the right. "Here," he pointed. "This one."

"After you." Skinner motioned him into the room, then raised a hand like a school crossing guard, indicating to the others that they should remain in the hallway.

"Oh," Jonah said, taking in the giant stuffed mermaid on top of a pink quilt dotted with colorful pictures of Ariel, Sebastian the crab, and other characters from *The Little Mermaid*. "Where's my stuff?" He turned and glanced at Lucie. "I mean, that other boy's stuff."

"If I may," Helen interjected, violating Dr. Skinner's keep-mum policy that made sense for Jonah's parents, but not for her. Of course, Danny's stuff wasn't visible. She'd stored most of it in boxes years ago when she converted the room for Lola. But some of his things, the ones she couldn't bear to box up, she'd stashed in her father's ancient leather trunk that they'd hauled from Oregon, and that Lola insisted on keeping at the foot of her bed. Every year on Danny's birthday—until last year—Helen would remove each object from the trunk one by one, as if it were made of the most delicate crystal, then tell Lola the story behind it. And though after a year or two Lola could recite the stories word for word, she always wanted Helen to tell them again.

"Please." The psychiatrist nodded at Helen.

"You're right, Jonah, this room is different. I changed it for Lola, but if you're interested, you could take a peek inside that old leather trunk."

He knelt down, slowly cracked the lid of the trunk, then peered inside. "Yowza," he exhaled, in a sort of stage whisper. "My stuff."

This time, he didn't correct himself to spare his parents' feelings and say, *Danny's* stuff. This time, he looked at Helen, who pressed her lips together and nodded.

"Gosh," Jonah said, pulling out a warped violin. "This is the one you got me at that store. When I was little."

"Thrift Town, over in Kingston," she said, gliding past Skinner. "That violin cost me a whole thirty-five dollars. I'd just started at the bakery, and we lived on toast and leftover pie for a week so I could pay for it. Little did I know you'd be so good."

She was aware of how effortlessly she and Jonah had shifted their pronouns from third person to first.

Jonah seemed to pick up on the switch, too. "I don't mean *me* me, Jonah," he mumbled in the direction of the hallway. "I mean, the other me. From before."

"I know, Bear, it's fine," said Lucie.

"Most kids who recall a past life refer to their former selves as 'me' or 'I' when they talk about that time," Dr. Skinner told Jonah. "It's perfectly normal." Then he crouched down next to the boy and said, "I bet you're seeing things you didn't even know you remembered until right now. Recognize anything else?"

"Yeah. My catcher's mitt." Jonah pulled a worn leather glove out of the trunk and slipped it on. "It's so *big*," he said, taking it off and setting it on the floor. "And whoa." He picked up a faded blue T-shirt and carefully opened it. Nestled inside was a mountain of baseball cards. Every Boston team from the infamous 1986 lineup when Bill Buckner blew the World Series, through 2002. Each set of cards had been carefully stored in its own plastic bag.

"Holy shit," Matt said, sticking his head into the room. He immediately put up his hands like a criminal under arrest. "Sorry."

"Please," Dr. Skinner said, his voice now sounding more like that of an exasperated middle school principal than Mister Rogers. "If you could keep your comments to yourself, you'll have a chance to weigh in later."

"I'm sorry, Dad," Jonah said, rifling through the sets. "I like the Mets, too. Pinky promise." He held out a pinky in Matt's direction without looking at him.

"It's okay, sport. No worries. It's only baseball." *Fuck*, Matt thought, the last thing he wanted was to make his son feel bad for liking the Red Sox, the way his own father had punished him for his devotion to the Mets. Could this be why Jonah had asked for the Boston hat when they went to spring training? Okay, so maybe he should stop being so suspicious of this whole past-life business, even if it could never be verified. But he was also sick of feeling like an asshole, when all he was doing was trying to protect his son. "Anyone like a glass of water?" he asked.

"Not now," Skinner said sharply. Helen shook her head *no*. Jonah didn't seem to register the question.

"No, thank you." Lucie was relieved when Matt went to get himself a drink. She just wished he'd calm down and accept what was happening so they could get past it. Not that she felt especially at ease herself. Watching Helen and Jonah interact like mother and son was making her skin twitch.

"What's all these?" Jonah was holding up two piles of envelopes bound together with red yarn, one pile in each hand. He glanced at Helen, who was seated on the edge of the girly mermaid quilt.

"Can *you* tell us what they are, Jonah?" Skinner asked.

"I don't know. Mail? Did I write them?" Again, he looked at Helen.

"You did," she said. Skinner raised a traffic-cop hand in her direction, but she ignored him. She didn't care about "keeping the investigation clean," as if they were mice in some ridiculous science experiment. She did, however, care about learning what had happened to her son, and if this little boy had any information, she needed to know what it was.

"One bunch are letters you wrote me from music camp when you were twelve and thirteen, and the others are letters you wrote to Mira. She left them here when she and Lola moved out."

"Mira?" Jonah asked. "You mean, Lola's mom? Why did I write her?"

"You don't remember?"

Jonah shook his head, which was starting to feel like it was filled with bugs.

"She was your girlfriend and she was pregnant with Lola when you . . . went away."

"Oh yeah, I sort of remember," said Jonah, brow wrinkled and lips pursed as he tried to fit the stray pieces of Danny's life together like a puzzle.

"Can you say more about that?" asked Dr. Skinner.

Jonah shrugged and began gnawing on a thumbnail.

"No problem," said the psychiatrist, "you may remember more later. But if there's nothing else in the trunk that interests you, I suggest we move on to another room."

"Just a minute, please. There's another T-shirt in there you might like to see," Helen told Jonah, expecting Skinner to scold her, surprised but thankful when he didn't.

The boy reached into the trunk and pulled out a neatly folded gray T-shirt. On the front was a rendering of a big black dog, with wings. He looked like he was flying.

"This one?" he asked.

"Yes. That one," Helen said. "Mira designed it."

"Oh." Jonah picked up the shirt and read the words spattered in bloodred letters beneath the flying dog. "Dog Radio. Was that my music band?"

"Yes, it was," said Helen, nodding.

"Charlie," Jonah whispered.

"Yep, that's Charlie all right," said Helen. "When he was younger. You can keep it, if you'd like."

Jonah glanced at Lucie, then dropped the shirt on the floor. "That's okay," he said.

Helen decided that as long as she'd already screwed up the interview, she might as well go for broke and show Jonah the one thing she was certain Danny would never forget. She reached into the trunk and pulled out Chester, his beloved sock puppet. "Recognize this guy?"

With a grin like a sudden burst of sunshine on a foggy day, Jonah took the ragged orange sock puppet from Helen, stuck his hand inside, and made swooping figure eights with it. Then just as suddenly, he yanked it off and handed it back to Helen. Then he turned to his parents and said, "Can we go home now? I miss Charlie."

"Sure," Lucie said, edging her way into the room.

His knees bright red from kneeling, Jonah stood and put his arms around Lucie's waist. "I'm hungry," he mumbled into her armpit. She took him by the hand, and they went into the living room, followed by Matt and Dr. Skinner.

Watching them leave, Helen realized that she'd drifted into a sort of reverie, back to a time when she was a mother with a son. As if this lovely little boy had once been her son. But that was a fantasy, a foolish fairy tale. Sock puppet still in hand, she sat down on the edge of the bed.

"WE'RE GOING TO get this boy some lunch," Matt said. "He's had enough."

"Understood," said Dr. Skinner. "Perhaps we could pick up this afternoon, after he's eaten and had a break." He looked at Jonah, who was still attached to Lucie. "What do you say?"

"We'll have to see. I'll let you know," Matt answered, in a tone that left no room for negotiation. "Ready to go, honey?"

"Wait. I forgot something." Jonah untangled himself from his mother and ran down the hall to the bedroom where Helen sat as still as a statue on the mermaid quilt.

Dr. Skinner, Lucie, and Matt stood clustered in the doorway and looked on as Jonah hopped up on the bed next to Helen, then got on his knees and whispered something in her ear. Like someone coming out of a trance, she turned and beamed at him, then stroked his cheek with the palm of her hand.

She could be heard saying *Thank you, thank you, thank you,* as if reciting a prayer.

And though for years afterward Lucie would replay the scene in her mind and try to guess, she would never ask and Jonah would never tell her what he'd whispered in Helen's ear on that sweltering summer's day.

BENJAMIN H. SKINNER, M.D.

LAKE HARRIET PROFESSIONAL BUILDING
11 LINDEN CIRCLE
MINNEAPOLIS, MN 55497

Preliminary Case Notes, July 3, 2010

Subject: Jonah Daniel Pressman, age 7

Interview dates: July 2 and 3, 2010

Persons interviewed: Jonah Pressman

Lucie Pressman, subject's mother

Matthew Pressman, subject's father

Helen Bird, mother of Henry Bird, aka Danny, missing
   since 8/31/2002

Interview scheduled: Miranda Brin, former fiancée of
   Henry Bird, July 5

Location: Aurora Falls, New York

SUMMARY

The case was brought to me by the subject's mother. She thought it likely that seven-year-old Jonah had "absorbed" the memories of a young man named Henry Bird. She was concerned about the impact of the memories on the boy's psyche. She'd already consulted a Tibetan Buddhist rinpoche whom she described as "very helpful" and who had lent her a copy of Dr. Stevenson's *Children Who Remember Previous Lives*. Since I trained with him, she hoped I could put her son's experience into a scientific context, especially for her husband's benefit.

Regarding the child's mental health, I assured her that among the 2,500-plus cases documented by Dr. Stevenson and other members of our team, there has been no higher incidence of psychological disorders than in the general population. Moreover, not only do the children in our research tend to be of superior intelligence and perform better at school than their peers, controlled studies have shown them to be no more suggestible than other children. I also stressed that nearly all children who spontaneously recall a previous life grow up to lead normal, well-adjusted lives, and that the memories generally diminish and all but disappear, much in the same way that early childhood memories fade with the passage of time.

My explanation seemed to ease Mrs. Pressman's concerns.

[To be continued . . .]

THIRTY-FIVE

BEN SKINNER SAT STARING AT THE SCREEN. HIS REPORT BARELY started, his thoughts were all over the place. This case was unusual and it was getting to him. Today's session had not turned out the way he'd hoped. Helen had hijacked it and he'd let her. Not very professional, including having her present while Jonah went through Danny's belongings, which was strictly against protocol. Nonetheless, Ben didn't regret going rogue on this one, even though it might not qualify as a legitimate addition to the literature. It was the first case he'd dealt with in which the body of the (presumed) deceased had never been found, and he wished for Helen's sake that Jonah had come through with some potentially verifiable information. But he suspected that anything concrete had been short-circuited by the trauma Danny had endured when he was killed. What's more, Ben didn't blame Jonah for wanting to hightail it out of Helen's house this morning and refuse to return for another round this afternoon. The kid was in an impossible position, so much emotion squeezing in on him from all sides. At this point, the best thing that could come out of this aborted enterprise would be for his PTSD symptoms to start to diminish. Ben just hoped the father wouldn't stifle further expression of his memories.

He sighed and watched the screen go to black. This was turning into one of those nights when he found himself alone in a hotel room in a strange town and wished he hadn't quit drinking. Not that this quaint little B&B had an in-room minibar to tempt him, though Vi, the proprietor, had graciously offered him a glass of sherry when he came in. Which his Higher Self had the good sense to turn down.

He shut the lid of his laptop and scratched the coarse hair sprouting from his cheeks and chin. He really should trim his beard so he wouldn't look like a Neanderthal when he met with Henry/Danny Bird's old girlfriend, Mira, the day after the Fourth, his next—and likely last—interview here. It was just past seven o'clock. Maybe he'd get lucky and the local drugstore would still be open. He left home in such a hurry, he'd forgotten to pack his razor and scissors. And he was starving, so he'd better get himself something to eat, too.

Outside the sun was still high in the sky and the temperature had dropped to just below blistering. Ben was used to the summer swampiness of Minneapolis, but here the air was just as oppressive. He scanned the shops lining the green. Down the block from the B&B he spotted one of those old-fashioned Rx signs with the mortar and pestle, but when he looked in the window, the drugstore was dark.

His mood improved the moment he set foot on the green. It was one of those charming town commons that seemed to exist only on the East Coast. With lampposts draped in American flags and a quartet of Beatles' impersonators crooning to a picnicking crowd, the Fourth of July hoopla was in high gear.

"Hello there," a woman's voice rang out, but when he looked around he didn't see anyone.

"Over here." The voice seemed to be coming from a small

wooden gazebo. "It's me, Helen. I've got the best seat in the house. You're welcome to join me."

"Thanks," he said, ducking low and sticking his head into the gazebo. "Actually, I'm on my way to grab some dinner. Any recommendations?"

"Without a reservation? I'm afraid you're out of luck. Everything's booked for the holiday weekend."

"Damn," Skinner said. He had to get out of this heat.

Helen eyed him coolly. "Look, I'm about to go home and make myself an omelet. I'd be happy to make you one, too."

Skinner made it a rule never to socialize with anyone involved in a case. Invariably, they'd want to discuss it, and if they happened to reveal any new information, he wouldn't have it on record. Or they'd want some assessment from him that he was unprepared to give. He studied Helen, who had closed her eyes and was swaying to "Norwegian Wood." What the hell, he thought, the case was already compromised.

"If you're really sure you don't mind."

"A LITTLE GOAT cheese in your omelet?" Helen asked, cracking eggs with one hand into a blue and white ceramic bowl. She was grateful for the chance encounter. After today's session and last night's dream, she needed to talk to him. Privately.

"You bet."

Ben watched her pour the beaten eggs into a white-hot pan and fold the omelet into thirds as deftly as Julia Child.

"Here you go," she said, giving the eggs a dusting of parsley and setting the plate on the tile counter between the kitchen and dining table. "Toast coming right up, Dr. Skinner. Please start while it's hot."

"Ben, please. And thank you. You have no idea how much I appreciate this." He sat down at the wooden table and shoveled a forkful of omelet into his mouth. "Fantastic."

Along with the toast, Helen set two goblets and a bottle of Sangiovese on the table, then sat down. "Care for a glass of wine?"

Would he ever. "No thanks," he said. "I'm not much of a drinker."

Helen traded his wineglass for a glass of water, then gave herself a hefty pour.

"You're not eating?" Skinner asked.

"I will, in a bit." She hesitated. "Actually, I'm glad I ran into you."

Uh-oh, he thought, savoring the omelet. "Oh?"

Helen swirled the wine around in her glass to give it some air. And to give herself a minute to figure out how to say what she needed to say.

It wasn't until late that afternoon when she'd spoken to Randy on the phone that she considered bailing on the investigation.

"We were driving west on Route 80 in my old Subaru," Helen said, telling him her dream from the night before. "Even though he was small, Jonah was sitting up front with me and I was so happy. It was just the two of us. 'I'm your mother now,' I said, but I think I just mouthed the words because I was afraid of upsetting him. Also, I was pretty tense, because if we got stopped, I knew I'd spend the rest of my life in jail for kidnapping. So instead of pulling over at rest areas, I found back roads where we could pee in the bushes. Our only stops were the drive-up windows at the International House of Pancakes. Which I hate, but Danny always loved their chocolate chip pancakes and so did Jonah. In the dream." Her words were starting to come out choppy, like a bad cell-phone connection. "Anyway, that's all we ate, the whole way from Aurora Falls to Laramie. I just wanted to keep Jonah happy so he wouldn't start asking questions about his parents. I drove straight through, day and night, and by the time we checked into the Mighty Oaks, I was so tired I fell into the deepest sleep of my life. And when I woke up, Jonah was gone. I was frantic. I ran around the motel banging on doors, then up and down the street screaming his name, but I couldn't find him anywhere and I couldn't go to the police or I'd be arrested. So I just collapsed on the sidewalk, crying, and that's when I woke up. Crying. I felt as if I'd just lost Danny all over again."

"Oh, Helen," Randy said. "Have you thought about dropping out of the investigation? Why go on when it's causing you this much pain?"

She tried to think of a good reason. "Maybe because Jonah said all these things about Danny that no stranger could possibly know, even though he was shy about it with his parents there. The poor kid probably felt like a traitor. Still, he recognized so many of Danny's things. His first violin. He even remembered where we got it. Baseball cards, other stuff, too." Helen paused. "And then, right before he left, he came running back into the room where I was sitting. His old room. He climbed up on the bed next to me and whispered something in my ear that made me so happy and sad all at once, it just about killed me. 'Chester.'" She managed to get the word out but had to wait for the tears to stop to tell him the rest. "Chester was Danny's favorite sock puppet that I made him when he was little, and Jonah knew his name."

Helen pictured Randy sitting out on his deck, blanketed by the vast, mutable Wyoming sky, fast-moving clouds darkening then breaking just enough to let in shafts of golden light like sudden revelations. He was right. She couldn't handle much more of this. Still, once she'd made up her mind to do something, she prided herself on seeing it through. "I'm no quitter," she mumbled.

But as soon as she said it, she realized it wasn't true. Hadn't she bailed on her marriage to Kip? Her relationship with Jock? Still, she wondered how she'd feel if she dropped out of the investigation. Relief? Guilt for disappointing Skinner? Jonah's parents? Jonah? Or regret for severing a thread, however fragile, that might in some mysterious way connect her to her son? She didn't know. What she did know was that whatever she did had to be her decision. She couldn't let herself be influenced by anyone, including Randy.

AFTER DR. SKINNER POLISHED off his eggs and toast, she said, "I'm sorry, I want to help you and Jonah and his family, but this is . . ." Her voice trailed off.

"Pretty rough, eh?"

"You could say that." Helen took a slug of wine. She'd hoped that by the time she turned fifty she would no longer care about disappointing people, especially people she liked. "About a Dead Sea's worth of salt in an open wound," she said.

"Understood."

No way, she thought, as she went to twist a hank of phantom hair around her finger.

Ben was tempted to tell her that in his own small way, he really did understand. That at age three his daughter Jenny began insisting that he and Marlene were not her "real" parents and begged them to take her "home." At the time he was chief of psychiatry at the VA hospital in St. Paul and dismissed her claims as childish nonsense. Until one evening before her fourth birthday, when she snuck out of the house to look for her "real" family. The police conducted a house-to-house search but missed his little girl, who was found asleep the next morning under the next-door neighbor's porch swing. During the interminable hours while she was missing, Ben wept and promised the Lutheran God of his childhood that if Jenny were returned to him alive, he would never again discount what she told him. He honored his vow and began spending Sundays driving her around to look for the "cow farm" where she said she'd lived with her parents and older brother. It was on one of those excursions that she described in detail how the little girl whose life she remembered died. "I smashed my head on a rock in the creek and drowned when my brother was supposed to be watching me," she'd explained. "I have to tell him not to feel bad because I have a nice new family." Though they never found the farm, Ben was blown away when Jenny's terror of water—including nightly baths—suddenly vanished. Around the same time, he stumbled across a book of Ian Stevenson's in a local bookstore. He walked out of the VA on a frigid February day two months later and, after training with Dr. Stevenson, set up his own practice working with families like the Pressmans. That was seventeen years ago.

"I'm sorry," Helen was saying. "But I can't keep being part of this."

"I get it," he said. "Do you want me to let the Pressmans know?"

She felt something hard and tight in her chest let go. Nodding, she said, "Thank you."

"I'm still planning to interview Mira Brin after the Fourth, just in case she has anything to add. And Jonah again if he's willing, but you don't need to be involved."

"For a minute I got my hopes up that I might finally learn the details about what happened to my son. I even played the tape you lent me for the detective who worked the case, but he said there was nothing to go on."

She looked so sad, Ben felt like leaping across the table and hugging her, an impulse he checked. "I'd hoped you'd get some clarity, too."

"Not meant to be, I guess," Helen said, rising. "As a wise woman I know says, we have only the present moment, and it seems that my present moments will forever include not knowing who murdered my son or what became of his body."

AFTER HE LEFT, Helen turned off all the lights and stretched out on the window seat. The adults had packed up their blankets and picnic baskets and hustled their children off to bed, leaving the green to the teenagers, with their sparklers, spinners, poppers, and Roman candles. Moments later, she saw Skinner stride across the green, but instead of dodging the noisy pyrotechnics, he stopped midway and appeared to be taking in the show.

Watching him, Helen realized she'd had it all wrong. The reason she needed to withdraw from the investigation wasn't because it was stirring up fresh sorrow over Danny. Well, yes, of course it was, but that she could handle.

It was Jonah. He was stirring something else in her, waves of tenderness toward a little boy that she hadn't felt in so long, it was like an atrophied muscle coming back to life.

Helen was terrified this might be love.

And she didn't think her fractured heart could take it.

She lowered the shades on the windows, then went into the kitchen to do the dishes.

THIRTY-SIX

THEY SAT ON THE CURB BY THE GREEN WATCHING THE FUNKY parade that took Lucie right back to her childhood in West Marin. There were kids decked out in silly hats riding bikes, and go-karts decorated with flags and streamers, while Uncle and Mrs. Sam wobbled by on stilts, trailed by a tall man in high heels dressed as the Statue of Liberty. Firemen atop an ancient engine were tossing lollipops and Tootsie Rolls to the crowd.

"What do you think?" Lucie asked Jonah, who was scrambling for candy and too busy to answer. Most Independence Days, worried about the blast of fireworks, Matt and Lucie kept him away from the festivities, but this year he'd begged to go and they decided to chance it.

"Whoa," Jonah cried, when a llama dolled up in a feather headdress was led past like a queen, followed by a marching band with baton-twirling cheerleaders and a garage band blaring "Born in the USA." There was the usual assortment of nonprofits and merchants hawking their goods, including Bella Vista Estates. From the back of a pickup carting a cardboard blowup of a model home, Mira, wearing large sunglasses and a red-white-and-blue sundress, waved at the crowd. Next to her, Lola, in matching garb with a white unicorn horn sticking out from her forehead, looked cross.

Glancing at the pickup's cab and seeing Jackson, Matt realized that the guy he'd run off at the mouth to at Humpty's was somehow connected to Lola and her mother. Who were connected to Helen. *Shit.* He had yet to mention his conversation with Jackson to Lucie.

As for Lucie, she was still trying to figure out how the pieces of their lives before and after Jonah's revelations fit together and found herself drawn more to watching the paradegoers than the parade. Across the street, squeezed in among a crush of onlookers outside her bakery, stood her son's "other mom," while the psychiatrist investigating the case was viewing the ragtag procession from a vantage point farther down the green. The filmy heat that coated the air like a glaze made the float carrying Mira and Lola appear even more surreal.

"Does any of this seem familiar?" Lucie asked Jonah, as an elderly man with a scraggly white beard and wearing a loincloth rolled past on an adult tricycle.

"I was here before," he said.

"And how does that make you feel?"

Jonah kept his eyes on the parade. "I don't know. Regular."

"Do you see anybody you recognize from before? Friends? Or just people you knew from the town?"

"*Mom*," he said, moving away from her. "I just want to watch."

Lucie had never felt so shut out of her son's life and the distance felt dimensional, like a bridge she could see but couldn't cross. She glanced at Matt, who appeared to be engrossed in the pageant. Was it possible he was starting to accept the new normal as normal?

When the parade thinned to intermittent stragglers, including a small boy tugging a turtle with a string around its neck, Jonah fluttered his thick eyelashes at Lucie and, clasping his hands in front of his heart in phony supplication, announced, "I want a hot dog."

"We need to get home," she said sharply. She craved just one day that didn't involve characters from her son's previous life, and this event felt like a booby trap. If, as Dr. Skinner predicted, Jonah would someday regard his past life as normal as Thanksgiving dinner at Grandma's, Lucie did not see it that way, at least not yet, and she hoped to make a clean break without bumping into Helen or Dr. Skinner or Mira and Lola. In fact, she was so desperate to spend time with her own family for just one day that in a generous moment she'd invited Phoebe—*Sonam*, she reminded herself—to join them for a barbecue and a sleepover.

"Momo's coming, we should head back. I can make you a hot dog at home," Lucie said.

"I thought she wasn't getting here until three and I wouldn't mind a hot dog myself," Matt said, pleased to see Jonah acting like a normal kid.

Lucie wanted to smack him.

THEY WERE SEATED at a picnic table eating their hot dogs and French fries when Jonah felt something poking his back.

"Yo, Jo." It was Lola with her horn.

"Oh, hi," he said and continued eating.

"I want to play with Charlie. Oma says he's still at your house." She leaned in close, arms folded, cheeks puffed out like an angry cartoon character. "He's my dog, too."

Jonah shrugged. "You can come over," he said.

Well, this was one good thing to come out of this booby trap of a day, thought Lucie. In spite of Lola's starring role in Jonah's past life, the two had bonded in the present, and Lucie knew he missed playing with her ever since they'd fallen out over Charlie.

"Lo, I told you I'd talk to Jonah's mom," Mira said, catching up. "She's been missing Charlie. And Jonah, too, haven't you, sweetie?"

Lola grunted.

"I've been meaning to call and set something up, but you know"—Mira raised a perfectly plucked brow—"life. Things have been a little crazy. Speaking of which, I'm supposed to talk to your guy tomorrow afternoon. Dr. Skinner?"

"We'd love to have Lola over anytime," Matt said, steering the conversation back to playdates. Like Lucie, he, too, welcomed a break from the supernatural. "We'll be home all afternoon."

"Actually," Lucie said, "my mother's coming over later, but tomorrow is good. Jonah and I have nothing all day."

"Perfect," said Mira. "I have an important meeting in the morning before Dr. Skinner. And it would be better if Lola wasn't with me," she added quietly.

Just then, a big man wearing a cowboy hat shouted from half a football field away. "Let's get a move on!"

Matt bent down to retie his shoelaces, praying Jackson wouldn't come any closer.

"*Now*, ladies," he was hollering. "I gotta move the friggin' truck."

THE FOURTH OF July bombs were still bursting in air but, remarkably, Jonah was sleeping through the uproar.

"I'll be right back," Lucie told her mother. Except for Charlie's freight-train snores, no sounds could be heard coming from Jonah's room. Which amazed her. Though she now understood why he'd always been so terrified of loud noises, she thought it would take more than saying he remembered hearing big claps of thunder the night he was killed to alter the way the neurons fired in his brain. Maybe having Charlie there with him was making the difference. Charlie, she decided, was Jonah's magic charm.

"This is incredible," she said, returning to the kitchen table, where Phoebe was sipping tea. She'd have to wait until morning to tell Matt, who had to drive back to the city at dawn and had gone to bed early. "Jonah has never, ever not freaked out at the sound of fireworks."

"That's wonderful, darling. I'm so glad I got him in to see Rinpoche right away. I knew it would turn things around for him lickety-split."

"Mom, *really*? Jesus." Narcissist that she was, Phoebe was taking full credit for Jonah's turnaround—*if* that's even what this was.

Phoebe looked stricken. "Did I say something wrong?"

Lucie felt the muscles in her body contract into a sheath of armor. She had no desire to get into it with her mother. "It doesn't matter, it's just a stressful time," she muttered as she heard the *ping*. She glanced at her screen and saw a text from Diana. "Shit." She put the phone on the table facedown. At the moment, all she wanted was to savor her son's silence during the fireworks blitz, not deal with her mother's self-congratulatory bullshit or her boss's mercurial demands. "Ten o'clock on the Fourth of July, this can't be good."

"So don't read it until morning. After all, it's a holiday, the people you love, hopefully including me, are all right here, so what could be so important?" Phoebe said, her large hazel eyes open wide, clearly seeking confirmation that she was wanted.

"You don't know my boss," Lucie snorted, withholding the love bomb her mother craved. "Diana's a vampire. She never sleeps or goes on vacation. Honestly, you'd think she was empress of the free world, not the editor of a women's magazine."

"Well, I still say it can wait until morning. Drink your tea, darling. That potpourri of herbs Sangye harvested for you from our garden is very calming. You met Sangye, remember? The little one from Brooklyn and my dear friend? It's her jalopy I borrowed to come here."

Lucie took a sip of the bitter-tasting tea. She would love it if her overamped nervous system went offline for a bit, though she wasn't sure that was possible under the circumstances. This situation was so unfamiliar—her mother spending the night, the two of them sitting up and talking like storybook mothers and daughters—she wasn't sure how to behave. Still, watching Phoebe lean back in her chair in a wash of moonlight with her white hair flowing, Lucie thought she belonged in a painting by Mary Cassatt. Age had made her even more beautiful.

"You know, darling, anyone going through what you're going through would be stressed." Phoebe rested a cool silky hand on top of Lucie's. "It's obviously taking a toll, just look at those bags under your eyes. I'm here to help, any way I can."

Lucie jerked her hand away. Why was her mother incapable of being sympathetic without being insulting at the same time? That was her special gift, daggers wrapped in valentines. Yet since she'd arrived midafternoon, she couldn't have been more agreeable. She'd patiently taught Jonah gin rummy, then played fetch with him, Charlie, and Matt while Lucie prepared dinner. Even Matt seemed to enjoy her mother's company, and Lucie had begun to imagine that she and Phoebe were on to a new chapter, one in which she wouldn't have to suit up in emotional armor every time the woman was within range.

But Lucie was not about to rise to the bait about how awful

she looked, so she picked up her phone and read Diana's text. *Trrbl nws!!!!! Ellie brk hr plvs bngee jmpng wth hr dghtr & in hsptl. Nd u hre frst thng tmrrw 2 edt hr stries, XOD.*

"Fuck," Lucie said, dropping her phone on the table.

"Didn't I tell you not to look at that text? That's one of many things I love about living at the monastery. No wi-fi between eight in the evening and noon the next day. World War Three could break out and we wouldn't have a clue. It's heaven."

"Well, lucky you."

"Just tell them no, darling. If there's one thing I've learned in my life, it's that *No* is the best complete sentence in the English language."

Which is why you never held down a job for more than ten minutes. You'd quit if you had something more pressing to do, like getting stoned and spending the day fucking your latest boyfriend. Lucie glared at her mother, who was staring so plaintively at her it made Lucie want to dive under the table.

"I'm sorry you're still so angry with me, Lucie," Phoebe said. "I only want what's best for you and Matt and my beautiful grandson. I wish you'd tell me what I'm doing that's so offensive. Please, darling, just tell me."

How much time have you got? Lucie did not say.

"I know I wasn't the world's greatest mom, but now that you're a mother yourself maybe you can understand that when I got pregnant I was very young, and my main goal in life was to not be anything like my mother. I know you adored Nana, but I was desperate to escape the shadow she cast over everything. I couldn't breathe in that house. She was so frightened all the time, especially after Pa died. I just wanted to have some fun. And be free. I realize now that my idea of freedom was pure delusion. But darling, as young and stupid as I was, when I found out I was pregnant, the one thing I knew for sure was that I wanted to keep that baby. I wanted *you*."

"Really?" Lucie had always been a little surprised that her mother hadn't aborted her.

"Yes, one hundred percent. Can I tell you something else?" Phoebe leaned in closer.

Lucie nodded, studying the bulging blue network of veins on her mother's hands.

"Something I've learned from Rinpoche, which I try to live by. And that is how at every moment our awareness dissolves, then reforms in the next moment. That's what happens when we die, but it happens in life, too. Who we were in the past, even who we were a minute ago, is gone and our future self has yet to come into being. I'm the first to admit that I made some terrible choices while you were growing up, and for that I'm truly sorry. But the mother of your childhood no longer exists. And you're not the same person either, my darling girl. Rinpoche says that regardless of what went on before, we humans have a precious opportunity to meet the present moment with an open heart and mind. To start again."

"I'm sorry, Mom, maybe that's true, but it also sounds like the kind of crap you were always spouting when I was a kid. *Be here now.* Only a lot of the time you weren't."

"You're right, I wasn't, and I'm not trying to defend myself. I loved you, but I screwed up big time. But I am here now. And I hope to be in the future, if you'll let me."

Lucie got up out of her chair. The wistful expression on her mother's face, her pleading eyes, were making her dizzy. She went and posted herself by Jonah's bedroom door. Still quiet in there, even though outside fireworks continued to shatter the late-night silence. She stood there wondering. Was she being unfair? Was she simply reacting out of her angry, wounded little girl self? Was her resistance to her mother so deeply baked into her cells, she couldn't give her a chance? Sonam really did seem like a different person than careless, supremely self-involved Phoebe. Wouldn't it be something, Lucie thought, to have a mother she could rely on? Especially now, with everything that was going on?

"Okay," she said, sitting back down at the table. "Let's just take it a day at a time and see how it goes."

"Thank you, darling, thank you. You won't regret it, I promise. And you know, I've been studying *The Tibetan Book of the Dead* for some time now and I've learned a little something about rebirth. Maybe I can help you understand what's going on with Jonah."

"Great, but right now I have to deal with this." Lucie held up her phone. "My colleague broke her pelvis and I need to fill in for her." She started compiling a to-do list in her head. *Text Jeremy's mother and see if Jonah can spend the day with him. Text Mira and tell her Lola can't play here tomorrow. Text Helen and let her know we have to drop Charlie off first thing in the morning.* "I guess we can ride in with Matt. His first surgery is at eight, so we'll have to leave by six. I just hope I can find a playdate for Jonah in the city."

"Lucie, hello! What have we been talking about? If you must go into work, I can stay here with Jonah and his friend. Please, let me help you."

The idea of enlisting her mother's help hadn't even occurred to Lucie. So much for starting over and meeting the present moment with an open heart and mind. "Are you sure, because I might not get back until late? And if Matt stays overnight in the city, which he probably will, I'll have to take the bus. I might even have to stay over, too."

"Of course I'm sure. You take care of whatever you need to

and don't worry about a thing. Jonah and I and that little girl will have ourselves a lovely day." Phoebe stood and attempted to rouse Lucie from her slumped position at the table. "Come on, darling, off to bed you go. You have a long day ahead of you."

Lucie let her mother take her by the elbow to help her up. She felt about a century past the point of exhaustion.

"We're all set. I can stay as long as you need." With her long, slender fingers, Phoebe swept Lucie's hair out of her eyes. "It's been so wonderful being here today. Your son is a very special person, just like my daughter," she said, her heart-shaped mouth quivering and her large hazel eyes appearing more liquid than usual. "It's just so good to be with family."

Lucie could tell her mother meant every word. She just wished she believed that this time there would be no surprise dagger hidden inside the valentine.

THIRTY-SEVEN

IN HER MIND HELEN ALWAYS THOUGHT OF IT AS BETSY, HER FAther's pet name for the brown leather trunk his grandfather had carted from Lincoln, Nebraska, over mountain ranges and across desert plains along the Oregon Trail, all the way to Portland—at least that's how the story went. Jonah had rifled through Betsy two days earlier, surveying some of Danny's treasures. Treasures Helen thought she couldn't part with. Until now.

Which was why at six o'clock on the morning of July 5, still in her pajamas, she was kneeling on the floor of Lola's room in the predawn half-light emptying the trunk, trying to decide what to do with each object. The old violin she would offer to Jonah, but only after she ran it by his parents, who might not want him to have it. The X-rated letters Danny wrote Mira, which she left behind when she'd moved in with Jackson, Helen would return to her or burn if she didn't want them. The letters Danny sent Helen from music camp, she'd give to Lola. But the old catcher's mitt and baseball uniform she didn't know what to do with. She pressed her nose into one of the uniform's armpits and sniffed, trying to pick up a lingering trace of her son's sweet, acrid sweat, any random molecule that, by some miracle, had defied the unforgiving thrust of time. But there was nothing left of him that she could detect. Same with his Dog Radio T-shirt, now dotted with pinholes, and that Lola coveted and would have. There were also a couple of records, *Doc Watson Live Onstage* and the Nitty Gritty Dirt Band's *Will the Circle Be Unbroken*. These Helen would keep, along with Chester and the rest of the sock puppet family. And buried at the very bottom of the trunk was the 1998 Aurora Falls High School yearbook. She took it out and slowly ran her fingers across the raised maroon-and-gold letters on the cover. This she would definitely keep. It was a shame Jonah had missed it. There were so many lovely photos inside that might have jogged his memory: Danny tossing his catcher's mitt in the air after the team won the county championship. Danny playing violin during the holiday concert with an expression of such deep concentration, it looked like bliss. Danny grinning and holding up a bunch of skinny carrots he'd grown in the school garden. She wondered briefly if it was too late to show the yearbook to Jonah, then decided that was a terrible idea. The boy needed to move on. And so did she.

"I need coffee," Helen said aloud. Usually, she relied on Charlie to nudge her into the kitchen for his breakfast as soon as she opened her eyes. But without him there, she had trouble getting her bearings, like a sailor whose compass has fallen in the drink.

Damn. She remembered she was supposed to be downstairs by seven to help with the early rush. Before she'd gotten herself tangled up in this business with Jonah, Helen told Izzy she could go home for the Fourth and agreed to work the register over the holiday weekend. The clock on the stove said six fifty-five. She'd be at least half an hour late. Oh well, Geo and Katy would have to fill in until she got there. What were they going to do, fire her?

She sat down with her coffee and began flipping through the senior-class pictures. There was Damian, with a glazed look on his face, even then. And handsome, dark-eyed Stuart, who a few years ago had given up playing music for designing some kind of music software that Helen didn't understand. What she did understand was that he was crazy rich and living in a pretty Craftsman in Santa Monica. She'd always adored Stuart, but thinking about him now, married with a ten-month-old daughter, was causing a burning sensation in her throat. She turned the page and there was Mira, looking not just beautiful, but forceful, resolute. "Artist, nature lover, free spirit, *carpe diem.*" Helen smiled, cheered that lately Mira seemed back in touch with her formerly feisty self.

She flipped to Danny's entry. "Henry Bird: music, nature, the f***ing Red Sox! *The future belongs to those who believe in the beauty of their dreams.*" In the photo he's squinting and looking more sober than in his other pictures, as if he really were trying to get a glimpse into the future.

"Oh, my love." Helen kissed the photo.

Then her eyes drifted to the shot below Danny's. When she read the inscription that went with it, she choked on her coffee. "I'll huff and I'll puff and I'll blow your house down, so you better watch your back, heh heh heh . . ."

She stared at the words, then read them again. And again, slowly, one syllable, then the next. "I'll huff and I'll puff and . . ." Could this really be him? The man Jonah claimed had killed her son?

The wolf!

Helen had to call Will. But it took several minutes for her hand to stop shaking long enough to punch in the number.

"STOP, STOP, YOU two. Oh, my goodness, uncle, uncle!" They were playing tag out back and Sonam was doubled over, trying to catch her breath. "Anyone for a glass of H2O?"

"What's H2O?" Jonah asked.

"OMG, it's water," said Lola. "Duh. Don't you go to school?"

"Of course I go to school! I haven't had the water class yet. *Duh.*" Jonah glared at Lola. He almost never fought with his friends in the city, but for some reason he liked squabbling with her. Even though now he knows that the boy who got killed was her FATHER! Which would have been him if he wasn't Jonah, which is NOT something he likes to think about. ICK! Anyhow, once he heard his mom call some lady at work her *frenemy*, and Jonah decided that's what Lola was. His best frenemy.

"Sorreee. JK. Just kidding, in case you don't know what that means."

"Do you ever talk English?"

"Come on, you two, it's too hot to argue," Sonam said. "Look at poor old Charlie, just think how he must feel running around with all that fur. Let's get him some H2O, too." The dog was trying to squeeze his large, hairy body under the picnic table.

"I'll get him some water, but I want lemonade," Jonah said.

"Me, too, lemonade, *s'il vous plait*. That's French for please," Lola added.

"*Toda raba*," said Jonah, hands on hips. "That's thank you in Hebrew." He learned that one time when he and his mom met his dad in Israel for a vacation after his dad got done fixing people's eyes in Africa.

"We could wade in the creek, that'll cool us off," Sonam said. They were seated at the picnic table sipping their icy drinks, while down below Charlie was slurping his water. She wrapped her hair into a loose bun, then watched Jonah and Lola thumb wrestle, silently pleased that her grandson was whupping the girl. Even though Sonam was steeped in reincarnation from Tibetan Buddhism and her beloved Rinpoche was a verified tulku, never before had she encountered a reincarnated being in everyday life, let alone in her own family! She'd tried to get in touch with her own prior lifetimes through past-life regressions, psychic readings, holotropic breathwork, even magic mushrooms back in the day. Once during a breathwork session she'd caught a glimpse of herself as a witch being burned at the stake, and another time as her maternal grandmother being gassed at Auschwitz. Yet, each time she came out of the trance, she wasn't sure if her vision was real or imagined. And since meeting Rinpoche, she'd learned that all those regression techniques were pointless. He said that people only remember a past life when it's important for their spiritual development.

But Jonah! Sonam was sure that on some level Lucie must be very spiritually evolved to have given birth to such a child. She just prayed that her daughter could truly forgive her. At least yesterday the door had opened a crack. If only Lucie could see how much Sonam had always loved her. Which was why on the day of the abortion, she'd jumped up out of those awful stirrups and ran crying from the clinic wearing only a cotton hospital gown dotted with teddy bears. Teddy bears for an abortion! Sonam hadn't told Lucie that part. There was no point, because just as they were about to start the *procedure*, she realized how much she wanted that baby. And now Jonah was the lucky charm helping her find her way back to her daughter.

"Momo, can we?" Jonah was asking.

"Can we what, baby?"

"What we said? Me and Lola want to go swimming at her house. She has a pool and air-conditioning and chairs with umbrellas. It's too hot here. Her mom said we could."

"Yeah, my mom said we could," echoed Lola. "She told me to tell you when she brought me this morning."

Sonam had not actually spoken to Mira, they'd just waved when Lola got out of the car. "Are you sure, sweetheart?"

"Roger that."

"And you know how to get there?"

"OFC. Of course. As long as I'm with a grown-up, it's A-OK with my mom. I have a key. Anyhow, my mom will be back soon. She has to meet some doctor guy at our house later."

"Well, swimming on such a hot day would be lovely. Do you both know how to swim?" Sonam asked, suddenly alarmed. "Because I am not a certified lifeguard."

"*Duh*," the children chimed in unison.

"My dad taught me before I could hardly walk," said Jonah.

"And I was a Whale at camp last summer," Lola said. "You have to be really good to be a Whale."

"Well, okay, if you're sure it's all right with your mom. Maybe Lucie has a suit I can borrow, I'll go look. And Jonah, you fetch yours," Sonam said, disappearing into the house.

Twenty minutes later, swimsuits, hats, towels, sandwiches, sunglasses, and sunscreen were stuffed into Lucie's straw beach bag. Sonam triple-checked to make sure she'd packed all the necessary items. Her rekindled relationship with Lucie was too precious to screw up, so she checked the bag once more before hustling the troops, including a panting Charlie, into Sangye's rusty old Toyota.

"Jonah, remind me to text your mom and let her know where we are as soon as we get there," Sonam said, unaware that her cell phone was the one thing she'd forgotten to pack.

SARITA BLANK, THE desk sergeant on duty, explained over the phone that Will was out of the office and wouldn't be back until after lunch.

"I've paged him and tried his cell, but he's not answering. Can you please get a message to him and tell him I need to speak to him right away?" Helen was trying her best not to sound hysterical. Hysterics, she'd learned, get you nowhere with the cops. In fact, the slightest show of emotion makes them treat you like you're the criminal, even when you're the victim. And Sarita was the meanest of the lot. "It's urgent," Helen said, trying to add a little sugar to her voice.

"Like I told you, Detective Handler won't be reachable until later. If you want, you can come down to the station and file your complaint or whatever with me. I'm here all day," the sergeant said, sighing audibly.

Helen could picture the woman, round as Humpty-Dumpty, with a face like a prune. "Thanks, but I really need to talk to Will, so if you could get a message to him, I'd appreciate it." Helen hung up before the woman could give her any more attitude.

She decided to take a shower. Still reeling from the morning's discovery, she wasn't sure what to do next, but she always did her best thinking under the soothing hot spray, and by the time she stepped out of the shower, her skin splotched a deep magenta, she had a plan.

THIRTY-EIGHT

COME ON, YOU TWO!" SONAM CALLED FROM THE POOL. "THE water's divine. Charlie will settle down if you just leave him be."

The dog was tied to a tree near the four-car garage, pacing back and forth.

"He hates being tied up. Why can't we just let him run around? It's so big here," Jonah said, eyes wide, taking in the gigantic property. "You can't even see other houses."

"FYI, we have to keep him tied up," Lola insisted. "Jackson said Charlie can never come over to our house *ever* because he sheds so much."

Jonah tried to scratch the wobbly pocket under the dog's chin, but he wouldn't stop pacing long enough to let him get close. "C'mon, boy, it's okay." Jonah turned to Lola. "He seems upset about something."

"Whatev, I'm going in."

"Me too." Jonah told Charlie in his most grown-up voice the same thing his mom and dad were always telling him. "I won't let anything bad happen to you, okay, boy? Me and Lola and Momo are right here with you, okay, Charlie?"

"Heaven, this is absolute heaven," Sonam sighed when both kids joined her in the pool. The truth was, she wished she didn't like it quite so much. The exquisite coolness of the blue water washing over her skin, the light bouncing off the glassy surface like electric snowflakes, the verdant hills and woods surrounding the enormous house. Sonam had gotten only as far as the kitchen, which was bigger and better equipped than the monastery kitchen that could feed two hundred people. *Stop*, she scolded herself. *Comparing mind is the root of all suffering.* So true, but she had to admit there were times when she longed for a space of her own that was more inviting than the cell of a nun who had taken a vow of extreme poverty.

"Come on, Momo, you keep letting it drop!"

"Oops, sorry." They were playing a three-way game of air volleyball, trying to keep a semi-deflated beach ball aloft. *Focus on the now*, Sonam reminded herself. She was determined to be the perfect granny. Maybe later she and Jonah would bake chocolate chip cookies. "Here you go," she called, tossing the ball in her grandson's direction, only to watch it go kerplunk a few inches away.

"This ball is stupid, it won't stay up," Jonah said. "I'm going back to Charlie." Without stopping to towel himself off, he sprinted past the covered cabana to the parking pad where the dog continued to pace. "This is so not fair! Why can't I take him for a walk on his leash?"

Sonam and Lola had given up on the beach ball and were floating around on foam noodles.

"Because!" Lola shouted. "You can't!"

Just then an extension of the landline began ringing in the cabana.

"Maybe you should answer that," Sonam said.

Lola, who had two purple noodles tucked under her arms

and was scooting back and forth across the pool by making angel wings, didn't see the point. "It's probably just my mom calling to say hi," she said. "I left her a voicemail telling her we were here."

"Good," Sonam said, glad that someone knew where they were. She was annoyed at herself for forgetting her cell. She'd tried calling Lucie from the kitchen, but Jonah, who claimed he knew her number by heart, obviously got the digits mixed up, because she kept getting some huffy woman named Roberta at an insurance company. Oh well, she'd have Jonah home, fed, and bathed by the time Lucie got back. With yummy chocolate chip cookies waiting.

Charlie was growling at the sound of the phone, and when the ringing stopped, he began to bark so furiously it looked as if his eyes would pop out of his head.

"Okay, okay, OMG," Lola cried from the pool. "You can take him for a walk but keep him on the leash and don't go near the house!"

LOOKING AROUND, JACKSON thought he might have slipped back in time a couple of centuries, either that or someone had spiked his Sam Adams with LSD. Some dumpy old broads in bonnets and long dresses were bent over weeding a garden, while a bunch of bearded dudes in straw hats were walking next to a wagon piled high with hay and pulled by oxen. Were these people real Shakers or actors pretending to be Shakers? All he knew was if he had a job wearing one of those outfits in the burning hot sun, he wouldn't be all smiley like these folks. On the other hand, maybe he should stay here and learn a trade. Blacksmithing. He could become a smithy. Even in the brutal heat, that might be a fuck of a lot better than having to declare bankruptcy.

He was so pissed off after the meeting in Boston, he got off the Pike near Worcester to grab a beer, and before he knew it, he was standing in line with a bunch of fat tourists. Well, hell, at least the bank that was going to feast off his remains wouldn't get the twenty-eight bucks he coughed up for admission. That was the good news. The bad news was that even though Mira thought it would be fun to take Lola to Old Sturbridge Village, they'd be lucky if they had enough cash left to pay for a dented can of beans.

Not that he'd mind going back in time for real, three years to be exact, before he bet their entire fucking future on Bella Vista Estates. And if he was going back that far, he might as well go the distance, ten years back, before he married Mira, before he decided he couldn't live without her ass. He tried never to think about that night, he was so young and, let's face it, suicidal without her. The truth was, she'd left him no choice. And now, that goddamn kid. Well, he couldn't let himself go there. The kid was the least of his problems.

He swiped the sweat dripping down his forehead with his tie. He had to get out of there, get his head straight. How was he going to break it to Mira that the investors he'd promised would come through on the Bella Vista deal had pulled out? *Unprecedented market conditions*, the head asshole, Walt, had said. *No buyers. Zombie subdivisions like yours are worth less than a bucket of piss.* It was all Jackson could do not to take a swing at the guy. Jesus fuck, was the whole goddamn housing downturn his fault? Was he the moron who invented subprime mortgages? He needed another beer, which didn't seem to be on the menu at Ye Olde Village.

Back behind the wheel of his Range Rover (well, his, until some other asshole came and took that, too), he decided he would drive straight home, dive into the pool, and not stop swimming until he figured out how to tell Mira they were about to lose everything.

Either that or until he drowned, whichever fucking came first.

"WHAT DO YOU mean they're not there? They have to be there. Mira was supposed to drop Lola off around nine. Maybe they're out back by the creek and didn't hear the bell," Lucie said, deleting lines of copy from her screen.

"Been there," said Helen. "No sign of them, except for three empty glasses on the picnic table, so obviously they were here earlier."

"Hmm," Lucie murmured. Having to trim this story was infuriating, but she had already fought—and lost—the battle with Diana. "What about Charlie? Is he there?"

"No," said Helen. "I'm in the kitchen now. The back door was unlocked and there's no one here." She looked at Dr. Skinner and shook her head.

"Christ, the one time I leave my mother in charge . . ." Lucie didn't know whether to be worried or angry and settled on a split decision.

"Your mom probably just took them over to the playground or to get ice cream. She may not know that Charlie can get spooked in public," Helen said. But it wasn't Charlie she was worried about.

"Could you look in the driveway and tell me if there's an old green Toyota parked there?" Was it unreasonable for Lucie to expect her mother to report in if she took the kids somewhere? She'd left her in charge, hadn't she? Was she overreacting out of habit? After yesterday's *rapprochement*, she didn't believe her mother would do anything reckless. She seemed determined to show up for Jonah and heal old wounds with Lucie.

"There's a car in the driveway, but it's white and looks new," said Helen, peering out the front window.

"That's my rental. Do you mind hanging on while I try my mother's cell?" Lucie punched in the number from her desk phone.

Helen went back to the kitchen, where Dr. Skinner stood towering over the scuffed-up wooden counter staring at a ringing phone. "Her cell is here, so they couldn't have gone far. Honestly, I'm sure they're fine," she said, trying to keep the worry out of her voice. After this morning's discovery, every cell in her body was on high alert, and the fact that the kids and Lucie's mother had gone AWOL wasn't helping. "I'll call Mira and see if she knows anything, but actually Ben—Dr. Skinner—and I were coming over to see you. He's here with me. Mira told me the kids were going to be with you today."

"They were," Lucie said, explaining the late-night text from her boss. "I'm sure you're right, my mother probably just took them for ice cream or something. But what's Skinner doing there? Wait, hold on a second." Lucie covered her phone with one hand. "I told you, I'd have it by two. Sorry," she sighed into the phone. "They want me to cut a feature on genetic testing so they can add one more useless spread on workout clothes. I gotta go, but when you figure out where my mother and the kids are, could you please let me know right away?"

"Of course."

"Before I hang up, though, just tell me quickly why Skinner's with you. Isn't he supposed to be meeting with Mira today?"

"There's been a development," Helen said. "We wanted to tell you in person, but . . . ." It all came pouring out: her discovery of the yearbook, the likely identity of "the wolf," her calls to Will, then Skinner. She hesitated. "Dr. Skinner says it's highly improbable, that in all his years of doing this he's never seen it, but if I'm right about who the wolf is, then . . . Do you want to talk to him?"

Lucie didn't wait for Skinner to spell it out. She didn't need to be told that her son could be in grave danger if Henry's murderer found out about Jonah. What if Phoebe and the kids happened to run into the guy in town and Phoebe started bragging about how her grandson was a reincarnation? Wouldn't this wolfman, who by now must have heard something about Jonah's claims, put two and two together?

"I'm on my way," Lucie said, grabbing her purse. "Just please check in with me after you talk to Mira and I'll try her, too."

As she ran from her office near Columbus Circle to Matt's office across the park, the one thought that gave her solace was knowing with absolute certainty that as long as Charlie was with Jonah, the dog would kill anyone who tried to hurt him.

"JONAH! GET BACK here right now!" Lola stood at the edge of the pool, scowling as she watched Charlie drag Jonah across the broad, sloping meadow toward the woods.

"Okay," he shouted, trying to appear in control.

"Jonah, do as Lola says. It's time for lunch, sweetheart," Sonam called. "Please come back here right now and tie that dog to the tree."

"Okay, Momo," cried Jonah. He yanked the leash as hard as he could. "C'mon, Charlie, let's go get some treats."

But the dog was going nuts, sniffing all over, like maybe he smelled bear poop. Or what if it was Bigfoot? Jonah tugged on the leash as hard as he could, but that didn't stop Charlie, who kept turning around and looking at him with his giant doggy eyes, like he was trying to tell him something.

"Charlie, please, boy," Jonah begged.

But the dog kept pulling him closer to the edge of the woods, and when he turned around, he saw Momo stumbling down the hill after them, still wearing his mom's bathing suit that was so baggy on her it was funny. But then she fell down and it wasn't so funny anymore, because she was crying and then he was crying and Lola was crying, and also yelling, "You can't go in there. I'm going to get in so much trouble! Jonah! You're not allowed, nobody's allowed, get back here right this minute!"

THIRTY-NINE

THEY'RE SAFE," A RELIEVED-SOUNDING HELEN TOLD LUCIE OVER the phone.

"Are you sure?"

"Yes, there's no reason to worry."

"Thank God." Lucie felt her pulse stop galloping like a spooked horse. "They're okay," she told Matt, then went back to the phone. "So, where are they?"

"It was so hot the kids wanted to go swimming and your mother took them to Lola's. They phoned Mira to let her know where they were, but she was in a meeting and just got the message. She called me to say she's stuck in traffic and won't be back in time for her appointment with Dr. Skinner. She asked me to cancel for her. I told her I'd check on the kids."

The spooked horse reared up again. "What about *him*?"

"He's in Boston and won't be back until late tonight, but I'm heading out there right now. I'll make sure your mother leaves with Jonah and Charlie the minute I see them."

"Thank you, Helen, thank you. Matt's with me, we're just getting on the West Side Highway. We should be there in an hour and a half, maybe less. Could you please tell my mother to call me as soon as they get home?"

"JESUS CHRIST," LUCIE said, shaking, after ending the call. "I can't believe it. Jonah's at the wolf's house?"

"Honey, take some deep breaths. Jonah will be long gone before the guy gets home," Matt said, taking a few deep breaths himself. He couldn't believe the wolf was the same asshole he'd sat around drinking with and who had tried to sell him a fucking McMansion. And Matt was the moron who'd tipped him off about Jonah. It was a good thing he hadn't told Lucie about that little encounter, or she'd really be freaking out right now. He'd confess sometime, just not this minute. "I think we should pack up as soon as we get there and head home tonight," he said.

"Agree." Lucie rubbed her icy fingers to warm them. "But what do we tell Jonah?"

"We tell him the truth," said Matt. "He's going to want to know why we're rushing back to the city."

"Yes, but we have to be very careful how we do it. Maybe during a session with Dr. Zager when things calm down? For now let's just tell him I have a work conflict, which is also true. The last thing he needs is to get retraumatized by this. I just hope he doesn't have to testify, if the scum ends up going on trial."

"Not to worry, Jonah will never testify. Never, I'll make sure of that." Matt reached over and squeezed Lucie's hand. "Luckily, he hasn't come into contact with the guy since we've been up there. And he's not going to."

"He better not." Lucie texted Helen to see if her mother and Jonah had left *his* house yet. After tapping the send arrow, she said, "The whole point of this summer was to get him out of the city, away from the scary scene on his birthday and to someplace new, someplace peaceful and safe where nothing would set him off. I was sure Aurora Falls was just the ticket. Great maternal instincts, huh?"

"You did nothing wrong, Luce, I promise you. Anyhow, didn't Skinner say that having Jonah spend time in Aurora Falls was the best thing we could do for him? He could be right. Jonah slept through the fireworks last night, and that was a first."

"I guess." Lucie wondered if Matt still secretly believed that Jonah's memories were a crock. At least he'd stopped behaving like a petulant asshole over them, and for that she was thankful. They'd had their differences over the years, but this one could have broken them.

Gnawing on a snagged nail, she said, "Remember the night we buried Jonah's foreskin and I did my little witchy number and asked Nana and Great Spirit and whoever to protect the baby and keep him happy and healthy and safe from every possible danger?"

Her heart still bucking in her chest, she checked her phone to see if Helen had texted back. She hadn't.

"Well, obviously there was one thing I left off my list of possible catastrophes."

JACKSON COULDN'T REMEMBER the last time he cried. Not that he wanted to remember, but he couldn't help it, because his eyes had turned into goddamn geysers the minute he crossed the New York State line. He was pretty sure the last time was when he saw Mira with the asswipe in ShopRite, her belly so gigantic it was hanging over the potatoes. He was one aisle over, in toilet paper, when he spotted them slobbering all over each other. That's when it hit him that she was never coming back, not with a kid on the way. He'd been laying low for years, hooking up with other ladies but never letting any of them get their claws into him, just biding his time and waiting for the big romance to peter out. Mira was his. For life. He'd told her as much when she broke up with him in high school, but she just laughed and swung her big fat bush of hair in his face. But he knew someday she'd come around, even if she was too dumb to figure it out for herself. And then that day in the supermarket, he felt like such a jerk, slinking out because the geysers started going off in the checkout line. That was when he knew he had to do something, and fast, before the brat popped.

In a million years he never could have imagined that the fucking asswipe would come back to haunt him.

He swabbed his face and neck with the tie he'd been wearing since six o'clock that morning, then yanked it off. It was some overpriced Armani piece of shit that Mira said would impress the investors more than his dead father's good luck bolo. As if.

His cell started ringing. Mira. He wasn't ready to talk to her. He set the phone on vibrate.

He could hear his heartbeat crashing in his eardrums the closer he got to home. Every fucking thing he'd sweated his balls off to give her was about to be taken away.

Well, not every fucking thing. She'd still have him. Which better be enough, but he couldn't tell what was up with her lately. She'd been acting snippy and stuffing her face with all kinds of shit. If she didn't watch out, she'd chunk up and look like she did before he got his hands on her, before he bought her all those fancy designer clothes and paid for three-hundred-dollar hair-cuts. If they had any chance of selling a house before the whole shit project collapsed, she better not start looking like a goddamn house.

As he punched in the code to open the gate to their private road, he wondered if she was home. That's when he heard it, coming from the woods. He rolled his window down and stuck his head out just to make sure he wasn't hallucinating. What the fuck? It was a fucking dog. Barking its goddamn head off. How was that even possible? The whole twenty-three acres were fenced in, plus there was a gated entrance and *No Trespassing* signs every couple of yards. Not even a fucking baby deer could get in.

He pulled onto the fire road. The barking was getting louder. He turned off the engine, opened the glove box, and grabbed the smooth cool handle of man's real best friend.

FORTY

C'MON, CHARLIE, LET'S GO BACK, WE HAVE TO," I YELL, AND I am yanking so hard on his leash he would have to be a stupid idiot not to understand what I'm saying, and Charlie is not a stupid idiot. I am the stupid idiot, even though my mom says I owe her twenty-five cents every time I say something bad about myself. I wish she was here. I would pay her a thousand hundred twenty-five cents for how stupid I am for letting the dog drag me all the way into the woods. And now he won't move. He's sniffing and digging his paws in a clump of leaves and we're in the middle of the forest and it is dark and scary and I don't want to be here.

"I'm going to count to three and then we're leaving." I am trying to sound grown-up, like my dad when he gets mad. But I don't sound at all like him because when he gets mad his eyes are not all swimmy with crying and he doesn't have snot pouring out of his nose when he counts. "One . . . please, boy," I say. I'm scared . . . More scared than in my whole entire life, more scared than when the guns went off on my birthday.

"Two-oo." My voice is so crackly it hardly makes any noise, and now Charlie is barking louder and growling so loud he sounds like a wild jungle beast. And he is pulling so hard on the leash it breaks in two pieces and I am not even holding on to him anymore.

I want my mom. I want my dad. I want them so bad I'm starting to pee and the pee is hot and running down my leg like a baby, and I can't stop crying. I can't breathe either because the air tastes like fire. "Two and a half," I start to say, but I don't even get it all the way out when I hear the voice.

"Three." It is a man's voice, coming from behind a tree.

That's when I know. When I hear the voice. Even though I, Jonah, have never been here before, Danny was. Which means these big, tall trees with the wavy leaves are the ones I flew up in when I got killed in the head. Then I wasn't Danny anymore. I was nobody floating up in the clouds, and then I saw my mom and my dad and they were so happy I was coming to them.

But now I'm really scared I'm going to die again, because the man who said three is the Wolf, and when he comes out from behind the tree, he has a gun. I scream as loud as I can, but no sound comes out because the air is on fire and I don't want to die. I don't want to leave my mom and my dad. I've only been Jonah for a little time, and they love me so much they would be so sad if I left, and I would be really sad, too.

Then I hear it. The shot. It is so loud it hurts my ears and makes my mouth taste like throw up. I cover my ears with my hands and fall flat on the pile of dried-up old leaves where Charlie is digging, and I'm pretty sure I'm dead, pretty sure any minute I'll fly up in the wavy trees like before, only this time I don't feel all the way dead, so I don't know if I am or I am not. And when I can hear again, the only sound is Charlie and he's yelping and crying. Even though I'm scared that if I move the Wolf who thinks I'm dead will shoot me again, I peek anyway and there is blood coming out of Charlie's leg, so I scoot over and put my arm around him. If we're going to die, we are going to die together.

The sound of the leaves crunching is getting louder, and when I look up, the Wolf is right over me. His face is the color of a tomato and he is staring down at me and pointing his gun at my head.

FORTY-ONE

Driving back from Albany after meeting with Brenna Stephens, a horsey-looking divorce lawyer with the reputation of a pit bull, Mira knew Jackson would give her shit for not showing up at Bella Vista today. But instead of her insides feeling scrambled the way they usually did before he went on a rampage, she felt exhilarated, like a prisoner on the morning of her release. She was done. She and Lola would throw some stuff in suitcases and get the hell out of there before he got home. Stay at Helen's until she figured out what to do next. Brenna would see to it that Mira's soon-to-be ex would be served with divorce papers by the end of the week.

She yanked the retainer out of her mouth and tossed it on the passenger seat. Jackson was convinced she'd sell more houses if she fixed her overbite—and to shut him up, she'd gone along, one more soul-crushing bargain to keep the peace. His obsession with her teeth involved the same sort of magical bullshit that made him believe they were fated to be together for eternity. Or that the white-glove Boston investment firm would buy them out of the failing development. "They know a hot property when they see one," he'd said, sounding manic when he jabbed her awake at five o'clock this morning. And that wasn't his only good news: The Boston people wouldn't just pay peanuts on the dollar, they were going to buy them out at such a humongous profit, they could avoid bankruptcy and "within the week" they'd be "back on their feet." In Mira's case, the crippling high heels that had led to neuropathy in her right foot and deformity in her left. When she packed, she'd leave those murderous stilettos behind.

She was just thankful he wouldn't be back until late, because in her message Lola had mentioned that Charlie was at the house along with Jonah and his grandma, and if Jackson found out, he'd throw a five-alarm fit about his life-threatening allergy to dog dander. Mira had never once seen him sniffle or sneeze around other people's long-haired dogs and was convinced his "allergy" was specific to Charlie. No doubt because he'd been Henry's dog.

She punched in Jackson's number to make double sure he wouldn't be home early, but the call went to voicemail. "Hey," she said. "Just checking in. Hope it's going well with the guys in Beantown. See ya." In court, she thought, ending the call.

PUNCHING IN THE gate code Mira had texted her, Helen told herself she just needed to stay calm. *This is not an emergency. He won't be home until late. This is not an emergency.* Still, she couldn't take a full breath until she pulled up to the parking pad and saw for herself that Jackson's Range Rover wasn't there. The only car was the old green Toyota belonging to Lucie's mother.

Within seconds, Lola came flying out of the house, the bows on her pink tankini flouncing as she ran. She threw her arms around Helen and buried her face in her chest before telling her what happened. "Jonah's grandma hurt her foot and can't walk, and Jonah and Charlie ran in the woods and haven't come back, and it's all my fault for letting Charlie come, and I don't know what to do," she garbled between hiccupy cries.

"Oh, sweetheart, nothing is your fault. You've been wanting Charlie to come over since you moved here." Helen hugged her damp, frightened granddaughter and stroked her cheek. "It's all going to be fine. I'll check on Jonah's grandma, then I'll go find him and Charlie. They couldn't have gotten very far; this place is all fenced in. And after we find them, we'll go into town for ice cream and meet your mom at my house," she said, glancing at the yearbook that lay open to the damning page on the passenger seat of her car. "No worries, love, I promise."

But seconds later the sharp blast of a gunshot pierced the air, coming from the direction of the woods.

FORTY-TWO

NOISE IS COMING OUT OF ME NOW WHEN I SCREAM, BUT IT comes out squeaky, like a mouse.

"You and that dog can scream and cry 'til the cows come home," the Wolf says. "It's not like anyone can hear you. These woods are my personal space. My man cave."

He must think that's funny, because all the sudden he's laughing, but it is not funny. And I have not seen one cow.

"Nobody is allowed in my man cave except yours truly. And that goes for your pal Lola. She knows better than to come anywhere near here. But don't worry, kid. I ain't going to hurt you. Do I look like some scary dude who goes around shooting people?"

I peek out from the dirty leaves and the Wolf is still standing right over me. He has big white teeth coming out of his beard, and he looks just like the kind of scary dude who goes around shooting people.

"You tried to kill my dog," I say. Blood is still coming out of Charlie's leg, but he's yelping and breathing fast, so he can't be all dead. "You tried to kill him," I say again, but I do not look the Wolf in his hairy face.

"Now lookie here, cowboy, you got it backwards, because that vicious mutt tried to kill *me*. Here I am, coming home to my private man cave after one of the shittiest days of my life, and what do I find? Some little kid and a bloodthirsty canine who charges me with fangs bared for the kill. Now, what am I supposed to do? Say 'Here boy, nice doggie.' Well, I don't think so. No choice but to fire in self-defense. You know what else?"

I shake my head. I am scared to know what else.

"I could call the cops on you for trespassing on my private property. You don't want to spend the night in jail with other criminals, do you?"

"No sir," I say. "Please don't call the cops. My dog ran away and I just tried to stop him, but then you shot him and now he might die. We didn't mean to trespass in your private man cave." I call it that even though it's not a cave, it's the woods. Woods where very bad things happen.

"It's okay, boy," I whisper to Charlie. "Please don't die." He is panting hard, and I don't know if that's dying or living, so I snuggle closer to him and say, "Good dog, good Charlie." I wish I had some treats to make him feel better. But there are no treats here and I am still wearing my stupid bathing suit and my leg is sticky from pee and there is dirt and leaves all over me and I wish Momo would hurry up and send somebody to get us before more bad things happen. I put some leaves over the blood coming out of Charlie's leg to try to stop it the way my dad put a towel over my hand that time I cut it on the glass.

Then I close my eyes and do the thing Dr. Zager told me for when I get scared. She said as soon as I feel a scary thought coming, I should use my mind to change the channel, like on TV. Like, right away think something happy. Like cuddling with my mom or going on a boat with my dad or Rocky Road ice cream. I try as hard as I can, but the channel is not changing. I am still in this horrible place with my heart banging.

I didn't know yesterday at the parade when I saw Lola's stepdad yelling that he was also the Wolf. I did not know until today when I heard his voice and he shot us. Charlie knows, too. I don't know how he knows, because he wasn't even here that night. But he's a dog and dogs know stuff people don't.

"Please." I try to rub the snot off my face with my hand. "Please, me and my dog are very sorry we got lost and trespassed. Pinky promise, we will never do it again." I hold out my pinky, but he doesn't pinky promise back. "Could you pretty please just help me get Charlie back up to the house? He can't walk and I'm too little to carry him and my grandma is there waiting for us. I'm sure she's very worried."

"Sure thing, kid, I'll help you." He is leaning up against a tree, chewing on a stick.

"Thank you, mister. I'm sure you didn't mean to kill Charlie, just hurt him a little because he was attacking, like you said." I fake smile at him. "So can we go now?" I get on my knees, but when I rub the leaves off, my legs are filthy and I have prickles all over me and blood from Charlie and my stomach feels all funny.

"All in good time, sunshine. But first we need to have a little chat, so you might as well sit your butt back down."

"Okay," I say and try to act normal, like this is not scaring me to death. "But do you think maybe first I could use your phone to call the house so I can tell Lola and Momo, she's my grandma, we'll be right back?" I do not sit down.

"Gosh, I'd like to help you. The thing is, there's no cell phone reception in my man cave. No one can call us, and we can't call them."

I know the Wolf is lying because I heard his phone go buzz. "I have an idea," I say. "How about we go up to the house first and then we have our little chat?"

"I'm going to say this one more time, nice as I can. Sit your skinny butt down and tell me what the fuck you and that dumb dog are doing all the way out here where it's against the law?"

I don't want him to shoot, so I sit down on the leaves next to Charlie and I give him my hand so he can lick. "I didn't try to come here," I tell him. "Lola invited me to swim and we tied up Charlie to a tree because she said you're allergic and we didn't want to make you sick. But he doesn't like being tied up and started crying, so I untied him for a little walk. Just for one little minute, only then he started running. I think maybe he was chasing a squirrel."

"Well, he is one violent, out-of-control menace to society." The Wolf slides down to the bottom of the tree and sits with his knees bent, the gun at his foot. "So, tell me something, kid. You've never been in these woods before, am I right?"

"No sir, never, I swear." And that is not a lie, because I, Jonah, have never been in these woods before.

"Here's the thing," the Wolf says. "I heard a story that you've been running around telling people you're poor old Helen's son come back from the dead. Now, why would you want to do that? Why would you want to go and make a sad old lady even sadder, because we both know it isn't true? There's no such thing as coming back from the dead. Except maybe Jesus Christ, and believe me, the jury is still out on that one. So why do you go around telling such evil lies?"

I'm scared he'll shoot me if I say the truth, so I don't say anything. Charlie yelps a little, then goes back to licking my hand.

"Okay, kid, I'll tell you, because I don't think this come-back-from-the-dead thing was your idea. From what I hear, there's some wacko shrink who's been sniffing around. Some quack trying to sell you and your family and poor old Helen on the idea that people die and come back, when all he really wants is to make a buck. If you ask me, I think your parents should take him to court and sue his ass."

The Wolf crawls over and puts his mouth next to my ear. His breath is hot and smells worse than throw-up, so I try not to breathe. Charlie lifts his head and growls. He would chew the Wolf into hamburger if he could, but he cries every time he moves even a little.

"Because the way I figure it," the Wolf is saying, "that quack got you to say crazy things for his own selfish reasons. Either that or you are crazy. I bet you don't know what happens to children who are mental, do you, cowboy?"

"No, sir," I say. Then I look down and see the gun on the ground and wish I was a cowboy. A real cowboy who isn't scared and knows how to shoot.

I think he sees me sneaking a look, because he picks up the gun again. "So, tell me, kid, do you or do you not know what happens to children who are mentally ill?"

I shake my head.

"Well then, it's a damn good thing we're having this chat. Because obviously your parents forgot to tell you. Children who are mental live in a hospital. Only not like a regular hospital where people get better, then leave. The hospital for crazies is like a jail."

He sticks his mouth close to my face again, and I hold my breath to keep out the stink.

"There are bars on the windows and people screaming and rubbing their shit all over the walls, worse than a zoo. And once you're in, they never let you out. You get what I'm saying?"

I nod my head, but I don't believe my parents would ever put me in the hospital for mentals.

"So now, all you have to do is cross your heart, hope to die, and swear on a stack of Bibles you'll tell that quack and your parents you made the whole thing up. Just say you're sorry, you made a mistake, you're not Helen's son come back from the dead. Deal?"

"Yes, deal. I made the whole thing up. Cross my heart, hope to die, and swear on Bibles." But only my fingers are crossed, not my heart, and I do not hope to die.

"Glad we're on the same page." The Wolf winks at me.

"Now can we go?" Charlie is panting fast again and has a funny look in his eyes, like he is not really seeing me. And he doesn't lick my hand anymore.

"Sure thing, there's just one tiny problem." Now he's walking around in a circle, twirling his gun like a toy. "Actually, it's not so tiny. You're a smart kid, can you guess?"

I shake my head. I don't know what he's talking about, and I am scared to know. I start to scratch Charlie under his chin where he likes it, but he snaps. He's never snapped at me before.

"Exactly my point," says the Wolf. "You ever see those movies where an animal, maybe a horse or a calf, sometimes a dog, gets injured and they have to put him down for his own good? People cry their eyes out when the cowboy shoots the animal, but it's the right thing. It has to be done."

"No," I say, looking straight at the Wolf. "You are not going to shoot my dog."

"I thought we had a deal."

"Killing Charlie is not in the deal. You said you would take us back to my grandma."

"I said I would take *you* back. I never said anything about that fucking hound dog. Because here's the thing. If I go to pick him up, you know as well as I do, he'll go for me. Even with his bad leg he'll attack me, and I'll have to shoot him then. Only if he's jerking around, I might not kill him on the first shot, which could get pretty ugly, blood gushing all over the place, him yowling his guts out in pain. And you never know, I might shoot you, too, accidentally. But if I shoot him first, a nice clean shot right between the eyes, then *bam* . . . he'll be gone, just like that, and he won't know what hit him." The Wolf snaps his fingers. "Easy as blueberry pie."

I lean over to touch Charlie's nose. It is hot and dry, not wet like usual, and this time he doesn't snap. "Good dog," I say. "Good boy." And then very slow, very careful, not touching his hurt leg, I climb on top of him and spread my arms and legs as wide as I can, like flying. Then I put my head on top of his head. He's breathing hard and making little crying noises, but he does not throw me off.

"Kid, come on, don't be stupid. Get off the goddamn dog. You want me to kill you, too?"

I don't answer. The Wolf can shoot us, but he can't hurt us. I know this from before.

Charlie is my magic carpet ride, and we are flying. I close my eyes and feel his warm fur under me, and I am not scared anymore.

FORTY-THREE

I'M GOING TO LOOK FOR JONAH AND CHARLIE. YOU TWO STAY in the house with the doors locked until the police get here," Helen says after calling 911. Then she presses the remote to open the gate for the cops and grabs a pair of Mira's running shoes from the hall closet. Tying the laces, she tries to convince herself that the gunshot, if it really was a gunshot, came from farther away than it sounded. A car backfiring or a neighbor at target practice, something harmless that did not endanger Jonah and Charlie.

"Oma, I am very, very scared." Lola's teeth are knocking together.

"There's nothing to be afraid of, love," Helen says, kissing the crown of her granddaughter's head, hoping that what she just said is true.

"That's right, there's no reason to worry, sweetheart," Sonam adds, hopping over to the front door on one foot and putting an arm around Lola. "Just please be careful," she calls after Helen, then double-locks the door.

Helen takes off, praying her bum knee cooperates. It's been bothering her ever since the trip up the mountain to bury the map.

"Please, God, please," she intones as she takes off across the meadow toward the woods. Although she was raised Presbyterian, she's never had much use for God, and she doesn't think God has much use for her, especially since He abandoned her son. Still, calling on God seems to be a human reflex that has more to do with terror than faith, and at this moment Helen is begging God to show her the way to Jonah and Charlie, because she has no idea where the hell she's going, and her knee is starting to pinch.

She pauses at the point where the meadow gives way to a forest, unsure which way to turn, then decides west, or what she thinks is west, the direction the gunshot came from. There's no clear path forward, and she has to dart between dense thickets of trees and brambles and hop over fallen branches. Before today, she had no idea that Jackson the big developer owned this much land, and she's wondering why he never developed it when she trips over a gigantic limb camouflaged by leaves.

"Jonah! Charlie!" she shouts from the ground, rubbing her knee.

Silence.

Grabbing hold of a tree trunk to help her up, Helen recalls Mira once telling her that Jackson had forbidden her from entering these woods. Something about rabid coyotes. The warning struck Helen as overblown. *Wolves* is more like it, she thinks, thankful the fucker is in Boston until late tonight.

Panting and sweating, she does a jagged sprint down a steep hill, scanning the ground for footprints or pawprints, but comes up blank. If Danny were here, they wouldn't get lost because he could read the woods better than anyone. Then again, if Danny were here, Mira wouldn't be married to Jackson, and Jonah and Charlie—and now Helen—wouldn't be lost in this godforsaken forest.

She stops and shouts Jonah's name again, then strains her

ears listening for a response or the sound of barking but detects only the whistling of leaves.

Where the hell are the cops? She should be hearing sirens by now.

Moving at a slow trot, her knee buckling every few steps, she wraps her hands around her mouth like a megaphone and cries out once more, "Jonah! Charlie!" The next time she stumbles, she feels something sharp slice her ankle. Without checking to see if it's bleeding, she wills herself to keep going.

"Jonah! Charlie! Jonah!" She doubles over to catch her breath.

And that's when she hears it. Faint whimpering that sounds like it's coming from an animal. Charlie? She must be getting close. She follows the sound toward what looks like a clearing.

Through the trees Helen sees a half-naked Jonah lying facedown on top of Charlie. Jackson is standing a few yards from them pointing a gun.

"Jonah!" she screams, racing into the clearing.

Jackson turns when he sees her. "What the fuck? What the fuck are you doing here?"

"Put that gun down right now," Helen shouts, running past him toward the boy and the dog.

"You better turn your butt around and go back where you came from." Jackson raises his weapon and points it at her.

"You don't scare me, you sick fuck." Reaching the spot where the boy and the dog lie, Helen kneels down and takes Jonah's wrist in her hand, feeling for his pulse.

"I'm warning you, bitch," Jackson says in a voice so lacking in emotion it doesn't sound human. Whatever shred of decency he once may have had deserted him the night he killed Danny.

"I know what you did." Helen spits in his direction, then rips off her shirt and wraps it around the wound on Charlie's leg, which is trickling blood.

The dog whines faintly as Jackson moves a few steps closer. The hammer on his pistol clicks.

"Go for it. Kill me, too, the way you killed my son. You really think you can hurt me any more than you already have? *Murderer.*"

Then crouching with arms outstretched, Helen makes an arc of her body and leans over the boy and the dog, sheltering them like a tree that's been bent by the wind. She closes her eyes and waits for the madman to fire but hears only the chorus of leaves swishing through the poplars surrounding this unholy burial ground. She knows what this place is, has known it from the moment she set foot on this cracked patch of earth and saw Jackson aiming his gun at Jonah. She knows, too, what lies beneath, and thinks that if she has to die now, it should be here. It should be her, not this boy. Never this boy. No way will she let this monster kill Jonah, too.

"Go on, just do it," she says, bracing her body to take the shot.

But the next sound she hears isn't the shattering report of a gun.

It's a deep, confident, don't-fuck-with-me voice.

Will's voice.

"Drop the gun! *Now.*"

The cops haven't abandoned them after all. They've come by the fire road, without the fanfare of sirens.

FORTY-FOUR

HE'S BREATHING BUT OUT COLD," HELEN TELLS THE WOMAN PO-
lice officer, who identifies herself as Caitlin something. "I think
only the dog got hit. In the leg. He needs to be taken to a vet immediately." Helen can't stop shaking.

Behind them, Will cuffs Jackson, then reads him his rights
and signals to the two uniforms to take him away. "Get this filth
out of my sight."

"I'm no doctor, but I'd say this boy is in shock." Caitlin runs a
hand along Jonah's bare back, which feels clammy but not cold,
and rises and falls with each shallow breath. "I'm going to get
him a blanket. And as soon as the paramedics get here, I want
them to check you out, too," Caitlin says, examining Helen more
closely. "You're drenched. And do you know you have cuts and
scratches all over? That gash on your ankle looks pretty deep."

"From the woods," Helen says, wearing only a bra and jeans,
and shivering uncontrollably.

"I want you to come with me and wait for the EMTs in the
car. You're in shock, too. I'll send another officer to sit with the
boy until he wakes up."

"No," says Helen sharply. "I'm not leaving him."

"Are you his mother?" the policewoman asks, but Helen is
cupping Jonah's head with her hand and doesn't answer.

"Jonah, can you hear me?" she says, after covering him with the navy fleece blanket Caitlin brought and throwing a second blanket around herself. Out of the corner of her eye, she sees Will milling around with other officers, his cell phone pressed to his cheek. Helen is not ready to talk to him. Not ready to deal with what comes next. She needs to stay with the boy.

"Jonah?" she says again, lightly stroking his spine.

Someone is talking to him. Jonah turns his head, and when he opens his eyes, his vision is fuzzy like in a dream and he sees Helen. She must be in the dream with him. "Are you dead, too?" he asks.

"Oh no, love, I'm not dead and neither are you. You fainted, but you're very much alive."

"I'm alive?" Jonah rolls to one side and looks up to see if the Wolf is still there, pointing his gun. "But the Wolf?" he says in a tiny voice.

"The police have taken him away. You're safe now, Jonah. The Wolf can't hurt you or Charlie ever again."

As if on cue, Charlie makes a high-pitched whining noise and tries unsuccessfully to stand.

"Poor Charlie." Helen scratches behind the dog's ear. "You'll see, he may hurt for a while and end up with a limp, but the vet will fix him all up. He'll be back to his old self in no time."

Jonah nuzzles the dog's head, then sits up slowly. He brushes his fingers through his hair and a flurry of broken leaves rain down on him like giant flakes of dandruff. Then he rubs his eyes, his cheek, his bare chest, and scratches his leg, still icky from pee. He tastes dirt in his mouth and spits it out. He can't believe he's alive.

"You're a brave boy, Jonah," Helen is saying. "Even though you must have been so scared, you saved Charlie."

"I'm brave?" He thought he was a scaredy-cat, like what Lucas called him at school one time when there was a big thunder.

"Yes, love, very brave."

"The Wolf said he was going to kill me before the cows come home." His voice sounds funny in his head. "I didn't want to go in the woods, but Charlie kept pulling." He is shivery, even his teeth, and for some reason he feels more scared now than when the Wolf was standing over his head with the gun. It's like all the scaredness he had to squeeze inside his self before is coming out now. It feels good when Helen holds him in her arms, which smell like chocolate.

"Shh." She rocks him and leans her head against his and breathes in the sweet, boyish scent of him.

THEN TIME COLLAPSES.

Cradling this boy in her arms stirs a constellation of sense memories in Helen so fierce, so tender, her body is seized by the sweet, aching urgency of them, as if in a flash all the years since she'd cradled Danny vanish. As if in this unexpected moment of mercy, this moment of grace, she is a mother again, and in her arms the two boys merge into one boy, like an atom before it splits apart forever.

Jonah feels it too, though he doesn't have words for it. Still, something in him knows that for a time that is not like regular time, he is Jonah and not just Jonah.

He turns his head and gazes into Helen's eyes without blinking.

"This is where I died," he says.

He says it so quietly, he hopes she can hear him. "When I was Danny. The Wolf shot me. Here. In the hole."

He pats the pile of leaves, then gulps. He almost called her Mom, but she's not his mom anymore. Should he call her Alice? Helen? He doesn't know, so he doesn't call her anything, just has to tell her. But it's hard for him to talk and it comes out funny, like a frog. "I'm sorry. I didn't want to leave."

Helen removes a twig stuck in his hair, then wipes the glossy tears from his cheeks. "Oh sweetheart, you have nothing to be sorry for, nothing at all. What happened wasn't your fault. Even though I missed you so much, I always knew you didn't leave on purpose. You couldn't help it. You did nothing wrong."

"I missed you, too," he says in a tiny voice.

"I know, love, I know." Helen kisses his hair, his forehead, his velvet cheek. And then he curls his body into the hollow of her body, and she wraps him in her arms like a present.

MATT AND LUCIE come by the fire road, driven by Mira. Lucie jumps out of the car before Mira can bring it to a full stop and takes off running. A woman—Lucie assumes she's a cop—yells at her to wait, but Lucie can't wait. Soon, Matt and Mira catch up to her, the cop at their heels.

With the bent branches of trees like skeletal arms forming an arch overhead, the road soon turns into more of a footpath than a passable thoroughfare. It's nearly as dark as night, but they snake their way through the thick undergrowth as fast as they can. Up ahead shards of sunlight stream down through the green forest ceiling, then suddenly they're there and see them: Jonah coiled in Helen's arms on top of a pile of leaves. Charlie next to them, panting.

Later neither Lucie nor Mira will be able to say how, but as soon as they reach the edge of the clearing, both women know exactly what this place is. And though Lucie's impulse is to rush to her son, something holds her back. She grabs Matt's arm to stop him, too.

Seeing Jonah swaddled in Helen's arms, she remembers what Jampa Rinpoche told her about how consciousness is like a film loop without end. How it keeps running after the body dies, runs forever. If that's really true, then they're all part of the same unbroken loop: Danny, Jonah, Helen, Lucie, Matt, Mira, Lola, Sonam, Jampa, Nana, Dr. Skinner. And Charlie, definitely Charlie. Even Jackson. Everyone. Everywhere. Looped together. Lucie doesn't understand how, but something in her knows it's true.

But then she can't wait another minute to hold her boy and just as she's about to call out to him, he lifts his head and turns toward her. When he sees her, he bolts from Helen like a rocket and leaps into his mother's waiting arms.

THE REST HAPPENS so fast.

The paramedics rush in with their kits and usher Mira, Lucie, and Matt out of the way. They take Jonah's vital signs and examine every inch of him. As they do, an emergency crew from the animal hospital shows up and slides a wheezing Charlie onto a stretcher. Before they take him away, Jonah gives him a good long scratch under his chin. Then the team examining Jonah declares him in stable condition. And though the senior paramedic wants to admit him to the hospital overnight for observation, he relents when he learns that Matt's a doctor and agrees to release Jonah into his father's care.

While Matt negotiates, Lucie and Mira kneel beside Helen,

who remains huddled on the mound of moldering leaves. The two younger women drape their arms around her and stay that way, breathing together in silence, until Matt finishes signing the paperwork.

Afterward, snug in his father's arms, Jonah turns and blows Helen a kiss as he leaves the grove with his family.

AND HELEN.

Once the paramedics clean and patch her wounds and Mira returns to the house to be with Lola, Helen lies on her stomach embracing the earthen mound of leaves and dirt, quietly weeping. A few minutes ago, she was certain this would be her grave, too, and now she thinks she could stay here forever.

But a crew of men and women in white protective gear are gathering at the entrance to the clearing. Will holds them off for as long as he can.

"I'm sorry, Petunia," he says when he can't wait much longer. "We need to let the crime scene folks set up a perimeter and get to work."

But Helen is unable to move. It's as if a force greater than gravity binds her to this plot of earth and keeps her pinned down until she becomes part of it and it becomes part of her.

Leaves, brambles, Helen, dirt, worms, and the bones that lie beneath.

One body.

Later, she can't say how much later, she feels the mound let her go, as if coughing her up.

As if the earth itself is releasing her.

She reaches for Will's hand.

Imagine a plume of cigarette smoke. Blue, curling upward, riding on the outbreath of the smoker, drifting farther and farther away, thinning until it vanishes. My mother never smoked, but my father did. That's what I remember most about him. He did bad things, I know, which is why we had to go. But that's not how I remember him. I remember him inside a cloud of smoky blue like a scrim that separated him from everyone else.

That's what dying was like.

When it happened, I didn't expect to hang around all this time, even though my sense of time is nothing like yours. Where I am, years can seem like minutes, hours like decades. But when I was alive, when I was still Danny, I never could have imagined that my memories would show up in someone else's mind. Not my idea, and I sure didn't mean to cause any trouble. To be honest, I don't know how it happened, only that it did. It was as if some infinitesimal part of me clung to this world and kept me from dispersing like smoke into my most elemental particles and merging with the whole of the universe, as sooner or later all atoms must. Until eventually they regain substance and rearrange themselves into another person or maybe a tree. I suppose that whatever substance of me was left needed to let my mother, my daughter, and her mother know that love outlasts death.

And that I'm not lost.

Gone but not lost.

I can feel the particles thinning now, drifting higher, starting to fly apart.

I'm ready.

AFTER

FALL 2010

THEY RISE BEFORE DAWN AND REACH THE FOOT OF THE MOUNTAIN just as ribbons of sunlight start to break through the dense cloud cover. Helen, Lola, Mira, Randy, and Rosaleen. Yesterday, Helen tried to talk Rosaleen out of coming. "The path is narrow and treacherous in places. Between your bad hip and the A-fib, maybe you'd be better off staying home."

But her eighty-four-year-old mother-in-law was having none of it. "Phooey, Alice," she said. "Life is treacherous. If anyone realized just how treacherous, they'd never get out of bed. What's the worst that can happen? I drop dead on the trail, so what? You can leave my body out for the vultures the way they do in Tibet. Which is fine by me, I won't be there." Rosaleen tapped one of her walking sticks against the hardwood floor to make sure Helen got the message. "Danny was my only grandchild and I'm going with you to bury his ashes on the mountain he loved. Why else have I come all this way?"

THEY ASCEND SLOWLY. The trail is slippery in spots and choked with fireweed, goldenrod, and Queen Anne's lace, plants that hadn't begun to show their flowers when Helen was here a few months back. She takes the lead, with Lola right behind her.

Mira follows, the copper urn with Danny's ashes pressed to her chest. Next comes Rosaleen, supported by her walking poles, with Randy close at her heels to catch her in case she trips on the gnarled roots that crisscross the path. Yet though she has to stop frequently to catch her breath, Rosaleen remains surefooted all the way up the steep incline.

When they reach the spot near the first drop in the falls where Helen buried the map, everything that's happened since orbits through her mind, a kaleidoscope of revolving images. Jonah and Charlie seeing each other for the first time. Jonah remembering his life as her son and whispering "Chester" in her ear. The discovery of the yearbook. The scene in the woods where she prepared to die. Then, cradling Jonah when past, present, and future collapsed into no-time, and for a fleeting moment of grace she held her son one last time before embracing the unmarked grave where he lay, had lain, since the day he disappeared.

And later: the unearthing of his splintered bones, now scorched and ground to ash.

At first she'd imagined a public memorial. There were so many people who had loved him. The owners of Perennial Pleasures, the plant nursery where Danny had worked, volunteered to host, and Jock was set to lead the service. There would be nothing for Helen to do except show up. But every time she pictured herself in a crowd, even a loving crowd gathered to honor her boy, she felt her insides buckle and she knew she couldn't go through with it. Whatever she did, she had to do in private. With family. Here, on this mountain.

But today is nothing like her previous trip up the mountain, she thinks, looking around. As sad as she felt that day, the burial of the map was a metaphor. A dress rehearsal.

"Do you remember which tree?" Randy is asking.

"I'm not sure, maybe this one." Helen pulls a trowel from Danny's old backpack, then crouches down next to one of the hemlocks near the trail and starts to dig. As she does, she remembers something she learned about forests long ago, while helping Danny with a unit on trees. Apparently, each individual tree in a forest is connected to every other tree, and they communicate through a deep underground network of pathways that are undetectable on the surface, yet make the trees behave as a single organism. Maybe that's how it is with the living and the dead, Helen thinks. We appear separate, yet we're bound together in some invisible way, except during rare gaps, when a veil you didn't believe existed suddenly flies open and gives you a glimpse of what's on the other side before sealing over again. She has Jonah to thank for lifting the veil.

"Any sign of that old map?" Rosaleen asks, sounding a little cranky.

"Not yet, just a bunch of roots." Her mind spinning, Helen hasn't done much digging and realizes it was a mistake to have brought only one trowel. "I think it might be this tree," she says, scooting one hemlock over.

The plan is to deposit some of the ashes in the spot where she'd buried the map. The rest will be split three ways. Mira and Lola will find a place for them at their new house near the university in New Paltz, where Mira plans to finish her degree in studio art. Rosaleen will take her portion home to Eugene to place on her altar. The rest Helen will take with her to Wyoming, as soon as the pending sale of the Queen of Hearts is final—a deal brokered by Mira, which she calls "the swan song" of her real estate career.

While the others look on, Helen continues to dig and prod the sunbaked soil until her arm freezes up and her legs start to ache. Plus, she's really confused about which is the right tree. The stone cairn she erected to mark the spot is gone. "Why didn't I take a picture of where I buried the damn thing?" she mutters.

"Because you never thought you'd be coming back?" says Mira.

"If Charlie was here, he'd find it," Lola grumbles, realizing she's still miffed at Jonah for dognapping, even though she's getting her own doodle puppy when she and her mom move into their new house. They've already picked her out from the litter and her name is Kaya. And since Lola recently decided she is human after all and would rather be a cowgirl than a mermaid, starting next year she plans to spend summers with Oma on Randy's ranch out West. She's also decided that if they don't cause any more trouble, she'll invite Charlie and Jonah out for a visit, even though she's still not sure if Jonah really was her papa before he was Jonah. Her mom and Oma seem to think a tiny speck of him was, so Lola guesses she thinks so, too.

"Even Charlie would have trouble finding the map after all that rain," says Helen. "But you know what? I don't think it matters where we bury the ashes." She lets the trowel drop to the ground, sensing her son's presence in every twig, hollow, stone, and leaf on this mountain.

"Let's not give up quite yet. How about I dig?" Randy volunteers.

"I can give it a go, too," says Mira.

"Me!" cries Lola. "Me, let me dig! Look!" She flexes her biceps and sashays around as if she just took Olympic gold for weightlifting. Then for extra good luck, she rubs the pretty silver locket her mom gave her to wear around her neck. Her papa always kept it in his pocket, and inside is a tiny picture of her mom. A policeman found it in Jackson's safe, along with her papa's phone and his wallet, which is why Jackson is going to jail until he's dead.

"Okay, love, you dig." Helen passes the trowel to Lola. "Just don't get your hopes up. But maybe try over there." She points to the spruce across from where she'd been digging, then slides to the ground and stretches out her achy legs.

Randy and Mira squat down on either side of her, while Rosaleen leans against a neighboring tree. "I may survive the expedition, but I'm not sure I could make it up off the ground," she says, her voice sounding parched.

Helen sees rivulets of sweat raining down Rosaleen's forehead. She quickly retrieves Danny's old Boy Scout canteen from the backpack and hands it to her. Map or no map, Helen wants to get the ashes in the ground and start down the mountain before Rosaleen suffers heat stroke. The clouds have thinned and the sun is climbing higher in the sky.

"Lola, sweet pea, that's enough," Helen says. "Grandma Rosaleen is going to say some prayers, then we'll bury Papa's ashes in the hole you just dug. You've done a beautiful job, love, that's the perfect spot." Her voice catches on *perfect*.

"*Now*, Lo," Mira says. "You have to stop."

"OMG, okay." Lola sits up on her heels, her arms coated to the elbows in dirt.

When everyone is quiet, Helen nods at Rosaleen, who bows three times, chants several verses in Japanese, and with her hands in prayer position says, "May our great abiding son, father, grandson, beloved Daniel Henry, together with all beings, realize the end of suffering." Then she looks directly at Lola and adds, "We Buddhists believe that after we die, our awareness, which some religions call our soul, continues on as energy. My teacher says that each of us is like a wave in the ocean. Before it's a wave, it's just water. When it crests, it's water, and after it breaks, it's still water. And that water doesn't go anywhere, it stays right there in the ocean until it joins with other drops of water and becomes a wave again."

"You mean Papa is like a wave?" asks Lola, curled up like a kitten in her mother's lap.

"Yes, darling, that's exactly right. And even though we miss him, it helps to know that our love for him and his love for us is also like a wave in the ocean, and it never goes away."

After Rosaleen chants a closing prayer, the only sounds aside from a collective chorus of sniffles are the birds chittering in the treetops.

Helen thinks about what Rosaleen told her late last night when she broke down and said that the thing that pained her the most, even more than Danny dying, was the fact that he hadn't had the chance to complete his life.

"Oh, but he did, Alice, he did," Rosaleen said. "It may not have been what you wanted for him or what he had in mind for himself, but he did what he came here to do, and his life was complete."

Which hurt Helen to hear, but in a different way than losing him.

"Thank you, Rosaleen," she says, glad she hadn't been able to talk her mother-in-law out of making the trek up the mountain. Helen had needed this simple service, even the prayers in Japanese that she didn't understand. The rituals of grief are as necessary as they are without end. Burials, birthdays, anniversaries, flashes of memory that unspool into infinity, sometimes erupting like a volcano, at other times barely a ripple, a hushed undercurrent that keeps time with the heart.

No one stirs. But when Helen glances over at Rosaleen and

sees that her face has turned scarlet, she leans on Randy to help her up. Then she grabs the urn and carries it over to the small crater that Lola has dug. "We need to get this show on the road before we all melt," she says.

"Please, just one more minute," Lola begs, wiping her face with an earth-encrusted hand and jumping up from her nest in Mira's lap. "Let me dig for one more minute, please, Oma!"

"*Lola*," says Mira, also noticing Rosaleen's flushed appearance. "You did your best, sweetie, but that map is gone. No more digging. Over and out."

But Helen relents, knowing how important it is to her granddaughter to help lay to rest the papa she's yearned for every day of her life and will continue to yearn for the rest of her days. "One more minute," Helen says, "then we bury the ashes and hightail it out of here. Deal?"

"Deal!" Lola grabs the trowel, then gets down on her hands and knees and thrusts her nose back into the earthen bowl she'd carved earlier. About a minute later, with a grin so wide it seems to swallow her face, she holds up the map, then stands and curtsies before presenting it to her grandmother.

Helen can hardly believe it. She pulls Lola close, showers her head with kisses, and whispers, "*Hocus pocus abracadabra*" into her ear before taking the map from her.

The paper is so faded, nearly transparent, she has to hold it up to the sky to see what's there. When she does, she bursts out laughing and reaches for Randy to show him.

The eastern half of the country is gone, but if she squints and looks really hard she can make out all the states west of the Mississippi.

ACKNOWLEDGMENTS

Profound thanks to the amazing Anne Edelstein, my literary agent, who got *Jonah* right from the start and found the book its ideal home; and to my wonderful editor, Gail Winston, and the exceptional team at HarperCollins—including techno-angel Hayley Salmon and publicity whiz Heather Drucker—for providing that home.

Deepest gratitude to the three Marks: Mark Matousek, for his abiding faith in me, as well as dreaming up the book's title almost as soon as I dreamed up the story; Mark Epstein, for lending me his copy of Dr. Ian Stevenson's book *Twenty Cases Suggestive of Reincarnation* that got this whole business started; and Mark Wolynn, for teaching me about inherited family trauma.

Special thanks for his kind support to Dr. Jim Tucker, professor of psychiatry and neurobehavioral sciences at the University of Virginia Health System, who is continuing the late Dr. Stevenson's groundbreaking research into children who spontaneously recall a previous life. I am forever indebted to Dr. Stevenson for his published body of work, and to Dr. Tucker for his books *Life Before Life* and *Return to Life*—all essential sources.

Deep bows to Dharma teachers Adyashanti, Sylvia Boorstein, Tara Brach, Debra Chamberlin-Taylor, and Sharon Salzberg, for their wisdom and generosity, along with the many other teachers

ACKNOWLEDGMENTS

who have been pointing the way for decades. Profound gratitude, too, to the late Nawang Gehlek Rimpoche, whose book *Good Life, Good Death: Tibetan Wisdom on Reincarnation* has been a valuable source, as have Yongey Mingyur Rinpoche's *In Love with the World* and Sogyal Rinpoche's *The Tibetan Book of Living and Dying*.

I am grateful to Stephen Mitchell, whose close reading kept me from making a couple of serious blunders.

Abundant thanks to my writers' coven—Ronnie Cohen, Kathy Ellison, Ginny Graves, and Laura Hilgers (who read the book almost as many times as I did)—for their editorial insight and undying belief in this book that saw me through tempests of doubt.

Boundless gratitude to my wider circle of writer friends who gave *Jonah* a careful read, offered invaluable feedback, and cheered me on: Florence Falk, Audrey Ferber, Molly Giles, Geneen Roth, Marianne Wilner, Steven Winn, and Nina Wise.

Heartfelt thanks to Carmelita Thomson, whose enduring friendship and remarkable stories were an inspiration for this book.

Thanks to Laurie Liss, whose perceptive comments made all the difference, and to Sean Elder for introducing us.

Mega-thanks to the crackerjack team that has helped to spread the word: Julia Drake, Julie Coryell, and Madeleine Letellier at Wildbound PR; Steve Bennett and Laura Spinella at Authorbytes; and Frances Caballo at Social Media Just for Writers. To my many family members and friends—including dharma buddies Kevin Berrill, Eileen Harrington, Carolyn Klamp, Betsy Otto, and Jeff Rosenberg—who have offered love and encouragement along the way, deepest thanks.

Blessings to the children of my heart—my granddaughters, Isabelle Eva and Azalia Luce, who for much of their childhoods have been asking, "Aren't you done *yet*, Nonna?" The answer is, "Yes, my darlings, I believe I am."

And to their father, Clay McLachlan, who continues to teach me everything I know about mothers and sons, and who has believed in this book from the beginning, even when he had no idea what it was about, you fill my heart with joy. *Grazie Mille*.

Most of all, to my husband, Hugh Delehanty, whose love and optimism have kept me afloat for forty years, and who might have spared himself countless hours hunched over these pages if only he'd become a lawyer or a plumber instead of a brilliant editor, thank you.

ABOUT THE AUTHOR

BARBARA GRAHAM is an author, essayist, and playwright. She is the author of the *New York Times* bestseller *Eye of My Heart, Women Who Run with the Poodles*, and *Camp Paradox*. Her work has appeared in many magazines, including *Glamour, National Geographic Traveler, O, Time, Tricycle*, and *Vogue*, and in numerous anthologies. Her plays have been produced Off-Broadway in New York, and at theaters around the country. She lives in the San Francisco Bay Area with her husband, Hugh Delehanty. *What Jonah Knew* is her first novel.

barbaragrahamauthor.com